CALL BILLY
07899 232007

Sam McColl

McEllisons

First published in Great Britain in 2018 by McEllisons
4/6 Hillside Street, Edinburgh EH7 5HB

A CIP catalogue record of this book is available from the
British Library

ISBN 978-0-9957026-0-8

About the Author

Sam McColl is married, has three grown-up children and lives between Edinburgh and Tarbert.

For my grandmother,
who held me steady.

Also for Jamie,
Nell and Rosie.
And most of all for Steve.

PART ONE

Spring

ANDREW

'WHAT ARE YOU STARING AT? I do live here you know. I'm your wife, remember?'

'I didn't say a word.'

'I skipped my tutorial, Andrew, because I can barely see. My head … okay? So—'

'Here, let me help.'

Rucksack and jacket fall to the floor as I nudge the door shut with my foot and steer her through to the living room. Once she's stretched out on the sofa she waves a hand in my general direction.

'Be an angel, get me some water? And paracetamol – there's some in the dresser. Listen, about last night. I was pretty drunk. Sorry.' She half opens her eyes. 'I didn't do anything nasty, did I?'

Yes you did rather, I'm thinking. *No danger of a return invite – let's put it that way.* But it's pointless to go there. 'I'm amazed you went in at all – surprisingly dedicated of you.'

'Don't be childish, Andrew. How often have I missed a day?' she says, squashing a cushion under her head as I turn to leave the room. 'Com'on, don't sulk. I've said I'm sorry. Just get me those pills, will you?'

The Aga is belting the heat out, but the kitchen is cold. No wonder, the back door's open. Then I notice a row of teddies lined up on the lawn that Callum left outside 'to sunbathe' this morning. I should probably fetch them in before it rains.

On the threshold a house martin swoops low and misses me only because I flinch. Or did it know I was going to duck? Do house martins come back year after year to the same place like swallows? Is that the same one who was here last year? Will it find the same nest? I hope so – there's something sort of comforting about the idea.

I don't often miss Argyll, not really. Edinburgh has been great for all of us, but I'm missing the west now it's spring. Always makes me think of Abi and the swallow chicks. Cal was just a baby, I suppose, Abi must have been nine, nine or ten. I can still see that fixed look of concentration on her face as she fed them day after day, setting her alarm twice a night, the tears as they died one by one.

'Andrew, what's going on? I'm dying in here.'

'Cal's left a load of toys outside. It's going to rain. Won't be a minute.'

I gather the poor creatures up and dump them on the kitchen table.

The dresser drawer is a mess. I chuck several empty packets of paracetamol in the bin, eventually find a new ibuprofen and take it through.

Rachel opens her eyes, and pushes herself onto one elbow.

'Thanks.'

She pops four into her palm.

'I wish you wouldn't—'

'Just don't, yeah?'

I go and stand by the window. It's raining hard now, sheets of the stuff bouncing off the pavement. It's barely three o'clock, but the cars are already at a standstill. Who are all those people? Do they do this every day – do they mind? As a child I was always trying to guess people's thoughts. I still do. As a teenager I'd obsess about whether a feeling of impending doom followed everyone around like a stray dog, or if it was just me – I don't think I've changed much.

'Andrew? I've been thinking. Let's have a party – I could

ask some of the other students. And you're always saying how I should get to know your colleagues.'

I don't turn around because I'm trying to banish the ugly image that's muscling into my mind of the last time we had a party.

'Come on, Andrew. Please say yes. We haven't done anything fun for ages; it'll be good.'

It was a long time ago, that party. Things were different then. She was practically a junkie – it's the stray dog syndrome, I know it, but I don't have to take it home with me anymore, do I? Not this time.

RACHEL

WE SET UP THE BARBECUE yesterday, but now the forecast says it's going to turn nasty and I had the bright idea to dig out our canvas umbrella from the cupboard under the stairs. It went in easily enough, but now it's jammed and my arm's about to break – I swear we're talking a millimetre here.

'Andrew!' I snuffle through the cobwebs. 'Andrew! I can barely breathe for the dust. I could do with a hand if you're not too busy.'

'Mum?'

'Yes, darling.'

'Dad's outside, he can't hear you. I'll help.'

'Aw thanks, sweetie, I thought you were him. It's okay, I can manage. You go outside and help Dad. Sorry to shout.'

He gives me his oh-Mum-please look, because he's pretty sure he's smarter than me at most things, pauses to see if I get this, decides against pushing it and stomps off into the garden.

As well as fishing gear, two buggies, boxes of obsolete toys, wellies and waterproofs, there are a dozen croquet hoops knitting the whole lot together. By the time I drag it all out, the hall looks like a junk shop and Andrew's favourite rod has snapped. Do I care? No I do not.

A long ring of the doorbell has me picking my way through

the debris. I know it can't be *him* because it's only twelve and no one's due till one, but I'm that stressed I'm sure it will be, and suddenly I can't imagine what possessed me to ask him. Then I trip up on a hoop sticking out from a buggy wheel and stab my calf on the point of a second one.

It's not Ryan. It's my mother.

'*You*! What are you doing in Edinburgh?' I don't give her time to respond – I step back so she can see the mess. It'll be Abi won't it – that's why she's so cheerful. Conniving little—

'I suppose you'd better come in. They're all in the garden.' I'm trying to sound as vicious as I can, but to be honest I just feel depressed now. I turn my back on her and check out my calf. Barely a scratch, though it stings like hell and by the time I've stuffed everything back in I'm almost crying.

I drag the umbrella into the living room, but it's so bulky I ram the double doors to the study which fly open and smack the wall.

'Dad just painted that.' It's Abi, wearing a strange and horrible jumper. I know that jumper; it's the one my mother knitted for Andrew when we first got married – the one I thought I'd thrown out when we moved.

'Just keep her out of my way, young lady, and since you're so concerned about the paintwork, how about giving me a hand?'

She gives a little skip by way of response, pushes past me and wiggles down the steps into the garden and I finally lug the wretched thing outside and dump it on the patio. Who even cares if it rains?

Abi catches my eye as she hugs her granny. I could happily throttle the pair of them. This was meant to be a nice relaxed party – if it wasn't too late I'd cancel.

Andrew follows me into the kitchen. He's always following me.

'I knew nothing about this. Sorry. You okay?'

I give him a half-hearted smile and scrape fruit peelings into the compost bin. 'Yes, I'm fine. Thanks for asking. You'd better get the wretched thing up and I'd better shower.' He gives me a sympathetic grin and goes back outside. I pour myself a glass of wine and go upstairs.

Twenty minutes later I'm back in the living room. It's nice in here, especially with all the doors open. And it doesn't look like it's going to rain. Who knows – perhaps my mother will leave early. I can do this.

I check myself out in one of the two long mirrors that flank the bay window. I'm wearing the knee-length denim skirt I bought Abi from Topshop (which she's never worn of course), with a pale yellow cashmere cardigan. Beside my reflection I can just see my mother and Callum on the lawn. She's reading to him. In a heartbeat I'm pretty sure I can't. Do this. At least not without help. I study the rows of booze in the press beside me and in another heartbeat I've poured myself a wee brandy. Bracing myself, I take it through to the study, stand at the top of the steps and sip it. Medicinally.

Andrew and Abi are playing some kind of game. Burger Tiddlywinks? Sometimes I wonder about those two – the way he's got his hand over hers, the way he's leaning in so close. I mean, can't they see the flames from the fat? Is he trying to set her jersey on fire? That's all we need.

I'm about to shout at them when the doorbell goes again. It'll be Ryan won't it, and in his honour I down the rest of my brandy. But it isn't Ryan, it's Megan, our pretty, walking-talking counselling service – more Andrew's friend than mine – and *her* mother, over from the west coast. I take them through to the kitchen. Megan peers into the garden and hangs back, and together we watch her mum drift outside and hug the kids, before kissing Andrew and then, ugh, Mother.

'What's *Liz* doing here? I thought she was banned.'

'So did I. Pitched up out of the blue. I thought maybe she'd got a lift with your mum.'

Megan assures me she didn't. 'I'd have called you. I'd have put her off. I know the pressure she puts you under.'

'Oh well, it's done now. Pass me those, will you?'

I take the tray of rolls from her and slide them into the oven. Megan's okay – she's nice, even if she does make me feel shallow and neurotic most of the time.

The door again. I touch Megan's shoulder lightly as I pass. I've been practising this familiarity for some time – still feels creepy.

'Hey …'

'Hey.' I hide my burning face by scrambling up to kiss his cheek. He is so tall and his skin smells of strawberries. His hand is pressing on my spine.

'I wasn't sure whether you'd come,' I say, not meaning to.

He laughs and raises one eyebrow, like that says it all.

It's a cliché, I know, but I really feel weak at the knees.

'Come on. You going to take me through or what?' he says, releasing my spine and taking my elbow, steering me across the hall and into the living room as if this was his damn party. When we reach the doors to the garden he drops my arm and walks ahead of me, his boxers showing well above his belt. The sun hits him like a spotlight.

'You must be Andrew?' he says. 'Good to meet you. Nice garden.' A broad sweep of his hand sends spirals of blue smoke from the barbecue corkscrewing up. 'And you must be Abi.' He takes a bow, grinning, hands Andrew a bottle of wine. 'You look just like your mum.'

Andrew adds the bottle to the cooler beneath the table and asks what brought him to Edinburgh, and I can just hear Ryan drawl on about how he began life as a hack in some corporate bullshit set-up, first in the States, then London – how he came up for the festival one year and fell in love with the city – how one thing led to another. He says he reckons the university can't have filled their quota for blacks, because they almost begged him to come. Then he looks sort of confused, the way he does sometimes, and does this weird hop from one foot to the other, yanking up his skinny jeans which are slipping off his hips.

'You doing English too?' Andrew says, turning a sausage which drops through the bars.

'Nah!' and he grins back at me now. 'I'm doing Business. Getting practical in my old age.'

Andrew stabs the flaming sausage. 'Why don't you get yourself a drink – there's cold beer in that bucket, or wine. Maybe you could show him, Abi?'

'It's okay, Abi. I see 'em,' Ryan says, grinning again, catching my eye as he grabs a beer and snaps off the cap on a corner of the barbecue. 'Hey, let me get that …' Somehow he manages to flick the charred sausage from the coals with his pinkie.

I'm about to join them, when the doorbell goes again.

It's David, a colleague of Andrew's and Brad Pitt lookalike – a conceited fuckwit as it happens – and six of my uni friends, including Dawn and her children, and I see that Trish, who I'm not sure I even invited, has made a special effort to colour-coordinate an orange micro-skirt with her fake-bake legs. Hmm, lovely.

By the time I've said 'hi' to everyone and fetched Dawn's kids a drink, I see that Ryan and Brad Pitt have taken themselves off to the bottom of the garden. Looks like they're having a pee against the wall, or maybe they're just admiring the neighbours' flowers? Whatever.

I'm taking the rolls out the oven when someone rests their hand on the small of my back. It's fuckwit David. 'New haircut?' he says.

'Jesus!' I say, straightening up and shaking his hand off. 'Almost dropped the rolls.' I tell him I got fed up with the weight of long hair and how my husband (with emphasis on the word *husband*) had a fit.

'Your *husband* is a stick in the mud – it looks great. *You* look great, far too beautiful to be hidden away.'

Oh please.

'I'm not hidden away, I'm at uni.'

'Course you are. Well it obviously suits you. I presume these gorgeous young people are fellow students – and as for Abi, she looks stunning.' I confirm that it does, they are and she is. But that's it. 'Now if you'll excuse me, my husband's waiting for these.'

I leave the rolls with Andrew and help myself to a glass of bubbly, but before I know it Brad Pitt is shoving his face into mine again. 'Can I ask you something, Rachel?'

'I guess it's a free country,' I say.

'I was hoping for some female advice. Not here of course. Over a coffee or a drink – my flat's on Forrest Row, right near the campus. Perhaps—'

I'm searching for just the right ball-crushing response, when something orange catches my attention. It's Trish mincing across the lawn to where Ryan and a couple of my student friends are passing round what looks like a spliff and I wish I was with them. But instead of taking a hit, Trish takes his hand, holds it briefly to her lips and drags him off. Now what's she up to? She seems to be wagging something over her cleavage and I'm not sure which is more disgusting, her ridiculous tits or—

'I know where you live,' I say, shoving David aside, downing my drink in a oner, needing more, sprinting up the steps and through to the sitting room, where even the sight of the Remy Martin has a soothing effect. Clutching it to my breast, I turn my back on the whole damn lot of them and stare through the bay window onto the street. Maybe I'll go out. Leave. Find somewhere to be on my own. And then I hear someone behind me, see movement on the glass and break into a sweat. My grip tightens around the bottle. If he touches me or says a word I'll knock his fucking head off.

'Bit early for the hard stuff, huh?'

But it's not David. It's Ryan. 'You okay?' he says.

'Not really no. My mum turned up this morning. Oh, I can't explain! She's … she's banned from our house. We all hate her, but she never gets it. Listen, I'm sorry – I shouldn't be dumping this on you.'

'Can I?' He takes the bottle off me, picks a glass from the press, pours us both a shot and hands it back. He's smiling now, like he's shy. 'Well that's a relief. Cheers,' he says, knocking it back. 'Thought I'd done something.' He has perfect even teeth. 'All mums are crazy, Rachel – at least mine was. You got things well sorted: that husband of yours cracks me up, man – solid guy though – has anyone said to you how like Bill Nighy he is? I saw that film, *Love* something—'

'Everyone. *Actually*. It's *Love Actually*,' I say, trying to imply that Bill Nighy might look charming on the big screen but just try living with him.

'Yeah. Funny guy.'

'If you like that kind of funny.'

He gives me this weird look. 'You should take a peek at my world one day, sweetheart.'

I look at him, kind of wishing he could see inside my mind.

And he stares right back as though he can, and says, 'Big house, nice husband, two edible kids, and still the prettiest chick on the block.' He glances towards the garden, where David is chatting up Trish, and says, 'That guy's not taken his eyes off you since he got here. He's a piece of work – you seen his pupils? – high as a kite, that one. Special friend of yours, is he?'

'You must be joking. You seem very pally though?'

Ryan shrugs, taps his nose, and I say, 'He's no one, an idiot, really gets on my nerves.'

Knowing his eyes are looking hard into mine, I bite back the urge to tell him I'm going mad inside this picture of domestic bliss. But I don't. And he breaks the stare and touches my arm for a long second and turns away while stupid beginnings of stupid sentences surge and fade until it's far too late. He's gone.

Now all I can see is Abi, sitting on the wall, holding out the front of that horrible jersey, while Callum is running in circles around her, winding a ball of wool off it. Then Ryan's back in the frame, and Andrew's offering him a sausage which he takes between his teeth as he drops to the ground and hugs Callum, pulling on the thread too, so that Callum can't keep up.

Now what's he doing? He's grabbing Trish, pulling her down beside him and pretending to tie her up … Oh God. And Callum is joining in, with Ryan rolling over on the ground and lifting him high on his legs. And everyone is watching now, half of them laced together in wool, and oh yes, there's my mother, right in the middle of it all – everyone laughing like one big, happy, fucking family.

I finish the job I began and splash myself a large one.

ANDREW

'WHAT THE HELL GOT INTO YOU, RACHEL? What the hell did you think you were doing? Those were my colleagues you told to sod off, your children's grandmother you manhandled out of the front door. This party was your idea, not mine. What on earth's wrong with you?' I know it's the third time I've said it, but there it is, behind my anger is this gnawing fear that things are kicking off again – that everything we've done during the last year counts for nothing. Thank God Callum went home with Dawn.

She pushes past, heading for the stairs, and I follow, ready to catch her if she falls. With a faint taste of bile in my mouth, I lean against the bedroom door as she pours herself under the duvet and dismisses me with a familiar flick of her wrist. I cross the landing and open Abi's door; she's lying on her tummy snoring softly, her face towards the wall. I creep back downstairs and slump on the bottom step.

The house phone on the table beside me goes off like a siren. It's Sarah – brave and original artist, drama queen of the west, a close friend since childhood and temporary custodian of Nevis, our dog.

I tell her about the party and she laughs. It's a nervous thing – irritates me to hell. But she's practically family, has a huge heart and I don't know where I'd be without her.

She then trumps my outpourings with the latest episode in her daughter India's soap-opera life. There's no pleasing her. I would tell her that she should be happy that India has removed her dozens of body piercings at last, just like I told her last week that India's decision to be celibate is a lot healthier than sleeping with every lowlife in Oban. But I don't, because to be honest she won't hear it, and my head's filling with Rachel again, and now I've just noticed that Liz has left her bag on the hall table and someone is about to ring the doorbell.

'Listen, Sarah, I have to go – there's someone at the door. Give India a hug from me and a big pat on the back. Tell her that I'm proud of her – make sure you do. I'll see you all in a couple of weeks.'

Liz's silhouette is unmistakable through the frosted glass and I open it before she has a chance to push the bell. I'm guessing she'll be upset and I'd rather Abi stayed in her room.

'My bag.' She's been crying, her nose is swollen and red.

'Ah. Yes. I just saw it. Come in, come in, Liz.' I lead her through to the kitchen, take a dirty plate off the armchair by the garden door and shake crumbs off the cushion. 'I've got a bottle of brandy here – you look like you could do with one.'

She sits heavily, takes the paisley shawl off her shoulders, flicks it about a bit and knots it over her large bosom. I pour us both a drink. Then I sit too, wondering what the hell to say.

But I don't get a chance to say anything other than 'Liz' (with as much weight and affection as I can muster) because she cuts across me.

'She's always hated me, Andrew. God knows, Carl and I did our best as parents, we …'

I've heard it a thousand times before. I'm used to surfing over everything she says, used to thinking one thing and saying quite another, but this time, I don't know – perhaps I can't straddle the fence any longer, or maybe I'm just drunk. But it's not just about Rachel is it? It's my butt that's bleeding, and Abi's, and soon to be Callum's, and suddenly I can't see the point of it all. So whatever the reason, two decades of lies and pretence fall back like tacky theatre curtains, and I'm about to deliver lines that will alter everything. I take a deep breath, close my eyes and begin.

'Liz, there's something you should know.' Her eyes widen, and her serpent head lifts as if ready to strike. Normally this gets *truth* scrambling for refuge, but this time, I dunno, I feel numb, committed to deliver some or other version of the lines I've rehearsed for so long. 'A lot has happened over the last year, moving half way across the country, new schools, new job, Rachel going to university. But none of these explain why she's ... why she's so hostile.'

I take another slug of brandy. 'No. The reason her behaviour is so destructive, so seemingly unprovoked, is that she, she ...' There is the longest moment of drum-rolling silence, during which there is still time for me to pass out from stage fright, or suffer a stroke or even engage my feeble brain, but I don't. I deliver, instead, three words straight out of a poor amateur dramatics script. 'Carl abused her,' I enunciate carefully, projecting my voice as I add a fourth – 'sexually.'

I pause. It's her turn now, surely? And then it'll be mine again and we'll get through this, together, like it's meant to happen, like I've seen it happen so many times on TV. But no. She's up and shooting me a venomous look, before she snatches her bag, which I find I'm clutching to my chest (as though that might save us).

Idiot that I am.

I stand stupidly, struggling to gather my thoughts, to absorb what I just did – but before I can say anything else she storms through the hall and out into the street, slamming the front door with surprising force. A sensation of having been robbed seeps through me and I flop down heavily on her chair. There was so much more I had to say. She shouldn't have left.

Eventually I lift the kettle from the Aga without bringing it to the boil and make instant coffee. I hate instant coffee but the bitter taste jolts me back to a semblance of sobriety, laced by panicky justifications for what just happened. Isn't it always best to tell the truth? Isn't that the golden rule, the one we've drummed into our children every time they've tried to save themselves with lies? I mean, how can we hope for reconciliation if we're not honest?

Complete uncompromising sobriety creeps up on me unawares.

Having jettisoned a couple of decades of lying, I try a few ways of squinting at the name 'Liz' to see if it might go well with any form or derivative of the word 'reconciliation'. Nope. So I grab her untouched brandy and gulp it down too.

Oh shit, what have I done?

'Who was that?' Abi says, coming downstairs.

'Gran. Come back for her bag.'

'Oh.'

She wanders through to the sitting room and puts on the TV. I hear ambulance sirens. It's eight o'clock: *Casualty*. I follow her in with a plate of leftovers, salads and bread. 'Move up.' She flops across my knees, shoves a cushion under her head and strokes the bridge of her nose.

I stretch over her, pick a chicken leg and dunk it in mayo. 'I'm sorry about what happened.'

She half sits up, shakes out her hair.

'It's her should be saying sorry, Dad, not you. Why can't she grow up?'

'Well, you know, if Gran hadn't come round—'

'Oh come off it – Mum was gross. Why shouldn't Gran be here? I wanted her to come and so did Cal. Why does everything revolve round what *she* wants? Honestly, Dad, you're always making excuses.'

We watch a parade of near deaths, unhappy families and screwy relationships on *Casualty*. As soon as it's over she abandons me for her bedroom. I wish she wouldn't. I don't want to be alone. Because now I'm alone, a picture is beginning to form in my mind: a very frightening picture – one where I'm telling Rachel what I've just told her mother. A sudden urgency gets me to the downstairs loo, my bowels are like water and I feel faint. After what seems like an hour, I tug up my boxers, go into the hall, eye up the phone and enter the stored number.

'Bonnington's Guest House,' someone says. 'How can I help you?'

'Liz Coleman, please.'

'Hello, Andrew.' Liz's voice cuts down the line.

'Is that you?' I say, cringing, as though it could possibly be anyone else. 'I was wondering how you were.'

'How do you think I am?' Her voice is dull and blunt. 'What do you want?'

A perfectly reasonable question but not one, apparently, that I'm able to answer. It occurs to me that I've rarely heard Liz deliver an ungarnished sentiment before and thankfully it forces me to focus.

'Liz, I'm coming round.' I'm sure she's about to protest, so I quickly cut her off and call up the stairs. 'Abi. Abi?'

I find her sitting at her dressing table, dragging straighteners through her hair. 'Darling, I'm going to walk to Gran's hotel. You be all right for an hour?'

'Dad, is Mum going crazy again? She's trashed all the time, and you know she's smoking, don't you?'

'Yes I do, and no, I don't "think she's going crazy". You shouldn't have asked Liz to come without telling her, Abi. You knew it would wind her up.'

'She ought to grow up – it's really embarrassing.'

Unable to argue that, I change the subject. 'Abi, your hair couldn't be any straighter.'

'Whatever. Are you sure you didn't take Prozac or something? You seem very mellow.'

She gathers her fringe together and zaps it until it smokes. A faint burning smell fills the room.

'Very funny. Honestly, Abi, your mum—'

'Yeah, yeah – save it for Gran.'

It doesn't take long to get there. But I must've been waiting in the residents' lounge a good ten minutes before Liz appears.

'You shouldn't have come, Andrew.'

She looks older – years older. Normally the idea of touching Liz would be impossible, but I give her an awkward hug and steer her to a small round table in the bay window. There are no chairs, so we sit awkwardly side by side on the padded window seat and face the grate where a few tired flames fail to lift the gloom.

'Have you told her you've told me?' she says.

'No, not yet. She's sleeping.'

'Sleeping it off, you mean. How do you know she didn't make it up? She's spiteful enough. Carl wouldn't … He was, he was—'

'It's okay, Liz. I understand.' Her jaw is trembling and I say, 'Let's go upstairs. Come on.'

The faint tang of coal dust curls the hairs in my nostrils as we open her bedroom door. She makes her way to another bay window and sits heavily on the threadbare seat. I reach for her hands, but she moves them.

I stare at the empty space in desperation. 'It was never, well, never—'

'Never what?' she rasps.

'Never … you know, penetrative.' Agh, that word, surely there must be a better one? 'More, well … He used to bath them didn't he?'

Her head drops forward as though her neck just snapped. 'Not Sheena as well?'

I look around the room, as if something in this dump could help me. But there's nothing.

A sob breaks as she pushes the table with surprising force. Half expecting her to rise and strike me, I resist the urge to run. Instead I reach for her shoulder and pat it awkwardly. 'I told you to help you understand, not to hurt you. Carl did it, not you.'

'I was her mother – I was meant to protect her.' She glares round at me and shrugs me off.

'Yes you were. But it doesn't make you to blame. You would have if you'd known. Rachel's come to terms with a lot of it over the years. I shouldn't have said anything. I don't know what came over me. I wish I could take it back.'

She reaches for a paper doily and begins to shred it.

'Well you can't,' she wheezes, thumping her bony chest. 'My inhaler, I need my inhaler.' She flicks her wrist at me, just the same way that Rachel does. 'Over there, by the bed!'

ABI

I'VE A MIND TO JUST GO. But why should I? It's my house too. Besides, left my keys in the kitchen, didn't I?

'Morning, Dad. Where's Callum?' Mum looks rank – still off her face.

'Still at Dawn's,' they blurt out together.

'I asked Dad, not you. *Dad*, I'm going to see Gran, okay? Before she goes back.' Mum like gives me this evil look. 'I can see my own grandmother, can't I?'

'Did I say you couldn't?' Mum goes. 'Just make sure you eat something first.'

'Get lost. I'm not three, am I? It's not me that needs telling. You're the alchie!'

'Abi!' Dad goes, but I just snatch a banana and my keys and I'm out of there. I'm at the hotel in minutes. I ask the alien at the desk for Liz Coleman, and she tells me Gran checked out just after breakfast. I feel like crying but I am so not going home. So I walk down the road and into the park, head straight for the pond and sit on a bench in the sun. It's Baltic out here and I wish I had a jacket and some bread for the ducks. There's this super-cool willow that makes a kind of tent around me – branches totally touching the water. Some boys are mucking about on the other side, pushing and shoving. I recognise one from my school – Rory. Right prat. I pull out my phone and pretend to text, flopping my hair forward, but he's already pointed me out to his mates, and now they're all splashing over. It's like a rule to blush, which is totally weird because I'm not even one bit embarrassed, but I'm bright red anyway.

'Hi,' he says.

'Hi.'

'Hi *Ab-eee*,' he goes again, like my name is some kind of retard label. 'This is Jamie, and Aidan – that one's Leggy. *Ab-eee*,' he tells them, 'is at my school.' For some reason this turns out to be pee-in-your-pants funny. We all crease up, me too, which makes them fall about all the more, so I reckon they must have already had the joke before they came over – so it's me they're taking the piss out of, but somehow that doesn't stop me joining in, does it? I'm grinning like an idiot. They crowd round my bench, bunching up beside me, wriggling and squirming, making out they're like just getting comfy. Then this creepy silence happens, and I really, really wanna run, but there's totally no way, is there?

'What school do you go to then?' I say. I'm only putting it out there. It's not meant to be a joke, but of course everyone's creasing up again.

'Broughton,' the one called Jamie says, staring at his feet. And I notice for the first time that he's totally drop-dead fit.

'What's it like then?' And I'm blushing now, big time.

'S'okay – if you're intae music, I guess.'

'So are you then?' I ask, trying not to look at him, but like, grinning, you know, like I'm so totally stupid.

'Yeah, some. But it's pretty borin' if you dinnae gie a toss like these skivers,' and he shoves at Aidan hard with the flat of his forearm, and like he's grinning at me, and oh my God that's so cool.

Aidan picks himself up and kinda trips off, kinda limping towards the pond. He walks straight in, as though he doesn't have expensive trainers on.

'Ya fanny!' Leggy shrieks.

But Aidan doesn't give a toss. He reaches down, scoops up a load of minging water and hurls it at us. Half an hour later we're all sodden and shivering.

Then this parkie kicks off like he's been spying on us. We all crack up, acting like we're so scared, but once he starts punching his phone we scatter fast.

'Catch yous later,' Jamie shouts. And I hope he does.

'See ya.'

RYAN

SOON AS WE'RE IN THE QUEUE I see Rachel and Dawn at a table near the bog, heads together. I wave at them, nice and polite, and Dawn waves back.

'What's up with Rachel?' I mutter.

Trish leans in, kisses my ear. 'Dumbo. She fancies you, of course. She was well pissed off at the party.'

'No, really, that was about her mum.'

'No. Not *really*. I'm telling you, she's well pissed off.'

I keep ladling beans next to my sausage. I can tell Trish is pleased about Rachel's huff. I let her pay and tail her to a table like a puppy dog and daydream while she yabbers on about her family, how proud they are, la la la, that she's the first to go to uni. She's just a kid, twenty-two tops. It's sorta nice hearing how one of her sisters works in a bank and the other in a nail parlour. She tells me how brilliant it was, the day her results came through – how all the aunties and uncles, cousins and grandparents came round for a party.

I remember the day my results fell through the letter box, how I spent two days fighting off the craving to celebrate with a cocktail of Class A drugs. Still don't know how I did it. But hey, who cares, man, cos I'm a year in to getting a degree, and doing a little weed is about as high as I ever get. One lucky fucker is what I am.

Hang on – what's she saying now? Something about a visit? Her parents … I'm thinking, gotta get that essay done. Gotta drop by Andrew's pal, David, with some gear. Wait a minute. Meeting the parents? That's not me, surely? I mean we've known each other barely five minutes. Times, places, dinner, a tour of the castle … Jeez, baby. I say nothing, just push aside my plate along with the hangman's noose hovering over my head and walk outside for some air.

I slump on the wall, cross my legs, look up at the sky which is almost white it's so blue, and put my shades on.

'Hey.' Trish drops down close, mirroring me.

'Hey.' I keep staring at the sky. 'You done?' She does this half angry, half come-and-get-me pout. 'Jesus, Trish, quit running my shit will you?' She looks like she's going to cry, wipes her nose on the back of her hand, kind of looks sort of cute.

'I wasn't … I mean I'm sorry, Ryan. I got carried away. Sorreee.'

She rolls onto her knees and squeezes my cheeks between her palms. Her orange cleavage rushes forward like a wave and she plants a wet kiss on my mouth. It's embarrassing – people are watching. When she stands to leave, her tits slosh back towards her chest, settle like muddy water. I shift my pants to make a little room. 'Get out of here. Go on,' I say. 'I'll catch you later.'

She stares at my crotch and grins and dances off and turns again and giggles and points.

David's been texting all day. *What time will I be there?* Pushy. Still, I'm not complaining. Thanks, Rachel. You may think he's a dickhead, or a fuckwit or whatever term you posh ladies use, but when you strip off the business suit and the urban charm he's nothing but an addict – another poor fucker in need of a regular supply. Took him about four minutes to sniff me out and fix up some business. I text him back. *I'll be there by seven.* Then I head for the library, spend a few hours gathering shit for my essay and I'm outta there by six.

I get to David's early. Nice place, I'll give him that. He pours me wine, shares hot clips on YouTube, offers me a line (which I decline) – very fucking pally. One day I'll get myself a place like this.

I leave by eight, and who should be walking past his door as I come out, but the beautiful Rachel. 'Well, hello.'

'That's where David lives, isn't it? Blimey, you two haven't wasted any time.'

'Talking to me now, are you?'

'Just wondering what you and David are getting up to.'

She's cute when she's riled. 'You care?'

'Not really, no, but Andrew might. Eco Écosse wouldn't take kindly to the face of environmental issues being caught up with a small-time dope dealer.'

'Not my problem, baby. You want to join me for some chips? I've not eaten since lunchtime.'

She gives me a dirty look and walks off and I join the queue. And then I hear what I hoped never to hear again.

'Stevie?' I don't turn around.

'Stevie?' Next thing I'm tasting his rancid breath and he's pushing his ugly mug into mine, pinching my cheeks like he's seen a ghost.

'Shit. Where've ye been? Shit man; we all thought ye was deid.'

I think about running, or flattening him or just plain bluffing it out like he's got it wrong …

'Hey, dude.'

'I cannae credit it, man. This is so-o fuckin' unreal—'

'I can explain.'

He steps back, looks me up and down, tilts his head from side to side.

'Jesus, man, what is that ye're wearing? And where've ye stashed yer hair?' He cops a feel of my biceps.

I pull his cap down over his eyes, ruffle the back of his hair and pull him in, hold him there like I'm welling up, like I'm too moved to speak. 'Good to see you, man. Fuck, man.' I say, letting him go, shitting myself. 'Billy.' And then I punch him softly in the chest like it's all just sinking in. 'You're a sight for sore eyes, man. Can we talk?'

'Sure we can. Sure we can fuckin' gab. You got some real fuckin' gabbing to dae. Jesus, fuckin' Jesus fuckin' shite.' And he shakes me again, like I just might shiggle down into some other person or maybe he's just hanging on, case I run.

'You alone?' I say, trying not to sound like it matters, trying to stay calm.

24

'Sure, man, sure.' He spins me out of the queue, shoves me from behind, and with a vice-like grip round my bicep pushes me across the street to a low wall. We sit. He faces me square on, claps both hands on my thighs and peers in close. He's lost a lot more teeth since I last saw him.

'Ah reckon'd ye was deid, man.' He shakes his head, waiting. 'I thought we were – well, ye know. I thought we was for keeps, like.'

'I had to get out, Billy. You knew the score – I was dead meat back there.'

'But what aboot us?' he says, like we were married.

'Shit, Billy, you didn't want me – I was bad news.'

'That's no' for ye to say, now is it? I loved ye, man. And you know it.'

It takes all I've got not to leg it. 'Yeah, well. I'm sorry. It wasn't easy, Billy.'

'And what aboot ye maw – where the fuck is she?'

'Dead.' I say. 'Buried her a few months back – got pneumonia didn't she?'

He plucks my sleeve. 'Sorray to hear that, man. She was sound your mum. So what's this with the gear? What's with the new look?'

'I needed to get out, Billy – everyone knew what was coming.'

'An yer hair, Ah thought ye loved yer hair. Fuck, man. Ah loved yer hair.'

'Yeah, well – sorry.' My mind is working overtime. 'I'm only here for the day – job interview, mate. Now maw's gone. Living up north at the moment. You gonna say anything?'

'That's what fuckin' hurts the most, like – ye could've told me. Ah'd no' have grassed ye – ye ken that. What d'ye think Ah am?'

I tell him I wanted to, but it wouldn't have been fair. But he doesn't get it – never will get it.

'Ah'd have come wi' ye, Stevie – ye ken that!'

'I know, Billy-boy, and don't think it wasn't the hardest thing I ever did.'

'Ye mean it? Ye really mean it?'

'Sure. I loved you too – you know it.' I touch him lightly on his arm, smile at him. And he grins back – *fucking idiot.*

'They went mental, man, like Ah said they would.'

His knees, beneath joggers furred with age, are jiggling something crazy. He smells so bad.

'Hey! Yer lookin' good, man. Ye got any blow?' His eyes are swivelling in their sockets now.

'Sure. What you doin' here, anyway?'

'Free country, innit? What's it to dae with you?'

'Nothing. Course it is. Listen, Billy, I got a train to catch. Heading back north – if there was a later one I'd leave it, but with the connections and everything, it's the last one. You're not going to say nothing, are you?' I press all the dope I have into his thigh, and he takes it, flashes me a nervy smile. 'I'm a dead man if you say anything – you know that, don't you?' I say with feeling.

'Sure. But we can keep in touch, like. Give us a call next time yer in toon – neabody needs to ken nothin' – Jesus, mate, it's good to see ye.'

I put his number into my phone, punch him in the shoulder and eyeball him like I can see the future in there, and that somewhere in that rosy future we're together again, playing in shits-ville – happy as pigs, and shrug and walk away. And that's when I see Rachel and Dawn sitting at a table outside Petit Paris on the other side of the square, and Rachel is looking right at us.

RACHEL

'YOU LISTENING, RACHEL? You look miles away.'

'Y-es,' I say. 'You were going all dreamy about staying in a caravan on Eigg for the summer.'

'I was asking you about your mum, why you hate her so much. We were talking about Saturday – what on earth she'd done?'

'So we were – or rather you were.'

I'm trying not to look at Ryan, and failing – he's hugging someone. His son, maybe? I mean, would you hug *that* if it wasn't out of paternal duty?

'How could you get so worked up about her and in front of everyone like that? In front of the kids, Rachel.'

'Easy. You don't know her. I was restrained, actually. She is not welcome in our house and the sooner my family understand that the better. I've done some counselling, Dawn, I know what I know. Someone has to put some rules in place and I've married a weak man, so it won't be Andrew. Does that answer your question?'

'Not really. Poor Andrew. He seems like a lovely guy to me. But it sounds like you've been through some tough times, so what do I know?'

'Yes, some. Sorry, Dawn, but I've just seen someone – won't be a minute.'

I get up and cross the road quickly. The *chav* (I think that's the right name) is last in the queue outside the chippy, so I stand right behind him.

'I just saw you talking to Ryan – you know him?'

'Ryan? Who the fuck's he?'

'The guy you were just talking to. It looked like you knew him?'

'Ryan? Yeah, *Ryan*. Aye. *Ryan*. Old mate, used to be neighbours. And you? You ken him like, dae ye?'

'A bit. I'm at uni with him.'

He stares at me a minute like I've grown two heads, or more likely he's dropped something which just kicked in. Now he's patting pockets and looking around the pavement.

'What's wrong?' I ask, stepping back.

'Nutin. He's at "uni", ye say? Aye, right enough, he said that. Wa'the fuck – Ah wrote his number down, like, on a fuckin' Rizla. Lost ma frigging phone.'

'You lost your phone? What – just now?'

'Naw, before like. Fuck. Shit. But Ah've lost the fuckin' Rizla—'

He's pulling out his pockets.

'Can ye give me his number, doll? Dinnae want to lose touch with him, ken? Ah said Ah'd call him, got some stuff tae sort out.'

'You can give me yours if you like,' I say. 'I'll text it to you.'

'Well yeah, okay. Ye sure ye've no' got his number? Ah said Ah'd call him later, go for a wee bevy, like.'

'Sorry, no. Battery's flat.' I riffle through my bag but can't find any paper, so pull out my library book, open up the cover and hand it to him, along with the only thing I can find to write with – a blue felt-tip. 'Here you go.'

'Okey dokey.' He sits on the ledge and cups his palm as he writes, like a kid trying to stop me cheating. I turn, but can still see his tongue, similar in texture and colour to his joggers, protruding in a hard twist as he concentrates.

It takes him an age, and once he's done he comes up close and jabs his finger triumphantly at the last three digits. 'See tha'? Feckin' cool eh? Feckin' 007 cool dude Bond.' And he bows low.

'No problem, err, Billy – I'll get my phone charged and text you. Where was it you both lived then – somewhere down south, was it?'

'Nah. It was Niddrie. Ye should'a seen him two year ago – Ah hardly ken him.' He looks at me, pennies dropping. Then he smiles a smile I've only seen on warning posters at the dentist. 'Ye didnae know that did ye? Spun ye a line did he? Well, that's our Ste ... err, *Ryan* for ye. Ken, he did come frae London or the States maybe though like, once upon a time ... that's why he talks posh, like.'

'You're right, he so doesn't sound Scottish.'

'Ach well, he stayed in Niddrie ten years ken. Ah've got some stories that would frazzle those pretty ears of yours, Hen.'

The woman in front of Billy pays for her fish tea and leaves.

'Your turn.' I say, still absorbing this stunning revelation.

He gets his bag of chips and waits while I get mine. 'I'll need to go, Billy – nice to meet you, and I'll, well, I'll make sure you get his number.'

'Aye, ye dae that.' He says, pulling his cap low over his eyes with bling-encrusted fingers, his smile more of a smirk now.

'What was that all about?' Dawn says when I get back to the table.

'Sorry. Yeah. That was a friend of Ryan's. An old neighbour from Niddrie.'

'Niddrie? You're kidding. Ryan lived in Niddrie?'

'Yep.'

'I thought he—'

'London? Yes, we all did. And he wasn't christened Ryan either. Here, have a chip.'

Ryan

I'm shaking so bad, my last smoke's a live thing and it takes me to breaking point to fish it out of the packet. Once I've nabbed it and got some nicotine in my lungs things start to cool down.

Billy-boy might be a retard but he's not daft enough to tell them he saw me. Too fucking scared. And there's no fucking way Rachel could hear from there. So what did she see, anyway? Some junkie hitting on me – so what? I slip into a doorway, take a few deep breaths, finish my cigarette and look back. No sign of him.

I pull out my phone, delete his number and walk, and don't stop walking until I'm almost home and then only to buy more Marlboro and something to eat. Last time I went near my fridge, whatever was in there looked like it was setting up house, and right now I've no stomach for meeting its growing family or carrying out an eviction.

Agnes is waiting for me as usual. Sometimes she's watering her tub of geraniums, sometimes just talking to them. I reckon it takes her the four or five minutes, from her first sighting of me in the street, to get onto her feet and shuffle to our shared landing. She's lived here forty years, widowed for many of them, makes it her business to know everyone in the stair, if they'll let her. There used to be a single parent in my flat, Agnes was friendly with her too, and the kids, but they moved on and I moved in. Poor substitute I've no doubt, but I do my best – couple of minutes talking about the weather or a blether on the state of the young these days, don't cost much. Sometimes I'll sit in with her, have my tea and listen to her stories. She's lonely, her feet are bad – she seldom gets out.

'Is now a good time to do the light bulb?' she says. 'I put the chair there, son – shouldn't take more than a minute.' She sniffs at the air and grins and I grin back and remind her she forgot to put her teeth in. I even manage a smile as she claps her hand over her mouth and scuttles off. 'That's better,' she says, when she's back, swapping my carry-out for a new bulb. 'Honestly, I've not had my own teeth since my twenty-first birthday and I still forget to put them in.' She wags her finger at me. 'Yours all your own, are they, pet?'

'As far as I know,' I tell her, climbing down carefully. And to stop her launching into the drama of life before the birth of the NHS, I ask her if she remembered that tomorrow she has a doctor's appointment, that I'd be happy to walk her along.

'You're a good lad,' she says, 'but William's taking me – you remember – the nice man from the day centre? You coming in for your tea? The fishmonger slipped me extra – I'll never manage it all.'

'Can't today, Agnes. Stuff to do, got myself a carry-out,' I say, nodding at the parcel on the shelf behind her.

I put the chair back in her tiny kitchen and turn the light on and off a few times. 'I'll see you tomorrow though, after your appointment.' I bend down to kiss her on the cheek and pick up a mouthful of powder. I reckon she's the closest thing I have to family.

Between drags on a strong one-skinner, I scoff the two cold pasties and settle down in front of the TV, Billy-boy's face fading at last. But there's nothing but virtual bullshit, news, crap drama, so I knock over the stack of DVDs, looking for anything I've not seen a dozen times. But the anythings I've not seen a dozen times aren't worth seeing, so I call Trish and tell her I'm busy till ten thirty, though she's leaning on my bell at ten.

'You got here quick. I thought you stayed in Bruntsfield,' I say, once she's through the door. But she's not listening and doesn't care – she's pulling her shirt off, unhooking her flimsy bra. Man, she's in a hurry.

Damn, look at them jugs …

After we're done she pulls a stuffed bag onto the bed and begins sorting through what looks like a small chemist of beauty products. Right.

I drag on my boxers and spell it out slow. 'Trish, you're doing it again, muscling into my life. No one asked you to stay.'

She doesn't like what I'm saying, but I do. Her bottom lip quivers as she repacks her bag real slow, like I might change my mind, but I'm not even one bit tempted. Yet when she's done I lift her chin and kiss her – tell her she's a good girl, that it's been a long time since I've been with anyone, that I need to take things slow and easy. Two years and this is the truth. She shrugs me a coy grin, like maybe this is kind of cute after all.

I have her in and out of my place in an hour.

Next morning there is real warmth in the sun. I take a walk through the park, pick up the bus at Canonmills – stare out the window.

As the bus rolls round Charlotte Square I take a good look at one of my homeless junkies at the corner of Multrees Walk and Harvey Nichols. He's always there, same place, a dog under a blanket at his side. He loves that dog. Sometimes, as part of the service, I sit with him, take him a coffee. He's a nice guy, used to run a small bookshop down The Walk, good little business by all accounts. Never did junk until he found some in his flat – reckons one of his crazy wife's buddies left it there. Only totty wee shots at first, just enough to help him forget the debts, the fact that his missus was screwing around – just enough to help him get to work on time and smile at the customers. Hooked in quick though. Was barely two years before he was selling the house and living in the shop. Another four and he was sleeping on the street.

Now there's nothing left to sell but his arsehole.

Rachel

Eleven o'clock. Another scintillating evening. Megan's very nice, well of course she is – a good friend, part of the family even, what with her being so close to the kids. But sometimes I just don't get it – I mean, why does she like hanging out with us oldies so much? Doesn't she have single friends? Doesn't she ever go out and get plastered or have one-night stands?

I load the last of the plates into the dishwasher.

Andrew's taken to sitting in the garden after supper with an old overcoat round his shoulders, staring up at the sky. It's bright out there, moonlight's sparking off his crystal glass as he turns it slowly through his fingers. Even though the French windows are closed he can sense me – that's part of the problem – he's so fucking tuned in it's like we're hotwired. He swivels round and stretches out his hand. I put my empty glass down and go out. Don't know why – I'm already irritated. He pulls me onto his lap and makes room for me inside his coat – and strokes my back like he's trying to reassure me or something. I can just make out the dark smear on the flagstone of the sneaky fag I had earlier. I could do with one now. So why don't I just get one from my bag? I mean, what's that all about exactly? It's about pleasing Andrew, being good, being someone I'm not. I can't remember the last time someone actually gave a fuck about my needs.

Sitting here on his lap, even his legs are weighing me up. And there's something calculating about the way his hands are so carefully placed on my waist. Like, might this be a good night for sex? Is that what he's thinking? I mean, when was the last time we did anything spontaneous in bed? Not for months, not since he started sleeping like the fucking dead. Sunday mornings, Sunday fucking mornings. Oh God, give me strength.

'I'm going for a walk. I must stretch my legs – get some air. I can't breathe.' I twist round on his lap to face him. And then he starts up, ahead of the game as usual.

'I thought you were quiet. I could see it. What's up?'

'Nothing. Just fancy a walk, that's all.' Jesus, must we analyse everything – can't we take things as they are, just for once?

'Great idea. The kids will be fine for half an hour – it's such a beautiful night.'

Something deep inside shifts in that moment. 'Andrew, you've got work tomorrow, and I've just seen you taking your pills – you'll be zonked in twenty minutes. Surely it's bed time?'

'No, it'll be fine – I'd love a walk. You'll steady me up if I start to stagger.'

As he stands, he puts his arms around my waist and draws me into him. I struggle to get away. 'I'm going alone. Please, Andrew, just don't. I mean it. Just go away, will you?' I know how unfair I'm being, know he doesn't deserve it – but I'm going with it anyway.

And he'll forgive me, he always does.

He's looking weird, following me as I move through the kitchen, trying to edge in front of me. No way, he has no right. I lug the front door open, grabbing my coat off the peg.

'For fuck's sake, Andrew. Take a hint can't you? If I have to listen to another word about climate or dysfunctional families or, or suicide, for God's sake …. It's all so patronising. Trust me, I know my own mind, and all it does is turn you into the bore you dread being so much.'

I think he might grab me, he looks so distraught, and for a minute my interest is pulled back, but no, he checks himself – of course he does – and I walk away.

At the bottom of Canonmills a huge moon sits smugly on the chimney pots. It is so big and so close I think it might be planning to land right here, right in front of me. For a minute I imagine being drawn inside.

I light another cigarette off my first, go past the Colonies, half planning to cut across the bridge over the canal, but find I've missed it and come out on Raeburn Place instead. So I'll walk through the park, past Heels.[1] I'm in no hurry.

And then I see her – Trish, barely fifty yards away, stepping up onto the bus, snatching her arm free from Ryan's grip. We both watch her as the bus moves off. Then he turns away, strides across the road and disappears through a red door. While I'm standing there staring at the building's windows, I think I see him pacing his room on the first floor, before the glass switches from yellow to black.

I walk across the street and push the buzzer with the name Turner smeared across it. Seconds later the glass glows yellow again and I hear the whine of wood on wood as the window above me grinds open.

'What the hell do … Oh!'

There's a long wait. Then a buzz close to my ear beckons me up and I heave the tenement door open.

The last thing I feel like doing is talking, so when I walk into his flat I get straight to the point by turning the light off.

After, as we lie there with this feeling, this feeling of nothing I've ever felt before, I am sure I have done everyone a favour. No, I don't want to leave my family – I just want more. And the fact that I know nothing about him, that he has no past, sends rushes of pleasure through my soul. I roll over so that his dark satiny skin merges and divides with my whiteness, tiny rivers of moisture swelling and receding with our breath. I pull my eyes away, look up.

He is propped up on one elbow, grinning in that mocking way he has, like he knows something I don't.

I place my lips on his; they are soft and full and playful. I feel wide awake and wildly happy. I draw a line with my tongue from

---

[1] Heels, the name of the school, stands for Holistic Education for Edinburgh Learners.

his mouth down across his flat belly and cradle his soft penis between my teeth before giving the slightest nip. His knees jerk up and he pushes me off.

'Hey, you crazy?'

ANDREW

'ABI, THIS IS THE LAST TIME I'm going to wake you. You can miss school and deal with the consequences, okay?' I wonder if I can get to this stage earlier – skip the fury and just hand her a daily ultimatum. But I don't think so, because for Abi, rage and caring are synonymous and I wonder if that's the way it is for all fifteen year olds – I like to think Megan would say it was and this makes me calmer.

While Callum is guzzling Shreddies with one hand, and playing a drum routine with a spoon, an upturned sugar bowl, the cereal packet and a large pot of yoghurt with the other, Rachel is humming, humming something from *Les Mis*. This new-found bounce of hers is giving me the willies.

Abi mooches in, finally, and slumps at the table; thick shadowy lines that I hope are make-up frame her eyes.

'Callum, watch your bowl. Callum! Abi, don't punch him like that – leave him.'

She gives him one more jab in the chest for good measure. 'Jesus, you freak, Callum. Mum, stop him banging like that – he'll break it. For Christ's sake!'

Callum does a swift, and, in my opinion, rather promising finale, jumps down off his chair, boogies across the floor and out into the garden.

'It's not my fault you've got *per-swan-ability* issues,' he calls back, climbing onto the swing. And I thank God Abi lets it go.

'Mum,' he yells at the top of his voice, the swing gaining momentum. 'Will you take me today? Will you? You haven't been for ages!'

Even Abi's head swivels at Rachel's reply.

'Yeah, okay. But we need to go, *now* – I've got a lecture.'

Callum beams and jumps off the swing and runs at Rachel, and locks her in his world-famous bear hug. She may love Heels and rave about it to everyone, but I can hardly remember the last time she set foot over the threshold.

'Yes! Yes! Yes!' He charges up the stairs to clean his teeth, flies back down, almost pulls the hook off the hall wall as he grabs his school bag, and, with his chest pushed forward, stands to attention at the front door.

I nod towards his bare feet.

He scrambles back up the stairs and down again in about four seconds, new trainers in hand, flops to the floor and studiously ties his laces. I'm irritated by my reluctance to take Rachel's good mood at face value. But you'd never know by the grin I'm wearing as I wave them off.

Back in the kitchen, Abi is staring into space.

'Mum's in a weird mood – you fallen out?'

'No, she's happy, Abi. Didn't you notice her lips? They were smiling and she's taking her son, Callum, to school. Happy. You have a problem with that?'

'Yes.'

'Right. Well, fine. Good idea, good way to live. Yes, well done.' I leave it at that. 'I'm working here this morning – I think I'll make a start. You okay? Got everything?'

'You're crap at fake smiles,' she says, punching me in the shoulder.

I love the way she can rumble me. 'Okay. Well, sure.' But I'm thinking, *let's try to stop worrying so much, scanning Rachel's every move.* 'How about just for once we try to be happy for her.

She'll be excited about Sarah coming tomorrow. Let's just get through the weekend without any dramas, shall we?'

'Right, whatever. So it's all cool then, is it?' She turns inward and hugs me.

'Of course it is.'

We sway for a few seconds and then separate. I wait until the front door bangs shut before going into the study to phone the office. David answers. *My* David. My find. I allow myself a brief bask in the reflected sunshine of his success, and congratulate him on his latest corporation-bashing appearance in the tabloids, then ask him to tell Guy I won't be in for a while. As soon as I hang up, the phone rings.

'Is that you, Andrew? It's Liz here.'

Oh shit. Double shit. It's been almost a week and I still haven't told Rachel what I told Liz. Shit, shit, shit. 'Liz, just give me a few minutes will you? I'll call you right back.'

'No actually, Andrew—'

But I cut her off.

I need coffee to help me think. I feel a small rush of hope. It would be absolutely typical of Liz to want to bury this. I mean, she's buried every other blatant truth about her lousy marriage. And I was rash wasn't I? Horribly rash. And upset. And it's well known that we all say things we shouldn't when we're upset. I should rethink. Absolutely. What could possibly be gained by telling the *truth* right now? Nothing. I mean, did I really imagine she and Rachel were going to suddenly become bosom buddies? Laughable, Andrew. Best if it was out in the open? Madness, let's be honest. Far better if I swallowed my principles on this occasion. And if Liz is okay with that, well, it'd be downright childish not to follow suit.

Back at my desk, with my coffee half drunk and an almost steady hand, I pick up the phone and call her back.

'Liz, it's me. Sorry about that. It was someone from work – but they're gone. Liz? Liz? Are you there, Liz? I've been worried about you – that cough …'

'Well of course I'm here. And so will my taxi be in a minute. Have you spoken to Rachel – does she know? I've not heard a thing from her.'

'No, no, not yet – I've been waiting for the right moment.'
'Well don't – I don't want you to.'
'Are you sure?'
She was sure.

Abi

'So how's lover boy?' Sarah goes, before she's put a foot through the door.

I could kill her. No one knows about Jamie, especially Mum – so how the fuck does she? Oh shit. I remember now. That stupid email she sent me, going on and on about my zero love life – and how I was missing the best fucking years of my life – 'fucking' in italics, naturellement. I'm fifteen, for fuck's sake. Stupid. I should never have got riled, never have mentioned him. She is so gross!

I narrow my eyes as mean as I can, and check out my mum, who hasn't heard, obviously, and luckily, because my darling sweetest dog Nevis, who I miss so, so much, has got his huge paws on her chest and is licking her face off.

Sarah, though, is still having hysterics at her unfunny joke, and is about to repeat it, or a far worse one. I give her my most furious scowl, which must have hacked through her dense skull somehow, because now she's snorting and oopsing from behind her hand which she's squashing flat over her mad, purple mouth. I had totally forgotten how gross she can be. One minute ago we had a regular-size hall, and now it's like we can hardly breathe. And it's not cos she's really fat or anything (except for her size Zs of course), not really, but it's like everyone just shrinks when she's around. Maybe all artists are like that. Anyway, after she's squeezed me half to death and whispered 'Sorree darling, but have you shagged him yet?' in my ear, I just flop to the floor in despair, and let Nevis wash me too.

I'm just wondering why she's alone, when Todd staggers through the front door loaded with bags. Todd's nice and no one could believe it when they married. But I guess he's regretting it now, cos he looks like he's about to cry and I wanna ask where India is, in case she's crying too, but think better of it cos I expect she decided not to come, get some down-time without her crazy mother. I know I would.

I frown at him, the kind of frown that's a question, but he slips into the loo. And then Sarah yanks me off the floor and spins me around and gives me another bear hug.

'God, you look fabulous, darling. That's city life for you. Oh, I miss you all. I could kill you for leaving the west coast for a crummy city. You're our family for chrissake – Andrew's the nearest thing India has for a father. It's okay for you, Abi, you live here …'

I can barely breathe now.

'In fact I think I might stay on – would that be okay?'

'Of course you can, you idiot,' Mum says as she drags her off me.

'So where's Andrew, and Callum?' Sarah bangs on. 'I can't believe they're not here to meet us.'

'Andrew's at some kind of saving-the-planet conference and Callum is at school, as usual.'

'Thought he'd broken up?' she says, like Mum might be lying. Sarah's dead paranoid underneath.

'No such thing at Heels. It's sort of open all the time. He's building a canoe.'

'In the middle of Edinburgh?'

'I know, I know,' Mum sighs. 'But he wants to paddle down the canal between here and Glasgow. Oh yes, and he's tickling tomatoes, whatever that is.'

'Oh how sweet,' Sarah squeals. 'He's doing the gardening as well as building a canoe?'

'Yep! The kids actually run the whole shebang at Heels. Maybe that's why it's free – not really … But seriously, they do the accounts, pay cheques, garden, the lot. I tell you, he's going to be one scary guy in a few years' time – he'll absolutely never find a girlfriend. I'm convinced we've made the wrong decision sending him there.'

'Dinni be daft. He'll earn a fortune,' Sarah says. 'And besides, Callum's always been destined to become a grown-up, Heels or no Heels. Now come with me …' she says, towing Mum to the kitchen as if this was her gig.

Todd emerges from the loo and this time looks straight at me. I ask him if he wants to take the cases upstairs. He gives me this lame smile and nods, so I grab the yellow canvas holdall and this thing that looks like a giant strawberry (a case in disguise), which Nevis is snacking on. Nevis hangs on all the way up to the top floor and we both exchange guilty smiles when the giant strawberry makes this loud farting sound. Todd opens the spare-room door and heads to the window, and I follow him as if that's what you do.

Out in the street, Sarah's beaten-up blue car looks abandoned not parked, and it's so covered in dust it's turned silver.

'Todd, is there someone in the car?'

'Well yeah – India. They had a row on the way over. She said she was going back.'

'What about?'

Todd turns away, embarrassed.

That'll be over him then. What's wrong with that woman?

Then the car door opens and … You're kidding. Wow. That can't be India! She looks so hot – no wonder Sarah's upset. She's so thin and where are the piercings in her nose, and her eyebrows, and her lips? All gone? Spoo-ky. Why didn't anyone tell me? I thought we were meant to be family!

'Shall we go down?' I say, like in almost a whisper.

'Sure. Off you go. I'll be right behind you.'

I get carried down the last few steps by Nevis practising his snow plough – just as well he's so squidgy, eh – and heave the door open just as India's turning into ours.

'India. Hey. Come here. You look so different, I didn't even know it was you at first. Wow.' She's wearing low-cut skinny jeans and a white T. OMG, she's super cool.

'Thanks, sweetie. Don't s'pose Mum's said anything …'

'Like what? About you? No sorry – nothing.'

'Oh, never mind. Like she's ever going to change. Almost took the train back to Oban, but why should I let her get to me? Sod it. Look at you, Abi, I … You look amazing! I've missed you. Where's Todd?'

But I don't get a chance to say anything because I hear the spare room door open and I guess my face tells her it's him.

'Sorreee,' she says, taking the stairs two at a time. 'I should've seen it coming. I should've stayed at home. Poor you, silly sod. How can you stand her?'

But before Todd can answer, Sarah blasts through from the kitchen, coos up at them both on the landing, and spreads her flabby bingo wings wide, like they might actually be tempted.

'Oh, my darlings, I'm so sorry. I'm such an idiot – please forgive me, please. I don't know what comes over me – I don't deserve you, do I?'

Like they can answer this? Err no.

Two hours later Dad comes home with Callum to find Sarah, Mum and India half cut and flaked out across the sitting room floor. Todd's fucked off to the Botanics – to stretch his legs. Yeah, right.

Dad, being some kind of misguided saint, kisses them all and starts cooking dinner. Callum forces Sarah into a sitting position, presents her with a bunch of white flowers that he says he's grown himself, and tips carrot thinnings over everyone to munch on before dinner. I have to admit it's pretty cool being part of this family these days. I think I might even be happy.

RACHEL

WELL THANKS A LOT, ANDREW. Nothing like asking your wife before blundering in with an invitation to India to come and live with us. Do we really want her sharing our space, even for a few weeks? She's hardly a good role model for Abi. What if she starts ... Oh never mind. From what Sarah was saying, she does seem to have turned over a new leaf this last year, and I plan on being magnanimous. So I tell him how kind he is, that he's right, that he's the one who does most of the domestic stuff and with any luck India will help him out, and I concede generously that the kids have, after all, always loved her.

He looks at me warily for a second and then apologises. 'I was also thinking that Sarah and Todd could really do with some time alone. You should have heard her on the phone the other day – she's insanely jealous of India. Sorry darling, I didn't think it through.'

'Don't be silly – it's fine, honestly.'

'You think you'll be able to stand her?'

'Of course I will – she'll be fine. It'll be nice for Abi and Callum – like having their big sister back. Please, Andrew, don't worry about it.' I pat the space on the sofa beside me. Andrew rests his head on my shoulder and I stroke it without even the slightest quickening of my breath.

'However much you hate your mum, Rachel, it was her who got India to do retakes and get herself together. It must have had an effect.'

A few weeks ago a reference to my mum being capable of anything useful would have had me storming out the room – but I'm barely hot. He snuggles in closer and I push myself up a bit and massage the base of his neck.

'Hmm that's wonderful.'

Blimey, he's really happy. After a few minutes of contented silence I ask him what he's thinking.

'Oh, nothing much. The weekend. How crazy Sarah is, the presentation we're preparing with Greenpeace, the way the office is expanding so rapidly. I never thought work could ever feel so ... so alive, vital. I can hardly credit that only eighteen months ago I was collecting data off the seabed – did I really believe I could work on the rigs forever? Seems like one way or another all this is down to you, Rachel.'

'Not sure how I should take that.' He means my breakdown, my behaviour, my moving the family into crisis. Forcing him to think about a whole new deal: job, schools, home. I know there's a lethal pressure point round the back of the neck here somewhere. Just saying ...

'Oh sorry – didn't mean ...' He pauses, worried he's hurt me. 'I loved having you at that dinner last week. We never really spoke about it. Did you have fun?'

Give me strength. 'Yes of course.'

'I had no idea David knew so much about contamination – he certainly knew what questions to ask.'

'You must be chuffed it was you who brought him on board.'

'He certainly knows how to get people's attention. I saw you chatting to him after dinner, didn't I?' he says, yawning.

He begins to turn round but only gets half way before he relaxes back into the dip below my collarbone. 'Hardly chatting. You can tell there's friction with Guy.'

'He's jealous. He's jealous of David's pulling power,' Andrew says. 'Imagine waiting thirty years to get divorced. You wait, Guy'll be buying a sports car soon. *And* I seem to recall that it was when Guy was in the worst bit of his divorce that he almost begged David to cover the tabloids for him. Do you remember my saying how surprised I was that David had been so reluctant to step up?'

'Why was that, d'y think?' I say, like I'm at all interested.

'Fuck knows. Probably a few husbands out there he'd rather avoid, and wives for that matter.'

'Do you think David does drugs?'

'Never thought about it. Why?' Andrew yawns out.

'Nothing – just something Ryan said.'

'Speaking to him again then, are you?'

'Actually no. He mentioned it at the barbecue. He said that David was off his face.'

'Ah, well that wouldn't surprise me.' He turns his head. 'You'd be amazed at how many people self-medicate, and David's always strung out. Still, I'll forget you said that – it's down to David's mug on the telly that we've got so much work coming in. Best I know nothing. Did I tell you we're about to take on two more staff?'

'Yep. Hold still, will you?'

He leans back and closes his eyes. 'We're so lucky, aren't we?' he mumbles.

'In what way?'

'Nothing special, not really – just that we're here, that we're together, that Callum got a place at Heels. I can still hardly believe it's state-run, can you? I mean, there's not a single fee-paying school in the city offering half as much. Things really worked out. That was you, Rachel. Again. I was rather cynical, I'm afraid.'

'I do get *some* things right you know. I seem to remember you thought we should find a house in the centre – something modern and minimal. You thought Inverleith suburban, rather stodgy.'

'Yeah, well, it is a bit, isn't it? But I like it anyway.'

He sits up, works his shoulders and neck in circles. The clock on the mantelpiece says eleven. I get up, offer him a whisky, and end up pouring two. Looking sheepish, he takes it from me. 'I shouldn't, really.'

My cue to yawn now and down mine in a gulp. 'Darling, I'm going to bed. It's been one hell of a long weekend – do you mind?'

'No, no of course not. Go ahead – I'll be up soon.' He pats his pocket. 'I'll just wait until these kick in.'

Hooray for his pills. I've already got my foot on the stair.

'And Rachel?'

'Yes?'

'I love you, you know.'

As soon as I'm in the bedroom I pull out my bag from the bottom of the wardrobe, go through the list in my head. Wait till Ryan sees what I've got … I shove the lot in the bottom drawer of the chest on the landing, shower and set my phone to vibrate at two o'clock and put it under my pillow.

RYAN

ELEVEN A.M. Rachel left, what, six hours ago? Jesus, feels like I only just shut my eyes. Fuck knows how she gets up for the children. Who am I kidding? She'll have trained that long-suffering husband of hers, won't she? And she's got India helping out. Rachel has it far too easy.

I feel my way into the bathroom and stare at the state of it. I can't resist taking a hopeful peek at the front door – but what fucker would bother breaking in here? I mean, they'd be doing me a favour taking some of this shit.

As my brain engages, pictures start flashing. We did this – me and her – last night. Seemed creative at the time, but I'm fairly certain some would lock her up for less. Just look at the state of that shower curtain and the rail's twisted beyond repair and where's my chair and the towel? As I pick my way round the puddles I see it upside down inside the cubical. Oh yeah, it's all coming back to me now. I even remember where the towel is – and wish I hadn't. Better left – leave it all until I feel stronger. Way I see it, I'm doing Andrew a favour, taking some of the strain.

I have a piss and flush, careful to avoid eye contact with the grime down the wall and under the rim. I wash my underarms in the basin. Then I run fresh water and dunk my head under. I need coffee before I fix the shower. I'm almost done when I hear a weak knock-knock on my front door.

'You in there, son?'

It's Agnes. What does she want so early in the day?

'Ryan?' her voices trills. 'Come on, Ryan, I know you're in there, I've just heard the flush.'

'Just washing my hands, Sherlock. What is it?' She knows everything about everything within a mile. She's been here so long it's like she and this building have worked out their own special language.

I open the door, and unfazed by my naked torso, she pokes a small jar of coffee at me, perched precariously between her gnarled fingers.

'No bother at all, Agnes,' I say as I open the jar, peel off the foil cap and hand it back to her.

She stands quite still, stares at the powder inside like I've just handed over her husband's ashes, the deep lines around her mouth puckering and gathering momentum. Finally she tells me about some unsavoury visitors yesterday, who were leaning on my bell in the street and shouting abuse when she opened her window and leaned out.

'It's not the first time they've been here, son. Same last week, sat on the bench outside the pub, staring up at me. Over an hour they were there. You're not in any trouble are you, Ryan? I mean, if it's money …'

'Nothing to worry about, Agnes – honestly.'

She doesn't look convinced, standing there. 'Agnes, I don't want to seem rude but I'm running late. I'll catch you later.' Her face crumples, so I add, 'I'll come in for tea – okay? I'm visiting Ma's grave today – Wednesday, right?' and push the door to and wait till I hear the shush of her soft leather slippers crossing the landing and the creak and clunk of her front door.

The kitchen sink is full of last night's dishes and foil tubs. Pulling up the blind always makes things look worse, but I do it anyway. Sun filters through the filthy glass, gathering into a sunbeam of solid dust which ricochets across the skanky work surface before dropping to the even skankier linoleum. I pick up a wine glass having its moment in the spotlight, and add it to the sink. Then I fill the coffee machine from the kettle and jiggle open one of the dresser drawers, before I remember there isn't any coffee. I open the other drawer for painkillers, and rummage there for a while adjusting to the beginning of another shite day. On my way to the fridge, I flick the empty kettle to 'on'. It pops and cackles before pooping out the 'on' switch. The idea of filling it from the sink is too much, so I grab a half carton of orange from the fridge, sniff it and swig back three Nurofen. Fuck the coffee. As I heave up the window, warm air drifts in from the street. I stare at the bench across the road. Fucking nonces – but I'm telling myself they're just students, man, wanky students needing a draw. Because there's no way Billy-boy … No fucking chance.

A few minutes shuteye is what I need, let the painkillers clock in. I consider another hour in bed, remember what my bed looks like and fall heavily on the couch, try to swing my legs up onto the low table, but can't, too fucking sore. Even my balls ache. The table is strewn with tobacco strands, discarded strips of ciggy papers and a patina of overlapping red circles from last week's drinking. I pick up Rachel's gold lighter, rub its smooth surface between my thumb and forefinger a few times and relight a roach from the overflowing ashtray. After a searing entry into my lungs I indulge a long, involved coughing fit, not altogether unpleasant, drawing a few smaller hits at intervals, but swallow them hard each time before tossing the butt into the fire place. That's better. My eyelids turn to lead and snap shut. Two things happen, first the excited sounds of singing, chattering, arguing, birdsong from the pub garden opposite bombard my senses, which is nice and mellow and full of innocence, closely followed by the faint tang of old semen drifting up from the couch, frizzing the hairs in my nostrils. I'm twenty-nine, still living in student digs, still shagging on furniture shagged on by God knows how many other losers over the years. I push the image away and pull up another one: I'm in Jamaica – the sea is right outside my window across a tiny dirt track, kids are playing old reggae hits. I have just finished a day's work, taken off my pale linen jacket, loosened my tie. There's a glass of wine on the table in front of me. Later I will swim. The sea is beginning to purple up as the sun sinks low – it's my favourite time of day; hummingbirds drink nectar from giant yellow flowers smothering my window, their wings a zillion mind-blowing bubbles of reflected colour. Wow.

An hour later I wake in a sweat; I'm swimming towards a drowning child, but never getting any nearer. I can see her tiny hands clawing at the air and she's going down for the third time.

The sun has shifted to a pile of washing behind my only armchair. I lift my legs free of the table and massage them awake. Once I'm upright I start folding from the tangle of clothes, lay some clean jeans, t-shirt and underpants along the sofa back and stuff the rest into the dresser that doubles up as my wardrobe.

At the back of one of the top drawers, rolled inside a pair of socks, are a couple of bags. They've been there three days and this is the first time I've been near them. I shiggle the toe gently and an innocent bag of bicarbonate slops solidly into my palm. Then I unroll its friend – the *other* one – and sort of wait for something painful to happen, but I feel nothing but pity for the poor fuckers who can't do without this stuff. I go back across the hall into the bedroom and take the mirror off the wall, along with the miniature set of scales from my bedside table drawer, and start weighing out, and once that's done I kind of step back – inside my head that is. Twelve bags. Nice one. Reluctantly I pinch and sniff, smear the dust across my gums. This is strictly business – need to be fucking careful not to disappoint, make sure I've not overdone the bicarb. Need to have something put by in case those fat fuckers come hammering at my door, and even if they don't I need to sort out the lousy back rent, buy myself some new gear. Man, I'm so hacked off with being poor.

I work quickly tying the bags up – not even tempted to have a proper hit. Twelve soft pouches – all ready to go.

I pull the bin bag up and out of its foul prison and add the foil trash from the sink – the stinking ashtrays, the fucked-up towel. I do the dishes, humming the tune we made out to. Can't fix the shower rail in any meaningful way, so I tape up the tear in the curtain and wrap it tight to the chair, which I jam over the bit of rail sticking out from the wall.

It's an awesome day, so I decide to catch a bus to Morningside and go on foot to the cemetery. I roll two one-skinners, one for the walk, and another for now. This Moroccan shit is so damn dusty I sneeze until my bones shake.

The hot sun has turned to rain and I'm wet. I remove Pa's ring, same as always, chuck the old flowers over my shoulder in case she's creeping up on me and replace them with the fresh ones. I know she's dead, man, but tell my brain that. She's still on my case, same as always, like it's my fault her bed caught fire. And worse thing is, however much I argue, however much I replay my warnings about smoking in bed, every bone in my body sees it her way. So I'm here ain't I, paying my respects, hoping one day she'll see fit to join her rotting body and get out of my head.

The skies are clear blue by the time I leave and glassy puddles on the pavements are blowing off steam. The street has that sickly smell of old fruit gone soft which makes me think of Jamaica, of the photos of the market places, of when my mum was young and laughing and in love.

ANDREW

I STARTED WITH JUST the one after I put the kids to bed. Should have eaten, that's the trouble – now I'm sort of drunk. Not that it matters much, and it *is* a very fine single malt. I pour myself another small one, perch on the stool that gives me a view of our raggedy front garden and on down Inverleith Row.

It's kind of weird Rachel being away – wish I was seeing Shakespeare in Stratford–upon-Avon. Fucking lucky I'd call it. Been a while since I slept on my own, had the kids to myself. I've enjoyed it, to be honest. Not that Rachel isn't excellent company these days – she is. Even the physical thing's improving and I've no doubt it'll do her good to have a few days away. Let's drink to that.

What is it – a month since India moved in? It's been good. She's popular in the office, surprisingly agile on a PC, always home by three or four – no sweat these days if I'm a few minutes late. A great addition to the family is what she is.

Fucking good whisky this.

It's getting dark. I glance at my watch: five past ten. Long evenings – that's what I like. No point staring down the road like a zombie, I should sober up, get something to eat. On my way to the fridge, I flick the telly on. I find the last of the blue cheese quiche in the fridge, take it back into the other room and flip through the channels. Nothing.

I wolf down the quiche, stab at the remote a few times before hitting the off button and trying the pile of CDs. I find an old *Jo Cocker Live* – nice. We used to listen to this when we first got together. Suddenly I'm brimming with happy nostalgia and set off across the room, tugging the curtains closed with hard rhythmical jerks, as my hips and shoulders start gyrating spontaneously. Oh yes! This feels great!

It's odd, but a few months ago it would have annoyed me – Rachel going away. I would have seen it as just another excuse to be off with some of her student friends, get away from the kids. But this time, well, she was reluctant, to be honest, moaning about everyone being so young, how she'd miss us. Just goes to show things can change – even Abi and her are doing so much better.

I must have dozed for a few minutes because the next thing I know it's midnight. I am way more drunk than I should be. I plunge my way to the kitchen and drink water, then manoeuvre an unsteady course back into the drawing room, open the study doors onto the garden wide, and suck up the night air. Shall I wait up for India, or shall I not wait up for India? Nice name, India – I remember Sarah naming her after her hippy tour of the Far East. I raised my eyebrows then, in disapproval, but now it's sort of old fashioned, romantic – kind of tragic and noble. She should be in by now. I am surprised by how paternal I feel towards her.

It's a very salutary thing and privileged thing to be drinking fine whisky and drinking a bit too much without ha, without Rachel shoving her oar in, or me shoving in mine for that matter. Let's step out of the fucking groove shall we and have another wee dram and play another tune? I'm half way across the room when I hear the front door shutting. She *is* late.

'I'm in here,' I shout. I'm having to concentrate to get to the table of drinks. A change of direction takes a moment and I find I'm following a new circuitous route to the hall, via the old pouffe that I inherited from my parents.

'Whisky or wine?' I ask, steadying myself against the door jamb.

She doesn't answer right away; then disappointingly she declines, says she's already had a few.

'Everything okay?'

'Yes fine, thanks. Everything's great. But, well, this is going to sound really weird, Andrew, but … well … I was having a drink tonight, and, well, I thought I saw Rachel.'

Although my gut has balled into a fist, I hear myself say with reasonable confidence and accuracy that I'd talked to her earlier on her mobile – she was in Stratford–upon-Avon having just seen some play or other, just as she was meant to be. 'And where did you make this remarkable sighting?' I continue, with a hint of impatience that I regret word by tortured word.

'She was at the window of a flat. Shutting it. So I've just got it wrong – of course I have. Forget it.'

Sodden words flop out with rehearsed elocutionary deliberation. 'And a window where, if you don't mind me asking?'

'Raeburn Place – I was having a drink in the Raeburn hotel, in the garden at the front. Ridiculous. Listen, I'm knackered, Andrew. I'm going to bed.'

'Sure, sure.' I kiss her lightly on one cheek and attempt unsuccessfully to make light out of dark by flapping my hand past my face a couple of times. Rachel is in Stratford-upon-Avon. She's absorbing Shakespeare. The whisky prompts some automatic sense of responsibility deep inside and urges my feet to the first landing from where I hear my voice slopping up the stairwell. India emerges from the bathroom with a mouth full of froth and brush, leans over the banisters and grunts questioningly.

'I might get some fresh air, India. Callum's asleep and Abi's staying at a friend's house. Okay?'

She nods with her hand cupping her chin, catching drips, smiling.

Not sure how the fuck I got here, but I'm on the street, maybe fifty yards from the house, steadying myself against a wall, until my legs threaten to give way and I half fall onto a bench, which happens to be empty and within reach. Dropping my head between my knees, waves of queasiness come and go. Rachel's in Edinburgh. She's screwing someone and that's why she's been cheerful this last month; that's why I've woken up alone some nights; that's why sodding everything. It's nothing to do with us, it's nothing to do with our life, it's to do with her fucking problems, her fucking problems and fuck-ups. She's doing what she's always done and I'm a gullible fucking coward just kidding myself that we might make this thing work – like uni or Edinburgh would make a difference, that we're a family, a proper family.

I start sobbing, unable to lift my head as my gut balls and forces the nausea to rise on a fresh surge. I puke on the pavement and watch the strings of bungee-jumping vomit link me to the gutter for good.

ANDREW

'AT LAST,' MEGAN SAYS once I've got settled at our table. 'Where've *you* been hiding? I was starting to think I'd done something wrong.'

'Don't be silly, we've just been really busy, and it's mad at work – I'm really sorry.'

But she persists. 'I was just sitting here updating my diary. Do you realise you've cancelled two lunches, as well as our walk on the Sunday Rachel was down in Stratford?'

'I know, I know. But I'm here now and it's wonderful to see you. How are you, anyway?' I hand her the menu.

'Good – well, good as can be expected.'

'I'm going to have the special – too much choice otherwise and I don't have long.'

'I'll have the same. Thanks,' she says as she closes the menu and hands it to the waitress. I pour the iced water. 'Where's Giorgio anyway?' she asks.

'On holiday apparently; he's owned this place for five years and it's the first time he's had a break. You're looking great by the way – been somewhere?'

How pathetic of me to think I wouldn't be able to cope. Nothing's changed, everything's the same. I'm not a book for everyone to read and Megan's not a mind reader is she? She's a friend and she thinks I'd tell her if there was something wrong – which I would, wouldn't I?

She smiles her lovely, warming smile. 'I've been back to Mum and Dad's the last two weekends. It's been baking hot, which nearly makes up for having to spend time with my fucked-up brother – at least Mum and I got a chance to go for some walks.'

'That bad, is he?'

'You're kidding me. In a sitcom – brilliant. Real life – excruciating. Honestly, Andrew, he pitched up with his latest bimbo last weekend and Dad spent the whole weekend staring at her cleavage, which Tom kept alluding to. The walls of those old flats may be thick, but not thick enough, believe me. You should have heard them.'

'Very glad I didn't. So have they given your dad a clean bill of health then?' I ask as our spaghetti arrives.

'Well, yes, kind of. So long as he's careful, keeps up with his medication. It was only a mild stroke. He's even been sailing a couple of times.'

'So that's all good then?'

'Well yeah, I suppose, though Mum won't let him go alone anymore – kind of sweet really.'

We finish our pasta in silence. Then she picks up the menu again and orders a pancake and smiles at me, a smile that makes me want to tell her everything, a smile that makes me believe she could take care of it all, but she couldn't and I don't. I return to the safe topic of her fucked-up brother. 'You mustn't worry so much about Tom. Something was bound to go down sometime – he wasn't just going to go away was he? Not from what you've told me. Things just don't. I've learnt that, if nothing else.'

'What do you mean?' she says, her dripping pancake half way to her mouth.

'Oh nothing, just that sweeping under the carpet thingy – well I've learnt something about that, haven't I?'

'Have you? Well yes, I guess you have.' She scoops up a dribble of syrup as it slips off her chin. 'But have *I* learnt anything? That's my point. No, nothing, and no, you're right, things don't just go away. Just look at me stuffing my face with pancakes. As I was coming here today I repeated over and over that I wasn't even going to look at the pudding bit ...'

'Does it matter, really?' I offer.

'Do I want a lifelong struggle with my bottom?' she says, ignoring me. 'No, I do not. But that's what I'm in for – that's where I'm heading unless I can stop blanking out these wise decisions I make most mornings. Shit. Here, finish it! Please, finish it, Andrew.'

'No thanks. And don't be ridiculous, you've got a great figure.'

'Shut up. You would say that – you're far too uncritical. I don't want to talk about it—'

'You started it.'

'You're right, I did. Oh God, Andrew, how do you do it? Hold things together, get so firmly back on track. You're all doing so great.'

'Oh yes. Best parents in the world.' I'm suddenly very hot. But clearly she's missed the sarcasm for she barely pauses.

'Look at me, thirty-three, single, childless, no boyfriend and only attracted to men who resemble my fucked-up father. Yipeedoo. Right, quite enough of that. Tell me about India.'

So I do. With pleasure. 'India's good actually, making sense of all our random paperwork, doing jobs everyone else hates. It's good to have someone so young and energetic. And great to have someone at home most afternoons.'

'And didn't you say she'd got a job in the evenings?'

'Four evenings, yes. Pizza Hut.'

'So she even gives you and Rachel your evenings together. Actually for all your misgivings, it couldn't have worked out better.'

'Well, yes, I suppose,' I say, staring hard at my lasagne. And then out of the blue I begin galloping on about Callum – an unstoppable bolt about the wonderful family atmosphere that permeates his school, about how the whole project-based principles of learning within groups of different ages was just so fantastically genius … and I can hear my voice taking on this strange distant pitch and moving on to talk about honesty and openness, and it all sounds quite marvellous except that – oh my God – from out of nowhere comes this single bloated hand from the world of comic strip with a fat flabby finger pointing straight at me. I screw my eyes tight shut. Yep that's worked. It's gone.

When I open them again, Megan is staring at me oddly.

'Andrew?'

I gallop on, this time swerving sharply from words like honesty or openness, and start recounting some half-arsed story that *The Sun* fabricated in Friday's paper. I explode into laughter. The freaky finger is back, but wagging this time, none of that accusatory pointing business, waggling and wagging. And so's Megan – not wagging, no – laughing, she's laughing. Blimey, that's so great, I haven't laughed since, since … and then I say, sort of tagged onto the laughter, in a voice that I disown – totally and wholly disown – 'And another funny thing – I mean you're really, really going to find this funny – because, perhaps in just the same way that you choose dickheads who don't last, I see fit to bury my head in the sand about my wife.' She's beginning to look anxious but now I've begun I can't stop. 'And you know how?' An almost imperceptible movement of her head to the left suggests that perhaps I should leave it at that. No chance. 'So get this – the real reason Rachel's been on such cracking form is that she's been having an affair. I mean, don't you just love that?'

Oh fuck.

I had absolutely no intention of doing that. I glance at my watch. I try to say that work calls me, but my gums merely form a careless square around bared teeth. It's as if I've undone the only nut on the only bolt that holds up the Eiffel Tower, but hey, there's always a slight chance that it can stay up without it, at least until the wind blows or someone leans out or, or some idiot … Yep, here it comes …

She puts a hand on mine but I pull it away and jump to my feet. The fucking tower – can't you see? It's falling!

'No. Sorry. Listen, this isn't okay,' I stammer finally. 'That was not fair. Listen, can you pay? I'm late for work. Can I phone you?' But I'm already through the door, making a left and then a quick right down the stinking mews behind Waterstones as twisted steel crashes and screams into the buildings around me.

That was absolutely the worst thing to happen – I fucking knew there was a perfectly good fucking reason why I was avoiding her. Shit.

Ryan

'LISTEN, RACHEL, I'M SORRY Andrew knows, sure, but this isn't my problem.' And I know this to be true, as clear as the pain on her face. I did not chase this one and I'm not paying for something I didn't buy. She pulls at my arm, about to start over, but I snatch it away. 'You're not thinking straight, Rachel. You don't want to be here in this dump. We'd end up killing each other. You know it – we both know it. We've been over this – goddammit, Rachel, you're making me crazy. Here, have some of this.'

She takes the joint off me and draws deep into her lungs. With the rush, her head flops forward between her legs. She's like a young boy. Her arms collapse across her knees like pale brown twigs. I watch the bones in her hands ripple as she flicks the ash to the floor, strands of white smoke coiling towards the window, which is wide open because of the heat. Like a girl, like a boy – that's the thing with Rachel. One minute she's driving everything and the next she's making out like she needs protection. But she doesn't, and I'm not falling for it.

Her jeans are torn at the knee, and her skin, blushed gold, is gleaming up at me, begging me. I slip across the space between us and wrap the crimson silk scarf that Trish left behind, around her throat. Her sweet lips pout at me, taunting me, convinced she only has to ask. I look at her now: hard red lips, a drowning tart, same as all the others, and I make up my mind that there is no way on this earth that she's pulling me in there with her.

I twist the scarf a little tighter; she gives me a look like she knows more than I do, like she can trade something. I twist a bit more – she likes this game. Picking up the joint from the ashtray she draws deep, exhaling hard in my face – blinding me. She laughs; she thinks she's won; she thinks she can just toss her head back and win any of these games we play. And I laugh too and place my hand under her stomach and flip her over. With her head over the back of the settee facing the floor, I pull down hard on the scarf. It morphs to a thread like blood. With my other hand I rip down her jeans, designer buttons rattling over the leather and onto the floor. A golden thong, damp with sweat and juice, divides her perfect butt, and I'm not sure how my dick has come free from my shorts, but as I look down he's there galloping on the spot like champion the fucking wonder horse. 'Now baby,' I say, greasing myself up with her juice and edging my way nice 'n easy. I've never done this with a woman before – it's tight in here baby. I tell her to relax, and since I know she likes being told rough I tell her stronger, pulling with the one hand and pushing with the other, until I find some space opening up to me. Oh shit, man, this is too much – this is too much and I can feel it coming, man, from every which way. Son of a bitch and I'm yelling and whooping and pulling out while she's gasping and pulling at that damn scarf.

'You crazy?' she says, spluttering and ripping off her t-shirt and kicking herself down onto the settee so she can lie flat. Her whole body is running with sweat and her red hair seems like she's just showered and she looks so sexy I almost feel like starting over. I don't though because I see something in the expression on her face which has nothing to do with anything we've just done. I surprise myself by kicking a chair across the room.

'Fucking hell, Rachel,' I say, pushing down anger. 'We're going to have to give up this shit. You got kids. You got to get back home and be a mum to those kids. You get me?'

She whips her head up like something bit her and grabs my arms.

'No way, Ryan. I need this. Without this I don't have a family, without this I can't love my children.' And now she's sobbing, and coughing, and I sit back down and hold her shaking and moaning and I feel her tragedy just for a second – and it hurts me too, cos to be that lost is to be dragged to the hole they're going to bury you in alive. And just for a moment I believe maybe we could face this together, that together the madness is tolerable, that together we could fix this thing, or if not fix it, then fight it at least, batter it back till it crawls away to die and leaves us in peace. After a while the sobbing gets quieter. She lays there with her golden thong twisted and torn and her red lips smeared across her chin and her perfect body used up and spoilt too many times. And all I can feel is contempt.

ABI

MUM LEFT TWO DAYS AGO, gone to stay with Dawn. It doesn't make any sense.

Dad says he tried to make it work, to keep the family together and he couldn't. But it was fine just a few weeks ago, things were better than ever between them, wasn't that what he said? 'I can't remember when things were so good, Abi.' So what the fuck's going on then? And all that crap about so many divorced parents ... 'It won't be so bad. You'll see.' I mean, what's he on? I think I'm going mad. I must be going mad.

I flop down on my pillow, yucky and smeared all over with old make-up – I've barely stopped crying have I? Not since she left. My eyes are so swollen I can hardly see, but I can't cry now, can I – just stupid dry sobs that hurt. I hear the door open. It'll be Dad again trying to make up with me for something he didn't even do. I just stay with my face down.

'Hi.'

It's Cal, dear sweet Cal, and he climbs up beside me and puts his head on the pillow too. 'It's wet,' I say. He doesn't answer, just wriggles into me. Next thing it's four o'clock. 'Are you going to Dawn's to see Mum?' I say. He's staring up at the ceiling, he feels so small tucked into my side. This is so shit – I mean, he's only a baby still, isn't he?

'Yeah. Please come, Abi.'

'I just can't.'

He pushes his face into my neck.

I sit up. 'Come on, let's go and find Dad, make some tea. It's not the end of the world, you know. Lots of people have divorced parents, you'll see.' OMG. I can't believe I said that.

Dad's slumped at the table, head in hands. But up he jumps, arms wide as he spins round. Jesus. I sort of put my arms around him but only because I feel sorry for him. Basically I just want to put the kettle on, and chat about normal stuff. Okay, so that's a crap idea. There is nothing *normal* going on in this house – not today, not ever. I shrug him off – I can't help it. She's gone and she'll never be back, she's having a good time at last – glad she's not got all the hassle of having to look after us, because she never even wanted to be here anyway, did she? And to be honest, if I were her, nor would I.

I get the biscuit tin from the dresser. I remember her buying these, I remember her words as she put them in the tin: about how I always wore baggy clothes to hide my thinness – how the chocolate chips were Fair Trade and organic. She held them right under my nose so I'd smell them. I remember wanting to knock them out of her hand.

Rachel

I'M A BAG OF NERVES. For some reason Andrew's bringing the kids *here* – to Dawn's – thinks it best if *I* tell them why I've left. That is so typical. 'You seen my black sweatshirt? It was here a minute ago.'

'Saw it somewhere,' she mutters round a ciggie. 'Must be here somewhere.'

This is all Andrew's fault. 'Maybe we should go out – shall we go out?'

'Here, catch.' Dawn lobs the sweatshirt across the room. 'Surely it'll be easier with my two here, we'll play a board game or something.'

Jesus, she does say some pretty stupid things. 'Somehow I can't imagine Abi or Callum being up to playing a board game when they're still reeling from the shock of their mother leaving home for no apparent reason. Sorry, but no. It'd be best if we went out, just the three of us – we'll go to The Meadows, get a burger or something.'

The doorbell rings. Thank God, it stops me from saying something really cruel. I let Dawn get it, ignore the look she gives me. I don't want to see him. Nothing is all one person's fault – he should know that. It's obvious he's bringing them here to punish me, making quite sure they can see the kind of squalor

I'd rather live in than be with them. Never thought he'd be so petty.

'Hi, Callum darling. Abi not come?'

'Nope.'

I am ashamed to be relieved that I don't have to face her. I lift him up and hug him until he makes it clear that I'm being weird. 'Listen Cal, shall we go to The Meadows, get something to eat, or would you rather stay here and play with Angus?'

He shrugs.

'Okay then, let's walk to The Meadows shall we?'

As we climb the steep stone steps to the pavement he takes my hand, but it feels kind of fake, like I'm holding a hand without a person on the end of it. 'How's school?' I say.

'Fine,' he says, hopping over the lines between the paving slabs.

'How's India?'

'Fine.'

'And Abi?'

He doesn't answer. Cut-the-crap Callum will not be distracted by cheating small talk.

We walk in silence down the path to the playground. Just as the swings come into view he stops and climbs onto a bench under this huge tree.

I feel like I'm about to sit an exam that I'm hopelessly unprepared for. My heart is hammering stupidly. It was raining earlier; the bench is wet and the grass is steaming in the sunlight. We watch boys kicking a ball and shoving at each other. Everyone is smiling.

'Are you going to come home – you know, when you've had your holiday?'

'Oh Callum, come here.' He wriggles away from me. 'Is that what Dad's saying – that I'm on holiday?'

'Nope.'

'It's not easy to explain, not so you'd understand. Living with someone is much harder than you think. When you're a child everything seems okay – it's different when you're grown up.'

'Does that make Dad a single parent then?'

'Yes I suppose it does, in a way.' I'm staring at his knees poking out beneath his oversized cord shorts. I want to hold him to stop him saying anything, to press him against me.

He kicks his skinny legs out, one and then the other, and they begin to swing. I realise they are like mine: my ankles, my calves, my very own son. This stupid obvious thing hits me like a punch.

'At school we've been talking about different kinds of families and I want to know which,' he kicks one trainer off, 'mine,' and then the other, 'is.' And then he hops off the bench, runs to pick them up, drops to the ground, rips the Velcro open and slides his feet carefully in, and skips back to our bench. I offer him my hand, but he ignores it. As soon as he's seated he starts swinging his legs again.

'You still have two parents darling, don't you? I mean, I'm still your mummy.' His legs swing and flop like rope or a pendulum counting down.

'One parent at home, silly,' he says, more like a researcher than a bereaved child. 'Not one parent *in the world*. One parent who *does* everything. And that's going to be Dad, isn't it?' He stares at me, legs frozen mid-swing, waiting for my answer. I do my best.

'You'll see, darling – it's just hard in the beginning. But things will get better. They will, honestly.' Laughable. He lowers his matchstick legs and starts kicking the bench with his heels instead. His little fists are clenched together and I think he might be crying. I'm about to gather him into my arms but he shuffles away from me, gives a big sniff and keeps staring at his feet.

'Mummy?'

'What, darling?'

'Why don't you want to live with me and Abi, then?'

'Oh sweetheart,' I say. 'There's nothing wrong with you or Abi. Nothing. I'll go on loving you both just the same and seeing you and having fun and coming to your school and being there for you. I'll always be there for you.'

'So it was Dad, then?' His shoulders slump as his head jerks back.

It's going okay, this makes sense.

'It's not his fault, he's always tried his best, and so have I, darling. We've both tried. Sometimes it just doesn't work out between parents – but we both love you, we'll always love you and Abi. You know that don't you?'

'Yep.' One shoe and then the other fly through the air.

I sigh and suggest we get a burger. There's a café on the lane south of The Meadows and it's a lovely evening. He looks up at me as if he's thinking about my offer. Then he jumps down, sweeps up his shoes, flops to the grass and puts them on. When he stands to face me, his arms are crossed and the way his little eyebrows pucker up makes me think of tiny swords.

'I know you're angry, Callum. But you'll see, it'll be okay. Honestly.'

PART TWO

Summer

ANDREW

THINGS ARE SETTLING DOWN. Once I got over my pride, and spoke to Megan like a grown-up, it's been okay. Not completely okay, obviously, but okay. Surprisingly okay. Kind of. Though there's absolutely no doubt at all, if she hadn't been so amazing, Megan, that is, I'd probably be on the floor. Really. She calls every day and checks up on us all and brings us meals and makes me see sense and well, I'd be lying if I didn't admit that she's pretty much holding us all together. But we're getting stronger, day by day and right now I'm sitting on a rock beside the chapel in Holyrood Park, facing the New Parliament building, and guessing which distant speck might be her. I've spent the last fifteen minutes arranging a picnic on a blanket in front of me, there's even a bottle of white wine chilling in ice and I'm considering having a glass before she gets here.

'Hmm, I hope that's not all for us, Andrew.' A voice behind me makes me jump.

'Jesus, don't do that, you'll give me a heart attack. Where did you spring from? I've been watching—'

'I had a client in Easter Road. It's further than I thought. I should have phoned, sorry.' She laughs and drops down beside me.

'You never phone and you're always late.'

'No, but I should. I always mean to. I will in future.'

'Right. Good. Here, have a glass of this.' I pour wine into two plastic glasses and place one in front of her. 'Actually, I was thinking this all looks a bit meagre – a bit savoury – not enough chocolate.'

'Oi! You making a dig?' She slaps my shoulder, and fills baguettes with tiny crayfish, pulling lids off plastic tubs. I describe my morning and we spend a good few minutes imagining how there'd be no need for prisons or police or social work if everyone went to Heels.

Then inevitably she asks me about the '*India situation*', which took place a few weeks ago and I skate over it and say, like the naïve idiot that I am, that it's all calmed down and gone back to normal. 'Thanks so much for your support. It was quite a week.'

'A pleasure. Nothing like someone else's dramas to take one's mind off one's own, especially a big fat juicy one. Poor India. I've been thinking. All those sexual partners she had in Argyll, all those piercings – you don't think she was trying to make you jealous, even then? I mean, that particular brand of hangdog you do so well, it's pretty irresistible …' She giggles, leaving me in no doubt that you'd have to be deranged or a nymphomaniac to find me attractive.

'Well, thank you, Megan. I'm glad you find it so amusing. Actually, she's mortified, and showing surprising insight into her behaviour, which is why she's not going to find somewhere else to live. She got drunk and misread the situation, that's all.'

'Really? Come on, Andrew, I imagine it runs a lot deeper than that. India never knew who her father was – remember? Then by some gleeful act of fate she finds herself under the same roof as her childhood hero – her now *wifeless*, *lonely*, all of a sudden *attainable* childhood hero …' She pauses to wipe her chin with her sleeve. 'Doesn't take Freud to work it out, does it?'

And I say, with what I've come to call my head-in-the-sand voice, 'Yeah, yeah. Whatever. But I can't bring myself to chuck her out or send her home. Can you imagine what Sarah would say? Besides, she's vulnerable. And the kids love her. But,' I add, wisely, 'I've stopped taking my sleeping pills as a precaution.'

'And are you sleeping?'

'No, not really, but at least I know I'm sleeping alone! Joke! Really Megan – it's fine.'

'I still think she should find somewhere else to live. You've got enough on your plate, surely, without having to worry about India climbing into bed with you or whatever ...'

'Nah, I had a paranoid moment – she's fine.'

Megan looks at me in that way she has.

'Besides,' I say, pausing for effect, 'the gossip *is*, she and Guy are shagging – well, flirting, but very definitely *flirting* of the soon-to-be-shagging variety.'

'What, Guy as in boss Guy? Guy who just got divorced?'

'Yep.'

'He must be thirty years older.'

'And the rest. Please, don't knock it. I'm hoping they find love and lasting happiness. Cheers!' I add, downing the remains of my wine.

She picks up the doughnut box, opens one end, raises it to eye level and squints at it. 'Sod it. Okay. Let's just have a good day shall we? Here, you have them both,' she says, snapping the box shut and sulkily tearing a branch of grapes off a bunch on the rug.

'Honestly Megan, I thought you'd given up dieting.'

'You're quite stupid about women aren't you, Andrew?'

'Whatever ... Come on, let's eat these and burn them off climbing Arthur's Seat. I've got a free afternoon and you said you were quiet this week. Then I'll persuade you to come back to ours for early supper, with the promise of a rhubarb crumble. Callum brought home a ton of the stuff from school yesterday – grew it of course – you'll thank me.'

'Okay, okay, give it here. The steep way – okay?'

Almost as soon as we've stuffed everything into my rucksack and begun the ascent the sun disappears behind a dark cloud. A breeze, damp and cool, needles my skin through my cotton sweater as we move away from the shelter of the hill.

'Andrew, you're shivering.' She rubs my arm, but then stops.

I badly want to take her hand, but there is no way I'm going to risk the only real friend I have because of my inability to stand and face this alone. So with my arm firmly by my side I stride out purposefully.

A persistent wind follows us, but we haven't reached the steep part yet and we just walk side by side. I tell her we've decided to go to the west coast in a few days' time, for the remainder of the holidays and stay with Sarah.

'Not doing a last minute to France then?'

'Nope – kids didn't want to in the end.' And then I ask something serious. 'Megan, has your mum said anything about Liz recently?'

'Not really. Why?'

'I've had a couple of very strange phone calls – I'm worried about her. So in a way it'll be good to go back to Oban – it'll be good for the kids to spend some time with their old mates and I can check out the mother-in-law. They miss Sarah and her craziness and the beach and Nevis – Nevis especially.'

'Good, aren't you? What about Rachel? Liz is *her* mother. You don't have to fix everything, Andrew.'

I don't answer that directly, because there just doesn't seem to be a right way. Instead I say, trying not to sound like my life depended on it, 'What about you? You going across?'

'I will if I can clear my desk a bit – how long are you playing Mr Flo Nightingale for then?'

I yawn it out. 'Couple of weeks – till school starts again. I guess it will depend …' But inside I'm already dreading the time without seeing Megan – and wondering if there's anyone on the west coast who I *am* actually looking forward to catching up with. Probably not.

'Well, just make sure you get a bit of a break, eh?'

We slip into single file now. It's got a lot steeper, the path has petered out and I'm trying not to wheeze. When we reach the top I'm too bushed to do more than collapse face down on the grass. But after the pain in my chest has eased and I've managed to prop myself on one elbow, I silently vow to come up here more often. For as far as I can see, creases of land roll and unfold until a million miles away what appears to be the softest, palest cashmere drifts just keep on rising, until somewhere, I realise, they have become sky. I wish Abi and Callum were here. And, as

I draw my focus down it seems that nearer in, nestled childlike in the dappled plump arms of Mother Earth, rests a contented and lazy Edinburgh. It's a long time since I felt poetic – and quite a long time since I felt my right arm. I unbend it painfully, and reluctantly roll away from my masterpiece only to be smacked by a seascape beyond Leith of such fantastical splendour that it's all I can do to suppress the giggles.

'What?' Megan says, beginning to smile too.

'This. Don't you feel it? Isn't it the best thing you've ever seen? I mean ever. I mean … Stop grinning at me. It's, it's … What is it? It's like melted mercury or stretched silk or, or Christ. I mean, don't you wish you could fly down there and touch it?'

She rolls onto her back. 'When we were children, we used to come here with our picnic every weekend, can you believe that – winter and summer? My dad is a bit mad you know: "A family tradition," he'd tell us, as we trudged through the snow. "Good for body and soul."'

'Rather cool, really.'

'I suppose it was. They have at least half a dozen hampers at home that friends have given them, which they never use. The one we used was ancient and full of glass and silver and gingham and weighed a ton …' She trails off and sighs.

'What?'

'Nothing. I just wish they hadn't moved. Mum says she loves the whole west coast vibe, but I don't know if she's just saying that. I mean, with Dad – well, it all seems so pointless …'

'You're sounding like me, Megan. If she says she's happy, then maybe she is.'

'Yes, maybe, but you know what she's like – she'd do anything for Dad.'

'Then maybe that's what makes her happy.'

'Maybe – well yes, I guess …'

I stand up and pull her by the hand. I'm feeling the cold again and we begin the descent. By the time we're walking past the New Parliament building I notice a wee crack of light has forced itself into my darkness. I try not to make sudden movements, I want to coax it on, but after I've dropped her off it begins to dim, and as soon as I'm home any residual glow fades, leaving me uncomfortable and large and lost again.

No one home, yet.

As I slide the kettle onto the Aga I catch the faint bleeping of the answer machine in the sitting room. I make tea and take it through as the first drops of rain fleck the windows. It's Megan.

'Andrew. Dad's had another stroke. I'm heading across. I'll call you later.'

ABI

WISH WE'D GONE TO FRANCE now. Oban's a dump. How did I ever think it'd be okay coming back here? And what's with no one even mentioning Mum's name? It's like she never existed – like they've all been warned not to say anything ... I mean, we wouldn't want to be up front about anything, would we? And Dad always asking me if I'm okay – I mean, really, he's kind and everything, but it's so annoying. And I'm sick of everyone telling me how brilliant I'm looking – as if I don't know what *that* means. They should just come straight out with it, yeah? And those kind of weird sussed looks whenever I mention that Dad's out with Megan or whatever – what's that all about? They're pals, aren't they? Not allowed pals, I suppose – that's what I totally hate about this place. Fucking shit-stirrers.

Mum loved this place. Didn't matter how totally bad things got, we still had some laughs here, didn't we? Now look where she's living – in Dawn's crummy basement. I just sort of scroll though my contacts, for no reason really, but then as soon as I see the word 'Mum' I just press it. And then realise I've called the house phone at Dawn's.

> *Sorry, no one here right now. If you want to leave*
> *a message for Dawn or Rachel we'll get back to you*

as soon as we're back. Actually Dawn is away until the beginning of September – you can get her on her mobile.

'Mum? It's me.' And then I add 'Abi' – like she might not know her own daughter's voice. Durr. 'Can you phone me on my mobile?' And then like a complete dick, I tell her I miss her. Fanfuckingtastic. I really hate that, it only dawned on me today that I miss her, after forever of totally hating her – so it like means nothing, anyway. Hell-ooo – so what am I on then?

Jesus, look at this dump. You'd think Sarah might have made an effort – I mean, we've got her skanky daughter living with us for nothing and she's been begging us to visit her for long enough. Why can't she get her act together? The dust is an inch thick and there's washing under the bed, India's washing of course, and it's probably been there forever. Yuk.

Perhaps I should call her on her mobile, like before she gets my stupid message, but I remember we're having lunch with Gran at one and I'll need to get my skates on if I'm going to make it in time.

It's like such a relief to get outside. I don't even mind the drizzle. I zip up my jacket and walk down along the beach past our old house. Feels like shit. I mean, I was here forever. I grew up here, Callum was born here. And Nevis. I know this beach better than anyone. That's Dad's rock over there; this was where I spent every day in the summer, where Liam and I ... Well never mind that. I speed up a bit, need to get away from here – too many memories.

I decide to get something from the bakery in the square. Gran's not herself these days and even if she's remembered we're coming, lunch is bound to have a nursery theme.

As I'm tagging onto the end of the queue, two weirdos from primary appear round the corner, a rash of acne gleaming like chicken pox. I turn my back to the window, yank my hood up. 'Pain au chocolate please. Hot.' The rush as it squirts molten chocolate into my mouth is the best, so good in fact that I feel suddenly happy and decide to run up the hill to Gran's wee cottage.

The first thing I think is that she's had bad news. I keep smiling at this flaky face that I suppose is Gran: a sort of fake Gran, with faraway eyes. I lean towards her and kiss her soft downy cheek which I know has left powder on my face cos these days she's spooning it on. I never ever want to be a hundred years old. She clocks me at last.

'What a lovely surprise. I thought you lived in Edinburgh, now.'

'No Gran, well yes, we do, but you remember, yesterday you asked me and Dad to lunch. You had tea with us at Sarah's. Are you okay, Gran?'

'Of course I'm okay, darling, and of course I remember – how silly of me, come on in. It's the high pollen count that makes me forget. How lovely to see you.'

Okay then.

I go through to the sitting room, cross to the window and stare down at the bay. There's this kind of pale mist, kind of drizzle. Can't stop thinking about Mum, kind of wanting to cry. She could be fun sometimes couldn't she, like really fun? I mean how can everything have got so heavy and how come I'm always so furious when I see her or think about her? I've been such a bitch.

Gran disappears into the kitchen and appears again a few minutes later with two bowls of soup. 'Here we are, darling, a nice chicken broth,' she says, all jolly.

Right.

'I do like a good warming soup, don't you?'

Well I do as it happens, and I don't ask whether she's going to wait for Dad. Best just get on with it. I get up from the table and collect two spoons from the drawer by the sink. She's waiting for me like I'm her mum or something, with her hands in her lap, just staring out the window.

'Were you working in the Cancer shop today, Gran?'

'No, darling, not for a day or two – I've been rather busy. What about you?' she says, picking up her fork.

I'm watching Gran trying to fork up her soup, and I'm getting really worried, because it's like – why? – when my phone goes off and Gran's phone goes off and for a moment neither of us moves as both phones kind of sound like an alarm.

Mine is Mum.

'I'm at Sarah's,' I murmur on my way through to the kitchen, gearing up to rubbish everything. And I'm just about to describe ex-slut India's (whose room I'm in) manky washing and the horrible weather, when Gran lunges at me with a sort of war cry and I slip out through the back door, and slam it shut real quick.

I can hear the edge to Mum's voice, like she's missing out on something and through the window I can see Gran's mouth opening and shutting like a fish gulping for air (I can so see what Mum meant now about her looking like a mullet) and I'm worried she might be about to fit, or something. 'Listen Mum, I have to go. I'll call you back later. Sorry, Mum.' I hang up, and rush back inside. 'What's up, Gran? Who was that on the phone?'

'That was your father, dear. I think he said that Megan's father, Brendon, died this morning.'

With that off her chest she grabs my arm and pulls me through to the table, settles back in her chair and gets all normal again.

'Eat up, darling, our soup's going cold.'

So I do. I sip my cold soup obediently. I think we're in shock – well I'm in shock. Obviously Gran has lost her marbles. Normally I would expect her to be right on the case, organising the funeral, upsetting everyone, but no, here is a new, quiet granny – another person I thought cared about me gone AWOL.

'Would you like a game of clock golf after lunch, dear? I'm sure your father would appreciate you joining us.'

Oh God. I'll just pretend she didn't say that.

'Where was he, Gran?'

'In hospital dear, he died in hospital.'

Dad said she might have dementia. He told me she'd been weird a few days ago, but this is the first time she's been like this with me. Everything is falling apart.

'No I mean – where was Dad?'

'I think he was next door, darling – I said so, didn't I?'

'Do you mind if I go and see him, Gran? Poor Mr Hyslop, poor Rhona and Megan as well …' I can't believe it. It's so awful. They said he was better, he was fine, we were all of us out sailing a few days ago – I mean yesterday – it was yesterday. God, I mean, it shouldn't just happen like that should it? Not when he'd got better, not when they said he could, that he was well and everything ...

Gran's admiring her nails. Honestly, I could slap her, a good hard slap, to get her back, so she can help me out here. But how can I? She's like gone, too. Totally fucking left, hasn't she?

I'm going for the door and then I'm noticing Gran's face which is kind of weird, upset and confused like a child, and so I'm rushing back, taking her hands in mine and telling her I'll come round later to help wash up and that.

I don't knock because I don't want to make any noise or anything. They have a bright green carpet, a new one, and I remember Megan telling me this story about how Rhona had bribed Brendon by letting him choose the colour, so long as he promised not to lay it himself – he was meant to be taking things easy, wasn't he? There's no one in the living room, but I look in anyway, mugs and cups and glasses everywhere like they've had a bit of a party, but I guess they've just had a lot of tea. I can hear voices now. I suppose they're in the garden on the other side of the lean-to, where there's like a table and chairs and stuff because it's mostly out of the wind. Through the kitchen window I can see Rhona sitting in her usual chair and looking away out to sea and I suppose she's thinking of him, maybe even seeing him in his sailing boat. I walk out the back door with loads of stupid thoughts going round and round in my head, making me dizzy. I'm just standing there for a split second before Megan comes up and hugs me. And that hug saves me, because I can't take any more of people being crazy or miserable or just dead. I can't take anyone else going away and I don't know what to say that won't sound stupid, but she probably knows anyway because she's a saint and a minute later I'm hugging her too, and crying a bit and it's raining again and Megan says we all need tea.

Rachel

It's four. I've been swithering about going to get milk for hours. What's wrong with me? I keep thinking the reason she called the house phone was that she might not have my mobile number – maybe she's deleted it. She was angry enough. I should have called her earlier, but I didn't think, did I? And I can't call her can I, in case she's busy *again* or changed her mind.

I go back to the hall, listen to her message, again. She does miss me, she's really choked up. I'll be quick. Could really do with a coffee. It'll be okay – she'll phone, she will, when she can. I should go. I will – I'll just go.

I start looking for the flat keys, knowing I'll never find them, get half way through the door when my mobile vibrates in my pocket. I wipe my palms on my jeans, heart thudding hard. This is crazy. She's my daughter for God's sake, my daughter. I haven't committed a crime and I'm not the first woman to leave her husband.

It's Ryan. His voice cuts painlessly through my legs. As I lean against the wall and slide heavily down to the floor, rafts of dust float out of my way and resettle against the skirting like an audience. He's been busy – he's got a job in a bar, been working

84

late. His voice slips into me like warmed honey, better than that. He won't apologise and nor will I make him. These last few days, well, I've had enough of going over things. He's called hasn't he? He's missing me, wants me back. Words, some from me, some from him, come swooping at me like swallows in spring time. I've been so scared – I've behaved so badly, said such awful things, done such awful things. I shouldn't have called his friend, shouldn't have said all those things. Billy, that's right, Billy … I've been so scared, so fucked up. And Billy was happy, he loved him – I need to stop worrying.

A surge of triumph mixes gloriously with the swallows and I'm weak with desire when he says he'll come over later. I'm nodding inanely, trying not to burst into tears.

I get up off the floor, brush the dust from my jeans and make my way shakily to Dawn's only half-decent armchair, reach for my cigarettes.

I tap out my third Marlboro. A celebration ciggy this time. I inhale deeply, blow a tube of perfect smoke rings through a lonely sliver of sunlight. I'll not ask him. Was I completely crazy to follow him? Yes I was, completely fucking mad. He'll have mates out there, maybe a relative or maybe his dealer – it doesn't matter … Does he act like he's shagging someone else? Well maybe he does sometimes, but that's just the way he is, isn't it – the way *I* hear him. I've had time to think, time to realise what I might lose, thought I'd lost. I'm paranoid, vindictive sometimes – but I'll change, I can change. I've waited my whole fucking life to find someone who gets me. I tried to make Andrew into someone he wasn't. I tried to be someone I wasn't. Almost gave up – almost. And then there he was – 'The One.' I pull hard on my cigarette, hold it for as long as I can. As I let go a rush of smoke streams out and I visualise all my negative energy rushing with it. It's this place; it's not good for me. I need somewhere with light – somewhere that's mine.

First Abi, then Ryan. I thought I'd lost them both, but now … I shouldn't be crying, I should be happy and I am, I am – just so relieved. It's not just about Ryan, God no, it's about me and her and making a new beginning. I go through to the bathroom and run the corner of a towel under cold water and press it to my ruined eyes and swear I'm going to clean up this dump. I drop the towel on top of the pile of dirty clothes and then take the whole lot into the kitchen and kind of sort them into two piles, grabbing other stuff off the floor. I shove one pile in the washing machine, and start looking for my keys again but can't find them. I'm near to tears, start kicking cushions onto the floor, pushing stuff off the work surface with my free hand.

Then my phone goes off again. I slip onto the floor, pushing the tip of a fresh ciggy into the glowing butt of my last one, blinking hard so I can see who it is.

'Hi Mum. It's me. Abi.'

I draw my feet up to my chin. She tells me of the rain, falls silent.

'We just heard that Brendon Hyslop died last night.'

I'm quite winded for a moment.

I take a long last pull and crumple my cigarette over itself on the floor. I've missed her so much. 'How awful,' is all I can manage.

'He and Tom hadn't spoken for years. Mum …?'

I hook the cigarette packet up with two fingers and peer inside but it's empty. 'Abi?' There's this rock in my throat, and all the words and ideas are piling up and crashing against it.

'Mum?'

'Why don't you come and stay next week? Dawn's still away, and we can spend the week, oh, I don't know – together.' She's not going to answer – I mean – we haven't talked for almost two months. Then she says, 'Yeah, okay, I could come.'

By nine p.m. a string of tiny night lights run down the passage and into my bedroom. I should say Dawn's bedroom really, but I've been using it since she left for Eigg. I've given it a good clean, taken most of the toys out, put the books in piles and my lovely linen on her futon. With the evening sun it looks almost pretty. I have whisky, and wine – a little dope.

By ten p.m. I'm a little drunk, trying to remember if we said a time. By eleven thirty I've run out of cigarettes again.

I found the keys – they were in the front door. It's nice to be out. I'm doing well, not angry, not really – we didn't say a time. I forgot to ask. He'll be here, he wouldn't have rung up if he hadn't planned to come.

As I'm leaving the mini mart and lighting my first, I see him. Some guy is pulling his arm. Ryan shrugs him off, but the guy is back flinging both arms round his neck pulling him in. Ryan brings his arms up, breaks away. The boy shoves his face into Ryan's, gives him the finger and walks off.

I start towards home, cutting across The Meadows, out of the glare of the street lamps and beating off the questions forming in my head. It could be anything, it could be random. He wouldn't have called would he, if he hadn't wanted to see me?

Ryan

I BUY SOME BENSONS and a half bottle from the off-licence on the corner and take a seat on one of the benches beside the path. Need to get my head straight. I roll myself a skinny joint and take a few wee nips of vodka. I should have phoned to say I'd be late. Despite my intentions, I finish the half bottle and chuck it behind me. It's been a bad week. Maybe I should call, tell her I'm fucked up or ill or had to work a late shift – rearrange for tomorrow. But it's only a minute away and she's going to be nice and on top of that my flat's a mess and there's no word evil enough for my bed, so I haul my ass over to hers and look over the railings. I can see from here that she's turned her living room into some kind of flickering spiritual shit, and go on down.

She's wearing a white vest top. Her skin is the colour of honey. Her jeans are designer ragged. 'Sorry, I got held up. Hmm, come here, you. You smell like sugared almonds.'

'You're here, now – that's what matters. Drink?'

'Yeah – anything. So long as it's alcoholic.'

She comes towards me, slips her arms under my jacket, pulls me close and stands on my shoes. 'Sorry,' is all she says. We kiss and I slip a finger through the latticed rip beneath her butt.

I push her legs with mine and we walk backwards like one person. 'You're pouring with sweat,' she tells me, tipping back.

'Yeah, been running to get here.'

'Start again?'

'Sure. You gonna get me that drink?' I tip her further back, roll up her top and kiss her belly.

'What now?' she says, waving her skinny arms, leaning and pushing.

'Something to help me unwind would be good. You seem like you've had a head start.'

She fake-falls back and totters to the cupboard beside the fridge wagging a finger at me, then changes her mind.

'Hang on a minute. I've got something better.' She goes into the bedroom. I sit on the sofa and pull off my trainers, and as I bend over I see the edge of a foolscap notepad and pull it out. On the first page is some kind of stream of consciousness bullshit that I scan pretty fast – wow she was mad at me okay. I get up.

She stops at the door, a bottle of single malt in her hand, a flicker of alarm in her eyes when she sees what I've got. Once she's heading towards me, I get up, hold her away with one arm and start reading it out to her.

So maybe I did ask him about his past – so what,
what's he hiding anyway …

'Fuck Ryan, give it here – I've been looking for that!'

Still holding her off, I lay it flat on the table and pull a candle towards it. 'Relax baby. What's this? *Emotionally what? Retarded?* Surely that's not me, is it?'

'So what? You know I was pissed off. Just letting off steam that's all. Read it if you like.' She stops pushing at my arm and crosses both hers across her chest.

'Nah,' I say and flip the cover back over. 'You're okay – I've been an arse too.' I pat the cushion beside me. 'Sit. I've got something to make amends. A kind of celebration treat. Just this once, mind.'

'What is it? What've you got?'

'Crack, baby. You ever done this shit?'

I cook. Then we drink a little whisky and sook a little smoke. Pretty quick she's on her feet, running for the bathroom.

After ten minutes, I raise my voice over the seduction of Cowboy Junkies. 'You okay?'

I remember my first time – aged twelve. Me and Billy, New Year's Eve, bollock cold and squatting in the snow, crapping our guts out with only six inches of community hall wall between us and the entire cast of *Shameless*. Fucking hilarious it was.

'Jesus, Ryan. Fuck.' She stands there for a minute with a smile, I know well, on her face.

My arm is almost too heavy to lift but somehow I pat the settee and she's here, melted into me and together we get lost in the lyrics.

'Look at your foot,' she says, beginning to giggle. I turn it one way and then the other and find she's right – it's fall-about funny. We both agree, in the moments between fits, that my toes out-gag most stand-ups, and it's with the deepest reluctance that I command them to the floor because other business beckons. I shove the one-skinner in my gob and stoop low and lift her off her feet and almost drop her – the toe theme still live it seems – and that, on top of dealing with some dude turning cartwheels in my belly, makes the journey from settee to bed seem like a long one.

Blinded by smoke I misjudge the distance and throw her from the door. Her head hits the low table but she won't feel it.

She lays spread-eagled on white linen, looking up at me though I doubt I'm in focus – looks like she's made quite an effort.

I stoop, hand her the joint and rub her temple. She bats my hand aside, rolls onto her belly, knocks over a pile of books, and giggles.

By my left eye is an open library book, and across the ticket in writing that I know better than my own are the words 'call Billy', along with the number 07899 232007.

Before I lose it completely, I manage to get her neck in an arm vice and maybe break her nose with the cover. 'Where the fuck did you get this?'

But I don't hear the answer because I've just seen the handcuffs and I'm dragging her to the window which has bars across it, and fixing her low, just like we've done so many times before.

'I'm sorry.'

'Sorry? Sorry for what, bitch?'

'Oh God, Ryan. Don't.'

I think I hit the side of her face with the book a few more times and do something with a bottle, but mostly it's a blur, mostly all I'm seeing is Billy and Billy's dad and Andy and the others.

'What did you do, Rachel? For fuck's sake what the fuck did you do?'

'Nothing – gave him your number—'

'Did you tell him where I live – did you?'

'I don't know – maybe. I think so. I was angry, that's all – angry. So, I called him …'

I'm trying not to break into a run. I'm leaving a crime scene and I'm pretty sure you aren't meant to run. Walking fast is okay. I'm shaking, sweating. Perhaps I should call the police or the ambulance. Next thing I know I'm on my knees heaving over a drain. They do that too, on TV. The taste in my mouth is so foul I heave again. I plunge my hand into my pocket, need a cigarette badly. I duck inside the Co-op, into the glaring interrogation lights, snatch a can from the cooler and almost run to the check-out. There are streaks of blood on my hands, my knuckles are torn. Jesus fucking Christ. My wallet, my fucking wallet. Then the chink of money somewhere, as I'm slapping my pockets. Backtracking to the inner pocket of my jacket I shake out four or five pound coins, which rattle onto the counter. I'm almost crying. I mustn't cry – the girl's looking freaked out. I wipe one hand across my eyes – there's grit scouring my eyelids – and wag the other at the shelves of cigarettes. I try to cover up the slick tracks of blood and grime on the back of my hand by pulling down my shirt cuffs. Once I've got the fags and matches, I skate to the door before she calls someone. I half expect a police car to skid to a halt beside me, to be hustled into the back seat, but the street's almost deserted: a few drunks in doorways, a couple of chicks tottering half-naked on long, spiked heels. I can't keep the match going long enough or strong enough to catch the tip. I stop and lean against a wall, force myself hard against it and cup my hands to make a windbreak. What the fuck did I do? Jesus, man, I'm well and truly fucked now. Finally I get the fucking thing to light, start striding out, need to get home, need to get away from the wind, need to call her, need to go back and get my wallet …

In my mind's eye I see her mobile, crushed across the floor. I pace round the flat like an animal. I feel like an animal. I shower, stick plasters over cuts. I think about going back there, but how can I? In the end I take a handful of barbiturates, drink a bottle of vodka and pass out.

ABI

As Dad put me on the train he said I was doing the right thing, but it doesn't feel right. Why's Mum not answering her phone? Jeez, I mean is that too much to ask – that she's actually in?

Once I reach The Meadows, the sun's sinking, making shadows – strong black stripes, like tubes across the grass. I kind of want to jump them, but I don't do I? If Cal were here I would. That's the thing with little kids, they get you to do stuff you kind of want to do but don't in case you look like a plonker. If he were here he'd be jumping them and yelling at me to keep up and run.

At the road I stare stupidly at a group of students racing through the trees and it makes me feel sad, kinda like I'm gonna cry. And for no reason I think of Liam and then Jamie. Like there's almost nothing the same about them. I'd have died for Liam, but I was a mug wasn't I? Nothing was real. He pretty much lied about everything – and now, with Jamie? Well he's different. Jamie couldn't lie to save himself, but well, sometimes I just want him to shock me, make me think of nothing but him, make me go weak at the knees, I guess.

I stare down over Dawn's railings – grungy as ever. My stupid heart's thumping as I tiptoe down the steps and press the bell. Almost jump out of my skin when Mum opens the door – like she was standing right there. She looks weird, but it's so dingy in the stairwell and so dark after the sunshine that I can't see really, not clearly.

She throws her arms around me and just stands swaying for a bit. Mum's hugging me – now I know something's wrong.

I stare up at the cobwebs that make a kind of awesome tent above us, and feel bad because she must have missed me more than I thought. When she lets go, she's all jittery – kind of grabs me by my sleeve, muttering and apologising about the mess as she half drags me into the kitchen. I sneak a sideways look at her in case it's someone posing as my mum. It doesn't even sound like her, not really. This is freaking me out. So now she offers me wine – like it's something she does every day. She's drunk – been drinking to steady her nerves. Okay. And I don't even care when she pulls out her fags. This is a fresh start for us: no more point scoring, we've got to be pals this time.

'Would you like coffee too, or just wine?'

'Whatever you're having,' I say.

The table has a candle burning in the middle and the curtains are drawn. I suppose she's trying to make it nice, like that's even possible. She picks up a dishcloth and starts wiping around the dirty cups and glasses and stuff, tops up her glass. I sit down at the table and sip at mine, trying to keep an open mind like Dad said, cos surely she must be pleased that I'm here.

'I'm sorry. I've had one of those days.' She's staring into the sink, but she like turns then and tries to smile at me and the dim light through the curtains kind of rests for a minute on her cheek.

'What's happened?'

'No. Nothing really, just waiting for you, just this place,' and she waves the room away with the back of her hand.

'Yeah it is a bit, well, you know. I would have phoned before …'

'It's okay Abi, it doesn't matter, what matters is that you're here now.'

'What happened to your face, Mum?' I say, cos I can hardly ignore the facts can I? She doesn't answer straight away and I'm guessing she's thinking up some story, but I'm wrong because she lets out this huge sob and I'm up and out of my seat like an idiot and grabbing her by the shoulders trying to hug her, but now she's pushing me off like she hates me, like I'm just nothing to her. Okay. So I stand next to her, leaning against the worktop like she is. There's a small gap in the curtains onto the skanky back yard and I try to see what's out there, like I care, but can't see a thing because everything's fizzing and blurry and I have to squeeze my eyes shut against the tears, cos why would I let her see she's upset me? I'll just leave, go home, go back tomorrow. This was a big mistake.

She moves back a pace and I can sense her behind me, hear her breath. Then she like tugs at my arm and pulls me towards the sofa, drags me down with her and starts patting my knee, like she's trying to remember something.

'Sorry. So sorry, Abi.'

'I thought you wanted me to come?'

'I did – do.'

'Doesn't feel like it – you're being so weird.'

She starts by telling me what a mess she's made of everything.

'No, you haven't.'

'Yes, I have,' she says, still patting my knee in small irregular pats the way some people do if they're listening to music with headphones. Only she's not.

Then she takes a stuttery deep breath.

It's midnight now. She's been talking for hours. I've been listening like I'm *her* mother. Oh my God. I mean I can't believe what she's just told me about this guy – this guy, well actually *the* guy, the *cool* guy, the guy who came for lunch, who messed about with Callum, who spoke to Dad, who Dad really liked … and I can't believe that she's told *me*. I mean she's my mum, and he's been beating her up, and not just a slap or something but really beaten her up like he's some murderer or something, and other stuff and everything. And she says she didn't do anything really, not really, just gave his number to some random guy she met who once knew him.

She won't tell anyone. She can't – that's all she says. "I can't", like, over and over. I reckon *he's* the reason she left us – must be. So why wasn't I told? I mean why? Did Dad know – or India? That day she sat on my bed – did she know that Mum was having an affair, that that's why she left? It would have made things better, not worse. Not knowing is the worst, why didn't anyone tell me?

Just look at her. She keeps trying to fill up my glass. She's chain smoking, but her hands are shaking so much and I'm scared of what she's going to tell me next.

I put my arm around her and tell her it's going to be okay, ask her when she last ate. I can tell from her face that she doesn't have a clue, and it's so totally obvious she's been drinking not eating. Oh shit. What the fuck should I do? What if there's internal bleeding? I ask her, and she says she's not bleeding, but she's so out of it – I mean, how would she know anyway? Maybe we should wait until morning, see how she is then. She needs to eat. Definitely. I should make her eat something. There's an old brown loaf on the windowsill. I sprinkle both sides with water and put two slices in the toaster. At the back of the fridge there's a piece of manky Cheddar and some of her favourite pickle in one of the cupboards. I could go out and get stuff, but I'm too scared now to leave her.

She shoves the bubbling cheese on toast away but I know I'm doing the right thing so I just look at her the way she's always looked at me, and she gives me a wee smile a bit like a naughty toddler. I stay calm and in the end she does eat it. She's pretty drunk now and after we've been sitting a while not saying anything really, she lets me take her through to Dawn's bedroom. There are dozens of used-up tea lights along the passage. Jesus.

All the furniture is brown and old and dusty. The light from the street makes the mauve curtains sludge brown. Mum must hate it. She shouldn't be here. She should be at home. Perhaps she'll come home, forget what's happened. Yes that's it. Suddenly everything seems like it's going to be okay. It wasn't right her just leaving like that, was it? She's always been impulsive. Dad's right, it's part of who she is, and besides, it's got its good sides. Like how she can be so fun, the way she always lets us do stuff when Dad's such a stick in the mud. She made a mistake, that's all. I mean he *was* drop-dead fucking gorgeous, wasn't he? And what with the pressure of juggling everything, being a mum, a student – just like Dad said – it got too much and that bastard was waiting. She just cracked, that's all.

She looks like a child as she looks round the room, sort of yanking at her clothes until they give up and kind of fall off her. Then she slumps onto the futon like a rag doll. It feels weird. The splodges of colour on her thighs remind me of that painting Callum did of autumn leaves. I climb in beside her and stroke her forehead until her breathing tells me she's asleep. Then I go into the kids' room and get into the bottom bunk.

> *She's covered in blood. Her eyes are shut and swollen but she's still gaining on me. Her legs are splayed out and back to front and her bones are jutting out all over the place but somehow it doesn't stop her coming and begging and pleading for me. Her hands, shit Mum ... Please don't Mum, please don't. Don't touch me, Mum, you hate touching, you hate touching, but I can't get away; I'm running but I'm not fucking moving ... Please, Mum, get away. It's not my fault, Mum, you'll have to find someone else, I can't, Mum, no! What's the matter with me? Please ...*

I wake up in a sweat. The dream was so real, it takes me a while to remember where I am. I must get her away from here. I'm not staying here another night – I'm not. I hug my knees up to my chest and check the floor for spiders. Someone's gonna have to clean this place before Dawn gets home. She'll go mental. I mean how could Mum let it get in this kind of state? Ugh. I'm not putting on my socks – no way, who knows what might have nested in them during the night. Gobs of dust stick to my feet.

I look in on her. Out cold.

By the looks of this place, Mum must have been sick for ages. This is like five years ago, when she turned the house into some kind of squat. What if she's taking stuff, again? Shit, I never thought of that – of course she fucking is.

I badly need a wee and tiptoe to the tiny bog with my hand jammed over my nose to keep the stench out – I'm feeling almost faint. It's like a junkie's flat. I pee without actually touching the loo seat. There's a bottle of sleeping pills lying on its side, the lid off and pills spewing out across the manky glass shelf to one side of the basin. She didn't even bother to hide it. So maybe she wants me to know. Who am I kidding? Reality check, please. Look at this place, does she really clean her teeth in here? Is this really my mum? I use her mingin' flannel to remove what could be mouldy trifle from the basin, except it isn't, it's something far worse – and chuck it on top of a pile of washing in the corner. I was going to wash my face and do my teeth, but something oozing from the overflow draws bile from my tummy and I give up.

ANDREW

'WHAT DO YOU THINK, SARAH? I mean, I can't just leave her to her own devices and Rhona's done enough. Besides, she's in no fit state to cope with Liz the way she is. Maybe I should phone Rachel or Sheena – what do you think?'

Sarah looks at me as though *I've* gone mental, while Nevis lays his slobbery muzzle along my thigh.

'So what did the doctor say? What's wrong with her?'

'He couldn't say for sure, but it could be something called MID.'

'Oh yeah?'

'Yes, a series of very small strokes, prompted by stress most probably, prompted by me – more than likely.'

'Okay – and how do you figure that out?'

'You didn't see the look on the doctor's face – or hear him. He asked me if she's been through any particular trauma recently.'

'So you told him.'

'Yep. And I quote: "Do you think it was wise, Mr Gillespie, to tell a fragile old lady that her deceased husband sexually abused both her daughters?"'

'Hmm – well maybe, but that's only because he's taken it out of context. You only did what you should have done years ago. This isn't your fault, Andrew – you know it's not.'

'Whatever. The fact is, she needs looking after and I feel responsible.'

Sarah grabs Nevis impatiently. He has placed his paws sympathetically on my knees and is now licking my cheek.

'Christ, Andrew, get a grip. It wasn't you that abused Rachel. Telling her might have been just what Liz needed to patch things up. You weren't to know, and nor does Dr Macey. He's just speculating. Why don't you stop beating yourself up? And for fuck's sake instil some discipline into this damn dog.'

I say nothing – no point.

And then I surprise myself by making a snap decision.

'Hi Rhona. I'm sorry to be ringing you so early but I've made my mind up to take Liz back to Edinburgh. Yes, this Wednesday, the day after tomorrow. I've talked to Sheena. Yes, Rachel's sister, and she's going to come to Edinburgh to get her from us in a couple of weeks. Yup. Well no, she's trekking in Morocco for two weeks and then she'll come up. For the moment I'm not sure there's much else I can do.'

Rhona offers to do the neighbourly thing for Liz, and I'm sorely tempted, but turn her down nevertheless – it wouldn't be fair. I tell her that I'm sure India will help out for a couple of weeks.

I decide to postpone calling Abi and India. I have a lunch appointment with Liz, which she probably won't remember, and I could do with a walk to clear my head.

I set off along the beach, at a skip. I am consumed by this novel, grossly inappropriate but overwhelming sense of wellbeing. Sleeping without pills helps, and I can't just ignore how much easier, quicker and crisper decision making is without Rachel.

Nevis leaps around, snapping at my shirt cuffs. I snap back. I run a little and then decide to walk the entire length of the beach, basking in this – this unfamiliar and welcome surge of enthusiasm.

It doesn't last. All too soon a nasty thought sneaks into my mind. I should leave it there, I know – not drag it out for closer inspection, but there it is: the image of Liz going madder and madder over the next twenty years, in my house. Unrealistic of course, and a piggyback for another much grubbier thought: I hate and detest Rachel, my wife. There – it's out. I say it again and again, and each time it fits better, sounds lighter, more right, more playful.

It felt like the end of the world when Rachel left – as though everything I'd lived for had disappeared. So how come in the space of a few months I'm beginning to feel things I've never felt before? Am I so fickle that I can dispense with almost twenty years of marriage so easily? Fuck it, so maybe I am – and for the first time ever I realise I'm in fuck-it mode.

I run a little, kick sand, look forward at my future with the children, my friendship with Megan, my work.

I'm not frightened anymore; I don't spend nail-biting hours working out strategies or worrying about how she'll react, or trying to bottle what I feel. Could this be the beginning of happiness, autonomy? Was I mistaking purpose for dependency – a dependency on fear? Maybe. Maybe I was. Well I mustn't. It's sick and depressing. Addicted to being scared – they say that don't they? We revert to and take refuge in feelings we know best. Wasn't Rachel the very one who introduced me to the concept, did it click? No, it did not. I drop to my knees and punch the sand in front of me. Nevis starts digging. I drop back prostrate and stare at the spattering of cloud above me.

I have twenty minutes or so before I'm due at Liz's. I mustn't let these insights slip through my fingers, but even as I think it, the clarity of the past few moments are blurring and drifting away.

The clouds are no good. I roll onto my stomach, press my fists into my eye sockets.

I sit up. It's obvious: having escaped the tyranny of my mother, and after a short sabbatical, I took up the tyranny of Rachel like the prodigal son coming home. Jeez!

ABI

I SWITHER ABOUT TELLING Dad and decide against it. I'm nearly a grown-up and it's my house too. Besides, Dad has too much to cope with just now – Liz and Megan and Rhona and everything. It's best if I do it on my own. I just need to bring Mum home and take care of her and she'll be fine in a few days.

I go shopping and fill the fridge with all the stuff she likes. I pick yellow roses and daisies from the garden and make up two small vases, one for the kitchen table and one beside her bed. I wonder if I should put her in the study on the sofa bed, but I can't do that – I mean I can't can I? Oh my God, oh my God – this is sooo cool. She made a mistake, that's all, and she's sorry, really fucking sorry.

Right, what's the time? Eleven. I've been gone two hours. I doubt she'll be awake but she may be. I should go. Get some croissants and milk and go, catch the bus.

My heart's racing as I rattle down the filthy basement steps.

No sign of her. I do a bit of tidying up, turn on Radio 1, open the curtains, put the kettle on, shove the croissants in the oven. I puff up the sofa cushions, make up a tray and take it to

Mum's room. She's lying in a weird way, like totally still out of it. I drop into the curve made by her stomach and knees and stroke her forehead. The duvet is covered in ash smears and her head's kind of twisted towards the ceiling like she's been battered. Her face is scary in the weak daylight. She doesn't move so I give her shoulder a wee shake. She murmurs something and drools saliva which spills over this wee spout made by a sag in her lower lip. She doesn't look like my mum. *Come on, wake up. This is important, wake up.* I shake her some more. She opens her eyes and looks up at me like she's seen a ghost.

As she struggles up I jam pillows behind her so she can drink. She's doing that naughty-girl thing again – does my head in. I'd leave her to it, but she's not holding the cup right and I know she'll spill it. Yep. I can't be doing with this and take it off her. She senses I'm pissed off and flicks me away with her hand, finally gets her legs out of bed and onto the floor. I help her up and she stumbles off to the bathroom. I fend off memories of her doing the same last time. Deja vu or whatever and leave her to it.

She comes through ten minutes later. She looks terrible. I settle her on the sofa, give her more tea laced with honey and once she looks a bit more awake I tell her she's coming home. 'Dad's been miserable – I mean we all have. You know him, Mum, he's so slow to do anything, and he might think it's all a bit rushed, but in the end it's what he wants – we both know that.'

'But I really messed up – he'll never want to see me again.' She's crying, like not making much noise or anything, but wiping her tears away before they reach her cheeks.

'I'll phone him. Don't cry, Mum, it's going to be fine.'

'Oh Abi! You really mean it – you really think Dad'll be pleased? I mean, I could get better if I was at home, you know, not just all the bruising, but in my head. Oh God, do you really think he'll be all right with it?'

It's two in the afternoon. Mum got some of her gear together but basically she's not up to packing. I tried to call Dad, like I said I would, but he didn't pick up and I could hardly tell him in a message could I? Why doesn't he call me for chrissake – or change his phone to one that actually works in Oban? How does he expect me to tell him stuff if I can't call him?

I open the cab door and she sort of spills out. She's really not with it. I pull out the bags and pay the driver who has given up telling stupid jokes and replaced them with these pitying looks. As I lug her bags into the house, I squash down a wave of sickening panic. She's never going to be that caring, stable person in my life, is she? We're going to be friends. But the word 'friend' doesn't really fit any better than the word 'Mum' – I mean, how can this beaten-up stranger sitting on the second stair up, who is really my mum, suddenly be my pal? I squat down, preparing to help her up, and she holds her bruised arms out towards me.

'I don't deserve you, my darling. I don't deserve you.'

I don't care what anyone thinks. I could just sit here all day. I promise I'll look after her and stay with her whatever she does. I know this sounds like totally stupid, but it's like, it feels dead right, like this might be a new beginning for us – like I might actually be doing the right thing for once.

ANDREW

I COULD KILL SARAH. As if there isn't enough on my plate without dumping Nevis on us for a month – my dog indeed! Yes, he was my dog, but he became her dog a year ago when she begged us to leave him with her.

'Fuck off will you, Nevis? No, Callum, I have not lost my temper and I'm not in a mood. I just don't think Nevis should sit on my knee while I'm driving. No, you can't take your belt off. Liz, could you just leave it alone? Classical is fine, it's what you wanted a moment ago. Please Liz, I'm really … Oh Christ, okay, no, don't cry Liz, please don't cry. Okay let's have the play, it's just that you said you didn't like it before.'

I stop at the first lay-by we come to, look around for Nevis's lead and realise I must have left it at Sarah's. I get out of the car, open the boot and grab some twine with which I'd happily throttle him, only I mustn't. Instead, I slip one end through the ring on his collar and the other through the grab handle above the door and winch his head in until it has only a few inches manoeuvrability.

'Take some deep breaths, Dad,' Callum says patiently.

Is he real or what? Annoying little shit.

I'm happy to say, Nevis looks contrite. Returning to the driver's seat I long to slap Liz's hand as she whizzes us through two seconds of each channel, acting at each pause like she's finally found what she's looking for. I can't stand this. I fumble below the dash briefly until I locate the fuses and pull one. Bliss. We set off again, Liz fiddling happily with a silent radio.

RACHEL

'WHAT DO YOU MEAN you never told him? You said he would be happy!'

I can see from the look on my daughter's sanctimonious, conniving, manipulative little face, as she vanishes through the front door, Callum in tow, that she lied to me. Andrew knows nothing about any of this. It gets worse. Staring at me like she's about to hug me or something is my fucking mother.

I'm screaming at him to stop, but Andrew grabs me and pulls me outside, slamming the door after us and shoving me into a chair.

'What are you doing here?' He's glaring at me like I planned all this.

I need oxygen, an inhaler or something. Heat starts rushing at me and before I know it I'm not angry anymore, I'm crying. He lets me cry at least. 'Believe me, Andrew, I thought Abi'd told you. I thought, oh God, it doesn't matter what I thought. I can see she never did … I'm so sorry.'

He seems different somehow. So hard. So terribly hard. For lack of anything else to say I ask him what my mother's doing here.

'Leave her out of this, Rachel. It's not about Liz, it's about you. You don't live here anymore, remember? Where's India?'

'I don't know. Staying with Guy, I think. For God's sake, Andrew, I thought you knew – I thought this was what you wanted.'

'Right. And this you deduced from Abi, did you? A child of fifteen who'd do anything to have a so-called normal family?'

'It wasn't like that. I've been ill—'

'Why can't your fucking boyfriend look after you?' Andrew lunges at me like he's going to hit me, but maybe he wasn't because a moment later I'm knocked off my chair by Nevis. I pull my knees up into foetal position and cover my face with my hands, but he's down on his side, digging at them like they're roots over a rabbit hole and I'm the cringing bunny. I'm hysterical, I can hear myself wailing – as if he's trying to kill me. Oh God, please get him off me, oh God …

'Damn it, Nevis, get off!' Andrew says, dragging me roughly onto my chair. 'What's wrong? What are those bruises? What happened to your tooth?'

'Take a fucking guess.'

He lowers himself into the other chair, stares at me coldly and bites his knuckles.

'Ryan beat me up … Abi came over – she's been looking after me. *She* brought me here. I thought she'd told you …' Now I'm fucking crying. Shit! 'I'll go as soon as I'm …' But I don't get to finish whatever it was I was planning on saying, because at that moment I pass out and slide off my chair into oblivion.

ANDREW

AFTER RACHEL'S TIMELY FAINT, Nurse Abi, followed closely by Liz, charges through the French windows, yelling at both me and Nevis to fuck off out of her way. Liz gets to her first and starts wailing. Eventually I prise Liz off, but it takes a good while to persuade her upstairs – my intention being to lock her in the spare bedroom. I'm just saying that I'll be back in a minute and I'm about to turn the key when I hear both Rachel and Abi's voices, and clock that they're coming from my bedroom, and wait for Abi at the bottom of the stairs. I don't believe this.

An hour later, (with Rachel settling in and no doubt having a nap on my bed) I manage to persuade Abi into the garden. I can barely contain myself. 'What do you mean you thought I'd be pleased – what gave you the right to do that, Abi?' But in my brain there's this other voice telling me that I'm a jerk, and that my daughter just did what any child would do, and that I'm an arse for expecting more … I mean, do I tell her how I'm feeling? Did I tell her about this new feeling of relief and joie de vivre? No. Have I been looking ecstatic these last months? No. So how could she know? This is my fault. Now, there's a surprise. Christ.

And it was only a few hours ago that my life seemed finally to be heading to a place that I could look at without wincing. And now Abi's face is going into meltdown. 'Please don't cry, if anyone else cries I might get violent – just don't cry, okay?' It's a struggle she's losing. 'Listen okay, I'm sorry. It's not your fault.' I give her a weak smile to try to hide the bricks I'm shitting.

'I tried to call you,' she sobs, 'but you didn't answer, and well, it was done wasn't it and when India came back to get something yesterday, she agreed it was best to wait till you were home. She wasn't just beaten you know, she was raped.'

My nostrils flare. I stall for time. 'What do you mean – raped?' She doesn't grace me with an answer.

I wonder, as I gaze stupidly at Abi's black eyes, whether perhaps it's fashionable to look beaten up. Because the last hour feels like an attack, intended to drag me back into a world I was just beginning to crawl out of. And besides, how do I know Rachel's not making it up?

'Right.'

'You've got to let her stay, Dad. She can't go back to Dawn's, not after what's happened.'

'I'm not saying she has to go this minute, but Abi, she can't just move back in. Things can't go back to the way they were – that's all I'm saying.'

'Okay, so long as you don't make her go back to Dawn's, so long as she can stay till she's strong again. She can, can't she?'

'Yes, well, maybe. But not in my room – it would be giving quite the wrong message. You need to put her in your room, or clear out the box room next to India's. Okay? Now!'

'Okay, that's fine – okay. I get it. But Dad, we've got to tell the police about what's happened, we've got to – you've got to!'

Abi

Jamie and me went bowling all morning. It was good – Jamie's super good at bowling. We got off the bus at the east end of Princes Street and stopped at the Bake House for coffee. He's been great about everything, really understanding, really sweet. 'Come for lunch? Ple-eease Jamie,' I go. 'It can be so stressed out with Mum and Dad and everything.'

'Yeah, okay. Won't they mind?'

'No silly, everyone loves you – you know that. In fact they all get really boring about you – apparently you're a good influence. Durr,' and I lean over the small round table and kiss him. 'Jamie? You do like me, don't you?'

He pushes back my fringe and lifts my chin up. 'Yeah – what kind of a question is that? You know I do.'

'Yeah, but, sometimes, well, you know – it's hard to tell.'

'Well I do, so stop worrying. I wouldn't see you almost every day, would I, and calling you and texting you and telling you how pretty you are, if I didn't like you – a lot.'

I flick back my hair and grin and run my hand along his thigh. And he takes my fingers and kisses them. Dead romantic. We finish our juice and pay and walk down the hill. I just hate it that I'm only fifteen. We're holding hands and swinging them bigtime and then skipping like kids and then suddenly he lets my hand go and says, 'Race yer.'

We fall through the front door and into the kitchen. Dad's in the garden reading a paper.

'Jamie's staying for lunch, okay?'

'Sure, but Abi …' And then he turns to Jamie. 'Sorry, Jamie, but do you mind if I have a word with Abi in private?'

Three o'clock and the doorbell goes. Gran's having her nap and everything's like really quiet. I'm with Mum in my bedroom. We set up a camp bed which I sleep on. Neither of us is saying anything much.

Then maybe it's ten minutes or maybe more and my heart's thumping like crazy and then Dad knocks and comes in and Mum goes, 'I've got nothing to say, Andrew,' – like biting his head off. 'I've told you!'

'At the very least, Rachel, you need to give them your name.'

'Come on, Mum.'

'I already said, Abi, I'm not saying anything.'

Then Dad tells her that they can make her give her name and address, now that a crime has been identified. That they can make her. Mum stands up suddenly and pushes past him.

'This is all your fault, Andrew. Why the hell couldn't you leave this alone?'

Dad and me follow her downstairs. She goes into the sitting room. The door's open a bit and I can hear them – the police, that is.

'Hello, Rachel. We really appreciate you coming downstairs – I know it must be very difficult. Myself and my colleague won't keep you long.'

The door closes and Dad and me go into the kitchen. India's reading the papers and the radio is playing icky Euro-pop.

'Want a hot chocolate or a tea or something?' she says.

I sort of nod, but before even the kettle boils we hear Mum's raised voice, the door slamming shut and Mum racing upstairs. I give Dad a look, like I'm going to get up and follow her. But he stands up too, and sort of blocks my way. 'You should go and talk to them, Abi,' he says. 'He might do it to someone else – you're the one who found her.'

And then the policewoman appears from the hall.

'Hello, Abi. Could we have a quick word? Nothing formal, just a chat.'

So I follow her. The policeman who's scribbling something on an electronic notepad thingy is sitting at Dad's desk. A woman is beside him. He stands and shakes my hand and nods towards one of the chairs. This is well weird, but I sit anyway and once he's settled again he bangs on about how Sheila is trained in sexual offences and that she's going to be asking me a few questions while he takes notes. I'm sweating – it's so hot, but I'm too freaked to ask them to open the garden door.

Sheila asks if I'd like my dad with me and I say 'No.' Then she says, 'Okay, if you're sure,' and smiles at me. 'Could you tell us a little about when you went to visit your mother?'

What does she mean? Which bit? I can't think what to say.

'I believe your mum was staying with a friend and you were visiting her?'

I suppose she's being kind. Jesus. I just don't want to get Mum into trouble. What if they think it's her fault? – I've heard that loads. Oh God, the way Mum looked at me.

'Can you remember anything? Anything at all? Take your time, Abi – there's no rush.' And I picture Mum in Dawn's mingin' little room sitting beside me, pouring it all out. And so I tell her a bit about that.

'He was a friend of yours – a friend of the family, was he?'

'Not really, I'd only met him once.' Now I'm going to cry, I can feel it.

'I'm sorry, Abi. This must be upsetting for you. I won't keep you long. I'm afraid your mum doesn't want to press charges, but we think she should. What do you think? We don't believe anyone should get away with hurting someone like that. Do you?'

'No.'

'Do you know where this fella lives?'

'No.'

'So you never met him?'

'Once. He came to a barbecue.'

'Oh, so he *was* a friend of the family then?'

'I already said. Not really – he was Mum's friend, like a student.'

'I see.' She tells me how rape is more about power and violence than anything else – that so long as he's getting away with rape, he might do it to other people and she asks me about Mum's clothes, if the clothes she'd been wearing were still around. Stupid, I never thought of that and Mum will have washed them. I tell her, and then say sorry like it's actually all my fault.

Then they ask me about Mum leaving home and why she came back and stuff, and I like say how things are really kind of great now that we're all back together again. 'Your father didn't seem as upset as we thought he would be, or as pleased about things the way they are, as you seem to be.'

'Dad never says how he feels.' And then I say, 'Typical man,' which sounds pretty good I think. 'But really he's over the moon – we all are.'

'Well that's what we like to hear, Abi. The more support your mum has the quicker she'll be able to put all this behind her. She's a lucky woman by the sounds of it.'

'Yeah. I guess.'

'Okay, Abi,' she says, all smiles. 'You've been great. We will be wanting to take a formal statement from you if that's okay. You'll need to have someone with you, someone you trust – is there someone you'd like?'

'Yes there is, a friend called Megan – she's a good friend of the family.'

'Well, that's good. We could come here or you might prefer to come to Gayfield Square – you can let me know.'

She holds out her hand. 'Good luck with everything, Abi, and you tell your father to show his feelings more – your mum needs all the love she can get. Here's my card – if you need me for any reason at any time, just give me a call, okay?'

Suddenly I can't wait to get out of here, and neither can they it seems, cos they're right behind me. Well that is until I *am* out, and now that I'm out, I'm desperate to go back in. But that's not an option is it, so we all just stand there and take in the show.

Gran is half way down the top stairs. She's wearing India's dressing gown – a kind of kimono. It's miles too small, and the first thing I see is the ribbon trailing on the stair behind her which … Oh God – it's fallen open. She's got totally nothing on underneath – good show, Gran, the police will be loving this.

She stops outside my bedroom. Use your left arm, Gran – your left arm, please Gran … She's seen me. No don't wave, please don't wave. O-kay. I do not wave back, obviously. To be honest I think I might faint, because her massive boob kind of judders and swings into full view as she hammers on my bedroom door. For God's sake, Mum, let her in, let her in – Christ. This is not good. Where the fuck's Dad? Oh here he is. Good. Taking the stairs two at a time. Ah. No. Not good. Not good at all. Please Mum – let them in. Oh great – vocals as well. Mum always did have a way with words.

'Go away, go away, leave me alone, haven't you done enough to me for one day?'

She's hysterical. I guess some of this is for Dad and some for Gran but the police don't know that do they? And, oh good – yes, it's getting worse. Dad's got hold of Gran's wrists and is backing her upstairs. I'll say this for her, she's fucking strong – putting up a great fight. I run to the kitchen and fling open the door. India turns the radio down and the tap off – she's totally heard nothing, but now that she has, well, she like flies into action and takes the stairs two at a time. Gran stops pulverising Dad and throws her arms around India, calming down immediately, but I don't think this helps, because if anything it makes Dad look worse. Doesn't he realise how this looks? Is he completely mad? Well yes, obviously. And just to prove it, loud as you like, in front of the two of them, as if they don't already have enough evidence to completely trash everything I said, Dad turns back to India and grunts at her to make sure she remembers to lock Gran in.

Good one, Dad.

Ryan

Man I'm high, high being just about as good as it gets these days. We've been doing this shit all afternoon, David flicking through his fucked-up porn videos like I'm interested.

'I should go, man.' I sort of float off my chair, in that I can't remember deciding I need a leak – it's great that these things are instinctive isn't it? On the way to the bathroom, I peek into his bedroom. Satin. Very nice. If I ever get my butt off the poverty line I'll be buying satin, but not this black shit – no, I fancy ice blue.

Soon as I'm back in the lounge I grab my jacket. I could do with some clean air.

'You going already?' he says.

'Need to, man – got someone to see.'

He tries to pat his nose but his finger floats on by. We crease up and high five.

I take my usual route through the Botanics and sit on the bench by the pond under the willow. The idea of going home sucks – it's pretty here, costs nothing to look.

So why's he staring, the black guy with the white hair? He's been eyeballing me since I sat down. He was here last week and the week before that. Could be anyone, one of them plain clothes policeman building up to an arrest, or Billy's hit man, sharpening his fists. Could be either of those. I've been expecting it, God knows. Or could be she wasn't hurt so bad after all. She's had plenty time to call the hounds out, so maybe it looked worse than it was – could be. As for one of Billy's lot? Nah, they'd want to admire their handiwork – make sure the job was thorough. And besides, they couldn't afford him. Let's be honest here, Billy's a drunk and an addict, the chances of him being sober enough to get the address down right, or find a pen, are, well, somewhere between slim and zero.

I should quit fretting. I should be pleased to have some dude in a suit like giving me the eye. Might be one of David's friends … But I think not, he's way too well dressed and far too, well, kinda shy I guess. Let's just imagine he's some lonely rich cunt looking for a fuck buddy. I shift up, and catch his eye without meaning to.

No way. He's coming over. He has the walk of someone half his age, smiling like he knows me, tossing the remains of his bread to the ducks as he heads my way. It's embarrassing. I mean, do I know him or what?

But I'm the clown as usual. He's just friendly, says he's seen me here often – says he's been admiring me from a distance for some weeks, says he's from Jamaica, that his name is Winston. I mean, who's he kidding?

'Where you from?' he says. 'If you don't mind my asking?'

Which I do, so I don't say nothing.

He smiles, jabbers on like I've poured out my life history. 'I was born in London with my roots in Jamaica – Montego Bay to be exact. I do business there. Lived there a while, but you know my problem?' And he leans forward and turns towards me like he's about to deliver a punch line, puts his hand up to his head and kinda teases out a white curl. 'I never settled, neither there or here really – always been on the outside. But now I find the outside sort of friendly. I like it here, in my way.'

So that would be the drug business would it? All I'm saying is, designer suits like that don't come cheap and his pale blue eyes look kind of spaced out.

'So how come your family moved here, then?' I say.

'Not here – London. My dad fought in the war.' He laughs. 'When he moved us up, there was only one other black family in Edinburgh.' Then he says something I don't hear fully because two kids start kicking up a racket behind us, but I hear the words 'half-breed' and I see his sideways glance, like he's talking about the two of us. Why's he telling me all this? Seriously, he's freaking me out. I'm still high, but he's bringing me down fast – could do with a top-up … I start kneading the gear in my pocket. He's eloquent, well educated, so what's he doing making out with some loser like me?

When he invites me to dinner, it comes as no surprise. I don't answer either way, just thank him for asking. He says he's always loved to cook, but cooking for one can make him maudlin, and this evening he would rather cook for two. I don't ask him whether he ever had a family. I mean, he looks like the kind of guy who'd have a family, so I'm guessing there's some kind of tragedy he's running from. Maybe that's the thing I can see in his face. When he stands up, I do too. Feels natural. Feels natural to walk beside him.

The sun drops behind the trees, like the end of act one. I pull my collar up against the cool breeze. We cross into Inverleith Park, past the school and down the Stockbridge main drag. I do not say that we are going past my place, and he doesn't pin me up against the nearest wall and wrench my arms off. His tells me his flat is in the New Town, just the other side of Scotland Yard Play Park.

Very nice. Main door flat: right in off the street – no crummy stairs or nothing. So I was right, he is loaded. He leads me through this crystal domed hall with these pale stone flags and into a room of pure white marble. I'm starting to feel freaked out. He's a drug baron of momentous proportion. Any minute he's going to punch me, or five guys in hoods are going to appear from behind a secret wall, maybe drop through the ceiling. Or Rachel's here and this is her father and any moment …

This chamber of ice is his kitchen and great gashes of sparkling granite kind of float off the ice walls like magic. I swear I haven't ever seen anything so rich and slick and pure. I shut my mouth, but not before I clock him smiling at me. As he pulls his jacket and scarf off (I don't let him take mine), he waves me into this dull silver chair that I swear is so skinny I hold my breath in the hope that I weigh less. Then he excuses himself, goes into a room to my left, his bedroom, I presume, but it could be his armoury. He returns wearing a sweat the colour of pale sand. No denying how beautiful he is, something about his manner and confidence brings up something emotional in me. But I'm not stupid, am I – doesn't mean he's not some crazy jackass planning to fuck me up. He spouts a long list of exotic teas, among which I catch the word mango and go for it. His elegant fingers arrange oatcakes and cheese on a flat piece of slate. The way he's standing with his back to me brings up a distant memory I can't fully place. This tea is nice, man, and I tell him so, twice. I'm not normally stuck for words, but my mind's a blank and searching for something to say is doing my head in. I excuse myself and head for the bog, top up, nothing too radical. When I come out, he's laughing, lays a small wooden box down on the table in front of me and lifts the lid. I am confused, but obviously my confusion seems to make him happy because all I'm seeing is his flashy white teeth as he flings his head back and laughs.

'You should see your face, Ryan. Take it easy. You are a beautiful man. I love beautiful things, no tricks I assure you. I just want you to enjoy a little hospitality, eat something with me, let me get to know you a little. Relax, Ryan, help yourself.'

I decline, politely – does he think I'm stupid? I've got my own drugs ta very much. He shrugs. We talk about bands. He asks me what I'm doing in Edinburgh; I lie, tell him I'm at uni – just finished second year. He looks at me like he knows damn well I quit.

He leads me through to a room at the rear of the flat. I've never seen anything like it outside of the pages of a glossy magazine. Floor-to-ceiling windows the length of one wall. Tall trees. Green light on a grand piano that's so slick and shiny it's more like water than a solid thing. I move past it and stand facing out. Below me are tennis courts and dark gardens and behind me guitar chords clear as crystal. I turn back into the room, no speakers, man, no controls that I can see, in fact nothing that has shit to do with music as I know it – just him, long fingers stroking what I can just make out is a small chrome panel on the wall. And by the time we're sitting on the stretch of pale settee, it's like Marvin Gaye's snuck right in there with us.

ANDREW

IT WASN'T HITTING THE BOTTLE that was the mistake – it was stopping before I'd fully passed out. I mean, I'm not even attracted to Rachel anymore. She's scrawny, not sexy … How could I have let that happen? Oh shit.

Something fell away – seeing Abi's face light up when she saw all her favourite people having dinner together … I suppose I just wanted life to be simple. What an idiot. What's it been – only five weeks? Feels more like fifty. Poor Megan, having to watch Rachel flirt with me like that … And what's with having Callum up till God knows when? And while I'm at it, no, it's not okay that she suddenly reinvents herself as the good wife, the devoted mother.

Yeah okay, she's starting therapy again, but why the hell couldn't she find her own therapist? Why did she have to elicit Megan's help in finding one? I should never have left them alone together. I might have known they'd be … And then I hear this snotty wee voice: they'd be what, Andrew? Planning to get Rachel the kind of ongoing support you've always wanted her to get? Making sense of the rape perhaps? Her father? Her compulsive secrecy, addiction to violence? Making friends? Yes, yes, yes – I know I'm being a shit, but I just wanted to move on and now it feels like the whole world is conspiring to force me back to a time and a place I'm done with.

The truth is there's only *one* adult I like talking to. I dial Megan's number.

Some bloke answers.

Is Megan there, please?'

'Yeah,' he says. 'She's in the shower. Can I get her to call you when she comes out?'

I squeak out a 'yes' and replace the phone. My heart is thumping. No wonder she left early last night – she was meeting someone. I remind myself that her private life is absolutely no business of mine – but still, you'd have thought she might have said if she was meeting someone. Well good. It's time she got herself a boyfriend. I wander through to the kitchen and shove a couple of bits of bread into the microwave to toast.

Outside there is a faint frosting over the grass. I grab the phone and open the French windows, pull up a chair and breathe in. A hint of wood smoke in the air confirms how much I like the autumn – it'll be nice later. I'm just wondering whether to cancel lunch with Megan, when the damn thing goes off in my hand.

'Thanks for dinner, Andrew,' Megan says.

'Hmm. Yes – it was nice wasn't it? Listen Megan, I've just looked at my diary – I think my meeting at twelve might run on. Can we change lunch to next week sometime?'

'Suits me. I'll confirm later when I've got my diary. That okay?'

'Your diary?'

'Yes, you know, the thing that tells you when you're busy.'

'So you're booked up with lunch dates are you?'

'I *might* be … What's up with you?'

'I'm fine. Just marvelling at your social calendar.'

'Riiiight,' she says, really patiently, like I'm some kind of imbecile. Then 'bye' really fast, like I'm doing her head in.

'Who was that?' Callum hops onto my knee and picks up my hand.

'Only Megan. I needed to ask her something. How are you?'

'Did Mum sleep with you in your room last night?'

'Yes, darling. Does that make you happy?'

'She'll be staying forever then, will she? Only you said—'

'I only wish we could see into the future, Cal.' He twists his little face round to stare straight at me and pulls my pinkie backwards.

'I know that, stu-pid. But what do *you* think? You know, about *Mum*?'

'I don't know. We just have to wait and see. What's brought this on?' Always has to know everything that's going on, doesn't he? Something to be proud of at Heels, so I'm told. Especially since I went to see Julie yesterday for a bit of a catch-up. Needn't have bothered, of course – she said how Callum seemed exceptionally open for a six year old … So come Monday everyone will know Callum's mum and dad had sex on Friday night. Perfect.

He splays my fingers out one at a time, as if they're telling him something, as if they're his. 'But is she going to stay with us forever, I mean.'

'Would you like her to?'

'Maybe. Depends. Is she going to sleep in your bed tonight as well?'

'I don't know, darling. Probably.' (And no, we won't be doing doggie style, we'll be saving that till the middle of next week – but I'll be sure to let you know.) I give him a friendly squeeze – more of a hopeful tickle (be six, child!), but he swipes my hand away.

'Don't, Dad.' He twists the trapped finger round in what reminds me of a sequence of brisk tango movements and rocks back and forth, giving me a grave frown.

'So why did Ryan hit Mum then?'

'I don't know, darling. People do strange things sometimes.'

'Even you?'

'Yes! Well, not hit people obviously, but other things – yes loads of stupid things, and Abi, and even you, scallywag.'

'So why then?' He starts with my pinkie, wiggling it.

'I think that as we grow up things happen to us that change us – some things make us into good grown-ups and some into bad ones, but most of us have a bit of both. We try to make the bad things less and the good things more until we die, more or less.'

'So how?' With my pinkie now gripped firmly against the one next to it, he uses his other hand to start making a very wide V; Jesus it's sore – but good, good sore.

'Well, one of the things I do is pretend things aren't wrong when they are – that kind of thing.' Pain denial's another one – close relation I suppose. 'Julie was saying you were really, really good at talking to everyone about your hurting things.'

'Yep.'

I'm not sure he's really listening, he's staring hard at the V he's created with my fingers, deciding, no doubt, whether to widen it or not.

'So you tell her about everything then, do you? Everything that, well, happens here? Not that you shouldn't of course …'

'Yep.'

'And do you really think that helps? I mean you could always talk to me, you know, if you felt that, well, some things weren't sort of "schooly", or if you were embarrassed or anything …'

'D-ad.'

'Yes, yes, I know talking is good, but you know I'd like to think you could—'

'D-ad.'

'Okay, okay.'

'What's the motto, Dad?'

'Yes I know, I know.' Everyone spills their guts – that was why we chose Heels in the first place; but then we were one of the happy, beautiful families, were we not? The family with experience, the family who'd been through the mill and come out the other side.

'You used to like me saying stuff, Dad, you used to tell me what to say in circle time – remember?'

'Well, not really Cal, no. Ouch! Crikey Callum, that really hurts. Yes, well, you're a very lucky boy aren't you? Maybe if I'd had a Ju-lie' – I can hear this childishly bitter twang as I say this – 'when I was growing up … Oh, nothing.' I take a breath and in a last bid to be supportive I say, 'You know, Callum, you'll probably be someone who'll help others when you grow up. You help me, you know.'

'Like Megan you mean?' He drops my hand like a piece of dead meat, turns to face me.

'Yes, like Megan.'

Then he looks up at me and his sweet eyes are beginning to fill up. 'You won't ever leave me will you, Dad?'

'Never, ever, ever—'

'Because I don't think I want to live with Mum, you know, without you.'

'Come on, wee man – what's brought this on? Everything's okay.' Oh yes, everything's just dandy: Mummy and Daddy are getting drunk and screwing like rabbits, Megan who used to be Daddy's best friend has got a new better best friend and everything is working out just the way it should. Hip, hip, hoo-bloody-ray. Tell that to Julie, why don't you?

'But will you?'

He rolls off my knee as the phone rings.

It's Guy. What a surprise. Since *India*, he calls all the time hoping she'll pick up. He witters on to me about work, the Leith thing – wants me to start the desk study and says if I get a whiff of contaminated soil he wants *me* to make an appointment with the developers. We discussed this on Friday – we could have discussed it again tomorrow *at work* … Christ. Give me a break, world – give me a fucking break. Goodbye Guy.

Andrew

I KNEW I SHOULDN'T have rescheduled for so soon.

'Sorry I'm late, Andrew.' Megan is flushed – she must have run here. 'The office is like a mad house, I nearly phoned to call it off and I can't be too long – sorry.'

'Well, I am flattered.'

'What's up?'

'Nothing. Let's order shall we? Something quick.'

'*Andrew*?'

Suddenly I'm feeling this awful weight pressing down on me like a slab of stone. I wave for the waiter – I just want out of here without making too much of a dick of myself.

'I'm fine,' I say. 'I don't know, I guess it's just getting used to it all. It's been five weeks – Liz was only meant to stay a couple. Wearying, to say the least, but I can hardly send her back.'

We order coffee, quiche and salad, and as I'm handing the menus to the waiter, Megan picks up the thread. 'Rachel's sister still in hospital, is she?'

'Sheena? Yes – she's fractured her femur in five places. I'm actively looking for permanent help and eventually a residential home – but meanwhile …'

'I suppose there must be quite a few emotions floating

around, what with half of Argyll living in your house,' Megan says, to the point.

'To put it mildly.'

'And *India* and Rachel, and *Abi* and Rachel?' she says.

'Oh fine – best of buddies.'

'Really?'

'Well, not Rachel and Liz, of course.'

'Of course not.'

'Liz keeps escaping. The police have brought her home twice now. I've got my suspicions—'

'What?'

'Rachel.'

'Letting her out?'

'Well, it's always on her watch,' I say, with my mouth full of quiche. 'But for some reason I'm always the one that takes delivery of her or goes and picks her up. The police are giving me some pretty evil looks. Anyway, I seem to be the only one finding life chez Gillespie …' And I'm about to make a fool of myself again, ruin what we've got, when a distance in her eyes takes the moment away.

'What?' she says, vaguely, spooning the cream off her coffee and sipping it.

'Oh nothing. Just that it's harder than I thought, but I've said that, haven't I?'

What I don't say is that things had begun to shift, that I'd begun to feel like someone with a future. Now it feels like Megan has one, while I stand back and watch mine being stolen. I swallow back a threatening wave of self-pity. She's not listening anyway, she's thinking about him, her new man, and why wouldn't she be?

She glances at me and smiles. 'Well at least life's not boring. Did I tell you Mum's coming across – to live I mean?'

'Is that good?'

'Yes, really good. I mean she might have agonised over what to do, but she's just going for the choice that seems right for her just now – she's an impressive woman, my mother … I'm sorry, Andrew.'

She's even beautiful with tears running down her cheeks.

'We're a sorry pair aren't we?' she says.

I hand her my hanky and she changes the subject. 'How's David by the way – still the golden boy? I only ask because I read a profile on him last week. What the hell was he doing on the rigs? It's hardly in keeping with his *highflying* career. Did you know he was in China for seven years, working as a consultant for the new power stations they're building, and before that in South Africa, mining? And much more interesting and juicy than that is the fact that he was born in South Africa and is an expert in explosives – that as a child he blew up the family home while making a bomb in the cellar and his mother was killed.'

'You serious? David killed his mother while making a bomb? You sure?'

'That's what it said. He was eight. Doesn't it worry you that he never mentioned any of that?'

'Not really, no. Not everyone spills their guts about everything – I mean we're hardly close friends are we? And yes, we knew he'd been a consultant in China *and* that he'd worked with explosives in South Africa – none of that detracted from his suitability for working with us. He's used to working in the public domain, he knows a lot about geology and he's good at his job, and as far as working in the North Sea goes, there could be any number of reasons, from a temporary attraction to the isolation, and cold, and generally poor lifestyle, to broadening his experience of mining – for a while. If you're that interested, he's due here at two – you can ask him yourself.'

'Well maybe I will. You're very picky, tetchy—'

'I know, I know, and I'm deeply sorry – it's been a bad week. David and I have got a meeting with those developers this afternoon – trying to figure out why they bought the Leith site *as seen.*'

'So you got that did you?'

'Sort of. It's a meeting – just a boring routine meeting with boring businessmen. Do you mind if we change the subject? I really would like *not* to think about work for an hour or so.' I stare at the table, push my plate away from me and revert to creepy-speak. 'Are you sure you've got room for Rhona at yours – I mean, won't it cramp your style?'

'No it won't. Honestly, Andrew, what's got into you? Who

knows, it might even be good for my darling little brother to see Mum more often.'

'Of course.'

'Couldn't get much worse.'

'Knowing Rhona, she'll do everything she can to make a success of it. Will she try to find somewhere of her own – you know, permanently?'

'I don't know. God, Andrew, give us a chance. I've no idea – I guess it'll depend—'

'Oh yes? On what?'

'I don't know – on all sorts of things.'

'Yeah, I guess.' Oh God, I can't believe I'm saying this.

'Listen,' she says, as though my poor manners might be her fault. 'I'm sorry I've been out of touch, and I'm sorry we've seen so little of each other, but it's only going to get worse for a bit. Mum's coming over tomorrow, she'll be needing my time, we've got quite a lot to sort out with Dad's stuff one way or another, and I've got Christ knows how much paperwork to catch up on at work. Taking that week off for the funeral, you know… It may be a couple of weeks before I've got a moment – you don't mind, do you? How about lunch Thursday after next?'

'Oh I don't know …' Very pretty speech I must say. Suddenly I feel so angry with her. How dare she? But she beats me to it.

'Listen, call me. I need to head off. I'll pick up the tab next time. Give David my regards. Ring me, okay? Misery guts.'

I don't give David her regards. I call him. He's pleased to go on his own to the meeting – more focus on him of course. And then I stare into my coffee for half an hour, before walking the streets until I have to get home for Callum.

PART THREE

Autumn

Ryan

So where am I? And what's that pain almost everywhere? Shit, this hurts. What is this – some black hole or what? I know that smell. What's that smell? I struggle to locate the muscles in my eyelids. But every time I get close I keep letting go, sucked back into a sea, not a hole after all, an oily black sea, no, not oily, not oily, no, it's like treacle, black treacle, soft and hot … I can't move in it, can't breathe in it. I'm going under, suffocating and going under, which might be okay, I guess. I start somersaulting downwards in slow motion. I'm going to drown, want to drown … I can't see – just pain, waves and waves of chopping, sawing pain and smells, that smell … I'm sure I can reach it. My arm reaching out, my arm but not my arm, just an arm swimming past, just a hand flexing and pinching, a crab's claw, snapping, missing, not trying, disappearing under the treacle. Now there's a voice swimming by, a word, my name, jumping like a fish – out of the inky, treacly sea, splashing and twisting like a fish … Where am I? I press through to the surface. The smell … A body. A face. I work on my eyelids, though it takes me an age to find them, and one eye cracks open; a sliver of painful light, the top of a curtain, large yellow flowers, a metal frame. And then the pain and the blood and the smell separate out; they are them, I am me: hospital, sick, dying. A flood of understanding unravels the hard knot of nothingness. But before I can make it my own it's running away, And the treacle and the ink and all the black evils are roaring back in, thundering, pounding back in drowning out smells and sounds, swirling and glooping, folding and rolling, somersaulting over and over into treacle.

Next time I wake I remember a dream. But it's gone again before I can grab it. Maybe it was a truck, but I don't think so. Something like a truck but not a truck – something built like a truck or maybe a bus.

I wake again. Some of the kicks and punches drift in and out of my consciousness and I try peeking again, cos the pain's getting worse and I need to figure out whether whatever did this to me has finished yet or whether it's getting ready for another round. Right there in the slit is Winston's blurred face, and from somewhere round where my ear used to be I can just make out his voice. I try to talk back, try to ask him to take the shit out of my ears, but all I can hear is this kind of gargle noise, so maybe I *am* dying, cos I'm hurting enough. I can just about make out his long fingers signalling me to take it easy, maybe catch a faint 'beaten up' and I think maybe I remember something about that, but what's bothering me is how Winston got here? I need to know. I try to sit, but he pushes me down and sort of nods behind him.

'Hi Ryan, Ryan, Ryan ...' kind of like an underwater echo. 'I'm Fiona, I'm Fiona. I'm a nurse.'

She lays her fingers across my wrist. A stabbing pain shoots up my arm and spears me in my armpit, ploughs on in, twists and pushes deeper. My eyes won't open a second time. I am fighting treacle and monsters with knives ... She starts talking, loud and slow, like waves on a pebble beach – telling me how I've been beaten up. I should sleep.

I'm still trying to figure how Winston is in on all of this, and I reckon he can tell my confusion, cos he's leaning in close.

'You've been beaten up pretty bad, Ryan – you remember much?' I would like to say something, but there's someone pumping up my eyelids and it takes everything I've got just to keep that crack open, get him in focus.

I'm trying to hang on in there, trying to follow you man, but your voice is so weak. Try harder, man – if you want me to hear, you need to speak up. *Speak up man*, I keep saying over and over like he might read my thoughts, but it's no damn good because he just isn't trying.

The next few times I open my eyes, I remember some and learn some. Like the guys who rang my bell weren't coming to fix the lights in the stair – they were coming to fix me. By the time they reached my doorway, they had hoods on. And it doesn't take a wise man to guess who they were. Fucking, Billy. Why man? Those smack-head dogs are mean, really mean … A loan, that's all it was, a measly fucking loan. I would have repaid them. Shite, even thinking hurts like hell. Where's my morphine? Where's my morphine, bitch? I hold my finger on the buzzer. Once the pain kicks in, I can't think anymore, just start living the nightmare over and over, like I'm that guy in *Marathon Man* and there's some mean dude drilling through my teeth and into my brain tissue. Jesus. It doesn't take her long to get here, only this time she's a *he*. I tell you I love these guys. I am hoping they'll give me one of those self-help morphine drips, though I'd miss their jabbering to be honest – keeps my mind off things. That's it: fix me up, man, cos I'm not doing so good in here.

Only one thing I know … Winston, he saved my life – came looking for me after I didn't show up. Mostly he's not saying much. It's the nurses filling me in – about how he got me this new room with a TV, and so many flowers it smacks of death more than life. And how till I woke up he was sitting by my bed, playing me my favourite sounds, talking to me, shit like that. The morphine kicks in. Shit. Whoa – going somewhere in a rush, rushing somewhere in a gong … Appreciate this fellas, really appreciate this.

I'm settling in, going one way flying up and up when I realise I'm heading somewhere else. This pink fucking cocktail of pain and drugs is making me see things I haven't seen for years – kicking off dreams, peeling back the years, spewing up stuff I thought I'd settled. I haven't blubbed since I was a kid. Now I'm blubbing and I can't stop. He was kind too. Like Winston in some ways, kindest person I ever knew. You can tell a kid all you want about how evil someone is, how they should be locked up. Makes no difference, not when the person you're talking about was the only one who ever showed you love – ever held you. My daddy was weak, that's all. Weak and lonely. Left me stranded. Wasn't her fault was it? Wasn't his fault – wasn't his …

ABI

I wait till Mum's left the house.

Can't believe what I just heard. I can't believe I used to respect him, and, and well, just that. I can't even believe he's my dad.

I knock just to warn him.

'Come in. Hey, you been crying?'

'Don't bother, Dad. Just don't even bother. I overheard. I was about to come in, and I heard you telling her that she had to go.'

'Oh.'

'So yes, I have been crying actually, cos you're kicking my mother out of her home! I mean why would you do that? Why?'

'Abi …'

'I mean, when everything's cool and Mum's doing great. Cos we're mates now. It's not the same, we're mates. You're just jealous.' And now I'm sobbing.

'I know you and Mum are getting on,' he says. 'I'm pleased you are – you know I am.'

I can't believe he's saying that. 'No, you don't know! You don't know anything or you wouldn't have said all that. You wouldn't be just chucking her out like that, you wouldn't – oh my God I just can't believe you're doing that.'

'You're right, I don't know. I don't know what it's like for you. I only know what it's like for me.'

'Oh right, so this is all about you, is it? Well it's not – it's just not. You bastard!'

'Okay, no, of course it isn't.'

'It's about me as well – me and Callum. Don't you think it's been hard for me and Callum, I mean when she left?'

'Well—'

'No you don't! And now, now she's back, and, and she's been punished enough. E-nough! Can't you understand that? Can't you get that into your thick skull? She can't take you doing this, Dad! She can't take it – you binning her like a piece of rubbish.'

'I'm not doing that, I'm— '

'Just don't speak to me, Dad! Just don't!'

I slam his door, run upstairs and slam mine, put a chair under the handle. Not that he'll try to come in – because he'd have to care to break the door down!

I text Jamie – really need to get out of here. C'mon, c'mon. *'Okay 15mins wots up?'*

Ryan

'RYAN? YOU AWAKE?'

It's Winston. He went home last night. They more or less sent him home. Things are beginning to settle down. I can see a little better and even say a few words – though I have this new lisp which Winston says he likes – he's so happy I'm going to live. And Jesus, fuck, I'm glad I'm going to live, almost religious glad I'm gonna live. I've been thinking, something good's come into my life – thinking that this time I could have something good brewing with this guy – with a bit of luck. I crack open an eye.

I'm lying on my side, in recovery. They gave me a bed bath this morning – some ungodly hour. It's the way they heave me around like dead meat, I go into shock – barely remember breakfast or the doctor's rounds.

'Ryan?'

Something about the way he hardens my name tells me we're not alone. For a fraction of a second a streak of pure terror burns through me. Winston touches my arm to reassure me. He helps me sit up a bit, pushes a pillow under my shoulder and heaves. I can't turn my head but I see two policemen standing by the door. They look sad and shy too, like they feel sorry for me – yeah right. Let's just sort this.

'I tried to make them wait another day, Ryan. Sorry. You okay, man – or what?'

He places another pillow behind my head and eases me up a few more inches. It's like every limb weighs as much as a dead body. Jesus, I hurt.

Winston signals to the chairs along the wall, and the young woman and older geezer pull them up close.

'Hello Ryan,' the woman says, clearing her throat. 'I'm sorry to disturb you. You must be in a lot of pain. We'll make this as quick as we can, but we were reluctant to wait any longer and the doctor says you're well enough to follow what we're saying and answer a few questions with a nod or a shake of your head. You okay with that?'

I nod. She looks at me with sympathy and leans in. I look at her with sympathy too, trussed up in that stupid uniform. I wish I could smile at her as well.

It's the man who kicks off. 'It's bad news, I'm afraid. We didn't want to break it to you until you were strong enough. But we didn't want to wait until you heard from some other source either.'

I nod. So my flat's been condemned or maybe they set fire to it or maybe it's nothing to do with the mugging. I'll handle it guys.

'Do you know an Agnes Burns?'

I nod as far as I can. My heart kicks in hard. It's Agnes. I've been kinda hoping she might find her way here – hoping she wasn't worrying, that someone else was opening her tins for her.

'We think she must have tried to help you – must have heard something.'

They say she was on the floor too, same kind of bag over her head. So maybe she's here in hospital, so maybe she's been asking for me. Jesus, man, you should have said – you should have told me before. I could make it down the corridor, in a chair, on a trolley, some way …

I look at him, knowing suddenly she's not here.

'She died here in hospital, just a few hours after they brought you both in.'

And then Winston chips in. 'I'm sorry, Ryan – so sorry, man. I know how much … You okay?'

Something is happening inside my head, making it hard to hear what they're saying, but I do hear something about head injuries, luck, and relatives.

The police ask a question, but I can't hear because my head has dropped off my neck. The nurse pushes through and bends in close. I'm thinking I might vomit, and start pawing the air.

Winston asks the police to leave. 'I told you it was too soon. I said he was too fragile – Christ, can't you see he's barely able to take it in'

Bullshit. I'm taking it in fine. Good as killed her. That's me. That's what I do. That's what I do best. What was it I was thinking? Only yesterday. That I was some poor misjudged lad whose daddy bunked off and left him to the humiliations of a mad mother … And what do I do? Learn from it? Try to figure out a few things? Live my life in a way that doesn't fuck people over? Who am I kidding? I just killed someone, someone good, someone who cared for me. Did I value her, take care of her? And even if I did, even if maybe I did – I was still too fucking evil to …

And you Winston – just one more sad fucker who's got me all wrong.

They give me more morphine, take the vomit bowl. I can see Winston about to say something. Fuck off man. You know nothing about me. Hard man like me's not going to own up to feeling something for some doddery old lady or lonely old black man. Please. People shouldn't live that long, especially people stupid enough to poke their noses into stuff that's none of their fucking business. The look in his eyes tells me he'd like to stay, comfort me, but I wave him away. His fucking kindness is doing my head in.

Abi

AND IT'S NOT JUST my family life he's fucked up. Any hope that I might actually be taken seriously at school is well and truly screwed, forever, yes, durr. Like there's been months of nothing but how totally cool my dad is, and how shit my mum is, followed by a few weeks of 'I've saved my parents' marriage,' – puke. And now a quick swap to the other side, and, err, I'm leaving my wonderful dad (who I now hate), to live with my mad mother! Cos that's what they're all thinking. I mean what does that sound like? Like I'm the idiot, that's what. I so totally hate him.

I open his bedroom door. He spins around with the usual goofy look on his face and spreads his arms open like he wants a hug.

As if.

'Oh, hello darling.'

Up he jumps. Stay away, alien.

'Sorry. Can I say something, Abi?'

'Go on then.'

'I should have done things differently, I should have spoken to you first. I never wanted to hurt you, Abi – and that's maybe partly why I messed up so badly. I just couldn't bear to let you all down. I kept telling myself that time would make it all okay, but it didn't, it just made things worse. I had to tell her, Abi, it wasn't fair on any of us.'

He reaches out towards me. Like as if that's all he needs to do to make things better. Get us back to how we used to be. 'We will get through this. I know right now it doesn't feel that way, but Mum says her new flat's nice – and there's a good-size spare room for when you and Callum stay over.'

'Back off will you and, pl-ease, give us a break? I'm not even interested in you being an idiot or getting through this shit. I've made up my mind to move in with Mum.'

'What did you say?'

'You heard – I'm moving in with Mum. It's totally my idea, not hers, so don't make it a big deal.'

'Don't make it a big deal?'

'Right.'

'Well I'm not sure I can do that, Abi – this is your home, it's where your family live.'

'Some of my family.'

'Bu—'

'Whatever, Dad. Not my problem anymore.'

'What about Callum? He'll be devastated. No, really, Abi, this isn't okay – I won't allow this.'

'Oh right, but you're quite okay about kicking Callum's mum out! Don't you dare say that! This is all your doing remember? I can't believe you just said that.'

'At least talk it through, at least … Hey! For God's sake – you can't just walk in here and tell me you're leaving home and then walk out. Wait until after the October break at least – please Abi! I've just booked …'

I'm down the stairs and out the front door before he's got his boots on. After a bit I'm sitting on the wall by the Botanics' entrance getting my breath back and feeling like I might cry when I see Megan walking towards me.

'Hi there. You look fed up. Can I join you?'

'Oh hiya.' I turn in to a hug, and sniff. 'Sorry. Just had a scene with Dad. Has he told you?'

'About your mum going? Yes he has. I'm so sorry, Abi.'

I let her hug me for a while and then I pull back and wipe my eyes and try to smile a bit.

'Let's get a coffee. I start ticking if I walk past Di Giorgio without going in. Have you tried the brioche?'

'Aren't you going to see Dad?'

'Well no actually, I'm not that keen to see your father just at the moment. I was on my way to that second-hand bookshop, round the corner.'

'I was just going to meet someone. But I'm really early.'

'Brilliant. It's time we caught up. I've not seen you properly for ages.'

She puts her arm through mine and we walk to Canonmills in silence. I remember how she'd take me off for long walks when we lived on the west – it was something about the way she talked. She always assumed I'd understand stuff. And when I said things about Liam, she really listened and understood, almost as though she'd been through it all and would have done what I did. And then I'd always see things differently for a bit, like a separate person. We always ended up in a café then too, and I'd eat cake or crumpets or something and she'd be squirming and nicking mine because she was always on a diet.

Megan orders two mochas and two brioches while I grab a table on the pavement. When she comes back I ask her if she's fallen out with Dad too.

'Not sure. Obviously he's got a lot on his mind. I think I've upset him. Don't worry – we'll be okay, just like you will.'

'You know what he's done, don't you?'

'Rachel? Yes, he told me. It can't have been easy for him, letting you all down.'

'Yeah well, it doesn't matter anymore because I've decided to live with Mum.'

'Ri-ght. Big decision.'

'Not really. Honestly Megan, you haven't seen him recently, and Mum's changed. She's not even angry about moving out – not even blaming him or anything. In fact if it hadn't been for her, I'd have just split. It was Mum made me talk to him, not that it did any good.'

'Oh Abi. You've got your standard grades next year, haven't you? Not a good time for more upheaval. And not so great for Callum either.'

'Yeah, well, Dad should have thought of that before he threw her out. And you can bet he'll get Callum to beg me to stay – do his dirty work for him.'

'I don't blame you for being angry – but I'm not sure that's his style is it?'

'Oh yeah, and what's that then? He's changed, Megan – he really has. All I know is that I'm going and nothing he can say will make me stay. I can't stand it. Liz isn't exactly easy, obviously, and India gets on my nerves.'

'How's all that going? How's Liz?'

'Don't know really – okay, mostly. Sometimes she gets stressed about stuff, cries sometimes, goes walkabout. But she loves India and Nevis and Callum of course. I think Dad's looking for somewhere – a care home.'

Megan swipes her finger across her empty plate and sucks it. 'Want another? Bound to end up with my mum's bottom anyway.'

'Better not – need to go in a minute. I'm meant to be meeting someone.'

'Boyfriend?'

'Sort of, yeah – Jamie.'

'Good, I'm glad you've got someone. Sometimes I wish I had – it would certainly be nice once in a while to share things. But all the good men are taken, I reckon.'

'I thought – I thought Dad said you had someone?'

'Now why doesn't that surprise me? You're right – he's being *really* odd.'

'See what I have to put up with, Megan? Why don't you go and see him, talk some sense into him? Tell him Mum's changed. I mean, he didn't give it a chance did he? Like not even two months!'

'I don't know, Abi. It's not really anything to do with me. He'd only bite my head off, and I don't think he's going to change his mind somehow – not from the little he's said. Perhaps moving on will be best for everyone in the end. I'm always here you know, if you need to talk.'

'Yeah I know, and thanks. But talking won't change anything – we'll still be a broken home, won't we?' I want to cry again and I open my eyes wide. Megan puts her hand on mine and squeezes it.

'Broken homes, unbroken ones – either one can be hell. You'll find a way through this, Abi. Your mum's looking forward by the sounds of it. Give it time. Keep talking to Andrew. You remember how when you can see what someone else is feeling it kind of makes it all a bit easier?'

I stand up. 'S'pose. I've got to go.'

I nearly text Jamie to cancel, but don't – just say I'll be five minutes late. I'm wiping at tears as I stride up the pavement, hoping my mascara's stayed put. He's never late. I like that about him. He's just so unlike the others, maybe a bit *too* unlike them. He's not tried anything yet, only kissing … which is good as well as bad I s'pose – least I know he likes me. As I come over the wee bridge I can see him on the bench. We often meet here, where we met the first time – romantic really. Dead romantic, Jamie. I hang back and look at him and wish he was taller, a bit taller. He's staring between his legs at the ground.

'Hey.'

'Hey.'

He stands and kisses me on the cheek.

'You okay?' he says.

'Yeah, I guess.'

'Wanna sit or walk?'

'What happened to your hair?' I say, like an idiot. It's fucking obvious what happened to his hair. He turns bright red and shrugs.

'Bit radical eh?'

I'm trying not to make it sound like a problem.

'Bit.'

He looks like years younger and I'm not sure why, but that makes me want to cry again – I shouldn't have come. I stand with my hands in my pockets and don't sit down.

'Walk then?' I say.

'Okay.'

So we start walking. Almost no one here. Then I look at him, wondering how he'll react when I tell him, and he says, 'What?' and I say, 'Told Dad I was going to live with Mum.'

So he gives me a million reasons why I shouldn't, which all sound like ways to tell me that he doesn't rate Mum. Wish I hadn't texted him now – what does he know anyway?

'I'm fifteen, durr, and I'm moving in with my mum. Her flat's nice, and I'm going to move next week – during October break – you can help me if you like. God, why is everyone making such a big deal about it?'

'S'pose. Your life I guess.' He takes my hand.

'Honestly, Jamie – it'll be easier with Mum. You've seen what Dad's like, checking up on us all the time. It'll be like having our own place, almost.' I nudge him in the ribs.

'What?'

'Oh I don't know. Just … We'll be able to do what we like.' I give him that look.

'Okay. Well yeah, I guess.'

But it's obvious he doesn't have a clue what I'm on about.

'Doesn't your dad mind?'

'Ye-ah, course, went ballistic didn't he? And? Come here. This is going to be so good for us babe, honest … I've had it with dumb grown-ups making dumb decisions about my life. Living with Mum will be just like having a flatmate. She even lets me smoke dope.'

'You smoke dope? With your mum?'

'Sometimes. It's like having a small glass of wine – really … Don't look at me like that. Mum says it's much better to do it with her than with some of those idiots at school.' He stops walking and faces me and he's got this expression on his stupid face that says – wow Abi, you're amazing. And suddenly it seems like it's all going to be okay.

I grab his hand and we go deeper into the bushes. I take his face in my hands, push him hard up against a wide tree trunk.

RYAN

NEED A PEE. BEEN needing a pee for the last half hour. Starting to go crazy in this dump. Don't sleep, fucking nightmares keep me up half the night. I'm tired of my music, my ribs are sticking into my lungs – they give me fuck-all morphine. I tell you man, I need more dope.

I press the help button. Years later a young nurse nudges open the door, peeks shyly in my direction. I love you too baby.

'Good morning, Ryan. Can I get you something?'

Soon as I can walk a few steps for myself, they'll let me out of here.

'I want to go to the bathroom.'

She pushes the wheelchair towards me, throws back my bed sheet like a magician unveiling a trick. Very clever.

I shake my head. 'I want to walk there – on my own,' I say, easing my legs over the edge. The pain shoots everywhere and I'm sweating like I've been running. She levers me off the bed. Then I'm shuffling like an old man, getting used to the shock waves. She moves in close as I begin to falter. The soft jelly of her stomach judders against my robe. I hate the feel of it, but I can't move away from her. By the time we make it to the bog I've sweated so much I no longer think I need it.

She starts nudging me around so I can sit. But I'm gonna stand, so help me God, and I lunge at the fucking handrail.

She fixes my hands to the warm metal, pressing down on them as though they might stick to it, asks me if I'm okay. I nod a few times as she tucks my robe out of the way.

'I'll be just outside, if you need me.'

I'm hanging on for life, barely able to support my own bodyweight. If I lean forward my legs will slip away under me. If I don't I'll piss on the floor. I start blubbing, but silent. No one gives a fuck, do they? Just a mass of damaged, bloody, broken, meaningless meat. Scum, that's all I am. A worthless scummy junkie. Do they think I can't see the way they look at Winston? 'Poor sucker,' that's what they're thinking, 'this dude is going to screw you for all you've got.'

'Hey nurse.'

She comes in quick.

'I'm done.'

'Whoa,' she says. 'Steady on there. Let's get you back to bed, sunshine. Quite enough excitement for one day. You're doing well, you know – really well. Hey, soldier …'

I'm blubbing again, or straining with every last bit of strength not to. Don't want to give her the satisfaction, but I can't help myself can I?

'Hey,' she says, bracing herself. 'That's it, let me take the weight. It's natural, Ryan – after something like this – takes a while to get your strength back.'

When we reach the bed, I turn my head away. She must find this funny, bet she'll have a good laugh later with her mates. 'Why don't you do as the doctor says, Ryan? The psychologist here is a really nice woman.'

I shake my head.

She frowns like she cares. 'Your choice, but you should keep an open mind you know. When someone dies—'

'I know what they say. I'm not interested in talking.' The lisp makes me sound like a faggot.

Agnes is dead. She died because I drag my shit around like I always do, till it's too fucking heavy and I dump it on someone. What the hell's talking got to do with it? Sure I feel guilty – it's the least I should feel and I tell you one thing, it's not enough.

You want to help? Give me more morphine, stop cutting it back.

She turns away with a grim smile, starts lifting the vases of flowers, wiping the surfaces. 'Your Winston's so kind – like a flower shop in here.'

She fills the water jug, places it beside my bed. 'He tells me you're moving in with him. Lucky beggar. He's lovely isn't he?' I don't answer. What's he doing telling everyone our business anyway? I mean, I wasn't about to go back to my dump was I? Did he really imagine I might turn him down? Just wish she'd leave, go and bother some other dude with her pseudo caring and inane fucking chatter.

She looks up again. 'Why don't I put the telly on? Richard and Judy today. I like them, don't you?' She turns back to her cleaning. 'Not speaking? Suit yourself.' A few minutes later she turns to me all smiles. 'That's me, Ryan. Back home for some shuteye. I'll see you tomorrow. And you be nice to Winston – he'll be here in a minute – good as gold that man!'

She's right of course, I am lucky. Without him, I'd be fitted with NHS dentures and God knows how long it would take for me to be back on my feet, but what with his posh dentist, and his personal physiotherapist and all those nice recreational drugs he'll be paying for – well, I don't deserve it, and I'm grateful.

I'm just drifting off when he pitches up and drops a dark blue orchid into a single-stem vase. 'They say you had nightmares, that they had to come in and wake you up,' he says, like it's any of his business. 'They say it might be good to speak with a bereavement counsellor …'

'I know, and I said I'm not interested.'

'You've been through so much, Ryan. Agnes was a lot more than a neighbour, and your mum passing last year … It can help to talk these things through.'

'What do you know about that shit?'

'As it happens – quite a bit. I saw one once, long time ago now, but she helped me accept things that had gone down in my life. Helped me move on.'

'Well aren't you the wise one. Maybe I don't want to move on. Maybe I just need to stay right where I am.'

'Sure. Well, if that's what you want.'

He walks over to the window. When he's thinking, or has something on his mind, he strokes the hairs on the back of his neck upwards. I guess he's wondering what or who the fuck he's got himself into. He doesn't turn to face me as he says gently, 'You're upset. No one's trying to get you to do anything you don't want to do. There's something else come up I need to run past you.'

'Oh yeah?'

'I got a call last night from one of the hotels in Jamaica. There's been a glitch in the building work. A strike. I need to fly out there for a few days and have booked a flight for tomorrow night.'

'Sure you do.'

Andrew

I CHECK MY WATCH for the umpteenth time and wonder how Megan can have such a responsible job, presumably making deadlines, turning up at appointments and all the rest of it – and yet never, ever make lunch on time.

'Oh God, Andrew,' she says, suddenly here and struggling for breath. 'I'm sorry, awful panic on at work – what's wrong? You look terrible.'

She stares at me in this weird way and then bursts out laughing. Giorgio runs up, laughing as well, taking her jacket and pulling out her chair. A menu materialises between us with a jolly flick of his wrist. He can be pretty annoying at times.

'Oh right. Hysterical. Andrew looks terrible, brilliant – good joke.' I don't even sound bitter, just dull and bored. Giorgio backs away quickly. I wonder vaguely whether he thinks we're married and suppose he does.

'Sorry, Andrew, think of it as a release of tension. It's different from usual that's all – so short, so spiky. Actually it really suits you.'

'Abi says it's almost as bad as Jamie's – he's had a "number one" too.'

'What?'

'A bad haircut. Funny how girls so often tell men that they don't like their hair, but if we men so much as—'

'Oh God, please don't look so tragic. Sorry, sorry, I can see you're not in the mood. I'm stopping now …'

'Thank you,' I say. 'And while we're talking about Abi – she said you took her out somewhere. She said she told you she was moving out and that you were all for it.'

'Did she now?' Megan raises an eyebrow.

'Pretty much.'

'I don't think you're trying to see it from her perspective, Andrew, she's confused and hurt and very angry. Rachel is her mother – it's normal for kids to stay with their mums.'

'Oh for Christ's sake. Rachel's set this up. Whatever Abi says, whether consciously or not, Rachel has wormed her way back and broken up the family.' I glance guiltily in Giorgio's direction.

'That's a bit hard, isn't it? Rachel didn't plan to get beaten up or raped – and surely it's good that she and Abi are getting on.'

'There is nothing good about Abi living with her mother. It's kind of you to put a positive spin on things but, well, you're not around, you haven't seen Callum recently. Nothing is going to get better or resolved.' I lower my voice, grateful that Giorgio is nowhere to be seen. 'Sorry, Megan, but you don't know her like I do. Rachel'll get bored with playing the caring mother, just as she got bored with playing at being a student.'

'So she's dropped out, has she?'

'Course she has. She needs a new toy – the secret affair at uni, all her young student friends, bonding with Abi. It isn't real, Megan, she's still a small child trying to forget. There isn't any space for Abi, or anyone else for that matter; everything is about creating her next brilliant hiding place.'

'You don't know that, Andrew. You're tunnelling down one scenario and you may be underestimating the significance that getting to know Abi; in a new way, has for her, especially when she and Liz, well, you know … The point is, we can't know, and Abi knows you're there for her – if she needs you.'

'If you say so.'

'Look, I haven't got long – can we order?' She fails to hide her exasperation. 'And maybe lighten up – just a little?'

'Ah, yes, sorry.' Giorgio is leaning against a pillar by the door. He looks our way and I catch his eye. He nods and smiles, pushes off with his heel and skips irritatingly towards us. I order roasted vegetables and feta in a filo parcel.

'Sounds good. Same for me with a large salad – to share.'

She tilts her head to one side. She doesn't want to hear about Rachel – she wants lunch with a friend who's not whingeing on about his problems all the time. I am quite alone. There is no one out there who sees what I see or who is in the least interested in trying to. I unfold my napkin, note again a recent tremor in my hand and gulp down a desperate urge to spring across the table, grab her by the throat and force her back to a time when we spoke the same language.

And suddenly ashamed, I ask how her mother is coping with everything.

'Good I guess, considering – feeding me up of course. No F words. No F words – a reasonably simple rule to follow, you might think. Sorry, Andrew, ignore me, it's sad – let's change the subject.'

'What you on about?'

'F for Food – I'm not talking about it, it's boring. Let's talk about something else. My new plans, for example.'

She tells me she's all but made up her mind to retrain into the educational side of psychology. That was my idea – her becoming a teacher. The last time we spoke about it we were sitting by the pier eating crab butties, just before Brendon's funeral. Laughing. I try to keep the bitterness out of my voice as I tell her how delighted I am.

Our food arrives. I start eating and force a swerve away from my own introspection.

'What?'

'Oh just thinking about Callum, his school, how he spends his days – something good isn't it?'

'Definitely. Focus on it. And Abi still comes over?'

I talk through a mouthful of cheesy comfort. 'Barely. She races in when she's forgotten something – says she having a great time.'

'So that's good, isn't it? Typical fifteen year old. This isn't her fault you know – she needs your support.'

'I know and I'm trying – I just can't believe how much I miss her. There's such a hole without her.'

'Of course you do – these things aren't simple for anyone.'

'Sometimes you do say some very unhelpful things. Sorry but—'

'And sometimes, believe it or not, Andrew, your sensationalism can be pretty hard work. It might be more helpful to see that Rachel's suffered too. Of course she missed Abi and Callum – she's as much a victim as anyone.'

'Rubbish. How often have you said that there's no point in blaming the past for everything, that we have to take responsibility.'

'Of course.'

'So?'

'So nothing – it's just not simple, that's all.'

'Well, how convenient for everyone.'

'Not really no, very *inconvenient* most of the time, but it's the world we live in and it's up to each one of us to interpret it according to who we are at that time. You're hurting, Andrew.'

'Amazed you noticed. And you've changed, Megan.'

She sighs. 'Now why's that I wonder? Oh yes, my father just died, and my mum has moved in and my brother is falling apart and oh yes I also have a full-time and incredibly demanding job. Listen, I haven't got long …'

'I just get the feeling that you're not being honest with me.'

'Not being honest with you? Not being honest with you? Ah, I get it. So that's what all this is about. Abi said something the other day – something about you thinking I'm in a relationship.'

'Well are you?'

'No.'

'You don't sound very sure.'

'I'm not having a relationship, Andrew, but I am seeing someone on and off.'

'Okay. Right. None of my business. Not unless you want to talk about it that is—'

'I don't think I do, if that's all right.'

'Absolutely. Right. Sorry. Absolutely none of my business.'

'Listen, Andrew. It's not so much that it's not your business, it's just that—'

'No, you're right, it's none of my business.'

'I never said that.'

'Yes you did, and you're right.'

She leans forward. 'It's just that you're not the only one who's been through it recently. At the risk of sounding like a stuck record, I repeat, things aren't always straightforward – much as I'd like them to be.'

'Obviously not.' I search wildly for Giorgio. I do not want to be having this conversation. He's near enough to have sensed the tension and throws me a desperate look before mincing our way. 'Two teas please, Giorgio.' He hurries away nodding, as though tea might save the day. She waits till he's out of earshot.

'I don't have time for tea.'

'No, of course you don't. Sorry.'

'I shouldn't really have come. We've got two staff off sick and I'm supposed to be covering for someone. I'm sorry, Andrew.' She stands up, opens her bag and rummages in its depths. 'You're the one normally on the run. Things slacking off then?'

'Oh! No, not really. At least, I don't know – I've been taking a bit of time off. Callum's been poorly,' I add lamely. 'You go. I'll get the bill. Honestly, Megan, just go.'

She gives me another exasperated look, zips up her bag and hoicks it over her shoulder. Half way to the door she turns back, but changes her mind, shrugs, as if I'm a hopeless case, and leaves.

Giorgio appears at the run, tea slopping.

He bobs, helplessly, staring after Megan like a wind-up puppy. I make a vague sign that I'd like both teas, and with a look of acute personal pain, he backs away.

Fuck. Nice one. Abi first and now Megan. And don't forget that Callum prefers to talk to Julie or, or well, anyone except me. I don't want to share things with India and can't share things with Liz, who loves me, but is mad, so doesn't count. Jolly good, Andrew – jolly well done. No friends left at all.

Ryan

TAKES ME AN AGE to climb the stairs to David's flat. Been a while. And I wouldn't be here now except I'm too fucking scared to call my old contacts. I lay my stick against the wall, take off my jacket and drop it on the chair in the hall. I still get the odd twinge, but mostly I've patched up real good. I shout through to the kitchen. My voice sounds steady enough. 'Who the hell were those dudes?' No answer. 'I'd hate to see them with their clothes off – those kind of muscles freak me out. Nice car though, nice chauffeur.'

He shouts back. 'Hey man. Thought you'd got lost. Help yourself to a drink. I'll be through in a minute.'

I bend towards the gaudy gold mirror and admire my perfect row of teeth. Winston's dentist was a trip for a start, like a fucking palace, his place – choose your own music, put on the head gear, open your veins, shut your eyes and lie back.

I can tell David's still pissed off with me. Tosser. I limp through to the living room. Once I'm sitting I reach for the packet of smokes on the table and notice my hands are shaking. I pull one out and light it from a fancy book of matches, which I pocket. He strolls in, whistles low, turns his back and goes directly to the drinks trolley. 'So look at you,' he says, 'Replay jeans, Armani shirt. Won the lottery have you?'

'Something like that. Who were those dudes, then?'

'What dudes?' He drops onto the black leather settee, puts a shot of whisky in my hand.

'The sumo wrestlers, the ones that were leaving as I came in.'

'No idea, mate.' He tips out a small mountain of coke from a tiny white wrapper and draws two lines with a scalpel, picks up the straw and taps it on the glass surface.

'That's more like it.' He leans back, shuts his eyes and hands me the tube.

'Because if those are the kind of people you're buying drugs from, David—'

'Don't know what you're talking about. Why are you so jumpy? Taking a beating made you paranoid has it?' he says, handing me a soft pouch, which I open, dip my pinkie in, and rub it over my gums.

'Just watching my back, that's all.'

He makes to punch my arm, but I shy away and limp to my coat in the hall, pull out a ball of foil and my lighter and go into the bathroom.

I'm gone for ten minutes.

'You want to watch a DVD?' he says, once I'm back. 'Still painful is it – your leg?'

'Not so much. But I should head. Stuff to do.' Which is true. Winston's off to Jamaica again tomorrow. Another crisis. Only I'm asking if it's here or there.

I zip up my jacket, take out a wad of notes from my chest pocket, count them out and hand them to him.

'Those guys you saw weren't my suppliers, Ryan. Now quit fretting will you?'

'Sure.'

'I'll call you. Must be nice to be buying rather than selling this shit. You got compensation or what?'

I tap the side of my nose and let myself out.

Winston isn't home. I head straight to my room and my laptop – take out the matchbook belonging to David's buddies, type in the web address printed on the back. Business International: it's one of a couple of dozen private business schools around the world. The site is convincing: photos of happy students against aqua marine seas holding up diplomas. This one in Beijing is positively luxurious. Isn't long, though, before I find reams of eloquent blogging – and accusations. 'My friend disappeared overnight. Very unlike her …', 'The accreditation is meaningless …', 'We were used like slaves in businesses while on so-called placements …'. And then other accusatory articles by academics – accusations of money laundering, human trafficking, drugs – but no convictions. So far.

I knew it. David's scared, really scared, and if I cared a fuck I might wonder what the fuck he's doing working with Eco Écosse.

I smoke a wee bit more to even up my mood. It's after six. So where's Winston got to? I text him, just in case he's been mugged. He answers right away, gives me this bullshit about heavy traffic, how he's taking a walk home by the canal – he'll be back in a minute. Coward. Truth is, he's been avoiding me all week, scared I'll have a go, cause a scene or mess up his precious *last night. Hurray*, is what I say – be a fucking relief to be on my own for a while, get myself some new company.

He tells me as soon as he's through the door that he's booked a table at The Witchery. Nice one. Put me in some fancy restaurant and I'll behave myself.

He touches my arm, kisses me. I let him hold me. He kisses my forehead like he's blessing me or something. But his smooching does my head in. I pull away and cross the hall and go into my room. Sometimes I just know it's a set-up, spend the night running from him or drowning, his kind black face smiling, wake up screaming. But the truth is, I've gone right through his past and he climbed his way to the top legit, which still doesn't explain why he picked me up, and why, having discovered that I'm no more than some paranoid scumbag, he hasn't thrown me back to the gutter where I belong.

I open the wardrobe. These clothes are all mine, racks of them. I take down the blue cashmere suit and pink shirt.

'You ready, man?' he calls from his room. We both have our own rooms as well as a shared one; we've got everything money can buy. When I first came out of hospital I was in the spare room – the one that looks across the road. I'd lie awake, weak as a kitten, listening to the cars on the cobbles. He took care of me like I was his child. Sometimes I'd fight it, him, his softness – other times I'd let myself drift off. He'd talk to me about Jamaica, tell me stories just like my own daddy did. I guess that's what he wanted, wants – a son, as well as a lover, and there were moments when I was his, I admit it, when he wore me down.

I check myself in the long mirror, try to fix my cufflinks, but it's awkward – my fingers still ain't healed right. I go through to the master bedroom where Winston is facing the mirror, knotting his white suede tie. He may be an old man but he still has style – no doubt about that. Now what's he grinning like that for?

'Ryan. You are one beautiful son of a bitch – did I ever tell you that?'

I raise my eyebrows as he moves towards me, his eyes sagging with lust. 'You'll need a tie tonight. Christ, anyone would think you was ashamed of those fine new teeth. C'mon, man.' He takes an ivory tie from the rack and loops it over my neck, but instead of tying it, he pulls me towards him – twisting it around his fist, while his other hand undoes the buttons on my shirt. His little finger slips under the supple leather of my belt, while his tongue flickers down my belly. He peels my trousers from my arse and takes me into his mouth. I stare down as his thick white hair moves back and forward, feel nothing much. Both hands knead my butt, desperate to have me yield, urging me to engage – his slim manicured fingers beginning to probe, but I resist. A picture forms in my mind: Winston, no longer the suave gentleman, but a desperate old man with a puckered mouth, now stretched to breaking point in some kind of supplication or scream. I know those faces. Some of them are art. I move slowly at first, gently kneading his scalp. Then I apply pressure, feel myself swelling, a slight push against my hands as he tries to ease back. But I'm building, tuning into his desperation to find rhythm again, hearing his struggle for breath. Then I clock that it's not the rhythm that's doing it for me. What's doing it is a picture of the only old man who could ever mean anything to me – my old man, choking; my old man, his hands, my hands, pushing and holding and rushing until I hear him gagging on my spunk. I let him go and turn away and hear him grappling for the bed. When I turn around he's sitting on its edge holding the tie out. I take it and stoop to kiss the top of his white head – my turn to be fatherly. I take my shit back into my room, open my bedside drawer. I've got just about every mood I need right here: poppy, cocaine, crack, dope, uppers and downers. I cut myself a line of David's coke. As I'm rolling a note, Winston chirps up from his room.

'Shall we go, Ryan? You ready, man – you okay?'

I shut my eyes. A cloudburst of the lightest snowflakes showers my troublesome brain and cools me down. I feel stupid, like I worry for nothing. I am one lucky son of a bitch; he loves me and I love him – it's so obvious I want to laugh. I haul myself to my feet, go through the second door that leads into the passage. He's waiting for me. I hand him the cufflinks, hold out my wrists. As he fixes them, he smiles, and I lean my head against his shoulder. He moves behind me and massages my shoulders. Glittering sparks sizzle from his hands as his voice joyrides through my veins.

Outside, the pavement's shimmering with frost. Despite the long wool coat the cold is like a solid thing. I'm not saying much, just watching some huge-breasted chick coming towards us wearing second-skin jeans and a paint-on t-shirt. I am mesmerised. Enough drugs and I guess we can even change the weather.

Turns out it's not just a table he's booked, we've got the best room in the place for the night as well. He must have planned this a while ago, took our stuff there this morning. If I wasn't such a cunt, I'd feel ashamed of myself. We decide to walk up the Royal Mile. It's a full moon tonight, pretty as a picture post card, and on the way I swear I see Rachel with that friend of hers, perched on a stool in a bar. My blood pumps in my veins. I knew it would happen sometime. Edinburgh is barely bigger than a village, but it's like, seeing her in the flesh, I mean, knowing she's all mended. She might have seen me, but I don't think she recognised me, not in the flash clothes and with a white haired sugar-daddy on my arm.

ABI

'HI DAD. IS CALLUM HERE?'

'Won't be back for an hour or so,' Dad says. 'He's got band practice. He practically lives at Heels, especially now you're—'

'Don't start, okay?' I walk past him and into the hall, take my scabby coat off and hang it up. I used to recognise the stuff hanging up here.

Dad's on my heels.

'I wasn't going to, Abi,' he says. 'But I can't pretend we don't miss you, can I? And now this arrived this morning.' He's got a letter in his hand which he's holding towards me. So that's what this is all about.

I snatch it from him and slump on the bottom stair, take a quick scan to see if it tells me anything I don't know already, and hand it back quickly. Sounds like they're well shot of me.

'What incident, Abi?'

'Mum went in about me missing a couple of days. Honestly, Dad, they were well out of order. They even had some kind of Welfare idiot giving her the first degree about parenting and some bullshit nonsense about unauthorised absences. And then they have the nerve to say "... wish her every success ..." Hypocrites! Like they care about me – like they've ever given a shit. I'm not going back and absolutely no one can make me, so don't even bother – okay?'

'So what about your prelims, Abi? It doesn't sound like you've thought this through.'

'That's typical of you. I'm doing home-schooling, if you must know. And prelims are ages away. Honestly, Dad, you don't know what it's like ... Actually you do, I told you enough times, you know fine well, so I've made up my mind – I've taken a *mature decision, and* I've got a part-time job where Mum works, at the Italian, and it's brilliant.'

'Goodness, Abi, without even talking to me about it – without even one word?'

'Yep. I'm a big girl now, Dad. I know it's hard for you to take on board, but I can make my own mistakes – if it doesn't work out I can go back.'

'I'm not sure about that.'

'About what?'

'About going back to school – it's not so easy, going back ...'

Can't be doing with this. 'Change the gig, Dad. I'm not telling you I'm pregnant or addicted to drugs.'

It's so dark in here. I walk across the hall and put the lights on. Then I go and lean on the windowsill that looks out over the street. Clouds, nothing but clouds and rain and yuk.

I turn back and face him. I used to love this hall. This was the rug we had in our hall in Pier Road, I used to play on it with Cal when he was a baby. Nevis chewed those edges when he was a puppy ... and that stain is wine. I just so hate being here ...

'God knows how many years you spent telling me how important the family is!' I suddenly yell at him. 'All that stuff about how much we'll love being in Edinburgh! "Oh Abi, you'll love it! So much for you to do, a new start."'

He looks at me with that sad innocent look he has.

'That's what I believed, Abi. I thought a new start would fix things for your mum and me.'

'Yeah right, but you didn't say that, did you? You made out that it was your job, the whole *schools* deal. I could have understood. It might have helped explain everything that had been kicking off – it might have helped me understand about me and Liam and why I so badly needed someone, anyone. Why didn't you tell me? I thought you ... I thought we ...' I'm about to fucking cry. No fucking way.

'Abi, come here. I'm so sorry, but this, this leaving school ...'

'For fuck's sake, Dad. Drop it, just drop it. Get off me – I'm fine.' I turn a few circles until my eyes stop stinging. I will not give him the satisfaction. 'This is my life, Dad. Even Megan says—'

'Have you seen Megan?'

I take a few deep breaths. Shouting at him is a complete waste of time. So why's he looking frightened then? What's he done now? 'It's just nice to have someone who actually tries to understand me, instead of just undermining everything I do.'

'Let's leave Megan out of this, shall we?' he says.

'Oh my God. Oh, fucking hell – you made a pass at her didn't you? That's what all this is about – you made a fucking pass at her and she turned you down. You're in love with Megan.'

'Abi. Stop this right now.' He sighs this enormous sigh and stares at the floor forever, like it might just swallow him up. Be doing us both a favour.

I'm just about to nail him to the wall when Gran bounces through the front door with this like totally fit guy, who I get must be the new nurse. I'm like ogling him and about to introduce myself when Gran lifts up her skirts and begins to squat. Awesome, Gran. Harry (that's his name) jumps in quick and escorts her to the loo. I stare hard at Dad, and he stares hard at me, and we both sort of shrug and shake our heads miserably. Dad picks up the mail off the floor and I stare at the coat rack and clock my old denim jacket which I used to love more than anything, and stuff it in my bag.

As soon as Gran's out the loo she lunges at me, kisses me twice on each cheek, grabs my hand and kind of skates me through to the kitchen, Dad on our heels. She sits herself daintily down while I put the kettle on, and finally get to say who I am to Harry, telling him that I hope he'll bring Gran round to our house. He says he'd be pleased to and asks where we live, and I tell him – and he says that Wednesdays are a good day because Gran does belly dancing class on Wednesday and she's always in a sociable mood and I tell him that Mum would love that and suggest he gives me his mobile number so I can call him. Result!

'How is your mother, my dear?' Gran says. 'How's Carl?'

I look at Dad, who looks totally freaked out. I pull my mouth into a smile with my fingers. So what if Gran doesn't remember stuff? Who cares? But Dad's up and out of his seat like a fucking jack-in-the-box.

'Dad, what are you doing? Leave her! It's fine. Dad!'

'Actually I think she should go to her room. Harry will take her tea up.'

'Why? She's cool, Dad – she's totally cool. Here you are, Gran. Back off will you, Dad?'

I tuck a chair in close to hers, sit on it and squeeze her hand and tell her that Carl died three years ago. 'Mum's good, Gran. She wants you to start coming to see us – with Harry!' She's not listening though.

'Carl's not dead, you silly girl. Is that what he told you?' she says, giving Dad the evil eye. 'No darling, he's with Rachel now ... You know, she was always his favourite, so now they're married. I think that's rather touching don't you, after all these years?'

Poor Gran.

'No Gran. You're confused. Rachel's your daughter and she was married to Dad. Andrew's your son-in-law.' She nods seriously. 'You know Andrew, Gran?' I yank him over. 'You remember, Gran – the really annoying one ...' I look up at Harry who's smiling at me and shrugging his shoulders. He's right, who cares? I let it go.

Now what's Dad up to for chrissake? What's that look for? I mean chill out, for fuck's sake. I take Gran's hand again and start patting. Ugh, just looking at him gives me the creeps.

I try to get Gran to make sense for a bit longer but she's getting agitated and Harry starts coaxing her upstairs. I follow them into the hall and try to kiss her goodbye, but she sort of shakes her head around as though she doesn't remember who I am. I watch Harry lead her up the stairs, but by the time she gets to the first landing she's crying and saying she wants to go home.

I think I'll go home too. I'm getting my coat when the bell goes. It's Callum, but instead of hurling himself at me, he just sort of looks around awkwardly. He does hug me in the end, kind of, looking the other way, and I kind of pretend how heavy he is, but he's like politely but totally pushing me off and climbing the stairs.

I follow him up, push open his bedroom door. Jesus.

He's standing hugging his school bag in the middle of the huge expanse of bare carpet. Where is everything?

'Can I come in? Wow, look at your room – where's all your stuff? Who did this?'

'Me. I like it like this.'

He shrugs as he climbs onto the bed, drops his school bag, picks it up, and hugs it to his chest. I sit beside him, but not touching. I quite like the silence so I just let it go on like that and then he does this big sigh and then I sigh and after ages I put my arm around his shoulders. And then after a while he just leans on me a little.

'Abi?'

'Yes?'

'At school today we all talked about sad things. And I wanted to talk about you leaving and stuff but we had to make it about things – you know, not people.'

'That sounds hard. Like what then?'

'Julie said one about a clock that's been broken forever and nobody cares enough to mend it, or a book that's slipped down behind a bookcase that everyone's forgotten about – stuff like that.'

'So what did you say?'

'I said about a teddy who was dropped on the beach for a whole night until he was nearly dead.'

'That is sad.'

He shrugs.

'Cal, will you think about coming over to Mum's? You could stay over.'

He shakes his head.

'We'd just really like it if you did, that's all. Jamie says he really, really misses you and everything. I mean, it'd be nice.'

After a few minutes his head becomes heavy against my shoulder and I nudge his school bag onto the floor.

The next thing I know Dad is jiggling my shoulder.

'What time is it?'

'Almost nine.'

'God, Dad – why did you leave me so long? I was meant to be home, I said I'd be home.' I leap off the bed like he's just told me there's a fire downstairs.

Cal is rubbing his eyes as I kiss both his cheeks.

'Abi don't go. Abi.' He begins to cry.

But I'm out the room stuffing my feet into my shoes and rattling down the stairs, trying not to cry myself.

I'm home by nine thirty. She's not even here. I don't believe this. She said to make sure I'm home by seven. She said she was going to rent a DVD, pick up a takeaway.

I drop the giant slatted blinds and it's like the walls have been painted with soft pink stripes, it looks pretty. I grab a can from the fridge and flop onto the massive turquoise sofa we got from Ikea. It's cool this place. I mean it wouldn't be so bad if she was doing the shopping – if I knew she'd be back in a minute. But for all I know she's run into someone, getting rat-arsed. And she never calls, that's what really pisses me off – I mean she's entitled to go out isn't she? So why can't she just say? I curl up into a ball and shut my eyes.

'Hi darling. Sorry I'm so late. Sorry.'

I hear her yelling from the hall and sit up. She flings her coat on the sofa and two or three carriers onto the floor. I can smell the takeaway, so I get up and start unpacking the bags. She goes to the fridge and takes an open bottle of white wine, pours two glasses and hands me one.

'Cheers,' she says, holding hers high. 'How was Dad? Did you see Callum?'

'Dad just heard I've left school, and how do you think Callum is?'

'No need to be so sharp, Abi. Things will settle down, you'll see. You're happy aren't you?'

She doesn't give me time to answer. She's fishing inside one of the bags, pulling out small foil boxes.

'Get the plates will you, while I change.'

'And Gran?' she shouts from her bedroom. 'Did you ask him about Gran coming over?'

'I asked the nurse – it's fine. Wednesdays.' I follow her through. 'She's getting worse though – we'll need the nurse.'

She throws her clothes in a heap, starts pulling stuff from her drawers. 'Your father always exaggerates – it's all part of his martyr persona.'

'Well, no, I'm not sure he is this time, she's saying really stupid things …'

'Embarrassing him is she? Peeing on the floor?'

'How did you know?'

'Your father told me, but I thought it was something he'd made up to put me off.'

'Well you're wrong then. Did you remember loo paper, Mum? I had to use the *Big Issue* this morning.'

'In the Co-op bag. Like what's she saying?'

'Stuff about you and Granddad, like you're married … like, oh yes, and that he was always very *keeeen* on you.'

I go back to the kitchen, start chucking the lids in the bin and scooshing curry onto plates. 'Great, Mum – this looks great. Oh and before I forget, India phoned, said it was urgent. You're very pally these days. I thought you said she got on your nerves?'

Then before I know it, like one second later, she sort of storms past me, grabbing her coat and bag off the sofa.

'Mum, where are you going?'

Rachel

I DON'T EXACTLY HAVE much in mind – just get to a bar, but then maybe I do, cos I'm moving past the pubs like they don't exist.

Can't think about Abi now. If I'd stayed I might have told her about her precious gran, and her precious grandpa. And to think I was really just beginning to believe Mum had no idea – that she was as much of a victim as we were. Jesus. With a bit of luck she'll die soon, go and join her bastard husband and leave us all alone.

I look up and find myself standing in the same place as I stood when Ryan and Trish broke up. I can see the way she shrugged him off – the way he stormed back through his door. I walk across the street and lean against the main door of his building.

Forgive me, Abi.

I press his bell. There are pale stripes framing the curtains. I hold the bell for longer this time. I think I'll wait a bit, so I walk across the street to the off-licence, pick up a bottle, and head over to the bench opposite his flat.

It's eleven now, I've been here an hour; people have been going in and out, but not Ryan. The whisky no longer warms me and I'm cold. Two girls stop at his door, speak to the intercom and someone lets them in. A minute later the pale line round his window grows brighter, as though more lights have been switched on. I can picture him bending low to the plug to reach the broken standard lamp, the curve of his back, the small muscles beneath his shoulder blades rippling his skin … I rummage in my bag for lipstick, remember it's in my jeans pocket. My mirror is small and smudged and my hands are cold and stiff, but the street lamp is right behind me and I do a fairly good job. I must be a bit drunk, I suppose. I cross the road. Press his buzzer again.

A girl's voice.

'Is Ryan there? I'm looking for Ryan.'

'Sorry. No Ryan here.'

I try the buzzer below. Maybe I forgot which flat he was in. No Ryan there. Oh God. I press the others and then walk back across the road and sit on the bench again. I need a drink, a lot of drink.

After a while someone sits beside me.

He asks me if I'm okay, why I'm all alone in the dark on a bench on the street, tells me I'm pretty. He has a kind voice. He is young. I tell him I've just had some good news and I'm celebrating. I offer him some of my whisky – he takes it. He has a nice voice. Cheers. To a nice voice.

I sleep in late, have a long soak in the bath, even manage to get up the road to buy a few essentials before checking my emails and listening to my messages. They're mostly from India. For no good reason I've been seeing a bit of her recently and I'd say she's being weird, weirder than usual, very hyper, very pleased with herself – very annoying. Mostly she's asking if I fancy a drink at The Basement later tonight. She's got a surprise for me. What? Another surprise – yippee fucking do.

I'm not normally on time for work, but today I get there early.

'Hey Rachel.' It's Toni my boss – looking exceptionally sexy tonight.

'Yeah?'

'You gota time for a drink layta?' Cute accent.

Never gives up, does he? 'I can't,' I say, 'I'm meeting my friend, Dawn, after work. Sorry.'

Twenty minutes later he suggests we 'change ze barrel' together. Half an hour after that I'm wishing I'd brought a change of underwear.

It's a relief when Dawn gets here on time.

'Get a sitter all right?' I ask. 'How are the kids anyway – not seen them for ages.'

'Yeah thanks, that friend from Skye's staying,' she says, deadpan.

'Ooooo.'

'Christ, Rachel – sex or nothing with you isn't it?'

'Maybe, sometimes.'

'Yeah well, we're not the same are we? What do you fancy, stay here or go out?'

'Let's go somewhere. I won't be a minute – just get my jacket.'

I wend my way down the narrow passage behind the bar but I'm met by an ugly howl. For the second time this evening I flatten out against a damp distempered wall. I edge towards the crack of light between the door and the door frame. And back up quick. Toni's girlfriend is paying a visit. How touching. But she's howling, so he's either decided to spill a lot more than his spunk tonight or there's been a bereavement. Either way my jacket can stay where it is – time I left.

I ignore Dawn's questioning look as I return empty-handed and head for the street. I pause at the door, choose a leather three-quarter-length coat from the customer hooks. Always wanted one of these.

'Forgot where I hung it. It's new – like it?' I say.

'Must have cost a bomb,' she says, which isn't really an answer, but I know what she means.

We head to The Basement – not too loud and most importantly not full of students.

India's sitting at the far end of the bar. She gives us a discreet finger-bend wave. She looks fabulous – and I'm not the only one who's admiring her. There are at least four young men, with eyes on stalks, talking to her – one of them will be the 'surprise' obviously. She's nothing if not a fast worker. Poor old Guy – that didn't last long then.

She doesn't exactly bound up to us, so I guess she'd rather be alone. Dawn and I shuffle through the bar huggers and I order two beers.

'I thought you'd given up drinking.'

'So I've given up, giving up. You should be pleased, you're always going on at me for being boring,' I say, giving her a warning look.

'That's crap, Rachel. Still, nothing to do with me.'

'You're right, so let's leave it shall we?' We draw up a couple of bar stools.

'Are you sure you're all right? Abi okay?'

'Abi's fine. I've not given up giving up drinking because anything's wrong, I'm drinking because I've proved I can be sober, and sober is boring. Have a problem with that, oh ye responsible mother of two – hmm?'

Sometimes I wonder whether Dawn and I are really suited as friends at all. I turn, catch India's eye and look pleading. She sashays towards us, grabbing someone by the hand who has just backed out of the 'mens'. He must have been gone a while.

'Hi Rachel. Hello Dawn. This is David,' she says, like she's just won him in a raffle. 'I guess you two know each other,' she says to me.

'Hello David. Surprise, surprise. Dawn, you remember David, don't you? He was at our barbecue.'

'Yes, I think so. Hello David.'

'Good to see you again, Dawn,' he says. 'I was just walking past and stopped in for a drink. It seems like it's everyone's watering hole.'

He manages to make these few words sound subtly insulting, which means, I guess, that India never told him she'd invited us.

'Now, you're all going to think me very rude but I was just leaving – got precious little sleep last night and I'm wiped out … No, please don't move. See you tomorrow at work, India.' And puff, he's away.

Dawn and I exchange glances and I turn to India. 'I thought you were seeing Guy?'

She picks up her drink, downs the remains. 'David and I

were just having a drink,' she says, nudging me in the ribs and frowning towards Dawn.

I dig her back in the ribs and speak softly. 'Pushing it a bit, aren't you? A colleague? Guy's bound to find out.'

'You obviously don't know Guy very well. He's quite blind – thinks we're in love – not exactly a turn-on is it?'

'So finish with him then.'

'You mad? One of the first blokes who's actually treated me right – wines and dines me, buys me chocolates, takes me on holiday. Besides, David's weird.'

Now why doesn't that surprise me? I nod to our glasses. 'Same again?'

Dawn raises her eyebrows.

As we wait for our round goody-two-shoes goes down the safe domestic route.

'Abi still with Jamie?'

'Yup. Abi's still with Jamie,' I say. 'And that makes Abi's life very dull.'

'Honestly, Rachel.'

'He's just like Andrew – nice, careful and boring. Did I tell you she's just started at the wine bar? And did you notice that gorgeous young man? No? Well never mind, you wouldn't approve.'

'And how's she getting on with studying at home? That can't be easy, especially if she's working,' she says, as if I don't know what that means.

'Not full-time is it? And standard grades aren't exactly rocket science. She'll sail through them if she wants to. Did I tell you how rude the head teacher was?'

'No you didn't. What happened?' she says, with her magistrate's hat on.

'They called me in – said that her attitude, which had never been "exactly enthusiastic", had "escalated to verging on the abusive" since she's moved out from Andrew's. Said that she had "crossed a line".'

'What did they mean?'

'Oh, something about her behaviour becoming a way of life, whereas before it had been an expression of her problems at home – bloody cheek.'

'Well you can't blame them for wanting to talk to you.'

'They want her to see the educational psychologist. Same again, please. They thought she might be depressed. Honestly Dawn, they implied that I wasn't a good parent.'

'They actually said that, did they?'

India kindly mutters the word 'bullshit'.

'They've already judged me. What the hell, she's my daughter and she chose me – in the end that's what counts. They put too much pressure on her – how do they know what'd be good for her? I'm her mother, I love her. Sod it, but you know what the real problem is, don't you?'

'Listen Rachel, why don't you steady up a bit?'

'Do you know what the real problem is, *Dawn* – the real problem?'

'I'm sure you're about to tell me.'

'*She*, Mrs. Bloody Harkness. Head teacher bloody Harkness, is a hideous dried-up prune and I'm not. That's what this is really about – she's jealous.'

India's giggling. There, she agrees.

'Oh, come off it! She's a professional, it's not always about you, Rachel. Not everyone evaluates life according to how sexy they are. Don't you think you've had enough?'

'Dawn, please, you are not my mother. Thanks, India. Half pint and a whisky shot – make it an Isla malt, okay? So, do you know what I did? I told her exactly what she could do with her poxy school.'

Thumbs up from India. I'm beginning to understand why I'm seeing rather more of her.

'Is that really why Abi left then – because you lost it in front of the head teacher?'

'They picked on her. Really Dawn, they did, didn't they, India? Remember the times she came home upset – you remember, don't you? Tell Dawn. Abi's had a rough ride from the beginning. No, we just talked it over and made a grown-up decision, and I backed her all the way.'

'Right,' Dawn says.

'Right,' I say.

'Right.' India nods happily.

Dawn says she's got to go. Well, good riddance! And don't

kiss me goodbye then, saddo. I turn to the lovely India with a sigh of relief. 'Poor Dawn – you don't know her really, do you? Well, you're lucky – she's one hell of a prude. She's got two very irritating small children that stay with her at weekends, works most nights in the week, and goes to uni during the day. Absolutely no fun at all – about as much fun as a pig in a poke. Don't have a clue what that means but it sounds extremely dull, well no, maybe it sounds quite fun actually. Aw shit, who cares anyway? Dawn is as dull as ditch-water – that's what I mean, dull as fucking ditch-water. Now for fuck's sake let's have something proper to drink.'

I order four margaritas. We take a table away from the speakers which are vomiting out some awful techno rubbish – take it in turns to go for a pee and pick up almost exactly where we left off last time. I'm all ears, and always surprised at just how much India dislikes Andrew, these days. I mean, this is the girl who called him Uncle Andrew, who used to practically live with us. She says he's changed out of all recognition and that he makes her feel like he hates her, and, if it wasn't for the fact that Callum needed her, she'd have gone, weeks ago. I'd have her with me, course I would – Abi and I would love to have her, but besides the fact that there's barely room for the two of us, it wouldn't be fair on Callum, not by the sounds of it.

'Why don't you try to get the house back, Rache? You'd be bound to win; they always give the mother the family home – that's what Mum says. Most men are incapable of taking care of kids, and I tell you, Andrew's no different. He might have been in the beginning but since you've both left, he's lost it – he really has.'

'But he's still very involved in his school and everything isn't he?' I say.

'Well, that's the point. Andrew'll go to the school, loves the school, but he's different at home, doesn't read to him or play with him. I do all that, and he's so often late back from work – he takes advantage, Rache …'

'It's weird because Callum never says anything – but maybe he wouldn't.'

'Of course he doesn't, little mite – he's not stupid is he? He wants you back. He doesn't want you to hate his dad, he wants you both to be his heroes. Simple psychology, Rache – I lied about my mum constantly to stop them putting me into care.'

'Haha. Your mum wasn't as bad as you make out. I almost feel sorry for Andrew. He's obviously having some kind of breakdown.'

'He's changed, Rachel. He's so changed and it's damaging Callum. If you got the house back I'd stay on and give you a hand. It'd be so good for everyone, surely you can see that.'

Ah! Now I can see where she's coming from – not clearly of course because I'm seeing mostly double, but yes of course I can, and it's good to know that India would be right behind me. 'Oops. Sorry, India. Delicious these, aren't they? What?'

'I said, you should go for the house – get it back.'

'Yes, well cheers, it's a good idea – let's drink to that.'

'So you'll try, then? You'll move back in?'

'Well, no. Well, maybe. I'll have to think on it, sleep on it. Do you know, if I just move my eyes just a wee bit this way – what's that – to the right, I can see four of you … That's great isn't it? Then back to two. Shit, can you do that?'

'I'm not quite as far gone as you, Rache – better get a refill.'

She slinks to the bar. I'm not so far gone that I don't see the looks the men give each other as they let her through. Just imagine living with that goddess and Abi even … and guess who'll be babysitting Callum? No. This way, this way, Andrew pays the bills and I have some fun. Fifteen years of babies, fifteen fucking years – I'm not giving up my little bit of freedom now, am I?

'Thanks, India! Here's to Andrew earning lots and lots of dosh, eh?' I'm starting to feel a bit queasy, should have eaten something. 'I'm slaughtered, and my legs are freezing. I should get home.'

'Oh come on, Rache – it's early, let's go on somewhere. What's wrong with your legs?'

'Freezing. Had to take my tights off – small accident.'

She wrinkles up her nose and starts giggling.

'No, not that kind of accident. Where's my coat? Have you seen my coat? I could have sworn I hung … Oops, there it is – pretty smart eh?'

I should get home. But first I need a pee, and finding the

ladies' proves almost impossible – am I that invisible? Can't they see me? I nudge and elbow my way through, practically knocking myself out. Who put a bloody step right there? I'm sure there wasn't one earlier, I'd have noticed – I'm not that stupid.

Bollocks.

'Hi fellas, don't mind me.'

ABI

So why doesn't she just tell me? Does my head in. Some sort of weird guessing game, maybe? Not hard, Mum, not when Toni's treating me like I'm some kind of family member all of a sudden. I'm not daft. And I don't mind – he's better than that guy I saw her with last week – and the one the week before – I mean *that one* was a real weirdo freak. And all the rest. She thinks I don't know – she really believes I'm that stupid. Toni'd be cool. He's dead tidy, and nice. And he's crazy about Mum. So no, I feel cool about it.

It's *my* love life that sucks. I can't talk to Mum, because she'll just tell me to dump him, most likely, and I don't want to do that because – because better him than no one. So why won't he sleep with me then? I'm almost sixteen, what the hell difference does it make? Mum's all for it – always staying out … And even Jenny's done it now with freak fuckwit Ferdie.

Makes me look at other guys and stuff, can't help it. I mean just the name *Ash* makes me go weird and that's before I'm imagining his rock star face. Yesterday, I actually got to see him at it. Through the bog window. OMG he was right there – could have touched him if I'd stuck my arm out. No wonder he's got them queuing up for it … Olympic kisser he is – creases me up, especially when they come back into the restaurant like five minutes after him, with their bright red chins and puffy lips.

Piss off. I can dream can't I? So maybe I'm a slut, cos I'd be lying if… I mean, if anyone like Ash did, well, you know, come on to me or anything …

Romeo-Toni creeps up behind me and puts a fatherly arm around my shoulder.

'Geeva your lovely muddur a hug when you see'er. Okay sweedie?'

When I get in my 'lovely muddur's out cold. She was so pissed last night I thought someone was picking the lock. Must've spent twenty minutes trying to get her key to fit. She'll have been kipping all day. This bugs me because the flat's a tip. I don't feel I have a mother in fact. She's more like a bum flatmate.

I play back the messages. Two from India, for fuck's sake. Then I bang around in the kitchen, washing up, chucking washing in the machine – stuff like that. The dishtowels look like used loo paper, which I know is Mum wiping out the wok because there's *never* any kitchen roll. Does my head in.

I pull the roaring vacuum cleaner down the passage and open her bedroom door.

'Ooops, sorry. I thought I'd vacuum …'

'Very funny.' She opens one eye, pushes up on one elbow and holds her forehead. 'Turn it off will you. Good shift?'

I stamp on the off thingy and collapse on her bed.

'Mum. Can I ask you something?'

'Yeah, what?'

'Are you and Toni, like – are you seeing him? Please Mum, please don't lie to me – he's banging on like I'm his little sister, and he sent you his love, and he's singing all the time, and you know he dumped Steph, don't you?'

'Would you mind if I was?'

'No, why would I? I don't expect you to stay single, Mum – you seeing him then?'

'You don't mind?'

'Just said, didn't I? How would you feel if I'd got a new boyfriend and didn't tell you?'

'He's hardly my boyfriend.'

'Well he thinks he is – you should hear him. It's like working in a friggin' opera.'

'He's Italian – they're always like that.'

'Well maybe you should tell him.'

'Don't you worry your little head about it, Abi. So what do you think of Ash then? Dead sexy isn't he?'

'I guess so, but I have someone, don't I, someone who really likes me, or have you forgotten? Anyway he's ancient and got a million girlfriends.'

'Okay, keep your knickers on – I was only saying.'

'Yes, well, I know *your* saying, Mum. You'll be making hints – I'm with Jamie okay? And so while we're actually on this subject, are you also saying that that's where you've been, at the café this week – with Toni – or have you really been seeing a lot of Dawn and India? I mean it's hard, Mum, not knowing.'

'Okay, yes – Toni. Sometimes I've been with Toni. Now, Abi, much as I love you, you're beginning to irritate me. Just give me another hour, will you? My head's still thumping.'

ANDREW

A FEW WEEKS AGO I came across an old photo of me as a child and found myself welling up. Four or five I guess, short trousers, Fair-Isle sweater knitted by my mother, large, grateful brown eyes, long, dark curly hair, hands tidily by my sides. Could be any kid in the sixties, I suppose, posing for a photo. But all I can see is the irony of it – the brick wall right behind me. They couldn't have picked a better backdrop – welcome to that small boy's world. And when he wasn't backed up against the wall, he was tight-roping on a barbed-wire fence. Since finding the photo I've been trying to claw my way back to that heart-stopping moment, just before my balance went, before I was forced to choose which side to leap, to feel the searing pain of my father's pathetic disappointment or the dull ache of my mother's terrifying resentment.

I doubt it's that unusual; childhood is a puzzling time for most kids, but isn't it also something most kids move through? And yet here I am over forty, still that small boy pressing into a brick wall, or climbing on and off that deadly fucking fence, or making imprisoned choices and futile attempts at reparation, or if not that – latching onto anything that feels like a way to escape.

And yet even now, I still can't accept Abi's decision. Not a day goes by without me spending a large part of it plotting to get her back – stupid and useless, I know, but I can't help it. It's like seeing myself all over again. She doesn't *say* she's unhappy because she doesn't know. Neither did I – that's part of Rachel's power. She blurs our judgement, confuses us. I only have to look at Abi's face to recognise *everything*: the defensiveness, the anger and depression. But it's really the hope that does us in, that keeps us hooked. And the worst bit is knowing that I chose her – couldn't wait – chose Rachel to be the mother of my children.

But sometimes, occasionally and even without trying too hard, I see how I can jump off that fence. And as I decide to jump, my parents skedaddle out of view. And hey presto, I'm a regular guy again with some shit on my plate, some bum stuff to deal with – like all those other regular guys out there … And I can breathe again.

And it's not all bad either. Like Megan once said, Abi might actually grow from what's happening in her life. She might. I can't know anything, not for sure. And then there's my work. It's good – we completed the soil samples on the Leith site yesterday and I'm up to speed, more or less, on all the office stuff. Guy's still behaving like a pillock, but even that occasionally makes me accept my singleness with more grace. And Nevis – a tremendous positive: saved me the humiliation of joining a gym and forced me to appreciate this wonderful city. Look at this place – what other cities have a mountain smack bang in the centre?

I can almost face thinking about Christmas.

Now where's he got to? He'll be chasing rabbits – there's hundreds of them up here, hence the lattice of burrows just under the surface which gives the unnerving illusion of walking on a giant sponge. I move further up the hill, pleased to have given myself enough time for a proper walk. There is a rock I often sit on which gives me a great view down the steep bank and across the valley. I should be able to see him from there. They say that gorse blossoms all year round; and it's true, despite it being winter, tiny clusters of sharp yellow flowers spangle the dull brown of the hill, and once I'm at the top, looking back, sitting on my rock, I can see him. Little shit, he's not chasing rabbits, he's begging. And surely that's not folk picnicking, is it?

I heave myself onto my feet. No way Nevis'll come to call if there's food involved. I inch my way round an unnervingly slippery bit of cliff to get a better look, and find there's something familiar about the group. A few metres more and I realise it's Rhona and Megan with her new boyfriend. I flatten out against the rock; they're beginning to look around. I could pretend not to have seen them and go back up, but from the way they're all staring in this direction and pointing, I'm afraid they've recognised Nevis and most likely seen me. Still, I stay flattened. I need to decide what to do. I have a pain in my shoulder and my heart feels like it's about to blow a hole through my chest. I should have been to see Rhona. I know that. I've not seen either of them for months.

I've been behaving like a tosser, obviously.

I'll have to go down. As I emerge from my hiding place I start waving and they wave back. Megan stands up, pulls on her gloves and scarf and shakes out the blanket. I can't see the expression on her face. It takes a lifetime to scramble down the scree and rock and I'm acutely aware they're watching. I try to dignify the last few feet of my descent by attempting a nimble jump, and fail. I've misjudged the distance *and* the ice under the scree and half stumble, half fall.

The new boyfriend holds out his hand. I pretend I haven't seen it and stagger upright.

'Hi, that looked tricky. I'm Megan's brother, Tom. We should have met years ago, but I think I'm considered too badly behaved to be introduced to Megan's friends.'

'Hi.' I stretch out a shaky hand to grab his, unsure whether to laugh or cry. 'No, don't be ridiculous, it's my fault. I haven't seen Megan for months – been so busy. Work's been hell, well not hell exactly, but hectic. Well, anyway, I've heard so much about you …' He begins to raise his free hand in defence and I rush on. 'No, good things, and, and yes, definitely good things.' I seem unable to let go of his other hand – something about the shaking rhythm. He looks nervously at Megan before jerking his hand out of mine, so I start jabbering at Rhona. 'Rhona, God, you look lovely. I mean, well, yes, I mean, really, well, really well, you – and isn't it a wonderful day? Shit. I'm sorry. I mean, I mean, I can't believe you're picnicking in November.'

Something passes between her and Megan, easily missable if you're not a paranoiac. They obviously wish I wasn't here, and so do I – badly. I wish I was dead in fact. Rhona bends down and grabs Nevis by the collar, yanks him off the rug. I mouth a silent sorry to Megan, but it's Rhona who speaks.

'It's been a long tradition. When Megan and Tom were children we'd try to come every Sunday – at this time of year, at the very least, it makes you so happy to get home. It was Brendon's thing really – his father had taken him as a child. Stupid, but there you are. It's three months since Brendon died – we thought ...'

'Oh God, I'm sorry, I've interrupted ...'

'Nonsense – it's lovely to see you. We were about to pack up anyway. It may be sunny, but an hour on a rug is quite enough.'

She takes my hand and pats it like she might a dog or a patient. I realise what a fool I've been. I realise how fond I am of both her and Megan. I realise how I'll get used to Megan having someone in her life – how I might even like the bloke. I am struck suddenly by another revelation followed swiftly by a painful lump in my throat: it's okay to be somewhere between places – a place in-between. Something opens up inside me as some hard knots unravel. Rhona must be living in that place, waiting to arrive on firm ground once again after her husband's death – Megan too, of course. I ask Rhona how it feels moving back to Edinburgh. She tells me that having her old friends around has been a great help and asks after Liz, and I respond with partial truths.

Calmer now, I turn to Megan and kiss her on both cheeks. She's looking wonderful – being in love suits her. Her hair has grown.

'I've been meaning to call ...'

'So have I,' she says, with the same familiar warmth that makes me blush with shame. '*Excuse me,* Nevis, but that was my roll. Come on, sit down, have something to eat, we've brought far too much. Have you had lunch?'

'Yes thanks. Well no, no. It's very kind of you. It's lovely here, isn't it? Still got a great view but cleverly tucked away out of the wind. Just look at these dinky salt cellars – and the napkins, they're so …' I turn to Rhona who has just sat down beside me, 'so, well, *you*, Rhona, really charming.'

'Oh, I don't know – it was Brendon really. He never liked the modern ones. Over the years folk had given us various far more practical picnic baskets, but he never wanted to use them – this was his father's. He was very into his traditions, I suppose.'

She stands up abruptly, smiles cynically.

'And I suppose that had its advantages as well as its drawbacks,' she says, and my philosophical mood latches on again. Grey areas, we can live without having it all. I have a sense of shedding a great burden. She takes another turn on her scarf, pulls her woolly hat down. 'I'm beginning to freeze,' she says, staring hard at Tom. 'Come on, Tom, I need to get walking, and you need to finish turning the compost.'

'Oh come on, Mother, stop nagging. You see, Andrew, they can't bear me to meet anyone – too ashamed.'

'Don't be ridiculous, darling. I'm sorry, Andrew, but we do have to go …' She raises a hand as I begin to get up. 'No, stay, bring Megan home – help with the basket, it weighs a ton. There you are, Tom – that lets *you* off the hook.'

She takes her son's arm, begins walking away but turns around and adds, 'I'll make you a coffee, a hot one, and you can see the alterations. Tom's been very busy.'

'Thank you Rhona, I would like that very much.' Cringing at the desperation in my voice, I pull a sheet of cling film off Nevis's nose.

I intend to begin again. I'm not going to lose these nice people because Megan and I… I rub my nose, which is prickling, and hold a warning hand up to Nevis who's tossing a slice of salami around in the dirt, coating it in earth before swallowing it whole, very undoggy behaviour – perhaps it's a little peppery.

I am aware that neither of us have said anything for what seems like a very long time. She breaks it.

'Shall we walk? Just look at that dog's desperate pleading eyes. Mum's always asking about you – how are things? Feeling any better?'

'A bit. How about you?'

'Besides wanting to murder my little brother, I guess things could be worse.'

I stab the ground with a stick I've been toying with. It breaks in half and jabs my palm. 'Listen Megan, I know apologies don't count for much and I know I've been a prat, but can I tell you why, and you can tell me to fuck off any time you like.'

'Oh please, please don't go off on one again – let's just keep this normal can we? Andrew, please …'

'I must ask you something Megan, but I promise I'm not angry or jealous, not anymore but—'

'Angry? Jealous? What could you possibly be angry or jealous about? That's what I mean, you've got a bit of a cheek, you know.'

'I know I have. Oh God, I know I have and there's really no excuse. But I was so vulnerable that morning and when, well whoever it was picked up the phone, twice, well I freaked, and then you didn't say anything and that undermined my confidence and our friendship. Oh God – and that's when I started to go weird on you. But I'm over it – I am, really, completely over it. Your boyfriend. And before you say anything, I know I've been a complete arse, but I felt so left out. I was so vulnerable, I suppose, and well it was just him answering the phone …'

'What the hell are you talking about?'

'The man—'

'What man? Christ.'

'The man I got at the flat early one morning – the man who sounded … intimate.' My heart is pumping hard again.

'Probably Tom, I don't know – he's been staying off and on, because he gets too drunk to move. And he always sounds intimate – it's a cover-up.'

'But you said – you said you'd slept with someone.'

'Actually I *said* I'd had sex with someone – I didn't mention anything about sleep if I remember correctly.'

I brush a dollop of mayo off my crotch. 'Maybe not, no.' And then look up and see her half smiling. A voice inside me orders me to lighten up. 'Mayo …' I say, pointing at the dark patch, trying to smile, remembering another time, in another life.

'I shouldn't have said it like that. I'm sorry,' she says.

'No, no, you should have. I was being awful, so needy and so controlling – I deserved it.'

'After you got back with Rachel, after everything, I didn't want to put any pressure on you. I was pleased, of course …'

'But? And?' I say, trying not to squeak.

'It wasn't easy for me …'

'Yes, I mean no—'

'Dad's death, it made me sort of crazy … I wasn't thinking straight.'

'No?'

'No. And you don't need to do that.'

'What?'

'Keep saying yes and no. Maybe let me finish, okay?'

'Yep, sorry.'

'To be honest I was all over the place. And … and because of the support you'd given me—'

'Had I?'

'For fuck's sake! Yes you had, you know you did, and I know it wasn't for long. God, a couple of weeks, that was all, but it sort of weakened me, and when you phoned to say you and Rachel … well I think I went a bit weird.'

'Really – you a bit weird? I find that hard—'

'You don't have a monopoly on behaving like an idiot you know, strange as that may seem.'

Blushing, I scoop a piece of mackerel onto an oat cake. 'No, no, I suppose not. But …'

'And it didn't help that you were so self-absorbed, it was like I'd become invisible – I didn't handle it very well. There was someone at work, he's always had a thing for me.'

'Someone at work?'

'*Yes Andrew*, someone at work. It was a disaster, of course, but at least my attention was somewhere else for a while. At least it was about something of my own making. I'd begun to realise I'd been living my life vicariously through yours. I suppose I might have been depressed for a while.'

'You didn't seem it.'

'Probably not – not that you'd have noticed, and I'm not the world's best at asking for help, not from men anyway. Nor am I very good at accepting my own limitations. Social work is full of people like us.'

'But—'

She holds her hand up. '*And*, if I'm *completely* honest, I suppose I wanted to hurt you – a bit of that anyway. On reflection, when Abi told me you thought I had a boyfriend, I think I was pleased. There. Bit of a mess really. And I suppose I was wanting to stop seeing you ...'

I flop backwards onto the rug.

'Andrew?'

I wave her to silence. I must let this all sink in for a moment. But the warm tingle soon peters out. 'But I'd left her, or rather told her to leave – I mean if, if ...'

'Not as simple as that, I'm afraid.'

'No?'

'You just didn't seem in control of anything. One minute she's off, the next she's back – then she's off again, you were all over the place. I had feelings, but I didn't think I could trust them, the man I'd seen emerging had completely disappeared – I needed some space ...'

'You did?'

'Yes, *Andrew* – I did.'

I prop myself up on one elbow – a piece of mackerel slithers down my fleece. She hands me a tea towel. 'Will you forgive me Megan – I've been so messed up, you have no idea how messed up I've been.'

'I think I may have.'

'Yes, but you haven't.'

'Whatever. Andrew, you've got your elbow in a tomato – you're covered in food. You're meant to be eating lunch, not wearing it.'

She doesn't have a boyfriend. This is the most extraordinary piece of news. I don't know what to do.

'Megan?'

'Yes?'

'I'm fucking freezing. Can we go and have tea with your mum and your darling younger brother and then will you come over for dinner with me later? Will you, Megan?'

PART FOUR

Winter

RYAN

I turn away from the screen and stand up. This sucks, man. Why am I wasting my time with this loser? Why am I wasting my time watching dumb porn?

I start pulling my jacket off the back of the office chair.

'Hey man,' he says, jabbing the pause button, standing up himself. 'You leaving? I thought we were going to make an afternoon of it.'

'Just remembered I've got an appointment with the physio – almost forgot. Besides, this kind of shit's not really my scene.'

He looks at me kind of quizzically. Decides to leave it.

'Okay, man. I'll call you in a few days, okay?'

I power walk to the Botanics, to the café on the hill. There's a dozen or so pushchairs and baby carriers stacked up outside, always are – it's a regular meeting place for young mums, ordinary, run-of-the-mill young mums. I like to guess which ones are the psychos. I mean, you'd have spotted my mum for a psycho at a distance, but here it's much more interesting – they're disguised – the Rachels of this world. I stand in the queue. There's a brunette over there, looks a bit like Nigella, busty, fat, corseted. She's often here – she's one to watch. She never gets anything to eat for herself, but shovels crumbs into her gob from her kid's tray. She despises herself for being fat. Her kid feels it.

191

I see myself in him, the serious frowns puckering his smooth forehead, frustration, the way he bites back the beginnings of questions he doesn't yet have the right words or courage to ask. And I watch him in the queue, the budding junkie angling for a way out, making deals, buttering and sugaring her up. I've seen it all – the way she'll squeeze his arm hard, really hard and then when he gives it volume, how she feigns surprise, puts on this great maternal show for the onlookers. She's a mind-masher, that one.

I get myself a coffee, take it to a table outside. It's bitterly cold, but nice, with the sun silhouetting the castle. And then I start thinking about Rachel. Ever since the night I saw her in that bar, she's been in my head, worming her way back under my skin. I know her shifts now – can't help it. Can't help wanting to know how she's doing, whether she's back at uni, where she's living, whether she's mended, obsessing. Not in that way, God no, never – but to say something, closure at least. As the sun snaps off behind the castle, I sip the last of my coffee. A little later, the street lamps flicker on like egg yolks through the sprawl of the city and just before the cold forces all feeling from my feet, I haul my butt off the wooden chair and head into town.

She'll be finishing soon at the Italian. I walk past a few times with my collar up, cap pulled down. Watch her drag on her jacket.

'Rachel?' I say softly, so as not to scare her.

'Jesus, you scared me.'

'Thought I saw you last week, but I wasn't sure. I'm not here to cause trouble.'

'You were waiting for me.'

'Yeah, didn't want to come in – didn't know how you'd be, seeing me. No, please, I want to explain, just a drink, one drink.'

'Well not here, then – wouldn't want to contaminate my regular—'

'Okay, okay, sure. I know somewhere around the corner. It's nice. Or we could have coffee if you'd rather.'

'Okay, but God knows why. I haven't got anything to say.'

She strides out, but I keep up, opening the door for her; her hair, now longer, falls from its band, oozing round her shoulders. We settle on stools.

She's looking well. Nope, she is looking poetic. I order whisky and coffee for two. I make out I heard nothing about her these last months. 'You not with Andrew then?'

'No.'

'And you're not staying with Dawn anymore?'

'No. I've got my own flat, like I said I would.'

'You're looking better than ever, Rachel. You still at uni?'

'So you quit then?'

'Didn't want to embarrass you,' I say.

'Right, well I quit too. Abi is living with me. How about you? You've moved.'

I turn my head a little and squint at her. She's been checking up or what?

'Yeah, kind of.'

'On your own?'

Something about the way this lady asks questions makes me jumpy.

'Yeah, I got some money together – got a flat, better than the other dump.'

'Got a girlfriend? Beaten anyone recently?'

'That's, that's why I had to see you – to ask your forgiveness. I was mad, like, out of control, man. I can't stop thinking about it, dreaming about it. I'm so sorry. Were you hurt bad? Fuck. Stupid question, man, Jesus, Rachel, I'm so sorry.'

'You were lucky I didn't press charges – everyone was on at me.'

'You never called the police then?'

'No, but Andrew did – he always does the right thing, remember? I just wouldn't tell them anything, and they couldn't force me. I thought at the time I'd provoked you. Now I'm not so sure. Let's just forget it, shall we? They probably think it was Andrew. Usually is, the husband, I mean.'

'Poor old Andrew.'

'Yes.'

'So what you up to?' Something in her face tells me I'm forgiven, and something else tells me she's got something on her mind – I can smell it. I swear I was planning on finishing the drive this very evening, putting this broken car off the road once and for all, but she's got her thumb out, hitching a ride. 'My mum died.'

'I'm sorry to hear that.'

She all ears now. Figuring out how she never found out I even had a mum, whether she jumped to all the wrong conclusions. Fifth gear now and we're cruising down the coast road. She should know better than to take lifts with strangers.

'She'd been ill a long time. I was expecting it, and with the money she left I got myself a new place, been busy making myself a real home. To be honest, I've also been feeling bad about all the things I've done – feeling pretty low – that's why I reckoned I needed to put things right. You know, apologise.' I pull my wallet out of my jeans. 'Better let you go … I mean, I just wanted to know that you were okay – just that, man.'

'Can't wait to get away – too many bad memories, eh?'

'Ain't like that.'

So that's how it is. One thing I know. Abi chose wrong. Something screwed this one up so bad, there's no iron heavy or hot enough to flatten her out. I look at her eyes, which are only saying the one thing as I can see it. She's tripping hard. I can almost feel my good sense shut down and something bad creep through me that I don't have the will to stop.

'Would you like a nightcap for old times' sake? My place is right around the corner.' All I can think about is getting my nose round something chemical. My left hand drops into my pocket, and like Gollum with his precious ring, my thumb and forefinger caress my very own bag of magic tricks.

'Why not?'

I hand the waiter a ten pound note and start walking towards the door. The only sound as we walk is the tap tap tap of her heels on the pavement echoed by the hammering of my chest. I'm hoping nothing of Winston's is lying around. Once we're inside I give her time to yank her jaw back to where it looks prettiest, and can't help but smile.

'You never said your mum was loaded,' she says, sliding me a look.

While she's still gaping at the décor I take two beers from the fridge, hand her one.

'I love it, Ryan. It's beautiful …' She prowls around the kitchen, picks up the cheese grater Winston bought just before he left, which is as much a piece of art as a culinary accessory.

I draw two lines of coke on the granite and offer her my rolled note. She doesn't hesitate.

'Thanks.' She sniffs, wipes the dust on her gums, hands me the roll.

I do a courtesy bow and lead the way into the lounge, open the million-dollar Chinese lacquered cupboard where Winston hid the sounds. He's into concealment, which is why I wonder if there's anything else he's not telling me.

Morcheeba trickles though the room, and I can tell from the way she's smiling that we're about to make some music of our own. I go back out to the kitchen and draw another wee line. White-out is what I need here. Tomorrow, man, I'm cutting down and that's a fact. On my way back through, teeth grinding their own damn tune, I pick up two glasses and a ship's decanter of the finest brandy. As I sit back down she places her neat little boot into my groin and pushes some. Class brandy. I take a sip and my teeth rest up. She knocks hers back like she's about to make a deal. I take the joint from her lips, take a hit and kill it while I remove her cute little pink boots, before those heels do some permanent damage.

ANDREW

'OF COURSE I WANT to "do it", Andrew – I've always wanted to, since that day I first saw you playing tennis with Abi. Okay, okay, so maybe it didn't occur to me then. I mean, you *were* with your child – you *were* married.'

I bring it up just to have it confirmed. One day soon …

We are in the Hermitage. Yesterday we were in Holyrood, the day before in those glorious woods behind Edinburgh Zoo: Corstorphine, yes. I never knew a city could be so beautiful. I never knew anyone could be so beautiful. Nevis is making friends. Sun-drenched tree trunks of grey silk shoot far into the sky and tangles of polished roots crawl across the hard-packed forest floor.

'I know you think I'm being unspontaneous and frumpy and there is the thing about you seeing my bum exposed, I'll grant you that, but, ouch, hands off, you! We need to get this right, Andrew. We don't want this making things worse.'

I hear her. Every word. And it's like being in a slow-motion psychedelic movie where words are exaggerated and meanings distorted and everything has shades, tones and colours that I've never seen before and I want to touch them and turn them inside out because, well, I'm forty for God's sake. It's like, it's like … and even now I can't grab the goddam words. She fits me. Oh my God, are those the words? They sound so trite. So fuck it, I'll be trite. SHE FITS ME. And, as I catch up with this vital truth, the meaning of those three life-giving words pulses with an intensity as sharp as crystal. Or not sharp, because they also stream and melt and drift through the flapping veils which have replaced the hard iron walls of my familiar dugout. She is holding my hand – her hand which makes my hand complete. No longer a hand going nowhere – a hand flailing around in the ether – but a hand which has meaning and purpose and feelings.

I tug her round to face me. I need to stoop to catch the smell behind her ears, under her hair: a powerful narcotic that I swear to God turns bone into sherbet. It's pathetic. For a week now I have been quietly, smugly brimming over. I love, I love. No drama, no unanswered questions, no doubts, no fear, just this soft, slow, chilled, certain, impatient frenzy.

She breaks it – a kind of croak or clearing of her throat. 'It's quite obvious we can't keep this under wraps forever – it's not going to be very nice telling everyone. Have you thought about it?'

'Yeah.'

'How do you think they'll be?'

'They'll be delighted – they'll be ecstatic …'

Abi, I want to tell you something.

Abi, we've got something to tell you.

Hey guys, we've got something to tell you.

Hey fellas, can we have a word?

They'll be fine.

They love her.

We'll do it together.

I'll do it alone.

And a few days later I have the perfect opportunity.

'Fine.'

'Fine?'

'Yeah, fine.'

'You don't mind then?'

'Like you mind if I mind?'

'I always mind.'

'Oh right, so what I mean is – when did you mind enough?'

'Please Abi – don't start. Can't we move on? Can we? This is good for us all, Abi – Megan is—'

'Megan's what? A good mate of mine as well? Someone who I didn't think would stab me in the back? How could… Yes, I thought she was my mate, actually someone I could trust. But obviously not, obviously she wasn't completely honest with me – and now I come to think about it, why should she have been? I'm only nothing, aren't I? So that's why you threw Mum out?'

'No.'

'Like I believe you. Mum didn't stand a chance – not with you lusting after someone else.'

'So maybe you should have asked then, Abi, about how I felt, instead of—'

'Oh, so you're admitting it now, are you?'

'I'm not admitting anything. But before you took it upon yourself to organise this family the way you wanted it—'

She points her chin at me and yells, 'She's my mother. It was my home – don't I have the right?'

'Please Abi – it's history. Please, can we move on? You're having a nice life aren't you?'

Her eyes are filling up.

'Oh sure, I just love living away from my brother and my home and my room and Nevis and everything. I'm having the time of my life, Dad. God, I mean, I couldn't be having a better childhood could I? You go ahead, Dad. You move on … I'm, oh sod it, your selfishness is way out of control and I hate YOU!'

She turns away, grabs her top from the chair in the hall and runs out the front door.

'I hope you're all very happy together – give Callum my love.'

'Abi. For goodness sake, please, Abi, come back.'

There's only rubber on the floor by the time I've reached the hall – and the only reason the door's still on its hinges is that Guy's holding it in one hand.

'Sorry, Andrew. Not a good time, I can see that – I'll come back later. You okay?'

'Yes, yes I'm fine. It's fine. Come on through – coffee? Or something stronger? Let's have something stronger. I'm definitely having something stronger. Whisky?'

'Bit early for me. You and Abi? Everything okay?'

'Yes, yes brilliant. Just giving her some good news. Say *when*.'

'Just a small one please – plenty of water. That bad is it?'

'Always that bad with Abi it seems. I was telling her that Megan and I—'

'Probation-Megan?'

'Yes, probation-Megan. We've been friends for a long time. I thought Abi would be pleased, but as usual I was wrong. What's the matter with everyone, Guy? I mean, you think one thing – or at least I do, but I'm so way off track it makes me wonder if I know my children at all. Well it's Abi. Callum's so different – Callum I can understand, but Abi, well, Abi …'

'Mine did too. Par for the course, I'm afraid, Andrew. Rocky times. Well, cheers – I for one am delighted. And relieved.'

'Relieved?'

'Well, yes. When India—'

'India?'

'Well obviously she mentioned it—'

'Me and Megan?'

'No, goodness no. I don't suppose she knew. No, certainly she hasn't mentioned Megan. No, it was your 'awkward' moment.'

'She told you about that?'

'Well yes. I think she wanted to get it off her chest. We've become close, as you know, and well, it's great that you've got Megan now.' He gives me this look – a look that's a mixture of pity, pride, shame, empathy and yes, a distinct dollop of smugness? 'No hard feelings then?'

'Well no, of course not. It's a relief actually, that you know about it – to be honest it was bloody awkward. I mean, I've always felt paternal, if you must know …'

'That's just how she saw it. That's exactly what she said.'

And then I'm hearing the distant whamming of gold bullion falling through the earth's surface.

'Sorry, Guy – I think I'm missing something here.'

'I shouldn't have mentioned it – let's forget it.'

'No, you should, course you should – go on. What exactly

am I meant to have done? Oh! Now I get it. I'm meant to have made a pass at her am I? Is that what she said?'

'Steady on, Andrew. She wasn't in the least bit offended – said she was flattered, but she thought of you as more of a father figure. And I, for one, am extremely grateful she did. And to be honest, since she confided in me, I've felt a little awkward about us – you and me, I mean. Well, I mean, you've been very generous about it, and I'm really glad you've got Megan now. And don't worry, the kids will come round. Megan is a much better bet – you'll see.'

Well of all the patronising… 'I'm completely gobsmacked, Guy. It wasn't at all like that. India—'

'Listen, Andrew, please, you don't need to. To explain I mean – I would have done just the same thing – honestly, it's fine.'

'I think I do. I mean I do need to – I want to …'

The front door slams shut. That'll be Abi coming back to give me a battering. Ah no, it's India. How jolly.

'Guy? Thought I recognised your bike – what are you doing here?' India air kisses him dismissively. 'I hope you're not coming to see me – can't stop I'm afraid, I'm meeting Rachel for a drink. I'll see you tomorrow yeah? Byee … Gotta go.'

Guy turns to me with a 'isn't she just gorgeous and she's mine and you've got the booby prize you saddo' look.

Instead of taking a swing at him, I help myself to another whisky. And then Guy calmly takes the bottle off me like we're mates …

'I know I said just the one, but, well, do you mind – I suddenly feel I could do with a top-up.'

Yes, I fucking well do mind, bollockhead. 'No, go ahead.'

He gulps confidingly. 'Andrew?'

'Yeah?'

'You don't think David's trying it on with India do you?'

Oh for God's sake, you pillock. 'Why do you say that?'

'No reason really, just something someone said. So you haven't heard anything? I mean, she hasn't said anything?'

'No, nothing at all.' A slight twitch starts up in my left eye. I'm becoming Bertie Wooster, a stuttering, stumbling fool misread at every turn – I'll dump her in it. My God I'll, I'll —

'Phew, that's a relief. Office gossip eh? You know, she means the world to me, Andrew – really.' Guy's eyes glaze over. 'Didn't think I'd ever fall in love again, not at my age. Sometimes I have to pinch myself … You know, just to tell myself it's real … Sounds stupid doesn't it – a man of my age?'

Oh God, he's going to cry. Please don't, for fuck's sake, man. 'No, not at all. I'm pleased for you, Guy – really pleased.' Urgh you wanker, you sanctimonious little wanker. I am tempted to squeeze one of my bollocks in self-flagellation but find I'm far too much of a coward. So I just squeak to an awkward stop instead.

'Thank you, Andrew – that means a lot to me. I'm glad we've had this opportunity to clear away any … cobwebs. Can I ask you something else?'

'Yes of course.'

'Do you like David? I mean I know he's 'your man', so to speak, but do you think he's the right man to deal with all this media attention we're getting?'

'Well he's certainly raised our profile. That must be a good thing?'

'Well yes, perhaps. But I'm concerned he gives out a message that I'm not entirely happy with. Saving the planet isn't glamorous, it's …'

Here we go.

'… it's serious and shouldn't be seen as sensationalistic – I'm not happy with the way David speaks to people.'

'Don't you think you may be bringing in your own personal agenda?'

'No, I don't think so. I've given it a lot of thought, I want you to front the Leith case – if there's any press involvement, I want you to deal with it, a more pragmatic approach would be far more in keeping with our ethos.'

'I'm flattered, Guy, but David won't like it.'

'Leave that with me. This isn't personal, Andrew – this is about giving the public the right messages.'

'Right. Well, okay.'

'Right.'

'Right.'

I don't ring Megan until after ten. By this time I've calmed down. Much more on my mind is Abi.

Megan is sympathetic and not really surprised.

'It can't be easy for her can it? Any of it. I doubt she's really thinking about the good or the bad of it – none of this is what she wants. Just *more* to her – *more stuff*, pushing her further and further into the background, away from where she wants to be. Do you think she's okay, you know, underneath it all – is she eating okay? I know there's not a lot you can do but the last thing she needs is to feel that you've replaced her. Perhaps I should give her a ring – see if she'll meet up with me. And Callum – how did he take it?'

'I haven't told him yet. He was tired. I'll tell him tomorrow … or maybe not. Christ, nothing's simple is it?'

''Fraid not, but sooner, yeah? Before Abi does, or Rachel for that matter. Mum's thrilled of course, but we knew she would be. How about Guy – still love sick?'

I tell her about India. She does not get het up.

'Forget the India thing, she's just a messed-up young woman – who cares? And it's only a matter of time before Guy'll be coming to his own conclusions.'

'But I lied,' I tell her. 'And not just about India. Guy asked me ages ago to see to the Leith thing myself – the day we had lunch.'

'Which day?'

'You remember. Dick day. *Me*, I mean. *Me, Dick.*'

'Oh that Dick day. What? So you didn't go, then – so David went, you mean?'

'Yes well, I wasn't exactly in the mood – so I went for a walk instead.'

'And?'

'Well, *and* nothing: he went to the meeting, he typed it up, filed the report. Only thing is, *I* reported it all like I'd been there – like totally.'

'Oh.'

'Yes, and I remember quite enjoying it, thinking that I had quite a talent for lying …'

'Oh.'

'"Oh" as in "so what?", or "Oh" as in "you idiot"?'

'Hmmm. Sorry.'

'Shit. It'd be bloody awkward to take over now. David would be bound to make a fuss and then Guy will start asking questions, and now he wants me to do all the media stuff. I mean, I'm snowed under, and David's good – he's thorough, perfect for the Leith thing – and he's already involved.'

'How can I know, Andrew? Guy's being neurotic isn't he? You're the project manager – I mean, shouldn't you be the one to decide? But to be honest, I think he's right about the press thing. David's got the air of a bullshitter, and he's a coke addict.'

'A coke addict? Why on earth would you think that?'

'Because you said he was.'

'Did I?'

'Yes you did. You said Rachel said Ryan said.

'Did I?'

'Yes you did, *Andrew*. And stop saying *did I*?'

'Either way, I haven't got much choice, have I? So you think it's okay do you, kind of ignoring the other bit?' Guy's smug mug of a few hours earlier suddenly assumes sharp focus again. Megan's right – make up my own mind.

'Oh I don't know, Andrew – barefaced fabrication isn't exactly professional, but you had your reasons, and Guy would probably understand. On the other hand, so long as the outcome's professional, does it really matter? Maybe it does – I mean he *is* your boss.'

I knew she'd see it my way – which is just as well since he also thinks I took the soil samples off to the lab on Friday. It sounds bad but David was passing the door, going somewhere for the weekend – he offered! Maybe I should explain to David how vulnerable Guy is. Shit, now who's getting involved?

'Andrew?'

'What? Sorry. Well yes, maybe.'

'Of course, you've got no actual proof that anything's going on between David and India have you? It's a tricky one.'

She quite right. Fuck 'em. Fuck 'em all. And I metaphorically tear the whole lot of them into shreds and toss them over my shoulder.

'I love you,' I say.

'And I love you.' And then she adds, 'As if I could have got myself a boyfriend and not told you. You really are a bit of a mess aren't you? Berk. Didn't you feel it, Andrew, in the summer, on the west? I was so dying to melt into you – I just thought I should—'

'Stand alone? I thought I felt it, but how could I risk anything with everything the way it was?'

'This is quite exciting isn't it?'

'What?'

'Just getting to know each other – you know, in a different way. I've been on my own for so long – you know.'

We both go quiet. Then she whispers. 'Still there?'

'I was just thinking how I had too – been on my own, I mean, so terribly on my own and well, just that really ...' Then I hear this noise. 'Hang on a minute. Something's going on downstairs. India forgot her keys most likely. I'll phone you back.'

Rachel

'Is she here? Don't look at me like that you sanctimonious smug bastard.'

'Is who here, Rachel?'

'*Is who here, Rachel*? Don't play Mr Innocent with me you cocky little shit – in bed were you? With her?'

'You're drunk. What the hell are you doing here?'

'Oooh. *What the hell are you doing here, Rachel? You're drunk, Rachel. Behave yourself, Rachel*. It's Mr Perfect Andrew Gillespie here, and I'm asking you a question. Excuse me—'

'What do you want?'

'Just passing; I'm allowed aren't I? How long has this been going on?'

'What?'

'Don't *what* me, Mr Smart Arse. You, fucking Megan of course.'

'Not long. Please don't shout, Rachel. Callum is asleep.'

'He's happy about this, is he? You and Megan. Is he?'

'He doesn't know. I haven't told him. And this is not the time to have this conversation. Please, Rachel, Megan's not here; but if you go on shouting you'll probably wake her in Hillside, and I imagine you've already woken Callum.'

'All the more reason to invite me in, so we can discuss what I've come to say. Thank you.' I push past him. He has no right –

this is just as much my house as his. I grab a bottle of his whisky and shake it at him. 'Yes, I'll have a whisky – thanks for offering. Actually I've come about Callum. It's obvious he'd be better off with me and Abi.'

That's shaken him. That's drained the colour from his cheeks. It's a good idea. Abi misses him. Yes, that's right – I've been thinking it would be a good thing for a while haven't I?

Not so smug now – that's shut him up. But he's right, I don't want Callum joining our little party. I may as well sit for a moment, think this through a bit. 'Come on, Casanova, stop gaping and give me a glass. I've cancelled my evening to come here, you could at least make me welcome – I'm still your wife you know, like it or not. Lost your manners?' I bounce onto the sofa. 'Always liked this sofa – got some happy memories around this sofa. Let me think now, that time Liz nearly choked – remember that, Andrew?'

'What?'

'The time Liz choked?'

'What you on about?'

'Aw come on, Andrew. You remember, course you do, when Callum hung the guinea pigs up in front of her, and Eddie sucked off Murphy.' I lean forward to grab a mug off the table. 'Sod you, Andrew. If you won't get me one, I'll just have to make do with this!' Christ, the table's tilting up. 'Oops. Lucky the carpet's coffee-coloured, eh? You remember, and, and oh God that was a good day …' Oh dear, well I think it's funny – he's not a happy bunny is he – so who gives a fuck? 'At last. Yes, how kind. A whisky would be great. Cheers.'

'Where's Abi?'

'What do you care? Crying her eyes out probably. Are you destroying her on purpose, Andrew? Are you sick or something? Don't you think she's been through enough?'

'I didn't plan to fall in love.'

'Oh, so it's love, is it? That's a joke.'

'Actually, yes it is. I wouldn't expect you to … Shit, Rachel, I don't know why this is such a big deal. I was hardly going to stay on my own forever, and it's not like I'm going out with a stranger. It's not like I'm putting anyone at risk. Can you please go home. We can talk about this when you're sober.'

'No, why should I? I thought you'd want to be the first to know I'm applying for custody of Callum and moving back into the family home. Abi would be happier here and Callum would be united with his mother and sister. I've been doing some thinking and talking to people – the courts will favour me.'

'Oh and why's that?'

'Because I'm their mother, and Abi is missing her brother and you've only just started taking an interest in the children, and you think you can just move your lover in. Don't look at me like that, *matey*. You think you're so clever, got your happy little family all worked out have you? Well listen up, *Andrew*, the sheriff won't like the way you pushed me out of my own home – made me so unhappy and confused – or your plan to do the same to my mother.'

'What the hell are you talking about?'

'About sending her to some awful nursing home. Locking her up. No wonder she's been running away.'

'That's what people who have premature dementia do, Rachel – they wander.'

'But she wasn't wandering was she? She told the police that she was running away. That's what she told them, that she was trying to get home – her home in Carlisle …'

He's turning purple – he might hit me.

'Oh for God's sake – as if you'd care anyway.'

'Well you're wrong. Relationships change and we've reconciled since she's been ill. You don't stand a chance, Andrew. You're an incompetent selfish parent and Callum should be with his mother before you do him irreparable damage.'

'What are you doing?'

'Having a cigarette. Matches, where are the fucking matches? One slip-up, Andrew. I slept with someone who was attentive, okay, so I fucked up, *once*. I didn't deserve to lose my home. I'm talking about getting it back so that both my children can have their mum back – I'm talking about fifteen years of being a mother while you played away on the oil rigs deigning to come home every couple of weeks for a few days. I'm talking about doing the best for the children. And don't kid yourself – one word, one hint to the courts that it was you who raped—'

'I'm taking you out of here, Rachel. Get out of my house right now. Give me that.'

'And what if I don't, eh? Hey, get your hands off me, Andrew. Stop it. Fucking stop it, you bastard. I always knew you were violent! Go on, go on, hit me why don't you? That'll sound good. Come on, you've been dying to for long enough. Ouch. Let go. Shut that fucking door – this is my house too!'

'Oh be quiet, Rachel, and get out!'

ABI

'Yoo hoo – darling. Abi? Are you decent? Are you alone?'

Jeez, what's she like? 'I'm in here Mum, alone and decent. Where've you been, anyway? You didn't need to stay out for me, you know you didn't. Jamie had to get back – he's got school, remember?'

'Well how was I meant to know he'd be so conscientious? Dawn and I thought you'd like a little space – had a bit too much to drink to walk home anyway, if I'm honest.'

'You weren't at Dawn's, Mum. I called her, and you weren't at work.'

'Don't be silly, darling, and please don't nag – you're in grave danger of sounding like you-know-who.'

'Why do you do that every time you don't like what I say, Mum? I sound like me.'

'So you're spying on me now, are you?'

'Christ, why would I spy on you, why should I have to? For fuck's sake, what the hell's going on? I mean you don't act like my mum and you don't act like a friend. I've tried not asking too many questions – but what's that all about? I mean, why shouldn't I know where you are? It's totally not about me and Jamie – why can't you just be straight? I mean, it can't be that bad can it? Do you hate me that much, that you want our lives to be so totally separate?'

'Oh God!'

'Oh Mum, don't cry. I mean, what's wrong with you? You're so paranoid all the time; I'm not the enemy – it's me, Abi. Don't you want to tell me where you were – I mean, why wouldn't you?'

'Okay, okay … I'm ashamed, that's all. I went for a drink. And before you say anything – no, not a man. A girl. Someone from the restaurant, someone who ate there. I've got to know her, that's all, and Toni was being so, so crushing … Which is another thing, cos I know he's great and everything. Anyway, she asked me if I wanted to go back to hers and of course I got far too drunk and stoned – I passed out, to be honest. I'm sorry, darling, but it's like I'm not sure I can do the Toni thing and I feel so bad. I'm so sorry.'

'Come on, Mum, for God's sake. You're not a bad person. It's okay.'

Mum sits there sobbing. I put my arm around her shoulders. Eventually, she looks up at me, mascara all over her face.

'You're wrong, Abi – I don't deserve you, or Toni or anyone. I am bad. I get drunk and I smoke too much. You don't deserve this, Abi. You should go back to your father – you should go home.'

'What? And leave you on your own? Come here *you* … Let's have a girly night in. Come on, Mum.'

She sinks down on my bed and plucks at the balloons on my duvet, sniffing and hiccupping, and stinking of old ashtrays.

'How was Jamie anyway?' She sneaks a look at me sideways and even tries to smile.

'Okay.'

No point in going there – she's still half cut.

'Well you don't look okay, sweetheart. So what were you doing when I came in just now?'

'Jamie gave me some maths past-papers. I was just looking at them, thought I might do one. I'll make tea, shall I?'

'Leave it, let's plan our party.'

What's she on about? 'What party?'

'The one we're having, silly. Oh let's, Abi, let's have a Christmas party, make a fresh start – can we? I'll have a quick shower, and you make us some coffee and toast and find some paper – won't be a minute.'

Thing about Mum is, you think she's going off on one and she'll suddenly change tack. That's what they say, isn't it? Growing up is all about finding out how fucked up both your parents are. So I'm bang on track then – hoo-bloody-ray.

No paper of course. 'I can't find any.'

'I can't hear you.'

So I go into her bedroom and slowly say it again.

'Just look, Abi.'

'I am looking. I have looked.'

I flop across her unmade bed. No chance Jamie'll come to a party, not one of Mum's. He like soo disapproves of her – and I wouldn't mind so much but he liked her to start with. Who am I kidding? She was quite together in the beginning, wasn't she? Now she goes out of her way to embarrass him. Seems like that anyway, either pissed or making gross hints about him staying over, stuff like that. Don't want to think about it – no point is there? What I need is a job, a full-time job with my own money coming in, not a few poxy shifts in a dodgy Italian with a lovesick boss who's measuring me up as a future step daughter. I could do what I want then – no more grovelling to either of my parents. Aahh it's just so annoying.

What's this? A notepad under the twenty tops she tried on before she went out last night – don't tell me she was actually making a shopping list.

'What are you doing? Leave that, Abi, it's mine.'

'Keep your knickers on – what is it anyway?' I get up and walk to the other side of the bed, hold it high.

'Nothing. Here give it to me.'

'Weird shopping list, Mum. God, Mum, I thought you said Toni was boring.'

'None of your business! It was a game – me and Dawn – a silly game.'

'Right, well, if you won't tell me, I'll ask her. No, okay, have it, have it. I don't want to know anyway.' I stomp through into the kitchen.

But I do want to know. Why is Mum making a list of sex toys and underwear? What the hell's she up to? I can hear her tearing off the sheet, scrunching it up and dropping it in the waste-paper basket. She's pathetic. By the time she comes through she's made up this stupid story about playing this game with Dawn that they found in a magazine – rating your sexual awareness. I can't even be bothered to catch her out. I mean, Dawn wasn't even here yesterday – she must think I'm stupid. Like I care!

Two hours later and we've scribbled down twenty-five people. Most of them won't come and the ones who will, will probably get us evicted. Whatever. Mum's got some excellent dope, we're on our second joint and giggling like spazzers.

Andrew

CALLUM IS NICKING THINGS and picking on younger kids. That's the story. Well as much as I like Marion, I'm not buying into this. I think she's got it wrong. Callum won't discuss it – and from what he tells me there are some pretty disturbed kids around here. He's depressed, well of course he is, but he's not a bully – so that's what I'm going to say. It may be a great school, and she may be a great head teacher, but that doesn't mean she, or they, always get it right, does it?

I tell her this straight.

'I understand just how you feel, Andrew. Listen, take a seat. We're not talking about a crime here, it's just an expression of his panic. He's lost a lot recently, and I gather there's a possibility of more changes?'

For a start, she couldn't possibly understand how I feel. 'What's he been saying?'

'Nothing, but Rachel came in yesterday.'

No way. 'And said what?'

'She's very anxious about Callum. We got in touch with both of you. Normal procedure, Andrew. Something wrong?'

'Yes, no, not really. Did she say she was going for the house, custody, the lot?'

'She did say how much Abi is missing Callum, and how much Callum is missing her. In fact she was very upset. I'm so sorry,

Andrew – things no better then? Listen, you don't have to fill me in, unless you want to, it's Callum we're concerned about – he's obviously very churned up at the moment, very confused.'

'Oh right, very upset was she?' I squeak. There are good people everywhere who'll believe her – who believe she's upset – and she well might be upset, she probably is upset, but … Something is blocking my airways, I can hardly breathe. I mustn't look down – a bottomless pit of regret yawns invitingly up. I winch myself back from it inch by inch and clear my throat. 'Well, that makes a first. She doesn't care about either of the children, not unless it gets her what she wants.'

'I know this must be excruciating, Andrew, that it must feel like we've let you down as well somehow.'

'No, of course not, you're doing your best, of course you are, but Callum just wouldn't – I talked to him – he just wouldn't. What did Rachel say?'

'She didn't seem to find it surprising, in fact she's offered to come in and help out a couple of afternoons, just to see a bit more of him. He's reluctant to visit her apparently …'

She doesn't say anything, but it's obvious she thinks that's down to me. 'I can assure you— '

'No, please, Andrew, there's no blame here and Rachel really does have a grasp of what's going on for him right now, knows a lot of it is down to her. But I think her spending time with him here will help too – he was so delighted when she came round the school with him that time. I know his feelings for her are very confused right now, and we'll keep an eye on things, but now she's left university – well, contact time, in a safe place, is always a plus. Every child longs for a reliable and loving mother – Callum will benefit from this, I guarantee it. I'm so sorry, Andrew, I can tell this is very hard for you. Lordy, you're still standing – where are my manners?'

She shunts a pile of folders off the only armchair. She likes Rachel. It's obvious she likes her – and why wouldn't she? I shouldn't be surprised. They've got the psychobabble in common, and not only that, but I spent the whole of last year telling Marion how wonderful she was.

'I so wish you could see this in terms of a process that he's going through; there really isn't any fixed line between what's healthy and unhealthy. All he really needs is our support and trust – and yours.' She smiles, hopefully.

'And just to change the subject for the moment,' she says. 'This pile of papers is the skate park project. Did Callum tell you that Edinburgh Council is considering building it from our model? It's such a great opportunity for the team – such an accolade for our work here.'

'No, he hasn't mentioned it.' I can't say any more because I think I might be dead. Her next comment confirms it.

'One more thing, Andrew, before I forget – and now this does sound like I'm trying to spite you, but I had a letter this morning from the curator ad litem. She's asking for a statement – she has to – in cases where residency is being sought. I'll be saying what a devoted father you are and how you've got so involved with everything. Okay?'

I go home and sleep for three hours. When I wake, I call Megan.

'Megan?'

'You sound awful. What's the matter?'

I will not dump.

'Everything.'

'Everything?'

I am an optimist. 'Well not everything, Megan. Just had a call from David – the soil results came back this morning. No major contamination, so they should be able to go ahead and get planning and we can file it and forget it, no press, nothing to worry about – and *Guy* can finally climb down off my back.'

'And how's Callum?'

'That's the *everything* … This is his third day at home. After the police brought him back …'

'Have you had a chance to talk with him, Andrew?'

'Not really. He says he doesn't like it here anymore, but when I try to talk to him about running away or the stuff going on at school, he just shrugs and walks off. Do you think I should make him go to school?'

'No I don't, not if he says he's feeling unwell. Give him a few days – give him some time.'

'You think he took those things, don't you?'

'I don't know. Who cares? He's under threat and he's reacting to it. Shit, Andrew, he's six years old – whatever he does is all about you guys. Andrew?'

'Sorry, but you should see him. He's not the same little boy he was – even at half term, which wasn't that long ago. He's jumpy and sulky and cross. I think this getting sick is more about him being accused. I mean, Callum does not want to go to school. Can you believe that? I mean can you believe that? I can't believe that. Can you? Can you believe that?'

'Have you ever thought that it could be more about wanting to keep an eye on you?'

'Can't say I have.'

'Well I don't know, but nor do you, Andrew. It could be for loads of reasons, including a virus, so for God's sake, get a grip. It'll be fine, just take a deep breath and a step back.'

'God, I'm sorry – I'm turning out to be so weak, and I was always the strong dependable one. It's all new territory, Megan – I just don't seem to have any choices or ways out and it's terrifying me.'

'Andrew, meet me at the Botanics – just for an hour.'

'But—'

'No buts. Who's there? Come on, sweetheart, it'll do you good.'

'Let me check it out with Harry. If you don't hear from me, I'll see you there in half an hour. Where?' I say.

'The café? It's looking pretty bleak out there, we can always get a coffee if it starts chucking it down.'

Ryan

'You're shitting me, Winston. You have a problem with that? What you want me to do – hole up in the back room while the rain pours through the extension? Yeah, man, other than the building stuff, things are good. Sure I knew you were kiddin'. Three – I got three quotes. What do you take me for? Okay, man. Sorry, but the weather's been shit – it's not Jamaica here, is it? Sure, I'm okay. What am I up to? Working out, listening to sounds, man – hey, man, you'd be proud of me, I've even started to write some stuff. Yeah, man. And I'm missing you too … Well I'm counting, man. Sure I am, seven weeks, seven weeks and two days to be precise. No worries, I got stuff to do too. Talk later. Yeah, good … Yeah, man, I'll find them – you just make sure you get the cash in the bank or you won't have a flat to come home to. Okay, man. Speak soon.'

I cut off. Lucky we don't Skype. Wouldn't want him seeing what I've got for my breakfast. I breast stroke through the debris on the floor; I can't look down in case my face falls off. My head is pounding so hard I wonder if maybe I've been mugged in my sleep, and I'm sweating like a pig. Third time lucky my fingers find and drag up my underpants. I'm having a problem with my legs too.

My guest, peeking like a lily out of a powder-blue lagoon of satin, gives me the sweetest smile, which triggers a surge of

217

blood to my dick. Help me out here. I manage finally to get my pants on back to front and my legs to the floor, hobble towards the kitchen. Just a smidgen should help me find the can and clear my head. The table is strewn with foil and clingfilm petals, half-cigarettes and torn Rizla; it takes me a few queasy seconds to find what I'm looking for. I need to make a shopping list, man. My fingers are shaking as I unwrap the tiny plastic bubble, scared I'll drop it or flick it or lose it – there's precious little here. I manage to tap half onto the tip of my pinkie and sniff. Jeez.

My phone bleeps. A text from Dave. Piss off, Dave.

It's just a few seconds before all pain and stiffness is gone and I'm floating clear-headed to the bog, and once I've sussed the mystery of the missing 'Y' of my underpants, I'm pissing like a stallion and trying to write 'sonofabitch' into the froth. It's nine thirty. Winston's due to call back around noon, confirm he's transferred the repair money. I flick the light on and move to the mirror. Did he seriously imagine we were about to grow old together? I clean my teeth, I can hear Jazzer moving about in the bedroom. I scoop up a condom from the closet and float down the passage.

'Hey man, get your nose outta my shit.'

'Keep ye claws in cat-boy. Ken Ah'm just needing a rag, man. Ma nose is cut tae shreds here. Ah've got a bleed on. Ah'm scared I'll bleed over yer classy sheets. Sorry, man. Like Ah say, dinnae mean no harm like. Ah'm burstin for a pish an-aw.'

I grab my t-shirt from the floor as he nudges the drawer shut with his long elegant pinkie – makes it look like a trick, and stares at me from under his thick white lashes. Looks like an angel – an angel with cat's eyes, and now I'm looking I swear he's not twenty-five, no way, more like sixteen or seventeen, maybe younger.

Once I'm settled, he nestles down with his head in my lap. I wipe the slight trickle of blood away from his lip, close my eyes for a moment to appreciate the gentle response from my dick to the pressure from his cheek. When I open them, the sun has snuck in through a gap in the curtains and is snaking over the bed, pooling in my lap and turning his soft white curls into tangerine flames – not the only thing on fire. Dick Turpin's rearing up, punching air. I clock the 'Y' of my underpants is still over my arse and flip him over the top edge, watch him bolt.

It may seem like a good idea at the time, but it never works out. Picking them up late at night … I should know better, fucking junkie, man – starts bleating soon as he's showered, 'just a line, man, just a fix …' If I'm not canny, he'll be moving in here before I can say buggery. Think again, cat-boy.

When I tell him we cleaned out last night, he totally fucking loses it, calls me names even I've not heard of, pulling out drawers, accusing me of child abuse. When he's finished, I tell him I'll call him later, when I've scored – make out I care. I think he's about to kick off again when something flits across his face, some other dumb punk no doubt. He leaves – kisses me on the lips and leaves. Little shit – what if he's seriously underage?

I snort up the last of the coke hidden in my underpants drawer and call my supplier. Com'on, com'on. But he's not picking up. Fuck, should have done this yesterday – meant to do this yesterday, should never have got so wasted, should never have brought that screwed-up little punk home …

Rachel

When I arrive, India is staring at the table, with her head bowed. I touch her shoulder and she looks up at me.

'Gorgeous coat. Guy?'

'Yeah – last week – nice isn't it?'

'Really. But it's boiling in here – give it to me and I'll hang it up. Hot chocolate or coffee?'

She peels it off and bursts into tears. I sit down, drape her coat across my lap and my arm around her shoulders and let her sob.

After a couple of squelchy minutes she lifts her head from her hands. Oh God, her nose. I rummage in my bag and pull out a hanky. 'Here, use this. Come on, India – it can't be that bad.'

I thought the hanky was rather bulky. Now I see India is wiping her nose on my tights – *the* tights. I grab at a small tail hanging down, which quickly becomes a long leg. The two women at the next-door table are staring.

'India, let go. You can't use those.' I win a brief tug of war, stuff them in my pocket. The woman, less than a foot away, hands me a paper napkin.

'Thanks.'

'Come on, India – I thought you said things were fine?'

'They were, they were,' she sobs, 'but he's changed – he's so paranoid, Rachel. I never know where I stand with him. It's like one minute he hates me, and the next he's like all over me saying all this stuff about me becoming a model. Like I'm so photogenic and everything. He can be so sweet, Rache … But today, well, he just went mad again. You should have seen him.'

She's wailing now. The waiter looks panicked. 'Let's go, India, before we get asked to leave. Come on, it's only a couple of minutes to mine. Abi should still be at work.'

I mouth 'sorry' to the waiter and exchange despairing glances with the next-door table. India slides into her long, woollen, million-squid coat again and we waltz the few minutes to my flat to a dubious melody of sniffs and snivels. Once we're inside she turns the volume right up and collapses onto the kitchen sofa, blowing her nose on my only clean tea towel. Honestly. In this light I can see bruising on her cheek, spreading into her hairline. I put the kettle on, press a wad of loo paper into her hand, and say the obvious.

'India, you've got to dump him. This is the third time he's hit you – he's a psychopath – he's never going to make you happy.' It all sounds very plausible and sensible.

'But I can't, can I? Not when I love him, and besides, when he's in a good mood, well, I've never had anyone like him, have I?'

I point out, as gently as I can, that his good moods are drug induced, but I'm wasting my breath.

'All those dorks I've been with – and Guy, he's very sweet, I know that, but he's hardly in David's league is he? If I could just get him to trust me.'

'Surely it's the other way round. Surely you're the one that needs to be able to trust *him*, India? Think about it. I mean, has he ever actually said anything, you know, to make you think he's not just playing with you for kicks? You don't know what he's up to behind your back.'

'That's not fair, Rachel. Last week he had a brochure of this, like, fabulous flat down in Leith, like a palace it was, and, and when I gawped at it he just laughed at me, not meanly or anything, said it was just the beginning, that in ten years' time … he said 'we' you know, like he was talking, like *we'd* be going places, like together, like we'd still know each other then – like he was really, really serious about me. Like he loved me …'

'So what are you crying about then, silly girl?'

'Because, because, like I happened to mention it in the office. I mean he never said not to or anything, and then one of the girls, Tanya, you know, the big one, well she went and said something to him and well, he didn't say anything, not at the time, but I could tell he was fuming. I could tell he was like really mad at me, and after, well he nearly killed me, said he didn't want people getting the wrong idea about us, that he'd told me it was confidential, that I was stupid, all that kind of thing – look …'

She yanks down her jeans and pulls up her t-shirt. All I can see are a few very amateur bruises.

'I mean, I know it's not much, but it hurt and I wouldn't mind but he's obviously planning on dumping me now, and I don't know why – I don't know why, Rachel. I mean, why? What's so wrong with telling a few people?'

'Oh India, are you completely clueless? It's obvious. Durr. He doesn't want anyone to know. He likes things the way they are. The last thing he wants is for Guy to find out. I mean, from what you say Guy's already suspicious. If he finds out about you and David, well, he'd sack him wouldn't he?'

'Who?'

Keep up – keep up, child.

'David, of course.'

'But I never told Guy did I?'

'Maybe not, but you can see why he thought you might. I mean, if you're blabbing to people in the office – it's going to get back to him, isn't it? Say you're sorry, and if you really want to keep him, grovel, dress up or something. I could lend you a few bits and pieces – course he'll forgive you.'

'I suppose.'

'Don't look so depressed. If you want to keep him you need to be one step ahead, that's all – keep him on his toes. Let me think … Another man, maybe? Andrew? Sorry, that's not funny.'

She whips round.

'Andrew?'

'It was a joke – a joke, India.'

'Not so much of a joke, maybe.'

'You're kidding – you and Andrew? I don't believe it – you have to be kidding.'

'No, not me and Andrew. What do you think I am? But he tried you know, he tried it on, just after you left. I wasn't going to say anything ...'

'But I thought he was in love with Megan? I thought he'd been hankering after her for years.'

'Maybe that's a rebound thing, or maybe they fell out. They did you know, for ages. Maybe *I* was the rebound thing. It doesn't even matter, does it? He did it, that's all you have to know. Like I said, I wasn't going to tell you, but why else do you think I've been trying to find an evening job? I need to move, but everything's so expensive, Rachel, and I don't know anyone to share with, but I definitely can't stay there with him, not after *everything*.'

'You mean there's more?'

'Well no, not really, but it's complicated. I mean I can hardly take people back there, not after that, and you never know ... I mean, David, well eventually, if we, well you know, I mean, it'd be different if you were in the house – you'd be cool about stuff. You're not involved, are you?'

'Well no, you'd be able to see who you liked. Of course you would. Um, I'm just wondering, India, just wondering whether you might, well, whether you would actually say this in court, you know, that Andrew made a pass at you. I mean, it's almost like your father hitting on you.'

'I never thought of that.'

Durr.

'I suppose I could. I mean, I can't see why not, if you think it would help.'

'Well it's hardly a good environment to bring kids up in, is it? I think it might.'

She nods.

Hitting on a young woman who he practically raised? Beating up his wife. This sounds more like it – in fact I'm feeling so optimistic all of a sudden I think I could just about stand to mention the forbidden 'L' word. And I do. 'How is my mother – showing any signs of dying?'

'Honestly Rachel, you are wicked! And in fact she's mostly okay – mostly upbeat you know, but she's difficult. Andrew's been to see some places. You know, somewhere she could live permanently – homes.'

'So even he's fed up with the old witch. And how's it going?'

'She's—'

'No, not her! The search for a place – how's the search going?'

'It's hard. He wants to find her something close by, that she'll like.'

'And what about Sheena? She's not offering to take care of her poor ill mother then?'

'She can't. She hasn't got the room, and Liz can't be left alone anymore. Sheena wants Andrew to have power of attorney, so he can sell her cottage in Oban. She'll not need that now will she?'

'I suppose not. But I should be doing this – I'm her daughter too, aren't I? And you know something, India – I'm suddenly thinking that mother and I are going to turn over a new leaf ...' She's about to protest. Give me patience. I do an exaggerated wink. 'See what I mean?'

'Oh, Rachel, you are clever. Are you coming round again, then?'

And you India are a durr-brain, a beautiful durr-brain, but a durr-brain nevertheless. 'Yes, well, so long as the children get back together again – they're really what matter aren't they?'

ABI

I OVERSLEPT. BIG DEAL. Means fuck all, anyway. I'm sure there's this song about night turning into day … So welcome to our world; when we're not working or partying, we're sleeping. Half the time I'm having breakfast in the evening but thinking it's early morning, or is it the other way round? Don't know, can't remember, don't care.

Better not wake Mum. She wasn't in till five – I know, because I watched the eye of her cigarette winking and flaring and then jolting in the dark as she crashed into a chair in my room. When she's totally off her trolley, it's not just the furniture she thwacks. Sometimes she thumps into the remains of her motherly instincts and decides to check up on me. And I wish to fuck she wouldn't.

In the kitchen the house phone is blinking at me. I listen to the messages. Four from India. For fuck's sake. What's Mum like? No need to answer that. I know what she's like. Useless. A message pings into her mobile. Six messages. Toni. Toni. Toni – boring. India, India, India. Might as well take a look. India: *Found something at David's flat. Need advice.* India: *Call me please.* India: *Coming round.* Jeez.

I set her alarm for four and write her a note to get something in for dinner or else!

SAM McColl

What's she like? We're talking about me having one lunch, one lunch with my dad, one measly meal … Does my head in – I hardly dare see them anymore. Not that she says much, doesn't have to. If I so much as mention Dad or anything she goes mental. It's just so childish, all her little jibes about a 'lunch party'! *Lunch party*? I mean, hel-lo? I mean, change the record, Mum. Most normal folk would call it a gathering for the sad, demented and infirm.

I keep telling her she should dump Toni. There's no point is there – not if it's not working out? And as for that new friend of hers, well I've got my doubts about her too – like why she never comes here, like maybe *she's* a *he* even; no, please no, don't even think it. Worst is, I'm beginning to understand that it really does take rape and a good bashing to bring her to her senses.

It's freezing out here. I could do with a new jacket – this one's rubbish. Better write to Santa, I don't think. You know, if I'm forced to choose between them, if it came to that, in court, it'll be her. It shouldn't be, I should choose Dad, but I won't, I know I won't, not if I'm forced. And I don't even know why – not really. All I know is that, however hard it is for him, it'll never be as hard as it is for Mum, and I hate him for giving up on us more than I hate her for screwing up. Besides, he doesn't need me – not now he's got Megan.

It's only a twenty-minute walk to Dad's, but my hands have gone numb, and my heart is banging in time with my knuckle on the front door. Why can't he get the bell fixed? Come on, come on, I'm freezing to death out here.

I'm about to piss off when the door swings open and wee Callum is looking up at me with a big grin. He looks so cute with leaves sticking to his jersey and poking through his hair.

'You took your time. You've been in the garden haven't you?' I squat down and hug him. 'Mmm, you smell so good – look at you, you're like a leaf man. Where is everybody? Is Sarah here yet?'

'Nope, and Megan had to go back to her house. It's just me and Dad, Gran and India and Nevis. India's with Gran upstairs, and me and Dad and Nevis are outside.'

So that's good, then. At least I won't have to lie to Mum about Megan. I make my way to the Aga and almost pass out with the fanfuckingtastic smell coming from the oven and suddenly I feel like bursting into tears, but India's coming down the stairs and I hug her instead.

Callum's made a sort of nest in the garden with rugs and cushions and Dad's got drinks all ready. I raid the winter drawer for scarves and gloves and pull on an old manky duffle coat of Mum's. I know I should visit more. And I would, wouldn't I, if it wasn't for you-know-who-my-mother.

'Okay Nevis, I love you too – now bugger off, will you.' In the end I give up trying to shove him away and lie spread-eagled on the grass letting Cal and Nevis bury me in leaves, which takes about a second. Once the leaves have settled and Nevis and Cal are back in their garden den, I open my eyes and try to see the furthest blue, but get caught up in the specks of light in-between. I used to think they were fairies – trillions of them, and maybe they are. If I try, I can hold one with my gaze and move it up and down or wherever, like the tiniest dragonfly wing, but it only works if I don't look straight at it – only if it's caught in my trying to look into the faraway blue.

I'm just thinking how I'd like to stay here forever, when I hear a faint hammering.

'It'll be Mum,' India screams from the kitchen. 'I'll get it.'

And the shrieks get louder and more mental until Hurricane-Sarah kind of balloons out the door.

'Oh Abi, I've missed you so much,' she says, helping me up. 'Get off, Nevis!' She kicks him away before resuming her bear hug. 'My God, you're so pretty. Bunking off school obviously suits you, darling.'

Dad looks morosely from her to me.

'Christ,' she says, fake-chattering her teeth. 'It's freezing out here and Nevis, your breath's like a sewer. Look everyone, vaporised poo! For fuck's sake, dog. Get off!'

I know she's gross, and like embarrassing and a terrible role model and crap mum, but I'm welling up anyway, because I'm so happy she's staying with me and Mum.

'Are you okay, Abi? Hey darling, oh how sweet, you're not greetin' are you? No one's ever cried at me arriving before, not from joy anyway. Aw, come here …'

She pulls me onto her enormous tits and squeezes. Most people I know have changed, but Sarah never changes – crap for her, obvs, but sort of lovely for me right now. I just miss so much stuff. Truth is, in many ways she was more of a mum to me than Mum, and now I'm like remembering all the times I snuck across the driveway and along the beach to her house.

I think I must have zoned out against her bosom for a few seconds, but now I'm feeling a kind of jiggling and shaking and I wonder if she's crying too. Gross – it's Nevis shagging her leg and the odd jerk is Sarah making small and totally useless kicks to throw him off. My eyes are open now and the choked-up thing has gone and there's this like other weird wailing noise coming from the house. It's Gran. I'm looking up now, my chin on Sarah's padded shoulder. Gran swings into view and kind of hovers on the kitchen steps. Awesome. Then she kind of checks out the scene, hitches her gross flowery skirt above her knees, and squats. Fuck, she's about to pee. I'm first to get to her and grab her hand.

'Come on, Gran, let's get you inside.' She folds forward and stares between her legs for a moment as though she doesn't understand me and then bursts into tears. Sarah's cottoned on to what's happening and between us we haul her up and get her through the kitchen and to the hall loo.

India's lasagne is awesome, but she's totally hyper. She keeps asking me if Mum's at home and then giving me this like heavy stare, as if she's trying to fathom a deeper meaning. Please, as if I'd bother. What's wrong with everyone? I only know mad people. Then she announces she's bunking off to 'keep Rachel company'. She says she's just had a really 'lonely' text from her (which is crap) and that she'll see Sarah later on – tells her not to be late.

I can't believe how much India's changed since Mum left; it's like all the stuff she said to me in the beginning about my mum being unstable and everything – like she disapproved … So now all of a sudden they're best buddies, and she thinks she can just like come round whenever she fancies. And Mum's weird too, cos she never says anything these days, probably cos she's so stoned she can't get her words out. So that means they'll both be in a coma when I get home. Fucking great. Excuse me for living.

I'm so not hungry anymore. Dad's staring at me in that cheesy way of his. Get off, Dad.

Sarah's being weird – good weird, which makes a change. Probably means she's feeling guilty for staying with Mum and me and she's not mentioned Megan and Dad once, or bitched about India or my virginity or anything. So maybe she's going to knock some sense into Mum after all. I mean, she'd better, because I'm so not going into that box to slag Dad off. I mean, like, how could she ask me to – I just can't believe she's that screwed up, that she's really going through with this court stuff.

'Gran, wipe your chin – Gran, your chin!' There's a piece of pasta like a flap of skin wagging from her chin.

'Why darling?'

'Don't do that, Gran. Here let me get it.' I dab it off the table before she flicks it at one of us. Harry's with his own family today, so lunch is about Gran control. I guess you get used to it, even the minging smell. It was Callum who told me that her last mini stroke messed up her bladder-mind link, so it just dribbles out more or less. As do her words. She doesn't even ask about Mum in any kind of secret way anymore – just comes straight out with it: 'Too busy doing the business with we-know-who,' she says, with giant winks at whoever's around.

Besides Gran, no one seems hungry.

Crumble next, plum crumble and Mackie's ice cream. As Dad ladles it onto plates, he announces he's made it just for me, and he probably did, but I wish he'd just drop it – everything we do together is so fucking heavy with stuff. I force myself to eat some anyway and it is nice – course it is. Then I get up and start clearing the table. Callum is very quiet all of a sudden.

Without warning, Gran picks up a plate and lobs it across the table. Mental. I try to catch it but miss and it smashes onto the work top. Dad's on his feet but Sarah gets to her first and snatches the next one off her. Gran looks furious for a minute and then bursts into tears again. Not good. She's so getting worse.

Cal tips his chair back and runs upstairs. Dad looks up from the floor. 'No, I'll go,' I say, and chase him up. His room looks so empty.

'Hey little man, what's up?'

He shrugs.

'Gran's not so good is she?'

He shrugs again.

'That's tough isn't it? Dad said she sometimes forgets who everyone is, but that some days she's back to her old self again?'

Cal shrugs again, eyes filling up. 'Come home, Abi – you've got to come home!'

'It's okay, it'll be okay, come on, wee fella … I'm here – I'll always be here—'

'Don't lie to me. You're always lying. You're never here, Abi. You're always with her—'

'I live there, Callum. I don't know what to say.'

'Nothing, Abi, don't say anything. I heard her, I heard her when she was screaming and screaming at Dad and I don't like her coming to school, so you can tell her that I don't like it … and I'm not going back either. I don't want her back here – I hate her. I'm staying here with Dad. Forever and ever, see!'

'Have you told Dad all this, Cal – that you heard Mum and Dad fighting?'

He throws himself at me, pushing me with his little fists.

'Promise you won't say, Abi – promise, okay?'

'Only if you promise to tell him.'

'Go away, Abi.'

'Promise me you'll tell him.'

He slumps down, sniffing and wiping his cheeks.

'Where are all your things, Cal? Where's Nellie-the-elephant and all the others?'

'I don't want them anymore. I'm too big for stupid teddies.' He bangs his fists on the floor.

'No you're not … Even I'm not too big for teddies. Where are they? Poor Nellie and Poo Bear and Piglet and Lilly and Angus. That's so silly. Where have you put them? Let's look shall we?'

I start towards the giant wardrobe which doubles up as his toy cupboard, but he leaps up and beats me to it. He sort of climbs in and bangs around a bit and then emerges with a tangled lump of trunks and tails and ears. Why would he do that? He's standing totally still staring at the pile and swinging Monkey by the arm … His back is turned to me. His tiny shoulders are shaking. I shuffle on my knees behind him and pull him onto my lap and stroke his head and pull leafy bits off his fleece. He's only a baby. What are they doing to him? What am I doing to him?

He goes on sniffing and wiping his nose on his sleeve and then wriggles off me and scoops up Nellie and Poo Bear and Tigger and Worm and Henry and crams them into my lap and I grab some cushions from off his bed and together we put them all in a circle and prop them up and the littlest ones we put in the bigger ones' laps. He's got his head on one side and gives me a little sad grin.

'Promise me, eh? You'll talk to Dad, and you won't hide them again – promise me Cal.'

He shrugs.

'Come home, Abi.'

'I can't, Callum. I can't just leave Mum.'

'She can come too then.'

'Oh Cal, I so wish she could, darling. I just so wish that was possible.'

He doesn't say anything. He just stares at the ground and then flops down, crosses his arms.

'Just go.'

'Oh come on, Callum. This isn't my fault.'

He shrugs again for the millionth time like that's all he has, holding onto opposite elbows, starting to swing from side to side.

'Cal—'

'No.' He stamps his foot. 'Okay don't! I'll go.'

And he stands up and looks at me like he might cry again and walks out the door, knocking over Nellie and Whiskers as he goes.

ANDREW

'ALL I'M SAYING, RACHEL, is, that Callum heard you yelling at me and he's worried sick that you're going to kick me out and take over.' I sit for a moment but it doesn't feel right, so I start another lap of her small kitchen table. 'He doesn't want you back there, and if Abi didn't feel so responsible for you, she wouldn't either. I mean, she didn't even think she should come for a walk on Saturday – you're forcing her to choose, Rachel, you're—'

'And you're mad. Of course she could have gone for a stupid walk – that was nothing to do with me, Andrew. You know what she's like.'

'I know what she was like in Argyll, when she starved herself to make room for your dramatics. I remember that all too clearly. I'm warning you, Rachel, back off, stop trying to get what you want through her – she's not strong enough.'

'You're jealous aren't you? Just cos we're close, just cos she chose me over you and now she wants her home back and her brother. She'll choose me, Andrew – she will, in court, if it comes to that, she will you know. You're the selfish one. Out with the old, in with the new. Well it won't work. Even Callum would swap you for Abi you know, if it came to it. Megan's got a perfectly nice flat, go and live there if you don't fancy this one. In fact, I've got an idea – put Rhona in here, it would make a great granny flat. There we are – the perfect solution!'

I don't believe this. 'For God's sake, Rachel – no one in their right mind —'

'Grow up, Andrew. Think about it for a minute, just like my lawyer has – he's quite convinced the sheriff will want to keep the children together, with their mother. And then there's also the small but significant issue of my mother staying there too and being pushed into a nursing home. Even India says you're not coping. Altogether I'd say …'

But she doesn't finish as Abi and Sarah come back with their arms full of groceries, and she's right of course – she might well win in court.

As Abi dumps the bags on the table she looks pleased, hopeful – incapable of seeing what's really going on. There's a reversal of roles going on here: Rachel playing the chaotic spoilt brat out to get whatever she can, and screw whoever gets steamrollered on the way, and Abi's behaving like a worn-down mother, too scared to say no – desperate to see her happy. Oh my God, Abi. Please start looking at what she's doing to you. 'I need to get home, Callum will be back soon and it's school tomorrow.'

'Oh Dad, stay a bit. Go on. India's at home, Callum'll be fine for once, come on pleeease … Make him Sarah – it'll be fun.'

She actually wants me to stay because it's like the old days. I get up and leave quickly, urging Sarah to stop by on her way home. I sit in the car and try to pull my thoughts together. I'm reluctant to involve her, it feels wrong somehow and childish, like I'm stooping to Rachel's level. But I'll need witnesses if it goes to court.

As I start the car, I feel so weak and helpless – how can I put Abi through this? And yet what choice do I have? And she'll never forgive Megan, will she? Not if she speaks out. Megan is her role model – her only role model.

What did I do that was so very wrong? Fall for the wrong woman? So how was I to know? God please tell me, how was I to know? We live in a chaotic universe full of damaged, abused children who happen to look like grown-ups.

The taste of tears is calming, nourishing. The feeling of drowning recedes. Maybe Abi's right. India is at home and Callum will be fine – so I turn right instead of left and minutes later pull into a parking space on Hillside Street. 'Can I come up – are you alone?'

'Yes, yeah – come on up.'

As I take her by the hand and lead her upstairs, everything slows down.

'I love you.'

'Yes.'

RYAN

ALREADY I'M PISSED OFF, *late for my visit to my psychedelic dentist. Last thing I need is running into my homeless junkie and his manky dog. We do a quick deal. I take the manky hound, he takes a full bag of poppy. Manky hound turns into Rottweiler. As manky hound and I walk past the shop windows my mood swings high – we make an impressive couple. No one's going to batter me again, are they? Not with Brutus swaggering by my side. I'm at the dentist in plenty of time, after all. The secretary curtsies and takes Brutus off me, shows me into the waiting room. I sit next to Agnes who gives me that look of hers, tells me she saw the way I kicked my homeless friend and took the only thing he loved in the world. Did I want him to die, she says, of drugs. I tell her it's not my fault he loves poppy more than his dog, but she looks at me again in that way of hers and I know she knows that really it was me that killed him after all because we both know he's dead anyway and all that nonsense was only a dream. I'm hoping Dodger-the-dentist will see me real quick because Agnes is doing my head in. I stare at the wall and put my fingers in my ears. The receptionist waves at me. I give Agnes one of my looks, climb into the dentist's chair (which is now in the waiting room) and rock back, stretch out my arm and clench my fist, my veins popping with excitement. As Daddy jabs the needle in, I open my eyes wide and lock into his.*

It's midday. Crazy dreams, man – crazy fucking dreams. A few weeks and I'll be back in Jamaica and I'll be finding some relatives, maybe even my old man, it's not impossible. Maybe once I'm on the other side of the world Agnes will stay away, though there's nothing she or Ma do to me during my sleep I don't see them doing when I'm awake. And the homeless junkie – well he isn't there anymore, because I went that way a few times. I hope he found a way out. I hope he's not dead, that's all.

I roll over, catch a tell-tale glimpse of spilt tobacco, a torn Rizla packet, and real stuff starts creeping into my consciousness. I spend several minutes hoping what I think may have happened last night, didn't. Hoping that Jazzer didn't talk me round because I was already wasted, that he and I didn't do crack, and that we didn't end up … Tell me it was a dream, man, like all the other fucking nightmares, that I'm not such a fucking idiot, that I didn't … I fully lean over the edge of the bed – no visible signs, but there's this smell, the smell of poverty and sweat and unwashed genitals. I doze a while longer, or try to. If he was here, then he isn't anymore. Wise move. And the next time he hangs around my door waiting for me to come home, he can expect a lot more damage than a bleeding nose. Fucking nonce.

Beginning to feel twitchy now, nothing spooky about that. I hop to the kitchen pulling on my sweats. There's nothing in the drawer, so I must have left it in the lounge. Argh. That's his snot rag … I remove it from the couch and drop it in the waste bin. It occurs to me his nose is beyond repair. Amazing how we begin to accept the damage as part of the badge, proudly almost – hard men.

I'm beginning to panic, break into a sweat. Where the fuck did I put that gear? Takes me a while to figure things out and by the time I do I'm knocking stuff over. Kitchen table first. He's taken the lot. That mother fucker has cleaned me out. And then I remember, I remember him pulling out the drawer by my bed, remember me yelling at him.

The stash, the money, the fucking twelve grand I'd taken from Winston's account to pay the builders. My ticket out of here, my new life … I'm running down the passage now, white heat building like a furnace inside my head, bile rising … I pull the fucking drawer out and throw it across the room, then the other one, then I start hallucinating. Maybe it's under the mattress, so that goes over, or maybe it's in the cabinet in the shower room. I pull that off the wall and throw it hard as I can against the door. So long as there's this crashing and splintering, it seems that it might still be somewhere – that I'd changed my mind about the drawer, wouldn't have put it in such a fucking obvious place. Nah, I'd have stuffed it under the sofa cushions, or in Winston's wardrobe or just anywhere at all … But in the end I've got to stop because there's nothing else to tear or throw.

Look at this place, who's gonna tidy up, man – who's gonna get me something, there ain't nothing here and I'm dying man, fucking dying, not a fucking lick, nothing, knocked the lot, enough frigging chang to run a fucking power station, must have been, there was …

So now where's my fucking phone, man? Where the fuck is it? You've taken my fucking phone, man, and you're dead. But it's here, by the TV. Thank fuck. C'mon beauty – dish out the numbers, c'mon, c'mon. He's fucking wiped them, course he's wiped them. This pain in my gut man; shit, there must be some dope someplace, man – gotta be something in all this mess.

ABI

JUST FUCK OFF, SARAH, will you? Go back home where they're all bonkers. I just don't get it. She emailed me to say she was coming to stay to try to talk to Mum, make her change her mind about the court thing, but here she is, eating our food, smoking our dope and basically just adding to the drama.

What's she on about, anyway? Todd's her husband – there is no fucking way he's eyeing up young girls, just as there was no way Dad set out to break up his marriage by pulling Megan. The truth is bad enough and it pisses me off to see them both cranking it up, behaving like idiots.

And why can't Mum just leave it? It's *so* not funny!

'Come on, Abi, tell us!' Mum says. 'Make her, Sarah.' Sarah is in the bathroom so Mum is actually screaming now. 'We saw you, didn't we, Sarah – so there's absolutely no point you denying it.'

I give her a 'back off' look. 'Sarah can't hear you, Mother – and saw what, exactly? Nothing's going on, and even if there was, you're about the last person I'd tell.'

Emerging from the loo, Sarah re-ties Mum's dressing gown, snatches the joint off her and drops down beside me, starts patting my knees, which I'm hugging. Then she sort of keels over against the bed her and Mum have been sharing. I should have left them to sleep – they're obviously still hung over.

Mum props herself up on one elbow and leans over the edge of the bed, pulling my chin round to get a good look. 'Don't lie, Abi, you've gone distinctly purple. And if you're worried I'd tell Dad, don't be. I'm the one who pointed him out remember? That's better, a wee smile even … Now come on, give us the dirt, come on, darling. Promise you'll not breathe a word, Sarah – I know what you're like.' She flops back onto the pillows.

Sarah sucks at the joint, stares questioningly at the dusty tip and sucks it again, slips her arm through mine and squeezes. 'My lips are sealed. C'mon Abi, I'd had half of Glasgae by your age. Been saving yourself have you? That Jamie of yours not up to the job then?'

As much as I hate the way they say stuff, maybe they've got a point, maybe I should *go for it*. I mean, at least Ash fancies me – unlike goody-two-shoes Jamie, on some permanent rant about us being underage and university and well, just being a plonker. Ash says leaving school early was the best thing he ever did. But I don't give them the satisfaction.

'Err, you're minging, both of you,' I say. 'Hey, give it here, it's not even alight, you idiot. Not everyone's like you, you know. Ash and I are pals. I work with him – he's Mum's boyfriend's brother for fuck's sake.' I take the joint, reach up for Mum's lighter on the bedside table, light it, then roll down flat on the floor. Fuck it – what do I know? At least with Mum I have a laugh, and Mum's right – Dad has Megan. And I can just picture him freaking out over Ash asking me out; no way he'd let me go to the gig Saturday. Knowing him he'd probably pick me up – as if that's going to happen. No, Mum may be a bit flaky, but at least I get to do what I like.

Then the doorbell goes.

Mum sits up, grinning, slaps the top of Sarah's head. 'Half of Glasgae! You idiot! You wish, more like.'

Very fucking droll, I don't think.

'That'll be India. Go on, Abi, I definitely can't stand – pleeease.'

'Go on, Sarah, you get it – she's your daughter,' I say, feeling very weak myself.

'Nae fucking way, ye fat lazy gits …' she says with her phony Glasgow accent as she tips sideways onto the floor. 'Now get off your fat arses, and if it *is* my dearest daughter, tell her I'm waiting to meet this new boyfriend of hers. You should take a leaf out of her book, Abi – if you can't choose, fuck 'em both!'

'Sarah!' Mum shrieks.

'Oops, forgot you weren't meant to tell me! Shushhhh, don't worry, Mum's the—'

The bell again. Christ, what are they like! I stagger up and go to the door. I've not eaten yet and I'm feeling a bit sick, but hey once I've opened the door the 'bit sick' flips into a 'fucking great overwhelming pouring sweat weak at the knees sick' because somewhere in the back of my mind I know about this – the letter I found on Mum's bedroom floor, the letter I only vaguely read, the letter that was from the education authority about a visit. Well thanks, Mum, I'll probably go to jail now – just so fucking long as I go alone.

'He-hello.' I stammer it out, like I'm used to being shot in the stomach when answering the doorbell. 'Can I help you?' Nice and loud, like I'm so giving someone (the responsible adult) time to hide the dope, get dressed, pull the other drunk off the bedroom floor, tidy the mess, brush her hair … Allowed to dream aren't I?

'Are you Abi Gillespie?'

Simple questions first eh? I nod the affirmative.

'Good. We have an appointment? Is your mum in?'

An immediate attack of exam nerves prompts the wrong answer this time. The right answer would have been a simple 'no', but I say, 'I'll go and see.' I mean, either she is or she isn't.

At least I don't invite them in.

But hey, I might as well have because they're following me, albeit at a polite distance.

'Hi, yes, I'm Rachel Gillespie. Forgive me, but we completely forgot you were coming. Please excuse the mess, and this is Sarah, a great friend from the west coast. We've taken the day off school work – haven't we Abi, darling? Sarah's here you see, so we've taken the day off.' She says, again, stuffing her hair into a stubby ponytail.

'I see. Well not to worry – I mean that's the heavenly thing about home educating isn't it? You can do it when you like and how you like.'

'I suppose it is.'

'And please don't worry about the mess – you should see my kitchen.'

Please don't get defensive, Mum, they're being really cool.

'Would you like coffee?' Sarah says, putting the kettle on. They are both blond. The younger one asks for tea, and makes to sit at the table.

In the middle of the table is a Rizla paper with some tobacco sprinkled over and around it … and right, oh cool, a small bit of scrunched-up tin foil – fanfuckingtastic. Mum brushes it into her palm along with some bits of toast and the lump of nicotine-stained apple we cunningly use to keep the tobacco damp. At least they'll be able to say that we eat fruit.

They ask me about the subjects I'm doing, and how I work and where I work. I think it's going okay; they just say that if I want any help they're always at the end of the telephone. They give me lists of websites and help numbers and resource stuff and libraries and for a while it all seems like it might be quite fun to get into it and ask these nice people to help me. It all seems very clear, not complicated like it usually does; kind of normal, like it might be simple to just work at home, and of course when they say it all like that, it is.

As soon as the door closes behind them, Mum bursts out laughing, but Sarah comes up to me and pulls me into her. 'I'm so sorry Abi – that was really crap. Shut up, Rachel, will you?'

It's not like I'm unhappy or anything but this terrible choke thing is building up again and I only just make it into my room and crush my face into my pillow before it kind of bubbles up and explodes.

After a bit I hear a row kicking off. First Mum's being all sarky about the education people and Sarah's all sort of concerned like she can be sometimes. And then Mum says something about Callum, and how it'll all be better when we're back home.

I push the door open a bit with my toe. Sarah is talking.

'I'm just saying that you're fine here. You've got your freedom, and Abi, a job – I mean why? Why would you want to go back to being a full-time mum? To be honest you're not that good at it. Sorry, but you're not.'

Then Mum goes. 'I'm not having Megan become Callum's mother – I'm just not!'

'For God's sake, she's not becoming Callum's mum, she's become Andrew's girlfriend, and I think they'll be good together – did you seriously imagine he'd stay on his own forever?'

'Of course not and it's not just that. It's everything – the kids need each other, and India would help out.'

'She's said that, has she?'

'Yes she has. And you know what? Oh nothing. I'm … I mean, you managed didn't you?'

'If you say so. All I know is that I've spent a lot of time resenting being a mother, putting my work first, making a name for myself as an artist, in other words being a fucking stupid cow. I should have put India first but every time anyone showed they cared for me, I told them to sling their hook. I wish I could say they'd all been bastards, but they weren't – some of them would have made great fathers, and some of them would have made great husbands too.'

'Well, you've got Todd now, haven't you?' Mum says.

'About twenty-five years too late for India though, isn't it? I could never understand why she always chose bastards. It's not useful to point the finger, but it's tempting …'

'You did your best.'

Oh Mum – you really are something.

'That's my point, Rachel – I didn't. I didn't do what was best for India. I loved her, course, but that's not enough.'

Then there's this big silence.

'All I'm saying, Rachel, is don't punish Andrew and the kids for things they never did.'

'I'm not.'

'Okay.'

Ryan

I crawl to the pyramid of post by the door. Where the fuck is she? Where the fuck's Rachel? I've been calling her for days, fucking sulky bitch. And you Winston, where are you, man, when I really need you? Got my story sorted out; how the builders found more rot, man … how he needs to call the fucking bank, man, and deposit another twelve grand. Truth is I'm dying here, can't buy anything I need with no money, can I?

I take the local paper off the top of the pile. What day is it? Wednesday. Makes it three days, man, since I've been out. No wonder there's nothing to eat around here.

My mobile rings, but I can't see it. I hobble through to the living room, start throwing cushions off the settee. That'll be Winston now or Rachel.

It's David.

'Hi man. Listen. David … You got something for me, man?' But he starts yelling at me, calling me names. 'Jesus, man!' I throw the phone across the room. But then suddenly phone numbers start popping up in my mind: 07977 … I kind of lollop through the flat, but the pain rippling through me like small electric shocks makes it slow. 07871496607, 07871496607. I finally make it to my bed, 078771496607, grab the pen, the newspaper. I scribble it down one way, then again another; now

I'm not sure, now I am. I pretend to tap it out, change the four into a six. I'm sure it's a four. Now all I need is some money. This picture of Gerry's puffy face handing me some gear chokes me up – it's his number, man, it's his number.

I'm shaking all over, can't move. No food, that's my problem, no fucking food – I need food man, got no food, no gear, nothing. That feels better, just need to wait till Winston calls or Rachel, get my knees right up here, man, in my chest, that feels nice. Maybe my hands will stop shaking after I've taken a wee siesta, when the money comes man, build my strength … I think there must be bugs in here, man, because I'm itching all over – and it's cold – so fucking cold. Winston's coming soon, just need to wait for Winston. He'll fix me up good again – just get some shuteye till Winston – or maybe David …

RACHEL

I HUG MYSELF AS goose bumps crawl up my neck and over my head: we're going to win this, with or without Sarah. No question, I can feel it. Even Abi's beginning to see the bright side – not that she says anything, not directly, but I'm not stupid, am I? I can see the way she fills up when I start talking about Callum, and the idea of having the whole top floor to herself. Well, it's every teenager's dream isn't it?

The thought of having a proper home again has changed me. Honestly, I feel so much more secure, so much stronger. I'm going to start looking for a new job, a managerial one in a club, and I'm not saying that Ryan won't be a part of it, my life I mean, but he won't be all of it, not this time. I'm not sulking like he thinks, I've just been giving myself a bit of space and I've learnt something in the process. I find my phone under a pile of clothes by my bed, plug it into the charger. Battery is so flat it takes a minute or so for it to kick-start. Fucking hell, Ryan's texted me a least a dozen times.

Ahh wee lamb, so he's been missing me after all.

I have no intention of running to him. I would have done; last time around I would have done. But I said to Abi I'd clean up and I will – show her I can be a good and responsible mum. Besides, he's not even texted me today, probably not even up yet.

It's after one by the time the flat's done and I'm showered and dressed and ready to go.

I stop just before his block to check my make-up. In my mirror I can see another door opening further up Scotland Street and a woman with two very small children shuffle out. They're coming this way, maybe to the park or toddler group or perhaps the shops or a café to meet friends. A sudden urge to swap places, swap identities, be in charge of two small children again, surprises me, but then almost as quick I remember how claustrophobic it felt, how isolated I was, how boring and mundane and mumsy I found all the other mums at playgroup. This woman looks nice. I like her jacket, her haircut. She looks in control, like she's happy to be her. As she draws close I can hear her daughter's questions: why couldn't she get in the buggy too? Her mum had let her yesterday, why was it different today? Why, why? She smiles at me as she answers, raises her eyebrows, shares something. I smile back, flattered, find myself wanting to cry. The little girl stops a moment as if deciding something, then takes her mother's hand and starts swinging it. They pass. How did she do that? Why didn't it escalate into tears and deadlock, like it always did between Abi and me?

As they turn in to the park, she looks back up the street and smiles at me again. I put the small mirror back in my bag and walk up the stone steps to Ryan's front door.

Come on, come on, open up! The curtains are still drawn. Typical. I read his last text: 'call me. Urgent.' I ring the doorbell again. Come on, lazy bones, answer. Come on, open up baby …

From behind the closed door, I can just about decipher a muffled croak, a gangster's voice in a second-rate movie.

He's mucking about. 'It's me, Ryan – Rachel!'

The door opens a crack, then a bit more. This bloke that I almost know is peering round it, blinking and squinting with a mixture of expectation and terrible disappointment.

'I thought you were … Wow, what's happened to you? Did I miss something? You been partying without me, sweetheart?

Aren't you going to invite me in? Ryan? It's me. Hell-oo. Stop fooling around. C'mon, let me in – it's freezing out here.'

I could turn away. Something bad's yawning up at me; something bad's happened. Walk away. You've got enough on your plate right now, Rachel. Walk away.

But I can't wait to get in there.

'Christ, what's happened – what the hell's happened here?' I hear myself say, incredulous. 'Look at this place. Hey, hey, it's okay – what's wrong?'

I don't know why I'm surprised really. He's been so wired up lately. The kitchen table's lying on its side, huge shards of broken mirror gleam maliciously up at me from the floor. Maybe he sacked his cleaner – bought a rhino? No, maybe not. An inside job more like.

Leave, Rachel. Leave now.

I can smell the drink on his breath or maybe it's rot. He nearly falls. He's not said a word yet and his eyes don't look right. I flash back to me being on the floor in Dawn's flat and he's asking me how my dad did it – over and over and giggling and punching. But this isn't that Ryan, this Ryan is defeated, cold … 'Hey, hey it's okay. Come over here. Tell me what's going on, who did this?'

But he backs away.

'Some cunt punk … Why the fuck haven't you been picking up?'

'I lost my phone – only found it this morning.' I lie. 'For God's sake, Ryan, what the hell's going on?'

'I was burgled, broke in and burgled. I need some chang, Rachel. I'll be okay if I can get some chang, okay?'

'I guess – but I thought, I mean you had loads.'

'And something to eat. Dope and something to eat.'

'I don't know, Ryan. I mean, I wouldn't know where to go would I? But I can roll a joint, I've got some on me. Look, I've got some. Shall I roll a joint?'

He folds to the floor and starts crying, crying like a baby. I crouch over him but he shakes me off and hands me some Rizla, practically bats me away.

Like a cat waiting to pounce, every quivering nerve is trained on me as I glue one paper to another, spill tobacco from a damped cigarette into the trough. A plume of Afghani smoke stings my eyes as I cook the tip of my small lump. I glance up, try to steady my hand – his nostrils are flaring, searching, sucking the air for it. I'm packing it down with a match, twisting it into a point, but he's on it before it's done, snatching it from me, along with the lighter, sloping off greedily like a starving dog with a scrap of meat, dropping to the floor by the door. He's pushed hard up against the skirting, his knees rammed into his chest to steady his hands that are cupped around the joint. A few false starts with the lighter but once he's got a flame and he's inhaling his first draw, he emits a deep groan of pleasure, eyes fixed on mine, his whole body shuddering with the force of it.

'Go and get food, Rachel.'

'Listen Ryan, I don't mind doing stuff for you but you'd better tell me what's been going on.'

Between ravenous drags, he tells me he hasn't eaten much since he saw me last Thursday. Five nights.

'Got money then?' I say, wanting some sort of recognition.

He stares at me with something like hate on his face. 'Gone, for fuck's sake. Do you think I'd be …' He goes back to his sucking. Then quietly adds, as if remembering reluctantly that he needs me. 'I'll pay you back.'

I doubt he knows where his keys are, so I go and get the spare set from behind the screen. He looks at them like I've just found a bag of smack. 'You need a doctor. You're ill, Ryan.' He starts saying over and over that he'd forgotten the spare set, over and over and laughing.

I'm away ten minutes, tops. He hasn't moved. I make tea, toast and bacon, eggs. I persuade him up off the floor and onto the sofa, sit close in beside him, help him hold the mug. I've been kidding myself – in control? What an idiot. Cocaine or crack during the day which he tweaks with dope and alcohol as the day progresses; take them away and he's fucked. His head droops low on his chest as if he's taking a nap, and I draw it into my lap and stroke his forehead.

An image of me, a long time ago, with my head in Andrew's lap settles queasily in my mind.

'You should cut down you know – you've been saying you might.'

'I need cash. Get me some cash will you? I need to get some gear, Rachel – I'll pay you back … I'll get cleaned up. I'll start to cut back but I need something now to get me started so I can get myself straight.'

He scrabbles up to sitting, looking wildly round for something. Then he stares at the floor holding a hand up to me. Something dawns on him and he staggers up, heads across the kitchen towards his bedroom and then he's back, a look of wild pleasure suffusing his bloodshot eyes. He shoves a newspaper roll into my chest, stabbing at the large numbers scribbled across the headlines. I'm staring at them as he stabs at it again and pushes me the phone with his foot.

He's too paranoid to make the call.

So I dial the number. As soon as it rings, he grabs it from me, shoots me an evil look and starts talking. It's his dealer – obviously. I move off back to the kitchen, pick one of the chairs up and sit on it with my back to him. I should leave now.

Then his hands are on my shoulders, briefly massaging my neck. I push back into him. Come on Ryan, come on, Ryan … Jesus, if you just move your hand there, yes, just there, just for a second more, no please don't move, don't move Ryan, stay, just stay just just … That's so good, darling – that's so good …

I don't think he even noticed.

I stand up and turn to face him, but he moves round me and slumps in the chair. I kneel in front of him. His trackies are spotted and streaked with dirt; he is always so particular about showering, his appearance. I slip my hand inside. Com-on wee man, cheer up for me, come on little guy. He's about to respond, I'm sure, when I feel a tugging at my hair, my head dragged back until I'm looking into his unshaven face.

'I'm not in the mood, Rachel – get that? I'll pay you later, but right now I need you to meet Gerry – okay? Meet Gerry, get me sorted out, and we'll have some fun later, okay?'

He shouldn't speak to me like that. He shouldn't take me for granted. I mean, what if I hadn't come round? What if I ran away? I could still run away. I swallow the hard lump in my throat and take the paper he's holding out to me. I won't look at him.

'The cannon on Carlton Hill. Take his number in case he doesn't show. He's got red hair and a beard. You'll need three hundred – I won't forget this.'

I get money from the ATM on Dundas – it'll leave me short, he'll need to repay me today. When I get there, there's no one. I sit on one of the seats that stare down Princes Street and check my voicemail.

There is one from India, of course.

> *Hi. I was wrong. He took those photos years ago – everything's great. Sorry to be such a pain – we're on our way to Skye for a romantic weekend. See you!*

What the hell's she talking about? That'll be David, I suppose? Does she honestly think I give a fuck about her petty day-to-day little dramas? No, India, I don't. I pretend I do, but I don't.

I'm back by three. Ryan's curled up in bed. The dope – enough to last me a week, is all gone, the foil licked clean on the duvet. I massage the soft bag in my pocket – he'd kill for it, he would – and click the edge of the hard square brick beside it, working a sliver loose. He's dreaming. His face is twitching and his jaws are working hard, his fists are clamped around the sheets, white knuckles gleaming through brown skin. I know those dreams. As quietly as I can, I crouch down beside the bed and make the merest breath of a stroke along his temple. He wakes instantly.

ABI

How DO YOU TURN A smelly old mattress into a soft feather bed?

'So where have you been, young lady?'

'Hi, Mum. Oh, Mum, you've nicked my question – not got one of your own?'

'I'm your mum, Abi. Oh forget it. I'm making brunch. Want some?'

'Just coffee. I'm not hungry.'

'You're not eating, Abi. Look at you – you're all bone.'

'Forget the coffee – I'm going to bed.'

'Abi!'

'Leave it, Mum, I'm not in the mood.' I need sleep. I need sleep.

I stand at the end of my bed and fall backwards. My bed, my wonderful bed. Oh God, *Ash's* was so minging. I tell you I won't be staying at his unless we go mattress shopping. I even loved my body, I did, I loved it. I was beautiful. For a few hours the world was beautiful. For a few hours I felt totally at peace and in love with the world, in love with the world, in love with Ash – in love with everyone there. Now I need sleep, my bed and sleep, so just carry on dear Mother with what you're doing and leave me be – there's a good girl.

How do you turn a mattress full of rocks into a feather bed? Easy mate – take a pill. I think I've forgotten the punch line –

something about a hat, dropping a hat, something like that, but pill's the best way innit?

Can't decide whether to tell her. I don't think she'd mind, not really, not if I got her in a good mood. No one dies of ecstasy, not if you're careful and drink water. And Ash was really good explaining everything, and everything. I needed a break, that's the whole point. He was so right. A break from my malfunctioning lifestyle. A wee break, surely even I deserve that once in a while. No one could blame me for a little time out, could they? Get away from thinking about all the shit that's going down round here for a few hours.

He said I was beautiful, more beautiful by far than Mum, said some pretty heavy things about her, in fact. Said she was mucking Toni around, and that families matter from where he comes from – like a dig at Mum, obviously. So tell me something I don't know. She's like a child, never thinks things through. You can tell the way she eyes me up sometimes, can't help herself: what if I get prettier than her? She totally thinks that – unbelievable. Well for one, I never will be, and for another she's not even meant to think like that, is she?

No good asking where's she been for the last two nights. I'm so sick of lying for her – how was I supposed to know she hadn't been with Toni? Fuck it, *she'll* have to sort it out, I've got my own life now, more important things to take care of, like stopping this massive lump on my chin from turning into some monstrous pluke.

Ten minutes later I'm trying to get some shuteye.

'Now what, Mum?'

'Jamie called. You awake?' she says through the door.

'S'pose. What did you tell him?'

'Told him you'd gone to a party. Why? Shouldn't I?'

'Fine. Now please, Mum.'

'How was it anyway – the party?'

'Fine.'

'And Toni – how was he?'

'For God's sake, Mum.' I drag myself up on one elbow. 'Come in then. Okay, I'm awake now. So what do you want to know – that he looked suicidal? Well yes he did, what do you expect? He was in a relationship, a perfectly good relationship actually.

You've only been with him for a few weeks – so where were you anyway?'

'Yeah, well, you've seen him pawing at me – you've seen him – what was I meant to do?'

'How would I know? Just not what you did, yeah? Get real, Mum, you were the one that pulled, or have you forgotten? Someone else come along? Is that where you've been?'

'No, actually I haven't. I stayed with Dawn, ask her if you want. I'm allowed time out with my friends, aren't I?'

'Yeah, yeah. I just feel sorry for him, that's all …'

'He's a grown-up, Abi. If he wasn't up for it he should have stayed with what's-her-face. He's an idiot, he makes my flesh crawl. In fact I'm leaving work, that's what I've been talking over with Dawn. She knows someone with a nice restaurant needing a manager – she's going to set something up for next week.'

It's impossible to know whether she's telling the truth. I just go with it, can't be arsed, just can't be bothered with it. And she's right, he'll get over it.

'Okay right. Now I'm going to sleep, don't wake me for anyone. Have you phoned Dad yet?'

'Just about to – *Mother*. You got the landline?'

Andrew

I SLIP AWAY, SHIFT Callum's head gently to the cushion and creep into the kitchen.

I spend too much time checking my phone. I'm always imagining I must have muted it, that she might have been calling, checking the call log, pulling up my messages, metering out the minutes before I can call her again, wondering who she's been speaking to if I get the busy tone. I'm a mess.

'Can I speak to Megan please?'

'Is that you, Andrew? It's Rhona. How are you? Things not so good at your end I gather – I'm sorry …'

'Apologies, Rhona. I didn't recognise your voice – thought you were still on the west. How was it? That must be pretty hard too – going back I mean.'

'Oh well, yes and no, Andrew. The weather was glorious; it felt like going home in a way, and considering we'd only been there three years. It's a very magical place. Strange with Liz gone though, sad to see the cottage empty. How is she?'

'Oh fine, I suppose. Her times out of reality are getting progressively worse – her long-term memory, well – it's quite hard to take, especially for Callum. On the other hand we've been incredibly lucky to find Harry.'

'Oh dear, you do have a lot on your plate. Megan's right here, champing at the bit of course. Ouch. God, she never used to be this demanding. Why don't you come for supper – get out the house for a while?'

'I'd love to, but I'll need to see how Callum is. No, actually that'd be great – he's got a friend round tonight and I can't go anywhere for the next few days because Liz is finally moving, so things will be a bit frantic. Thanks – I'll ask Harry.'

'Well, that'll be good for everyone, won't it, in the end – Liz I mean. Listen, I'll see you later, then. Here's Megan.'

'Hello you. That'll be nice. Hang on a minute,' she says.

'Megan?'

'Just shutting the door. Come early will you? Mum's exhausted. Whatever she says she's shattered after driving back. In a good way, I guess, but let's make it an early supper.'

'Well maybe another time if you think—'

'No, I don't think. She'd love to see you and strangely enough, so would I. Any chance you can stay over?'

'I can't – I need to be here in the mornings.'

'You are there most mornings, Andrew.'

'Callum is really down, Megan, and—'

'I know Andrew, I know he is, but I'm not sure you being there all the time helps. Surely India and Harry can manage, I mean they're putting him to bed aren't they, *and* he's got a friend staying over? I mean, maybe he might like you to have a little time off. Still, it's up to you – you do what you think best.'

'I'm sorry. I just think for now – especially if I'm not here to say goodnight. You don't mind do you? Things are beginning to build – that's why I rang actually – I've had a letter from her lawyers. She's going for it, Megan, and it makes sense – the way it's told makes very good sense. I can't really get my head around it, but it could happen, you know. I might lose them both. She doesn't work full-time, she's starting to ingratiate herself at Heels, India's searching frantically for a house because she hates me. God almighty, Megan, even *I* think it sounds plausible.'

'It's her word against yours, Andrew. It's one thing to think you can lie in court and quite another to actually do it, but that's what lawyers are good at – that's what you're meant to think. What does Abi say?'

'How should I know? She rang to say that she wasn't coming over today – I feel so helpless.'

'If, and that's a big *if* – *if* it actually comes to court, we may well be able to convince the courts that's she's becoming unwell in her mother's care. She was doing so well, wasn't she?'

'Maybe.' Maybe. But they'll both deny it – especially Abi – the main symptom of this fucking illness being 'denial'. Oh my God, I can feel this awful crisis rising up: a guy with a knife in the dark. No one can do anything – not Megan, not anyone. I never dreamt … I mean, this is not right, this is not meant to happen. 'But yes, she was, yes, thanks – you're right. It might not go that far, and with your professional opinion … But I should get a lawyer, shouldn't I? I mean I should, shouldn't I?'

'Let's talk about it tonight, with Mum – okay?'

'Okay.'

I've got to contain it – I can't just dump on her every time we speak. She's got her own stuff going down.

'Andrew? We'll get through this – she's probably bluffing. You know what she's like. Try not to worry.'

I spend the rest of the day longing for the evening.

David calls. Guy's been moaning about me taking so much time off – no surprises there then. We speak briefly about a new job in Skye; he was up there last weekend talking to the locals about proposals for a wind farm, trying to placate the community, educate them, talking to the press of course. I wonder if that's where India was. I had Guy on the phone sniffing around, asking awkward questions. To be honest, it's the last thing I need right now. Why the hell don't they just tell the poor sod?

'Was India with you, only Guy was snooping around.' My choice of words suggest a certain collusion between us, which I regret.

'Maybe you don't know this, Andrew, but India is a very confused young lady. I've told her dozens of times I'm not interested, but she won't listen, follows me around like a wounded puppy. Maybe you could have a word. It seems to me like she has a very imaginative imagination, if you get my meaning. To be honest I did flirt with her, but it's over, over weeks ago. Now, that really fucks me off.' I picture him shaking his head in disbelief.

Hallelujah. I apologise. I feel comforted, released. I tell him that nothing surprises me about India – that she did the same to me and that it's such a relief to actually find someone else she's targeted. He couldn't be friendlier. I find myself apologising for Guy's recent paranoia.

'Just as well the Leith job was given the all-clear then, wasn't it? No worries mate, I'd be doing the same in his shoes and he's right, you'd look good on the box. I'm just glad there are no hard feelings between us. I owe you one, Andrew – it can't have been easy with Guy bending your ear. You've been a good mate. And don't worry, as far as I'm concerned we were together right down the line, don't want to upset the boss now do we?'

Well that's something. We replace our handsets bosom buddies, and my serenity stays with me for all of three minutes.

Callum watches telly most of the afternoon and Abi shows up as though she never cancelled this morning. She has dark circles under her eyes, but is wildly cheerful in spite of this.

I have begun to shuffle, literally. I wonder how it would be if Megan … I'd be on my knees too afraid to move. She's like a safe house. Every nerve and fibre of my body longs for her minute by minute, hour after hour, and even this makes me feel guilty, because my children have nothing to long or hope for and the assassin is closing in.

I try to shrug my gloomy thoughts away. It is good to see the children together as they climb the stairs to Callum's room – to force myself to think of something positive about the imminent massacre of our family. The courts attach great importance to the children staying together. So maybe they're right. Well of course they're right, it's been horrible without her – but it's not that simple, is it? And Abi will most likely be away in a couple of years.

They're laughing – my children are laughing. I can hear them from here and I'm gripped by a terrible dread.

I get to Megan's about six thirty and let myself in – my legs are like jelly.

'Hi Andrew.' Megan hugs me hard and then peels away, taking my soul with her. I follow her into the kitchen.

'Hi Rhona. Smells great – curry?'

'Yes, Thai: from the internet. I get loads of stuff off it these days – don't I, Megan?'

Megan throws me a grimace-cum-grin.

Rhona continues. 'What'll you have to drink, wine, sherry or gin? That's about it, I think. Megan?'

A house without tension – a pale golden oasis and I try to breathe some of it in.

I could have stayed, I wish I were staying. Callum doesn't benefit from my intense caring and if I'm honest I can see how much it suffocates him. I fix my eyes on Megan's, and slide into the window seat. 'I'll join you in a sherry please, Rhona.'

'For Christ's sake, Andrew – she likes you already.'

'Ignore her, Andrew. This is a very dry, light amontillado. Absolutely delicious.'

'Mum, there's smoke coming from the oven – something's burning.'

'Good, it's ready then. Open this wine, will you, Andrew? I meant to do it earlier.'

'Megan?' I venture some hours later, after we have made love for the forty-fourth time (ha! not so very drunk after all).

'Megan?'

'Yes.'

'Don't you mind that most of the time I'm confused and unhappy and act like an idiot?'

'Not really.'

'Okay then, because you know, I'd hate for you to be under the impression that I'm like you or Rhona – you know, coping.'

'It's okay, Andrew, I'm not. I accept you're neurotic. Now, it's four o'clock, I don't think we've slept yet and I'm getting up in three hours and if you're staying then please shut up and let me sleep. I know you're a mess, okay – does that make you feel better?'

'Yes thank you – that feels good.' I lie gazing at the lightest down on her jawbone – and within a few minutes her steady insistent snoring seems to be urging me to either sleep or go. I go.

CALL BILLY

On my way home, I pick up David's new car in my rear-view mirror cruising down Broughton Street. India is with him. I don't think they've seen me and by the time I hear the front door clunk shut, fifteen minutes later, I'm in bed. I want to call Megan, but I daren't till the morning. I'm no longer tired, so I lie staring up at the ceiling watching the occasional car headlights push through my window, bounce off the walls and leave. Then I hear faint sobbing coming from India's room. I place one of my pillows firmly over my head and punch it into my ear.

Abi

It was nice to talk to Rosie, I guess. But it's not the same anymore is it, nothing's the same anymore. And I'm hardly going to blab that I'm scared my boyfriend might be cheating on me, and have all my old Oban mates calling me a loser – duh? In fact I don't know why she keeps calling – it's not like we speak about anything real.

And I've been staring at this sum for about twenty minutes – makes no sense at all, never will. My brain feels like it's turned into sludge, just can't be arsed with it all. Maybe tea will help. On my way through to the kitchen I tread on the fairy lights Mum bought yesterday – fucking stupid place to leave them, as if a few lights is all you need for a happy Christmas. And like, why would I want to go to Dad's for Christmas Eve, making out we're some kind of family for a few hours – like they care? If it wasn't for Callum and being there with him to open his stocking, there'd be no way I'd have said yes – no fucking way. At least Mum's got some kind of a Christmas do on at her restaurant. And as for Christmas dinner, how's this for happy families? Cos we're having ours with Dawn and her kids and her ex, while Dad's having his with Rhona and Megan and Tom which'll be crap anyway, cos they'll be missing Brendon, and so we'll all be miserable won't we?

Bollocks, she's home.

No need to shout, Mum, or slam the door – I can tell you're back by the rank smell of tobacco and booze.

'Hello, darling. Look at you, working away. Well done *you*. How you getting on then? How's the essay going?'

She's peering at the text book.

'See those, Mum? Numbers, maths, sums. Thought you were coming home early today.'

'Oh yeah, so they are. Clever you. I was, but in the end it was the only time Dawn could meet me about the court thing. No don't worry, she's not going to say anything bad about Dad, just going to say about me going to live with her, how upset I was and everything. Do you mind?'

'Nope.'

'Right. Well, I'm not back for long now either – what are you doing tonight?'

'Seeing Ash. Why?'

'No need to sound so defensive, I was just hoping you weren't going to be alone again. How is he?'

'He's good. And I like being alone. I'll be fine.'

I don't ask where she's going anymore – no point. As soon as she's left my room, I throw the maths at the wall, but I can still see it, so I crawl over and stuff it under my bed, click on the telly.

'Finished already?'

Like she's interested. They all think I've done my prelims and now I'm working steadily towards the summer exams. We are so close, me and my family.

'Roll us a joint then, darling, and come and chat to me. Been missing you. Everything okay? Ash okay?'

'I said he was, didn't I? Where is it?'

'On the bedside table. You don't need much, go easy with it, will you?'

As I'm cooking it up, I break off a bit, at least if he shows we'll have something to smoke.

'Thanks, sweetie. Be an angel will you and put a bit of toast on for me – I've not eaten yet. Thanks, darling. Did you do the shopping?'

'Err, well, yes – who do you think did it? Which reminds me, have you got some cash? I've done the shopping twice now out of my own money.'

'Some. But I need to pay bills and you are earning, and you do smoke my dope you know.'

'Fine. What about the lawyer? Did you see him?'

'Of course. Is that what you're worried about? Well don't be. Everyone thinks we're going to win.'

'I thought it wasn't about winning. I thought this was about me and Callum and what was best for us.'

'You know what I mean, darling. You sure you're okay?'

I hear the toast popping up and give her a dirty look as I turn away. 'Yep. Just think it's a bit unfair that Sarah and India are going to speak against Dad … and now Dawn. I thought you'd fallen out with Dawn.'

'They're not speaking against Dad, darling. They're speaking up for me – it's totally different.'

'Well you would say that wouldn't you? Just hate it, that's all.'

I slop jam on her toast and take it through to her bedroom. She's sitting at her dressing table.

'Saw Gran today,' I say, knowing this'll rile her.

'Where?' She hands me the joint, starts backcombing her hair.

'At the residential place. It's lovely, Mum. She goes full-time soon.'

'Great,' she says, flattening a blue scarf over her forehead and tying it at the nape of her neck. 'Do you think this suits me, or would orange be better?'

I tell her it looks great.

'I thought I'd drop in on Gran one of these days.'

'Oh, really?' I hand her back the roach.

'Yes, really.'

'Why's that then?'

'She's my mother, Abi, and she's not ill enough to be thrown into a home.'

'This is all because of going to court isn't it? Same with going to Heels so often – it's just so you can say—'

'No of course it isn't, Abi. I just feel better about things, and

I love going to Heels – if uni hadn't been so demanding I would always have gone.'

'I remember when we first moved here, Mum, you said Dad—'

She gives me one of her 'back off' looks, grabs the second half of her toast along with her jacket and swoops out, flicking her wrist at me. I follow her through, don't know why.

'For God's sake, darling, leave it will you? Why do you have to remember every little thing I do wrong, whether it's about Dawn or Heels or Toni. It's all the same, you just use it to have a go. I'm not perfect, okay – never ever said I was – and if I … Well, all I'm saying is, Abi darling, no one's forcing you to do anything. Just stop stressing over everything so much, it's not good for you. Why don't you just try to appreciate what you have?'

'Like?'

She turns round, grabs her keys off the table.

'Like being with a parent who lets you have your own life. I mean, just look how things have changed for the better for you – leaving school, being able to explore stuff that would be absolutely banned if we still lived with your father. Honestly Abi, you don't know how lucky you are.'

'S'pose.'

'Why don't you just concentrate on this evening and relax for once, stop being so suspicious of everything? You're turning quite bitter you know.' And then she's gone.

It's true really, what she says. I know I'm being a bitch most of the time, but I feel so crap about everything. I just can't believe this is happening. Maybe dope is making me paranoid; maybe it's me that's the problem. After all, in an hour's time my fanfuckingtastic boyfriend is coming round, we'll smoke a bit more, watch the sexiest DVD of all time, and then he'll make slow divine love to me – and here I am having a go at her. Why don't I stop a minute and picture the same scene at Dad's? Err, no, I don't think so. So maybe I should do what she says and try to be grateful.

Six thirty. I run a bath, fill it with bubbles and almost fall
asleep in it, stoned dreams fading in and out my vision. It's nice.
Mum's doing her best. From tomorrow I'm going to be nicer,
try to understand what it's like for her without Cal, try to think
more positively.

I borrow Mum's floor-length white towelling dressing gown
but can't decide whether it makes me look fat or not. Ash says
I'm beautiful. Fitter than my mum anyway – which is so cute
considering he's lying. I pull the cord tighter, turn this way and
that – we are going to have such a cool evening. I throw the
packets of nuts and stuff and the DVD on the table, pour myself
a vodka, and turn on *EastEnders*.

It's ten, yeah. Get real, Abi. He's not coming. Don't know why
I thought he would. Practically had to beg him – well not *beg*
maybe, but bribe – fucking obvious he only said yes to get me off
his back, or because he was guilty for having been a shit all week.
So why didn't the scumbag just say?

So how does Mum do it, I mean how does she just get them
falling all over her? Toni's still in a crap mood all day every day –
well, kerching, it's fucking obvious isn't it? Mum's beautiful and
sexy and confident and I'm fat and ugly and Mum only tells me
I'm skinny because she doesn't want the competition. And it's
totally obvious to anyone but Muggins here that he only wanted
one thing anyway. I knew what he was like, didn't I? I should
never have told him it was my first time, and now that he's had
me, well, it's obvious, isn't it – no one wants a tart. No one but
saddo Jamie.

No point in saving this is there? Might as well skin it up and
get more wrecked, more paranoid, more fucking unhappy. I
make myself hot chocolate and get into bed, stare at the balloon
pattern on my duvet. 'Virgin', my whole room shouts 'virgin'. I
hate my life. The twisted paper tip, which I should have chewed
off, flares up and drops, melts a small hole in one of the balloons.
I take a puff and nudge it around, so what if I burn the house
down. It fizzes out anyway. I hold each draw down and go on
holding till my chest is bursting and I'm totally wasted. A kind

of fog coats the flicking pain in my tummy with something soft. I can hear the sea though. Roaring. Like when Dad used to put sea shells to my ears. Being nowhere is better than being somewhere. I rest the flattened butt on the edge of my bedside table. Sagging into my pillows I can reach that sound if I stretch far enough with my toes – I can imagine I'm an eel and I'm flipping somersaults and I'm dizzy spinning over and over in this like bright green frothy wave that just keeps on coming.

ANDREW

'MEGAN? YOU'LL NEVER guess what's happened.'

'So tell me, Romeo.'

'Callum's shown me his stash – can you believe it? He actually took me upstairs and into his wardrobe where he showed me the things he'd taken from school … Aw, he was so sweet. It wasn't even as though he actually felt that guilty even. I mean, why didn't he? If I'd—'

'That was the whole point wasn't it?'

'What?'

'He didn't feel guilty, Andrew, because Heels didn't put those sorts of values on it. His behaviour wasn't criminal, was it? Actually, I'm not even going there with you – we've been over it enough times. I'm glad he did, that's all, he must be feeling safer. Be grateful.'

'Oh God! Yes I know, I know, and I've rung Marion, and she was great of course. But it was just so terrifying for me to see him so wretched and shut off, and now, well, yes I know I'm a bigger prat than ever but please, please come round, please, because I've just got to see you this instant. I'm so relieved Megan – it's been so awful.'

'Okay, yes, but let's go for a walk. Honestly, Andrew—'

'I know, I know – you'll never know how much I know. Isn't

it great though? I mean not the 'prat' of course, I mean that's just crap, obviously, but Callum, you know that … that he took me there!'

'Yes, Andrew. It's marvellous – it's just great.'

I'm hardly ever in the manicured wilderness that lies beyond these gates on account of there being no dogs allowed, hence Nevis and I are always looking longingly at it from the barren wastes of what remains of Inverleith Park. Not for long though. Finally, in January, the Botanic Gardens is opening its gates to the canine population – about time too.

Megan is early, blowing into her gloves, glancing at her watch. I wave and she smiles and hurries towards me and we link arms and go through the park gates and walk briskly, heads down.

I'm struck by an odd sharpness to the air. Not cold sharp, though it is cold, bitterly cold, but it's not that – it's more of an electric tension felt on the scalp as if something is waiting to happen. I remember yesterday, how the pines glowed lime-green against a yellowing sky. Today they are blue, blue-green and fernlike, a child's painting on deep mauve brushstrokes.

I listen. I'm all ears. If there is sound, I can't hear it: no birds, none of the usual kids' voices. I am reminded of a stage where the curtains have gone up and no actors have appeared, and I'm sure she feels it too. I tug my glove off and hold her hand tight. I am so glad I have hands so I can hold hers and for some time I'm simply glad for everything in my life that has led me to Megan. Countless 'what-ifs', incalculable coincidences, have tripped me along blindly until I've arrived. I am in love – in love! Could it be she doesn't know? Could it be that she's in some doubt – doesn't understand that she's the pivot upon which my fragile universe depends? She might not … she might not know that unless she's with me till I die – I'll die? Well, how would she?

I pull her around. The air is charged with electricity, no mistaking it now, fizzing with it. I take centre stage, clasp my hands together, bend a knee and wobble ungraciously to the ground.

She looks around – probably for help.

'Megan, I want you to marry me, to be my wife, my best friend and mentor. Please will you? Will you promise to continue to be my reason for getting up in the morning and my reason for going to bed?' A low rumble – God's orchestra probably, shakes the ground beneath our feet. Several people stop feeding the ducks, check out the sky and turn towards us. Some move away, imagining the rumble is a storm warning. But I don't care – I have just been moved to ask the most important question in my life, and all of a sudden I don't feel anything but confidence and joy and excitement.

At the margin of my vision a rabble of ducks is heading over. I've always found ducks to be a bit threatening and persistent once you start feeding them, especially en masse. Any pause and they switch to automatic, robotically padding towards the food source. Their bodies may be little, but there's something unmanageable and hardcore and pushy about them. And if pushy moves to attack and you grab them, their feathers, like alien limbs, come away in your hands – gives me the willies. But right now all it does is unnerve me to such an extent that whatever entrenched patterns I ignored thirty seconds ago slam into my brain now and almost knock me over. My knees are aching, early rheumatoid arthritis probably, and it occurs to me that I am already married – okay, okay, only legally, but these things matter don't they when you ask someone to marry you. And even if it didn't, *matter*, this is merely the winciest pothole when compared to some of the massive roadblocks that are erupting like mines on the long desolate highway to hell, which for a few pathetic moments I had smudged clean away.

Breathe man, breath.

God – how could I forget, how could I do anything so dumb? My past races in front of my eyes, along with a lightning flash, I swear, lightning – real as you like – as with horrific clarity I relive my most poignant moments: I place her in impossible positions, make lunatic demands on her time and sympathy, virtually ignore the grief she is going through while demanding full attention to my own trail of unhappy dramas. I withhold secrets, misread our relationship almost entirely and without compromise, behave like a selfish prig and blame her for my depression. Pictures and snippets whiz by. While avoiding looking at Megan, I prepare to bolt from the ducks who are barely six feet away and sneak a glance at the faces of our loyal but misguided audience, and it's blindingly obvious that they are already feeling terribly sorry for me.

I can't stand now anyway, my knees have locked – how the hell did I get down here? I bet she's really enjoying this, really rubbing my nose in it big time – and it's all my fault. From now on, the Botanics and winter and gloves and my knees even will forever be associated with humiliation and shame. Oh God.

'I'd love to.'

Little claps from the crowd, and Julia Roberts bends down to pick up the now prostrate Hugh Grant who has fainted, but despite being quite unconscious he is still babbling on like an idiot. 'I'm sorry, I should never … I mean, I don't know what came … Oh Christ, I'm a bastard, what an impossible position. Please, just forget I ever—'

'Oh do shut up, Andrew. I will, I'd love to. I'm thrilled you asked me – you left it long enough.'

I'm on my feet now, kicking wildly at the earth, trying to get my head around it. Giant blobs of rain hide my tears and the ducks flutter about in feigned panic.

'Come on, you lunatic. It's about to piss down, I'm starving, and you're due back for Liz in an hour.' She wraps me in a hug and for a blissful moment we rock and turn circles under an opening sky. Thank you, God.

ANDREW

I ORDER A COUPLE of beers and notice I've got the shakes.

'So, Andrew, I gather congratulations are in order: the lovely Megan. Cheers. She'll make a wonderful wife, well done.'

'Thanks. Can I ask you something, David?'

'Anything you like – fire away.'

'You know what we talked about the other day?'

'Remind me, Andrew – we do work together.'

'About whether India was with you in Skye?'

'Vaguely. Why?'

'I checked, well, not checked so much as took a call from one of the delegates who was at the seminar you gave, and it came up.'

'So I lied. Not a biggie, is it?'

'Not in itself, no, but I wondered why, that was all. The lie, well it wasn't just a lie, it was, well, very damning, very elaborate. I mean it's left me with a bad taste, in fact the whole thing with India and Guy is beginning to get to me. I've tried not to let it, but I'm beginning to feel like an accomplice, like I approve. To be honest, it's making working with Guy rather awkward.'

'Know how you feel, mate – covering up for your absences on the Leith job puts me under a hell of a strain. What do you think we should do? Spill the beans? Make a clean sweep of things?'

'Come on, David, it's hardly the same thing. I'm his mate. He talks to me about India, a lot.'

'It may not be the same thing for you, but I find it slightly weird that you presume to know how I feel about it.'

'Can't you encourage India to dump him at least? Stop the deceit?'

He laughs. 'I find it amusing. I find it hilarious. Call it a job perk. Pulling the boss's bird has always been, err, a hobby, a kind of gamble. India would love to dump the old wrinkly, but I won't let her. It amuses me – if he dumps her, or she dumps him, there's a knock-on effect: I lose interest. She gives me all the details, makes them up probably, but so long as it's good I don't care. Poor old Guy, eh?'

'Is that why you were sacked from your last job?'

'Been doing some homework have you, Andrew?'

'No. Megan saw a profile on you.'

'You're too soft, Andrew. I owe you one for getting me this job, and now I owe you another, and that's precisely why I'm prepared to keep schtum about the Leith samples. Don't look so glum – just be grateful it isn't you she's shagging. Same again please.'

I leave David to it and head into town to get presents for Christmas. I have cobbled together a vague list and pull it up on my phone. A new jacket for Abi, a basic computer game for Callum – along with the usual stocking fillers and extras. I'm hoping a couple of hours of retail should calm me down but I seem incapable of putting things aside and David's words are still twisting my gut into painful knots two hours later.

I call Megan.

'So what should I do? I mean God, what a bastard – he was blackmailing me, Megan, virtually. And poor India – what the hell did she do to deserve a creep like him?'

'Hold on a minute! Am I missing something here? I thought you'd told Guy about missing that afternoon.'

'Well no. You said, just do whatever was professional.'

'Yes, and I also said, if I remember rightly, that you should tell him. Is that it?'

'What do you mean?'

'I guess I mean, is that the only thing David's guarding for you?'

'Well no, not exactly, nearly, but not quite. David took the samples to the lab – and before you say anything, I couldn't be that petty, he was going right past their door. I was with Callum – he was ill. Come on, Megan, Guy was being paranoid. David may be a chancer, but he's not a criminal – Guy was being an arsehole. For God's sake this is ludicrous – what shall I do?'

'Talk to Guy. It's probably time some shit hit the fan. David's a wanker. Guy'll forgive you and I don't see that you've got much of a choice here do you? And to be honest David's a professional liability. Get rid of him, Andrew – it's only a matter of time before he starts playing around with Eco Écosse.'

'Great, just fucking great. Tell Guy that I didn't research him properly, that I never checked out his references, that I skived when asked specifically to do something by my boss, not once but twice – fucking brilliant.'

'Just do it, darling – sooner, rather than later. And while you're at it, you should talk to India – or speak to Sarah. But to be honest, she'll probably sort it out herself and she might not thank you for interfering. I barely know the girl, do I?'

She pauses for a fraction to long. 'Tap into your famous intuition – it could do with a bit of exercise.'

I get to the office early. Wanker David is already there.

'Guy?'

'Yes.'

'I need a word.'

'No can do, I'm afraid. You've forgotten I'm flying to Orkney today and I'm already late – I'm meant to be at the airport in forty minutes.'

'Shit, yes. When are you back?'

'For God's sake, Andrew – don't you have a diary?'

'Yes, yes, of course, day after tomorrow isn't it? So can we—'

'I'm actually pretty much out of the office till I get back from Paris on Monday. That's if the weather holds up and planes are flying – I gather it's been snowing over there. If it can't wait, email me. Have you seen that conference information on sustainable cod farming – the red folder?'

'Yep over there.' I nod. 'David, it's on your desk.'

David throws the perfect frisbee. Guy only has to open his hand.

'Right then folks – don't bunk off to the shops the minute I'm out the door. Andrew, that means you too.'

Very droll – very fucking droll. Still, a few day's grace is very welcome – get the whole Christmas thing over and done with. Now where's she off to? 'India – are you leaving?'

'Just saying goodbye to Guy. Then yes, I don't work Wednesday afternoons do I?'

'Okay yeah, forgot. Callum and I are out tonight at the Heel's Christmas dinner and then he's staying with a friend and I'll go on to Megan's – okay?'

'Yeah fine. Liz?'

'She's got another night at Fairweathers.'

David doesn't even look up, smug bastard – just answers a call, grabs his jacket and makes for the door himself.

Ryan

EVERYTHING'S DONE. Snoop as much as you like – you'll find nothing here, baby. Been a while since I felt so friggin' sorted: tickets, passport, new gear, all snugged up in a locker in Waverley. I leave a week today. Winston is due back the day before I go. I will meet him at the airport and have the cab drive us direct to The Witchery for their special Christmas Eve dinner, where I have booked a room. Everything will be just the way he likes it. We will wine and dine that evening and take a late breakfast. We'll spend the following morning at Scotland Street. I'll speak about the trauma of the repairs and we'll marvel at the neatness of the job. He'll be impressed. After lunch, one of us will fetch a few things for the evening meal. Either way I'll head for the station, collect my things from left luggage and catch my train to London. I will leave him a letter, though right now I'm not sure how much I'll tell him. Maybe everything, maybe a piece of it. And he'll forgive me, just because that's the kind of man he is.

Come on, Gerry, answer the phone. He never said anything about going away, I've been calling three days now – pick up, cunt.

First thing I'm going to do, after finding me a chilled-out Rasta, is a tourist trip around the island, stay a few days in a nice hotel in Montego Bay and hit the beach, man – it's the perfect time of year out there. Then I'll track down my daddy, trace some family. He'll most likely be dead, man, but I still need to pay my respects. I am what he made me, I need to see his grave, say goodbye once and for all. When I've done that I'll set myself up in business, buy a beach café, enjoy the good life, make a few friends.

Hell, that sounds good.

I roll out of bed, make some coffee and settle down to finish off last night's movie, keep my mind busy, till fatso picks up. I'm stiff, man: sore cock, sore balls. Bruce Steroid Willis: now that's a torso to envy – someone gives him a battering and he doesn't even dent. Fucking mental, man. Oomph!

I'm sick of this town. Sick of looking for Angel Eyes; been up on that hill most days, been all the places those kids hang out. He's gone man, dead most likely, pushed too hard and some blessed dude's gone and finished him off. To be honest I've lost the taste for revenge – too much hassle – I've got a future now, away from this piss pot of junkies.

I roll my post-breakfast draw and place my last few crystals on some fresh foil for later.

Maybe I won't wait. Just thinking about that cunt's got me twitching. Beautiful. I hold it down in my lungs till I'm cruising through heaven. Jesus, fucking Jesus, I swear my head's floating someplace in Nirvana. Wrong. I have no head. Just a smile in paradise, floating someplace away from all the shit. Woo, can't move. No need to move – cool. Come on, baby, come on Brucey baby, kick arse man, fucking kick her butt. That's funny, man – that's so funny. Now I come to think of it even Gerry's probably dead meat. That's funny too – shit that's funny: Gerry's dead, Gerry's dead. Mean cunts these guys – they'll kill you if you so much as look sideways at them. All dead. And then I get this idea, a flashing idea, like a beacon right between my eyes. Jazzer's junkie friend. I've been seeing that smack-head, every day one hour on from the day before, every day, meeting his faggots, doing his petty deals – punk. So maybe he killed Jazzer. Who cares? Who the fuck cares, man? These punks care for nothing but their dirty habit.

I try calling Gerry one last time – picture him lying in a gutter with a knife in his back, his phone singing out his funeral march.

I take a shower, consider shaving off my two-day growth, but don't. At two fifteen I snort up the last few crystals. A splinter of cold metal shoots up behind my right eye. Then my left. My tubes are fucked. I've been spotting blood. I should ease up. I will. Soon.

I know the punk don't know me, but just in case I put on Winston's black wool coat and mohair hat.

I walk fast; it's only just past three but the sun is already low. For no good reason I have a dumb tune my dad used to sing, mooching round my brain.

> Show me the way to go home,
> I'm tired and I wanna go to bed
> I had a little drink about an hour ago, but it's gone
>   right to my head
> wherever you may roam, on land or sea or foam
> you'll always hear me singing this song,
> show me the way to go home …

Twenty-five years it's been since I heard that song. So anyway, fuck me, cos just as I'm humming my way down the alley behind the cinema, and thinking how pretty the trees look in this fading light, I swear I see those white corkscrew curls, bobbing gently up and down, pressed against the crotch of some giant mother-fucking piece of horse shit.

I stay in the shadows, move behind the big fella; my new teeth grinding. Can't ten seconds go by without some bullshit cropping up? I guess it must be the tune, or a mixture of the tune and the drugs, or the fact that I'm already flying away from this dump. Whatever the reason, I'm not angry anymore, can't be fucked, poor miserable sod.

And then something strange happens: maybe it's the big fella, maybe he's about to climax, or maybe Jazzer can smell me – whatever – cos before I turn to go, his mother-fucking eyes fly open and lock into mine.

As I said, I'd nothing planned. But the shock of those pale blue eyes impact someplace out of reach, somewhere in my subconscious, must have. Before I know it, I hear myself sprouting this bullshit, nice and slow, that I just been diagnosed with Hep C and that they'd better head on down to the clinic. Shoot. Soon as I'm through speaking, that mean cunt grabs those child's ringlets as if they were coils of rope – or maybe Jazzer just bit the bitch. I think he's been bitten. He twists Jazzer's head towards me, drags him to his feet, and zips up all in one move.

'What the fuck's goin' on, like?'

'Nuttin' man, the fuckin' poofs a fuckin' liar. Ah swear, Ah've never seen the fuckin' radge afore.'

I keep on going – start humming that dumb tune and keep on walking – I've got stuff to do while I'm still high.

I take a seat, read the paper in the fading light, my fingers fumbling with the cold. But I'm smiling too, feeling lucky that I'm not Jazzer right now, my ears straining as I try to figure out if it's crows roosting in the trees or Cunt Blockhead seeing to Jazzer. Whatever.

Here comes the dude, mongrel at his heels. He's careful. Same every day – no money changing hands. Just handshakes and the gear's passed over. Small deals. I'm gonna make his day. I take my time, make sure the punters have done.

After business he shambles off to circle the tower, gazing out over Edinburgh as if he's interested in the views. He even nods at the locals who live on the hill's fringe as they walk their posh dogs before the light goes and the hill slides quickly into an underworld of pervs and poofters. I wait till he's round the corner and walk in the opposite direction so I meet him face to face. His shaggy dog trots towards me. I stoop to make friends and give him some biscuits I bought specially. Cool dog. I'd like a dog – one day I'm gonna get a dog. As his master lopes self-consciously towards us I'm smiling, crouching down and ruffling his shaggy mane. Good boy. He folds down and rolls over and I'm grinning first at Lassie here and then in a friendly way at his boss.

'Nice dog you got, okay if I give him some biscuits?'

'No worries. Go ahead mate.'

'What's his name?'

'Dofo. After the pet shop that used tae be doon Leith Walk. His ma wis' a favourite so it wis' an obvious choice.'

'Can I ask you something?' He stiffens like I'm honking … 'It's okay, man, a mate told me about you.'

'Away tae fuck. Who's he when he's at hame then pawl, and told ye what onyways?'

'Gandalf man. He's a mate – he said you'd be cool.'

His puckered mouth slackens off into a toothless half grin.

'Nae bother, nae offence, man …' He holds out his hand. The relief makes me smile too – the use of Gandalf's name was a long shot: Jazzer used to talk about him like he's some drug guru. Bullseye.

'Wa can Ah dae for ye pal?'

I check no punters are in earshot and tell him what I need.

'Nae bother man.' He takes a step back, stoops suddenly – peers at me. 'Hey man, ye Jazzer's friend. You're the radge alaways askin for um right?'

Despite the freezing wind, I break a sweat.

'That cunt man, I got better things to do with my time – why, you seen him?'

'Fucked off tae Glasgae, man, too many fuckers after his arse, fuckin' ripped me off, man – he'll no be showin' up here in a hurry, Ah can tell ye.'

'You got gear or not, man – freezing my bollocks here.'

'Sure, man – but like Ah say this would take an hour tae get taegether.'

Cunt. 'Like you mate, I'd rather not carry too much cash, take this as a down payment okay?' I push two fifties into his greedy little mitt. He's all ears now – flapping like flags.

'Okey dokey. Nae bother. Gie me an hour, man. Number eight Scotland Street ken? Save ye stayin' out in the cold eh.'

This takes me back, the shadow of a punch in my gut. Fuck knows why, probably every punk's got my address. I won't think about it; if they were still interested they'd have paid me a visit by now. Besides, by the looks of that grin, he's already making plans to wipe my arse, fancying himself as my contact now I'm living in style – he'll not be fucking this up, will he? His phone blasts out *Auld Lang Syne*. Princes Street is in full fairy lights now – pretty as a picture. He gives me the thumbs up – covers the handset. 'Sorry, man.'

As I nod back at him, he holds out his hand. I take it, but instead of a handshake he slips a small bag of charlie into mine – I like that.

ANDREW

As SOON AS I'M in the door, I pin her against the hall wall like
Brad Pitt would. I can't believe she's mine and that one day we'll
be married, and have babies and live happily ever after. Is that
fair – when so many are starving? When Callum and Abi …
But I swing a right hook before the fuckers ruin it. I deserve
some happiness – it's been bad for a long time and I deserve to
be happy and if I'm happy the world will be a better place. She
has the softest lips. She has the smoothest skin. The air becomes
bloated with sex thoughts and within seconds this pulsating,
pressing, fleshy, hot, urgent something sweeps away the rational
and irrational until we begin pulling each other towards the
nearest horizontal surface. Actually that's not true; we don't do
it on the floor or the kitchen table, we rush upstairs and emerge
starry-eyed a good hour later.

We have tea and chocolate and then I ask if she's coming to
Callum's school dinner the following night.

'I'm not sure – I think I might have promised Mum I'd do
something. I'll check with her when she comes in. You didn't
talk to Guy then?'

'No, I'd forgotten he was going to Orkney. I tried, honestly,
but he was only in the office for minutes. It's for the best,
Megan – now we can all have a hassle-free Christmas. We'll all

be so much less stressed out in the New Year. Have you checked the forecast by the way? Guy said there was snow on the islands.'

'Mum did. It's meant to be cold but clear – if there is going to be snow it'll be around Tyndrum, and it'll be mid-morning by the time we get there. It'll be nice to get away – look out to sea, give Dad a bit of time, do a bit of walking.'

'Thanks for getting the tree by the way. It looks, well, normal doesn't it?'

'Yes it does – it looks great.'

'What's up?'

'Nothing really. But you have to admit – it's pretty exhausting.'

'What?'

'Oh, come on, Andrew – last night you were raving about Heels …'

'Yes – and?'

'And – it's just been a bit draining that's all. I mean, last week nothing was going to get you back to a dinner.'

'Well that's because Callum said Rachel was going.'

'Well I know that. But she didn't in the end, did she? And so there was no one for Callum. I'm just saying that, well, like the stealing thing, no one but you made a big deal about it. That's all, really. Life goes on, Andrew – it's kind of even maybe a bit sad to see you so, like, *excited* that Guy's away. You're a grown-up, this isn't some kind of game, you know? It's not about getting away with it or not. Sorry.'

'Finished?'

'Sorry, yes. I just feel a bit overwhelmed by your stuff.'

'I thought you wanted me to tell you what was going on in my life?' I manage.

'Well I do, but maybe just not quite so much. I mean, I know that that sounds bad but I've got so much going on in my life right now and there just doesn't seem to be any space. Oh God, why did I start? It's not what I mean.'

'No, no carry on. I can see what a disappointment I am, ringing you all the time. Forgive me for being a bit neurotic about losing my children. God, I mean, how selfish is that?'

'Andrew, you're doing it again – building this up out of proportion. Rachel's not a psycho is she? Of course what you're going through is hell, but half the world is involved with difficult separations. You'll survive, the kids will grow up. She loves her children and she values you as a father. Honestly Andrew, you should see what some of the kids I see are going through. You should, you need to—'

'You know what, Megan – actually I don't know. Actually I'm doing the best that I can – but I'm really sorry to burden you with my dysfunctional life—'

'Where are you going?'

'Home. While I still have one. Okay with you?'

I didn't bring the car. Jesus, fucking Jesus, fucking freezing out here. Shit, I left my scarf and gloves and hat beside the bed. Well I'm definitely not going back. Talk about mixed messages. So okay, I'll just not, okay? I'll just not.

Fucking great – all the lights on. Brilliant. No chance of any peace then.

So what does Megan want? A weekly report, carefully balanced and thought out? Right. Well maybe that'd be best, a weekly report – if that's all she can cope with, that's fine.

And then my ears tune into something going on inside the house. Jesus, what's that fucking row? What the fuck's going on here? Don't mind me folks.

I open the outer door very gently and listen. It's David.

'Listen, India, it was a business meeting, she's a designer. She works for that company in Leith, the one we've been checking out – ask Andrew if you don't believe me.'

'So why did you lie then?' India says. But I can barely hear her, so I go into the hall and stand beside the door into the sitting room. 'Why did you say you were meeting Alex then?' she says.

'Because I knew you'd do this, because I knew you'd freak out, because you always do.'

'That's because you're always cheating on me, because you're obsessed with the Chinese – chatting her up were you? Told her about your fancy new flat?'

'She's been there, yes – of course she has, she can hardly do the interior for us without looking at it.'

'Fucking liar, you just can't help it can you? Promises, you're all promises, making yourself out to be some hot shot—'

'I wanted to surprise you. It'll be finished in a few months. Christ, India, I was doing this for us—'

'Like hell you were. Just like I can move in at Christmas, like I can give Guy up, like we can be a proper couple? Bullshit. You're all talk, David. You're a – a liar. A liar and a cheat and you were chatting her up. I'm not thick, you know; I'm not just one of your tarts.'

Poor India. Something bad is happening here, I can smell it. David has a new flat – how the hell can he afford a fancy new flat?

'No, you're not! What've I got to do to prove it? Okay, move in. Okay, dump Guy. I'm telling you, India – it was business.'

'Right, so, if it's yours then let's tell everyone – come on David, prove it.'

'Not yet, sugar, I'm afraid you're gonna have to trust me on this one, baby – we'll have to wait.'

I'm shitting bricks out here. I should have spoken to India – I should have made time. She may be naïve, but she doesn't deserve this, I should have done more. The conversation we had when he boasted about bosses' wives. Now he's got a Chinese woman in tow and the Leith project was bought by a Chinese conglomerate? That, along with Megan's discovery of his connections, begins to make coincidence seem unlikely. Could he possibly? Is that why he's been so keen to get involved? No way.

I can't restrain myself any longer. I cross the hall and open the sitting room door. 'Wait till what, David?' My voice barely holds. 'What fancy new flat is this then? This a picture of it, is it? Very nice. That must be setting you back a bit – I thought you were meant to be broke.'

India faces me furiously. 'How would you know?'

'Obviously I wouldn't, India – it was only what David's been saying. But no, I can see I wouldn't know, just as I wouldn't know from David that he had any feelings for you at all.'

'You're jealous, that's all – we're going to live there. I'm giving up Guy, and we're moving in, aren't we, David?'

'Be quiet, India – go and wait for me in the car. Get whatever it was we came here for and go. Here.' He throws her a set of keys.

India turns beetroot. 'Why should I? This is nothing to do with Andrew, tell him to bog off!'

'I think you should do as he says, India. I need to have a word with David, in private – do you mind?'

'Yes, I fucking well do.'

'*Now India – go now!*' he says.

And before she bursts into tears, she splutters, 'You think you're so clever, Andrew, but you're not, you're cold and selfish and … and deserve everything you've got coming to you.' Then she heads for the stairs and the clack of her stilettos on the wooden floor rings out like warning shots.

My hands are shaking, and my knees feel like they are about to give way. Shit, what have I done? Oh God, what the fuck have I done now?

'You're looking pale, Andrew. Whisky?' He picks up the half-empty bottle and peers at it. 'Sorry, I owe you. We seem to have demolished most of that. India can get very possessive, very tiresome. I was right when I said you were lucky you weren't shagging her. Well maybe not, she's pretty good at what she does. Last night – shall I tell you? No? Well all right – maybe some other time. How's the lovely Megan? India said you were staying over, otherwise I would never have presumed. Something happen? Had a row?'

'Shut up. Shut up, you toe rag. Don't you dare help yourself to my whisky, don't you dare talk about Megan – what have you done? Give me that. No, on second thoughts, I need a clear head, you slimy little snake, you stupid … Jesus Christ.'

I need to think, pull my head together. The site in Leith, my God. 'But how could you have?'

'Simple mate, very simple, made simpler by your co-operation. Well, and your, what shall we call it, "breakdown"? A bit severe? Perhaps you just took your eye off the ball, and who would blame you – the lovely Megan?'

'What the hell are you?' It sounds such a cliché.

'Don't give me that. You've been taking the micky – using me. But don't feel bad about it, I've been quite happy to fit in with your complicated domestics – so happy in fact we've prepared a small reward.' He looks at me over the rim of his glass. 'How does half a million sound?'

'They gave you – they—'

'It's called fraud, Andrew. Don't underestimate yourself, what we did could lead to corporate manslaughter. Come on, Andrew, think about it; you can pay the ex-missus off. If what India says is true, she's going to win you know. She's going to have the house, the kids – the lot. And once she's got the house – well, even a man of limited insight can surely guess what her and India'll be getting up to? Not something I'd like my five year old to witness. Oh come on, Andrew, do you really think she'd go ahead if you offered her hard cash?'

'You're mad.'

'I'm ambitious. Nothing wrong with that – so are you.'

'I'm calling the police. Does India know?'

'Does she fuck. I told you, India amuses me. For now. Go on, here's the phone – call them. They'll find out there's been a cock-up. Nothing criminal has happened, Andrew – a few mistakes made by a minor employee, some samples got mixed up. I think you'll find it's your arse you'll need to be covering.'

He takes the whisky bottle from between my knees and pours another slug into his glass and raises it.

'Cheers.'

I barely sleep. I barely move from a rigid foetal position. I'm in too much of a state to go to the bathroom to either empty my bladder or find my sleeping pills. All I am aware of is a voice, an all-consuming voice. 'Corporate manslaughter', it chants, until the repetition becomes hypnotic and gives way to another loop, 'dead children from cyanide poisoning', which tightens like a noose in my head and all I can do is lie awake and listen.

Megan was right. I'm self-obsessed. Just a simple job and I couldn't even do that. Don't deserve to have my children, don't deserve Megan or this job.

Sometime around six a.m. I muscle through the solid fog of voices and stagger downstairs, pick up a white envelope from the hall doormat. I must have missed it last night. I remain staring at the floor rehearsing – pleading my excuses to Megan, to Guy, to the sheriff as I recall his words before he left. 'You go public with this, Andrew, and I'll take you with me – don't for one minute think I won't. I'm good at spin – remember that. And while they'll never be able to prove you had anything to do with it, the fact that you hired me without references, covered for me while I shagged the boss's bird, and encouraged me to take over the soil testing for the Leith job against the governor's express wishes – well, it will create enough smoke to asphyxiate your job chances in Edinburgh for several years to come.' He's right about that – though that's not enough to prompt me to cross the line from blithering idiot to criminal.

I drag myself up to put the kettle on and while I'm waiting for it to boil I open the letter more from reflex than either interest or intention. It's from my lawyer.

> *Dear Andrew. I tried to call you today but didn't reach you at the office or on your mobile. You will be aware that things are pressing on, and with this in mind I decided to drop this off on my way home from work. Finally I met with Megan today in the hope, given her line of work, that her evidence would provide the sheriff with a semi-professional report on the family with the added weight of being a good family friend. However, I gather relationships have changed between you. I have to tell you that her evidence could now been viewed as prejudiced, especially as Mrs. Gillespie suspects her of manipulation etc. Sorry, Andrew. Perhaps you might like to supply another witness who could confirm your view that Rachel is unfit to provide the children with a stable home. At the moment I must warn you that things aren't looking too chipper. Look forward …*

I don't even need to think about it. I simply won't, There is no way I'm going to let my name be smeared across every newspaper as the guy who facilitated a major fraud, at least not until we get through the court business. That's it. No question. This may well be my last Christmas here, probably will be, and I'm not letting that fucker ruin it. I just can't let that happen.

I walk to work in a vacuum.

As soon as the office door cracks open I see David's coat hanging on a peg and hear voices.

'Hello, Andrew – I thought you were out for the day. These guys are from the *Scotsman* – came to see you actually. Dougie, this is the man you really want – the man in charge. Andrew, this is Dougie Wilson and Andy McFarlane – they're doing a feature on soil contamination.'

'So you're the boss then, Mr. Gillespie? Sorry to spring this on you.'

I already despise his checked sweater. 'Err yes, I suppose I am, though actually David's far too modest – we work as a team here. Sorry, am I missing something? Did you have an appointment?'

'Do you mind, Andrew? I was about to make a brew.' David interrupts.

'Go ahead.'

'Much appreciated, I'm sure,' Dougie says to David before turning back to me. 'No mate,' he says. 'Just thought we'd drop by on the off-chance of finding someone in. We're doing a Brockovich – digging for dirt on soil contamination, if you'll excuse the pun. Don't look so worried, it's only a feature. What with the deal over the M74 extension, and half the folk at Highlights Estate popping their clogs, environmental issues have become very in vogue.'

'I suppose so. Thanks. No, just black,' I say to the milk jug hovering by my shoulder.

And then Andy, who up until now has been studying the posters on the walls, perks up. 'You boys have been dealing with this theme park haven't you? Some Chinese conglomerate bought it, I gather. That's what's interesting isn't it? That's nerve for you! I mean with such a contaminated site just down the road and with that whole coast line a dumping ground for God knows how much industrial waste over the years.'

I'm pretty certain they can hear my teeth clattering against my mug.

'You've got kids haven't you, Mr. Gillespie – bet they were delighted, same as mine, when they saw the centre spread rendering we ran last month? Fancy having our very own Disney park right here on our doorstep, eh?'

'Listen guys, you've caught me at a bad time. I'm just here to collect some papers.'

'One favour before you go. We were hoping we might be able to shadow you – get out to some sites, see some of the action.'

'Well yes of course. When did you have in mind?'

'It'll have to be today – we're running this for Sunday and tomorrow we're scooting around Glasgow.'

'Impossible, I'm afraid. As I said, I'm in meetings all day.'

'Our loss.'

'So if you'll excuse me …'

'No worries mate. Come along *Erin*, drink up. And thanks, David.'

I grab a random folder and leave, almost fall down the office stairs. Once outside I move quickly up the street and into the nearest shop, which happens to be a flower shop, and pull out my phone.

'I don't know what the hell you're doing in the office, David, but I presume you're clearing your desk. Tell your buddies the deal's off. Do it David, or God help me, I'll—'

I'm shaking so much I'm actually holding the phone with both hands. I have a meeting in half an hour. I'll go without my papers, I'll make something up. I walk to the West End.

The meeting is tedious; all I can think about is Megan driving through Tyndrum for a 'hassle-free' two days. It finishes early. I go to the lab and collect new containers. It's driving sleet. There'll be snow on the hills. It'll be white-out in Tyndrum.

I'm on site by two. He's late. Although the ground is still frozen, I'm worried the car might sink, so I walk the hundred yards or so to where I want to probe – the same spot as last time. The ice splintering up under my boots looks yellow. That's what I can't believe: that I didn't smell a rat. There was a gas works here, it's probably steeped in cyanide, and just half a mile down there …

Two fifteen. He's not coming is he? I walk towards the car. Guy'll be back soon.

Then a blue Land Rover pulls up and my heart kicks in again.

'You must be freezing, man. Sorry I'm late. Jump in. Got caught up in traffic – everyone coming in for a last shop before the big day. Year's getting shorter, I reckon. Wasn't there someone more local you could have used?'

'Not today, no.'

He offers to pack the samples, reaches for the cooler box, but I hang onto it.

'Okay, mate, I was only offering. Take a pew in the Land Rover, it's warm in there.'

'Yes, thanks. I think I'm getting flu. Thanks, I will – just warm up for a minute. Tell me when you're ready, okay?'

It takes an hour to get down to the probe's limit of about four metres. Despite the warmth, I'm still shivering.

By four thirty, I'm at the lab in Broxburn. A technician I've not met before lets me in. He takes the new samples, looks at the labels and scrolls down a computer behind the desk.

'Are you aware you've already run tests for this site? Came out damn near squeaky clean if I remember. One minute and I'll tell you.' After a few seconds he straightens up. 'Yeah, that's right, nothing to worry about. Still want to go ahead?'

'Please, there's a slim chance the samples got muddled – we want to double check.'

'No problem. Wasn't you last time, was it? It was that guy who's always in the papers – good-looking chap – that's why it stuck.'

'David Stein. Yes. You said two days?'

'I did, didn't I? But I was forgetting Monday we'll be closed – it'll have to be late tomorrow.'

'Yes, yes, great – thanks.' I ask him to invoice me directly. He looks at me for a second too long, clocks that it's my call, gives me paperwork to sign and sees me out. It's already pitch dark, and beginning to snow. I stand in the overhead light on the doorstep and reach into my coat pocket for my mobile. It's a text from Harry. He needs the Fairweather's address for some reason. I look in my wallet for the card they gave me and text him back. Thank God for Harry.

Then a bomb goes off. Blinding flashes fix me to the door.

'Sorry to startle you, mate – good meeting was it?'

It's that idiot reporter, what the fuck! 'I, I forgot I had to be here.'

'No problem at all. Could you just move a little to the left so we can get the Wimtex plaque in frame. Yeah, that's great. Ta very much, Mr. Gillespie. Before we go in, perhaps you could tell us a few specifics about the theme park in Leith, give us some good news for the parents – something we could quote perhaps?'

The other one butts in.

'Dougie, we've got a lot to get through, and I'm dying of cold here.'

'Quite right. We'll call you if we find any gaps – okay? Be seeing you, Andrew – hope the mug shot does you justice, and enjoy the article.'

They open the door and bustle inside.

I wait in the car for a few minutes – try to calm down, work things out. This won't be a problem – it's just an article – nothing's going to happen. I call Fairweathers. Then India to make sure she's at home for Callum. Then the office. No reply.

The beep of a text: it's Megan.

'Sorry. x.'

I sit staring at the screen, fretting over how to reply then fumble out a text.

'Sorry – lv u.'

I nearly crawl up the stairs to bed – my arms and legs feel like lead. I'd call her to say goodnight, but there is no way I'm going to ruin her time with Rhona. This'll all be over in a couple of days, no one has been hurt, and no one's going to be, and if I tried to explain, well, I'd probably get it wrong and she'd probably think I'm a worse prick than she already does. She's right, I don't need to tell her every little detail of my life. I'll get an email off to the planning department in the morning. I'll tell them about the muddle with the samples. They'll have the right results by the time they're back at work after the holidays. We can put a small announcement in the paper. We're okay, that's the main thing.

RACHEL

I'VE BEEN IN BED all of five minutes. Someone is at the front door. No one would be so crap as to come round at this time, not even Dawn. Go away – go away. Christ's sake – okay, okay … I drag on my dressing gown. It's India – who else.

'What on earth are *you* doing here? Calm down for God's sake – some of us have only just gone to bed. Bit early to be half cut isn't it?'

'Shhhhh. I've got something, Rache. You're going to love this – can I bring my bike in, just in case?'

'In case of what? No. Don't tell me. It's Sunday, India – my morning off. I was planning on a lie-in … Christ, India, Abi's still asleep; for God's sake sit down and skin this up while I make some coffee.'

She fills the tiny hallway with her bike. I go back into my bedroom and pull on my jeans under my dressing gown. The heating's only just on.

'I've dumped him this time Rachel! Shit, burnt my finger – shit, shit, shit, I'm all over the place. Shit!' She rummages in her bike bag. 'Here, get some glasses. Bubbly? Two of the best, courtesy of David. Got any orange? Nae bother – just the fizz then, never did enjoy the bucking bit much, did you?'

'What you on about?'

'David of course! Well, and Andrew. Here take this, and this, you've got some catching up – Jesus, Rache, what's wrong with your neck?'

'Nothing. What?'

I turn my dressing gown collar up.

'Fake tan – I did it in the dark. Hand me the Pashmina will you? Thanks.' She passes me the joint and I take a cautious hit as the coffee grumbles behind me.

'Right, here's your coffee, the sugar's on the table. Okay, so tell me.'

'Okay, okay. So he was on a real downer last night. Jesus, Rachel, you should have seen him, drank a whole bottle of whisky in one go. Remember me telling you, you know, about the videos and, and him like proving to me that they were before my time, yeah? Well he just fucking lied, Rache. He just like fucking lied to me, and last night, well, the night before last, him and Andrew treating me like shit, like I don't matter, like I'm just rubbish.'

'Oh India, you already knew that – he's a freak, a perve. I've been telling you for months.'

'Yes, yes, but now I know for sure don't I? Cos I saw the bitch, first in the pub with David and then—'

'Shhhhh, you'll wake Abi.'

'Sorry.'

'Is that what you've come to tell me? That you've dumped him? Christ, India …'

'No, not at all – much better than that, I told you. You are going to love this.'

'What? Get on with it then.'

'Okay. So last night, foul mood, bottle of whisky, God knows how much gear, flaked out – comatose. Just about to go to bed myself when an email came through on the laptop. Re: Andrew Gillespie.

'Really? And?'

'I've got it here … read it, Rachel. It's something about that theme park – I've been filing all the paperwork and stuff at work. Something dodgy's been going on. Jesus, Rache – what if David's done something really awful and Andrew's found out?'

'Give it here.' She hands me a sheet of A4 paper. David's

email details and those of a company India hasn't heard of clearly legible.

> Re: Andrew Gillespie
> Okay. Disappear. We'll make contact when things
> have settled.

I'm intrigued, especially by the email thread: David's original email. 'I am leaving Eco Écosse with immediate effect. Andrew Gillespie has information which precludes us from continuing with the Leith project.'

'What do you think it means, Rache?'

'I don't know – yet. Anything else?'

'Well, yeah! This morning after he'd left the house – it was like a bolt from the blue! I'd seen her hadn't I? On David's laptop. Fucking whore, and now I'm thinking, I'm sure I've seen him with the other one – you were right, Rache—'

'India, can you call me Rachel? My name's Rachel. As interested as I am in his infidelities I'm not really that surprised. What did you do with the email? Might he know you've seen it?'

'Here, take a hit of this.' She stabs the joint at me, almost burns me. 'I deleted it, didn't I? Sent it to myself and then deleted it, after printing it, of course. Not stupid am I? Fucking hell, we ought to go to the police, you know.'

The espresso kicks in and suddenly I'm wide awake. 'They're not going to be interested in this, India, we need to show them what it refers to, what it means – you know, in the *grand scheme.*'

'Okay then. Guess what we're going to do?'

I cough and nod at the same time. I'm catching on and it seems like a good idea.

'We'll go to the office, get all the relevant papers and stuff and then we'll shop them, that's what,' she says, slumping back triumphantly into her seat.

We spend the next hour drinking champagne, eating toast and making a plan. We check out India's email and sure enough it's all there. We drink to our imminent success. By next week David's languishing in jail, Andrew's conceded to all my demands, and me and India and Abi and Callum are living happily ever after in Inverleith. Her giggles wake up Auntie Abi.

'What are you doing here, India?' Abi says. 'Don't you have

a home anymore, and why the fuck are you both drinking champagne?'

'Celebrating. Here, darling, have one – it's scrummy.'

'No ta, I'm already late for work. That's my laptop you know – make sure you don't spill booze on it.'

'Yes, Mummy.'

It's after ten by the time we let ourselves into the office, midday by the time we've got down the road to Gayfield Square Police station and a while longer till we're outside the *Scotsman's* HQ in Holyrood. It's so friggin' cold we are forced to buy a half bottle of voddy just to keep from freezing up. India does this kind of Scottish jig on the pavement before she screams 'sod the cunts' and drops the package through the letter box. And then we run as if it's some kind of bomb. Which it is of course.

RYAN

RIGHT ON TIME. Scrubbed up pretty well hasn't he?

'Hi, man – how's it goin? Fuckin Baltic oot there. Wa' I wouldnae give tae be fuckin' off tae someplace warm right now. Great gaff byraway. Gonny ask us in like, pal?'

I show him into the kitchen. He thinks he's so smart – really landed on his feet this time. Not many dudes from Scotland Street been up to his patch before, I bet. Just look at him, taking it all in; he must think I'm stupid – as if I'd score from some flea-ridden junkie unless I was desperate.

He sits himself down, draws out two lines – big fuckers. I do them both.

As I hand him back his note he brushes my hand. Punk. What's he playing at? He thinks he can pull – he must think I'm dumb or what? My head is fizzing and popping and rolling out. He places the two bags on the table. 'Good gear, man, you got some draw?'

'Like Ah says – Ah can get any shite ye want any time ye want. Afghan or skunk? That Moby?'

I'm not interested in making small talk with some crackhead but this cocaine has other ideas and I see or is it hear words about Moby's new album floating round the room in colour.

Cash is in my back pocket. He tells me the score and we divvy up, nice and civilised.

'Ye wanna' do some crack, man? Like Ah say, nae charge for a good mate.'

I shake my head, I'm high enough. He asks if I'd mind if he has one for the road. I wave my hand in a circle. One for the road, he says. He'll be gone in a minute. He's cool, just as fucked off with Jazzer as I am – said so didn't he? I walk through to the living room, turn up Moby a tad and by the time I'm back he's rolling a joint – not from my stash mind – the perfect gentleman.

Rachel is with Abi tonight – bonding. I'm happy about that – that's cool. So no harm in having some company for a while is there? I'm watching the silver trail whip up his nose – and him swallowing till his eyes pop and that kind of frozen look as the rush punches in almost like he's eyeballing some kind of ghost. He's tripping, man ... Shit. I wasn't planning for this but now I'm finding it hard to remember why not exactly. Let's face it, man, this may well be my last hit – because I don't think Rastafarians or Jamaica even heard of crack. Believe me, I'm counting on it. He's arching his eyebrows trying to focus – blissed out in some dream that I want to be part of. Now he's watching me and something in my stare must have made him read my mind cos he sits back down, gives me the joint, drops some crystals onto the foil, burns it and hands me a straw. I'm pulling hard, fuck.

We're pretty high; my head's doing stuff I'd pay to watch, and his hand, creeping over my back, sends some mean fucking charge to my dick. Whey ... Something's going down, man, because suddenly I'm wasted – something else man, something behind the crank rush – too weak to even raise my eyelids let alone return the favour with my hands. He's unzipping my fly and I'm trying to help him, I swear, but my hands won't move, they're just floating somewhere in the stars up above, and that moon is so fucking full – well it's blinding me. Turn off the moon, fucker!

No sweat man, it's cool.

Shit. I'm being peeled and rolled around, and somehow we're down on the floor and I'm drowning, can't get my head back up; he's got something everywhere and I'm yawning open for him like a crying baby. I can feel my flesh smooth out, and then just as quick it puckers up and throbs, and now these cute shocks start ripping through my knob, but only for a split second or maybe it's more – at any rate it's not long before the point of focus somehow shifts into my arse, and I'm thinking that maybe he's made some kind of tunnel or something like some underground Tube system linking all erogenous zones … He must have – I can see, no feel, see and feel this surging, falling shit pushing and whooshing down these fucking tunnels, man, electric lava yeah, red-hot lava that's heat, tremendous heat taking over like pure ice. That's funny, man. No it isn't. This ice burns, man, and this is burning my guts. I almost open my eyes. I mean I'm trying, cos his head's in my crotch, though I don't know that for sure cos there's this damn volcano in the way, and I think he may be eating my dick cos that heat's a kind of pain heat, but he's already eaten my hands, because they aren't there anymore, I mean, I think maybe they're there if I could just see them … I'm trying, man, but like there's this problem with my head, someone's treading on it – maybe they are and maybe they're not! There we go – thanks mate, I'm up now, yep, he's gobbling man, I can see his head stubble – fuck, shit, whoops, over we go man, pumping me full of dick big time whispering and muttering stuff which I can't make out … Someone says something about a condom, that's so cool, that's what I was worried about: catching something. Steady, man. I'm starting to tingle; it's starting in my toes darting and twitching, maybe not my toes, maybe my finger-tips, no it's my toes and I can see words now, I'm seeing them, jeez, they are expanding and throbbing all over the fucking place – like a million lava lamps of multi-coloured dripping words, hot wax. There's the bell, man! Open the fucking door. The door, man – open the door – cos we're having a party here. Ecstasy! I got it, someone's given me E. I need to stay with that, but I don't because it keeps falling away as soon as I grab onto it – them. I'm trying to remember cos it seems real important like getting my head round all this shit and I'm trying to open my eyes, I am so trying – there we go, but now I know I'm tripping out, because there's this dude, man, and it's Jazzer, fucking hell, like right in front of my face, and Billy's Uncle Shawn and Tyler. Jesus, maybe I'm gonna say something … I'm about to say something, man, when there's this new thing happening and I'm too stoned to know whether it's pain or if I dig it. It's pain, it's definitely pain. I'm trying to open my eyes to find my lost hands, but I can't, everything's shooting to my arse, long spears, great shafts of wood – fucking hell, of the purest pain and I know there's a better word but I can't get my hands on it. I think I'm being shot, but there's no sound, perhaps he's got a silencer, my rectum is being stretched up into my head. I don't know what's happening to my dick because there's just a hole there and I'm trying not to fall through it. I can see and hear this howling all around me like someone is hurting real bad. I don't think I'm gonna make it to Mama's grave today, but I should be okay by the time Rachel comes round, hey.

RACHEL

My head is pounding. What time is it? Ouch. What's that noise? I try to scream for Abi but it hurts far too much – what's the time for fuck's sake? Jesus, who the fuck's calling the house phone at this time? Abi, answer the phone. I knock it off my bedside table and then fumble for it on the floor, but head down is worse than head up. Much worse. Who the hell is that squeaking at me? Somehow I manage by process of elimination to get the right end to the right place.

'Hello,' I say, trying to sound sulky, angry, and bored. I don't need this, whoever you are. And I certainly don't need Andrew. What the hell time is it anyway and where the fucking hell is Abi? I desperately need a pee now I'm awake.

'Rachel, is that you? Rachel? Are you alone?'

'Of course I'm alone, Andrew. Hang on a minute, I need a pee.' Once I'm settled on the loo, I ask him what he wants.

'I've had the police here. They need to ask you some questions—'

'Abi!' Something's happened to Abi – I've been neglecting her. Oh God. No, no she's here, she was here with me all last night, out of our skulls – I remember, out of our tiny minds.

'It's not Abi, Rachel. They were here about your friend, Ryan. Seems like he's had an accident, at any rate he's dead.

They found things in his flat, your things apparently. They assumed you still lived here. I've told them it's unlikely you'll know anything, but they're on their way to you now. Just thought I should tell you.'

The phone falls away from me and clatters onto the tiles. His stinking vomit is all over my hands, crawling into my nose, the stench is making me retch. I must have drunk too much. Ryan's not dead – how could he be dead, I only left him a few hours ago, no, that's not right, a day ago … I needed to spend time with Abi – the court case – Abi was in a state. Andrew's a bastard. Just trying to upset me. Of all the disgusting cruel tricks. I need to get back to bed, forget what he said, forget … He's so jealous, he always was jealous, but this is too much, this is just cruel. I'll never forgive him for this, never.

I use the basin to help me up and open the cabinet. I need something to calm me down. I wouldn't normally, not in the morning, but this is different isn't it? Look at my hands. Where are my pills? They were here – I'm sure they were, right here! Honestly, Abi, this is all your stuff. I try to feel behind the bottles and tubes and things, but my hands aren't working right. Now look what you've made me do. Shhhh. Fuck. But at least I've got them. I'll take two. Or three, maybe three – I'll take three. Then I'll go round. He won't mind, not this once – not when I've been told something so cruel and abusive. I mean – he'll want to see me, of course he will. Abi's make-up is all over the floor, best pick it up. Bastard – how could he …

'Mum, what the hell are you doing?'

Abi's voice – Abi's cross voice.

'Oh Abi, you're safe, I thought, the police they, Andrew—'

'What are you on about – what police? Mum, what are you doing on the floor? Why's my stuff everywhere, what's the phone doing there and … Give me the glass before you drop that too.'

'I spilt it darling – Andrew, he said you … he said you were—'

'Get up Mum, I'll get it. What, what did he say about me?'

'Nothing, nothing, I just needed something for my hangover – I'm not well and I've got to go out.'

'You working then, are you? So early?'

'Yes … yes, I'm working. So just let me go, will you? I'm sorry, so sorry but Andrew, your father, your bastard father—'

Why is she following me? I don't want her to see me. I need to get dressed, go out. I need to see him. I'm late.

'You don't look well, Mum. Why don't you pull a sickie? I could phone if you want. You must be ill, come here, I thought you'd stopped … What the hell did you drink last night?'

'Please Abi, you don't understand. It's just a headache. I'll be fine when the pills kick in, I'll be fine. I'm late, just leave me, will you?'

Abi's giving me one of her looks – like she's always doing the work around here and starts picking up her stuff. I escape into my room and pull on the stuff I took off last night. See? They haven't come, have they?

He hates to think I'm checking on him – but I'm not, am I? I'm just passing, woke early. Now where's my make-up – where the hell's … Oh God, Ryan. Ryan, oh my God, please God, be okay, Ryan.

Abi's back. 'Mum, they weren't paracetamol, they were Valium – see? You'll be fucked when they kick in. Mum!'

I won't listen. I put the rest of the dope … Jesus, there's precious little left (she uses me that girl) into my bag, shove Abi out the way, and almost run out the flat and into the street.

'Mrs Gillespie?' A strange man steps out in front of me.

'No, I'm late, I'm meeting someone … at work – I'm helping out at work.' Words rushing out, riding on words to get out and past and away. 'Please, I'm late. What do you want? What could you want? Abi's fine, we're fine … what do you want, please, I'm late …'

'Just a word please, Mrs Gillespie. Just a moment of your time – please.'

I must have collapsed because I don't remember how I got here; maybe I'm dreaming and they're about to tell me that my father's died: 'A car crash, I'm afraid, with a woman – no not your mother …' Yes perhaps I'm dreaming, I could handle that – Dad dying, but no, it's Ryan, they found Ryan, dead, beaten and raped and dead and raped and dead and dead and dead … No, I'm not listening, and no, I'm not answering, not even you, Abi. I mean, I don't ask you what you've been up to, do I? You could be fucking anyone you wanted and I'd not stand in your way – and as I'm saying this I can hear that it's not sounding right because I do care, did care, cared more than anything, because – because I loved him.

ABI

I STILL CAN'T GET my head round this. Mum and Ryan – how could she? How could she go back to someone who raped her, who beat her up? Unreal, wasn't even ashamed, not really, says it's the first time she's ever loved anyone. Actually went to identify the body. No one else pitched up, did they? No friends, just my freak of a mother. Hate her. How the fuck could she do that – forgive him after what he did? She's not normal, honestly she's not, she must be so fucking sick, been sitting like that half the night, just staring out the window – won't let me put her to bed or draw the curtains. She says she wants to see out towards his flat, that it's her way of staying in touch.

The phone rings. It's India, only the third time she's rung today. She leaves a message.

No, airhead, Mum hasn't bought the *Scotsman*. Christ, is she on drugs or something? Can't she get it that Mum's *grieving*, that Mum's not going anywhere, especially not to buy some stupid newspaper to see some stupid article that I presume features something about her in it. And you are? Bog off, India, and leave us in peace will you? Just go.

I make coffee. Mum just waves her hand at it. The police say it could be weeks before she's back to normal – before reality sinks in. They said seeing him dead usually helps, but I don't think it has, she's still totally zombie, keeps going on about how much they beat him, how they must have hated him.

'Come on, Mum, it's your favourite. I bought that artisan one you like and I made the milk froth – please Mum, just have a few sips.' She looks at me like she's a child and takes a sip. Sometimes I think she likes it when I'm looking after her. 'Now have some of this Jaffa cake Mum, it's yummy, and you'll need your strength if you're going out. That's it, well done.' I explain again what's happening today, how I'm going to stay over at Dad's tonight, cos she's going to Dawn's. She looks so lost, I remind her that Dawn's going to collect her kids off the train and then come back for her. And then all the arrangements for tomorrow, Christmas Day. But she's not really listening, just nodding sadly, looking at her watch and then at the door, craving for the kind policewoman to come so she can try to persuade her to take her back to Ryan's flat.

'Is that okay, Mum? You happy with that?'

She waves at me and raises her eyebrows like she's not telling, like I should know, like I should *know*. I should know. Tears start rolling down her cheeks, but she doesn't move. Then she murmurs 'Thank you,' and takes the coffee off me and tries to smile.

Dawn stayed over last night, been totally great of course, and blitzed the flat.

I answer the door, let the policewomen in. Dawn makes tea for everyone and I kiss Mum and leave.

It's snowing: a million flakes dropping silently from the sky, nipping my cheeks. As I pull my scarf up over my nose the snow in the creases melts against my neck and tickles. If it goes on like this, it might be a white Christmas. But I let the thought pass, no point …

I can barely see the screen on my phone or press the right key. 'Luv ya babe when r u cumin bk 2 wrk?' Cute hey? Poor Ash, desperate to meet up, especially since Dawn, who by the way is racist, gave him an earful for turning up trolleyed at two in the morning.

By the time I get to Dad's, the pavement's white. Cool.

Callum lugs the door open.

'Come here wee man!' I drop to a squat and drag him to me.

'Oh Cal, you were fantastic last night – it was the best concert I've ever been to, really cheered me up. You were brilliant on the drums. Know what? I think you might become a very famous pop star one day.'

He wriggles until I let him go. Says nothing. Then he turns his face to the sky and opens his mouth. I copy him. Large, soft icy flakes thaw on our tongues and slip under our chins and down our necks. 'Do you think it'll be a white Christmas? Wow, think of that.'

'Will you come tobogganing, Abi? Will you? We're going up Arthur's Seat tomorrow if they don't lock Dad up. Will you come, Abi?'

'What d'ya mean – lock Dad up? What now?'

'Those policemen are here again.'

'What policemen?'

'You remember, the ones about Gran running away, and about me stealing and everything, and—'

'What?'

'And the ones who came round about that man being dead.'

'Where's Megan?'

'She's in the kitchen – she doesn't know though.'

I take his hand and pull him. Megan looks wiped out.

'Hi Abi. Callum's said, has he?'

'That Dad's in trouble again – what's going on? What's he done now? What are these boxes for?'

'Nothing, he's done nothing. But David has apparently. Do you remember talking about that theme park in Leith?'

'Not really – maybe. Why?'

'I think David had some fake soil tests done.'

'What do you mean – how?'

'I'm not sure – Dad's really shaken up. And David's disappeared. I think someone found out and told the police. I think they want to check out your dad's computer – they're taking it away.'

Shit. I don't say anything because it's just dawning on me that this could this have something to do with India and all that excitement I interrupted the other day.

'You've gone quite pale Abi. No point in worrying – we'll just have to wait until they've finished talking to him. It's obviously nothing to do with him. It's just that it seems like it's one thing after another. How's your mum?'

'Awful. Not speaking. Well she does talk a bit, but only about him. I doubt she'll make it to court. When is it anyway?'

'The preliminary hearing is the end of next week. Well, maybe that would be best.'

'Best for you and Dad, you mean. Oh I'm sorry, it's just ...'

Callum looks at me, frowning.

'Dad might go to jail and then what would happen?'

'Come here, my wee star. Of course he won't go to jail, he hasn't done anything wrong, he won't be going anywhere.' And I lead him across the hall and into the sitting room. 'Hey, just look at that tree, all those presents – did you decorate that?'

'Megan and I bought it and me and Dad decorated it.'

'That's lovely, Cal.' We lie under the tree and try to count all the fairy lights as we always do. I pick off one of the chocolate Santas and pop it into his mouth. Eventually the study door opens. Dad and a police guy (the one who was here all those months ago about Mum) stand there and we sit up.

The police guy says, 'Hello. Abi isn't it?'

Then he turns to Dad who looks really nervous and a hundred years old.

'I recognised Abi at Toni's the other day. A very good waitress. You must have left school then?'

'Obviously.'

'I was just saying to your dad what a relief it was with prelims out the way. My daughter ...'

Another policemen clears his throat from the hall. 'Ahem.'

'Sorry, yes, you'll be wanting us out of your hair. Well, we've probably got all we need – for the time being anyway.' And then to his colleague. 'You go and get the car – I'll start packing things up.'

Once the policeman's left the room, Dad squats down and picks up a reindeer. I ask him what's going on.

Dad spreads his hands out like he knows nothing. And then the one who was here about Mum says, 'I'm sure everything must be very difficult for you at the moment, for both you and your mum. Just wanted to say how sorry I am.'

'Right.'

'This David, was he a friend of your mum's too?' he says.

'No way – she can't stand him.'

'No, well – she's got that right. Nasty bit of work, but not everyone seems to think so – he was bailed after court this morning. Well, anyway, look at the time, if you wouldn't mind showing me where your computer is.'

'And how long will I be without it then?' Dad says, standing up and leading the way into the study.

I want to listen for some reason.

'A few days. Why don't you call us on Thursday? You were about to say who you thought might hold a grudge against David? His girlfriend, India? You say it's a volatile relationship and that she's been going out with your employer as well – so he might—'

The doorbell goes. Megan gets it. It's the other policeman.

Dad is as white as a sheet. 'That is completely out of the question – Guy knows nothing about India's relationship with David.'

'Okay. Well, let's wrap this up shall we? You say your boss is due back from Paris this afternoon? Tell him we'll be wanting a word with him – tell him we'll be in touch. You'll have quite a press statement to prepare, I imagine. Come on, Nick.'

Pillock. After they've gone we all collapse round the kitchen table.

'Coffee?'

The garden looks like it's draped in thick white pastry and the skinny cherry tree, normally almost invisible, is completely awesome, bristling with snow crystals. It makes my tummy all weird.

'Can we go to the park, Abi – please, can you pull me on the toboggan?'

Megan and Dad look at me with a kind of pathetic pleading. Actually, there is no way I'm ready to even think about whether India and Mum did this to Dad, let alone talk about it – and especially not with Dad.

'Where is India anyway?' I say.

'She went back to her Mum's for Christmas. I guess we should phone her.'

'She won't know about any of this then?' Megan asks.

We gulp down our hot chocolate and rummage in the top drawer for coats, hats, scarves and gloves. Stepping into the garden is like stepping onto a giant marshmallow. It's like being inside one of those paperweight thingies. Something about it, the heavy silence, snowflakes landing on my eyelashes, the way the snow thuds off the shed door like pie crust – even the smell inside the shed, it's all so awesome. I feel like curling up and just lying down in it – forgetting everything. My throat is aching, forcing tears … But I push through all this because it's Christmas Eve, because next year might be better, because my darling wee brother is staring up at me, his eyes shining with excitement. I yank out the plastic sledge and Cal drags it back up the garden and squeezes my hand with his free one.

'Can we make a snowman too, Abi?'

ANDREW

A HUGE SOFT SILVER pillow, ochre at the margins, hangs over Edinburgh. We watch from the porch as Abi and Callum fade, inhaled by falling snow. 'We should have gone with them – it would have done us all good.'

Megan sighs, lays her head against my shoulder. 'Maybe, tomorrow – we'll all go to Holyrood tomorrow. Have you thought about how you're going to present all this to Guy?'

I draw her in close. She shivers. A faint breeze sucks the snow into small funnels which flex and move like wraith dancers down the street. She straightens up and I rub her back as we turn into the hall, close the front door.

'Kind of. Megan, we need to speak – I need to tell you something, something I've been trying to find a way to tell you since we heard that Ryan died, since we were out of threat from the court case.'

The phone rings. I reach for the phone trying to hold onto her hand with my other one but she pulls away.

'It's Guy, his flight from Paris might well be delayed because of the snow. He'll call me around three – keep me posted.'

'This sounds ominous – go on.'

I tell her everything. How I took new soil samples, the reporters, David's admission, bribe, the flat in Leith, India's

308

probable involvement – how I was too weak to tell her – that I didn't want to ruin her time in Oban. She doesn't say much, just looks at me as though I've grown two heads, picks up her coat and leaves.

RACHEL

'RACHEL?'

'Why won't you take me there? I need to go there!'

'We can't,' The policewoman says. 'We've been through this. It's a crime scene, Rachel.'

'It's not right you taking all his stuff away.'

'We all want to find out who did this to him, Rachel. We were hoping you might be able to tell us a little about the man who owned the flat. The land register says it's owned by a company in Jamaica – and according to the utilities, a man who goes by the name of Winston Lawrence takes care of everything. But you say you've never heard of him.'

'I've told you – it was Ryan's flat. Ryan Turner. He had a lot of clothes … maybe it belonged to his family. His dad was Jamaican.'

They keep doing that, trying to say he was unfaithful to me, trying to make him out to be a bad person, trying to make out I'm a bad person.

'So you say, Rachel, but so far there's nothing we've found to confirm that. Ryan's phone is missing, as is his computer, no documents – bit of a mystery really. Ryan lived on the Stockbridge main road, you say – before he bought this flat?'

'Yes. I told you. He was under a lot of stress, his mother was ill.'

'Yes and she died, yes we know.'

So why's she saying it like that – as if she doesn't believe me? Frump.

'*Mrs* Gillespie,' the other one says, emphasising Mrs, 'I think we've taken up as much time as we should today.'

The young one, the one who's always trying to make me talk to her, wishes me a happy Christmas and takes out her keys – car keys, probably, and that's when I remember … I took a set – after you got burgled, my love, I had an extra set cut. I'd forgotten that. I'd always meant to give them back. I can now, can't I, darling? I can come and look after you, do some tidying – tidy up after those horrid policemen.

After they've gone, I tell Dawn I'm going for a sleep and she helps me into bed. She asks me if I'll be okay for half an hour while she picks up her children. I smile at her and tell that I'm feeling okay, that she should take her time, that's she's not to worry about me. She's been a good friend, Dawn, and I tell her this and she hugs me and I think I'm going to cry again, but I don't.

I wait for ten minutes, call Dawn on her mobile and tell her that Abi's just come back. Would she mind, I say, if we stayed here for the night and came to hers in the morning? I can hear the metallic sounds of the station behind her.

'No of course I wouldn't. I think it's nice that Abi is with you, after all. You have a nice evening okay? See you tomorrow!'

She's pleased, I can tell. There's only so much even Dawn can take.

I have three missed calls on my mobile and three voicemails.

It's me Mum. Abi. Just checking you're okay.

It's me, India. Just to let you know that I've gone back to Mum's – I can't believe you haven't phoned me. It's really crap over here … Phone!

It's Andrew, I was wondering if we could talk?

Andrew thinks he's won, now. He thinks he's got everything. He thinks this proves something.

I get Ryan's keys from my bedside drawer. This was never really my home was it? Never really belonged here, or anywhere

SAM McCOLL

else for that matter. Spent my whole life trying to fit in, and for what, for who? Fuck knows. There's not a soul out there who knows me, not the way you do – there's nothing here for me.

God knows I've tried.

I rip away the tape across the front door and stuff it into my bag, let myself in. It's cold – cold as death. I turn the heating to its highest setting and begin tidying. At least they left the wine. I open a few bottles to let them breathe. We all need to breathe don't we?

I choose six CDs: all our favourites, and swing up the volume so that Cowboy Junkies drowns out the ghosts of all those horrid people.

After I've closed all the blinds and the heavy velvet curtains in our bedroom, I click on the soft-red orb light beside the bed. The flat is rippling with music as I wander round puffing up the cushions, hugging everything to my face, finding the smell of you. There are chalk marks across the floor, in the shower. I pull out towels and cover the floor.

I choose the black satin sheets from the linen cupboard and stretch them tight till they disappear into their own reflection. And a blue satin throw: I toss it high – creamy blue satin swirling red from our light as it floats and flops into soft pools of deep rose, leaking one into the other. I open your wardrobe and pull out everything they left behind, and build myself a nest out of you.

It's beautiful.

I line up the wine beside the bed like we used to, and light a dozen of our best church candles.

I look for the silk scarves – I had an idea to hang them round my neck like a kind of symbol, but they must have taken them along with the sheets and all the other stuff.

Did you see the way that policewoman kept looking at me? She must have read the papers. Mother of two, deserted one of her children, affair with a drug addict. Oh how the press will love it.

I keep expecting you, listening for the shower to come on

(I could always tell which bits you were washing by the way the water changed key) or to catch a glimpse of you as you move around the flat, your honey skin gleaming in the candle light – it's so hard being here alone.

I throw my bag on the bed, shake out the stuff inside. See what I've got – see?

How many times have I taken my clothes off here, right here, by this bed? How many times have you torn them off? I slip under the throw, the satin feels like soft warm water; this is *me*, not the plain, crisp white cotton in my pretend home.

I open the plastic bottle and spill it all out, a long stream of pills and tiny wraps puddle into the well between my legs. Lovely.

Look at them darling, look at how pretty they are – they're for us.

I unwrap the foil ball. I remember the night you gave it to me – only a week ago, a lifetime ago – it was in that drawer. A special gift, you said. I was astonished. You rarely gave me stuff to take away, but you said I'd be needing something, that I was to keep it for rainy days – you were almost tender, like you knew you'd be going away. Did you know?

I roll a few joints.

A glass of wine in one hand, a joint in the other, a mouthful of pills.

A toast. To the lot of you.

I should write something down, leave my children a wee note. There's a pad here somewhere, I saw it. Ah, here it is. Only a wee scrap – just a line; blimey, can hardly hold the pen, can I?

Jelly fingers. Jelly fingers, that's the one, that's what they said, nasty, nasty people. All gone now.

I have it. Right, good.

Dear Callum and Abi. I'm sorry this is so late, but I'm sorry I really am …

Blimey, I'm all over the fucking place aren't I?

Sorry. I love you Abi, I love you Callum. Be happy will you …

My hands – all rubber … Sorry guys but wow, this is mad – better have that smoke now – don't want to waste anything do I? More wine, madam? Yes don't mind if … more pills? Certainly. Bring them on! Hmm all gone – all gone? Where've they gone?

Down the hatch, madam. Good, well no chance of fucking this up then, eh? Oh fuck – spilt it. Oops, wet myself, Daddy, nearly did the nose trick – mucky pup – come on, Daddy, wipe it up, Daddy, I'm coming, Daddy … say goodnight, Daddy …

Time to snuggle down, Daddy …

Andrew

It's Christmas Eve, snowing hard. I decide to walk to the office. Guy isn't due for forty-five minutes and he'll call me from the airport. I have time to buy a few extras for tomorrow, maybe grab a coffee. The snow on the pavement lies like pale gold dust under the yellow street lamps, like a scene from an old fashioned post card.

I tilt my head to the sky, open my eyes and stick my tongue out.

A couple of hundred yards down the road, I regret this childish reversion and pull my hood up, my neck freezing now against my wet shirt collar. As I walk past the garage and into Rodney Street, I realise my feet are wet too. The snow, a few inches deep on unused ground, is already slushy on the pavements and blackened with exhaust and road dirt. The few cars left on the road are painfully grinding their bellies over the high ridges as they try to keep to the narrow furrows cut by the car in front. Those with less confidence of making it up the steep slope of Broughton Street are beginning to abandon their cars, parking before they start shimmying sideways into trouble. Staring at the pavement, I am drawn to the interesting array of impractical footwear: trainers, stilettos, court shoes tiptoe past me, their occupants no doubt praying that the buses won't stop running – giving up on ideas of last-minute shopping, hoping they'll get home in one piece and in time to get everything done for the big day.

Then a pair of yellow slip-ons, just like David's, pass me. I swing back. I don't believe it! It's David all right, his hand glued to his ear as usual, talking into his phone.

I see him let himself into the office.

I check my phone is switched on. Maybe David's planning … What the hell could the bastard be planning – destroying records? Surely it's too late for that – vandalism? I wait a couple of minutes before retracing my steps and following him in.

Mentally I crack my knuckles. I want him. I'm gonna pulverise the fucker – knock him out, extract his toenails one by one with my teeth, bludgeon his … I let myself into the small office off the left of the hall, lean against the desk in the pitch dark and wait for night vision.

When it comes, I'm in for a surprise. The office is much bigger than I remember, huge in fact and a technological makeover seems to have taken place. In the distance a bank of screens glow dully and I move towards them. As I get closer I am fascinated to see myself on each screen. Me as a teenager with Sarah, building a sandcastle with India on the beach outside their house in Oban. Me with Abi, again on a beach. She's crying. I remember the moment. She'd been caught with Liam – I was grounding her. I move on to the next one and each time I do, the last one fades out. Now it's me and Rachel, another beach. We are about to have sex. It pans in, something's not right. The I on the screen turns towards the camera, only it's not me after all – it's David with that sly grin on his face. I move on to the next screen, aware of my heart now, a slight thumping. Fear. It's Callum on the drums at the concert. He's thumping great style as it pans in once again and I'm canny now, and sure enough, when Callum turns around it's David again, not five, no, more like nine or ten, and it's not a drum stick he's holding but a stick of dynamite, one in each hand, and they're lit and he's grinning. There are other screens – the mess of my life in full colour. I drag my eyes away.

'David?'

He's behind Guy's desk with the diary spread out in front of him.

'Ah Andrew. I was hoping you'd be early.'

'I saw you come in, David. What on earth are you doing here?'

'Just tying up loose ends, before leaving.'

Cocky little shit.

Just as I'm building to an authoritative but restrained response, I am lifted off my feet by two of the largest men I have ever seen. I say seen but I'm struggling to see anything as I float through space to a chair positioned this side of Guy's desk.

'I'd rather sta—' I begin as my feet touch the floor.

'Shut up, Andrew – no one's interested.'

One of them takes my mobile, switches it off and hands it to David. I confirm they are giants.

'Guy's due here in what – forty-five minutes? Gives us plenty of time. Okay lads, tape him up.'

Gaffer tape is so much more effective than rope – quicker, no loose ends to get hold of or work loose. On first appearances they might have seemed Neanderthal, but their finger work is impressive – it takes about twenty seconds to mummify and bond me to the uncomfortable office chair. I imagine they'll wait for Guy, and do the same with him. I'm finding this hard to get my head around. I can't think where this is going, it doesn't make sense – why Guy? But I'm scared, really scared, and the fact that I obviously don't have anything they want to hear or have just makes it scarier – I mean, who are these guys? And who is David? I'm scared and ashamed and trying hard to hold onto the contents of my bladder.

They have not blindfolded me and I've never seen David so animated. 'Da, daaaa!' He dances a magician's jig around a duster covering a small package on the desk, and whips it off. Dynamite Dave. Dynamite fucking Dave – Jesus. Megan was right, he's a maniac. Okay, I get it now. He's going to blow me up. Right. I wonder how scared you have to be to pass out – or if some people just don't. I want to pass out.

He tapes the device to the underside of my chair, millimetres from my balls. Then his two helpers turn the chair to face the door so I can see what he's doing – he's running a wire or cable from my nether-regions, more or less, across the floor and the small hallway and out the office door. He keeps glancing up at me; despite my imminent vaporisation he really believes I'm going to appreciate his cunning plan.

'And just in case Guy is stuck in snow,' he says, grinning, 'we'll be inviting the lovely Megan and your sweet daughter Abi to our small Christmas party – I guess you'll have their numbers in here, eh?' He giggles, points at the door, wags my phone at me.

'I'm so glad you chose the mystery prize, Andrew, instead of the money – it's just so much more, *fun*, isn't it?'

My eyes shut, in silent horror initially, giving way finally to prayer – something, if you'd asked me, I would have sworn I would never do. They open again though, as David bends my chin upwards. 'I want you to watch, Andrew – it's so much more fun to watch. Do you think Abi will bring Callum?'

And then David levitates – more magic no doubt. But no, one of my Neanderthal buddies is lifting him away from me while Big Ears pushes a second chair up against the back of mine and tapes it fast – and then I hear this screeching of tape as they do the same to David as they did to me. Five minutes later they're out through the back door leaving us in pitch dark.

David is crying, and I wonder why this release never occurred to me.

I wake up crying and turn on the light; it's two, two in the morning. It's okay. I try to pull myself back, but it was so real.

After several moments, I push myself to sit up against the pillows, heart still racing. Jesus. Megan went back to her flat. She is angry, but she's alive. It's Christmas Day. Guy came back from Paris. I dealt with it, it was gruelling, yes, but it's over. And David? David's a jerk, a nasty bit of work – forget him. Abi is sleeping in her room for the first time since she left. There are small stockings hanging from their beds, bulging with gifts. The tree is glittering with fairy lights and Abi is sleeping in her room. Abi is sleeping in her room. Abi is sleeping. Abi is. Callum. Abi.

Megan. And then I almost jump out of my skin as the house phone rings. I stare at it, my heart pumping and hammering. As I pick it up, I half expect it to be David.

'Is that Andrew Gillespie?'

'Yes it is – how can I help?'

'My name is Staff Nurse Reeves at The Edinburgh Royal Infirmary. We have your wife ...'

I leave a note for Abi on the bottom step of the stairs. I don't know what else to do.

Had to go out, call me. Won't be long. x

All I can think about as I pull away from the kerb is that I won't have her here. That's it. I don't want to deal with her again – does that mean I wish she'd died? Well maybe it does, and as I'm driving down Inverleith at two in the morning these thoughts take up an immediate rhythm with the wipers, and together they act as an anaesthetic to the bleak rumblings in my soul.

I pull to a stop.

Abi. Abi would want to be here. I should go back. I should have woken her up and told her. Why didn't I do that? She's just a child, that's why. She's been through enough these last few days. We're all in a state of recovery; I am that far away from a breakdown. It is Christmas Day and I couldn't bear that look on her face: the panic, the despair, the guilt. I couldn't face the drama of Abi on top of everything else. Besides, who would have been there for Callum? There is no way we could have woken him up, bundled him into the car, taken him to see his mother, unconscious ... This way I can explain when I get back, we can both tell Callum.

I ease into the road again. The drumming and hissing and pounding has become a complicated and engrossing symphony without which I may start screaming and pill-popping myself. Oh yes, truly. I pull into the hospital car park.

From time to time sirens scream past me and blue splintered light spits into the ambulance bay. I don't want it to stop; I don't want to swap it for the drone of polishers on the soft disinfected linoleum lakes that await me inside. And especially not with the old croc who is waiting in the shallows to swallow me up whole.

Without deciding to, I find myself sloshing across the car park towards the blue light. I find the admissions station and after too few questions they walk me down the long gleaming corridor and into a small side room. A stunningly elegant black man with crystal white hair is sitting beside the bed. He stands and holds out his hand to shake mine.

'Andrew Gillespie? I'm Winston Lawrence. I would invite you to sit down, but the circumstances are somewhat strange. I found your wife. I'm afraid I don't know what to offer – except my deepest sympathy. I'm rather jet-lagged I'm afraid. I only flew in from Jamaica a few hours ago.'

His hand has a slight quiver as he withdraws it from mine. I move close to Rachel. She is linked to monitors and I'm longing to lose myself in the bleeps and flicks and drips – I'm missing the drumming of the rain. I suggest we go and find some tea.

The vending machine in the waiting room splutters out tea for me and hot chocolate for Winston.

'So you found her. That must have been rather a shock.' An understatement of monstrous proportion, but it's the best I can do.

'It was. I'd just got back from three months away. Looking forward to seeing Ryan, my partner – in fact surprising him. I wasn't due for another week, but my last bit of business finished early. I managed to get an early flight. You often can on Christmas Eve. I thought I'd surprise him. Yes, well. As you know I found, instead, a young woman making an attempt on her life, in my bed, in my flat.'

'I'm sorry. I'm so sorry. How horrible for you. She and Ryan … Well, I believe they were lovers. I …'

'Go on.'

'When did you get back – just a few hours ago did you say?'

'Around midnight. Why?'

He doesn't know. He doesn't fucking know. 'Ryan. Do you know about Ryan?'

'About him being bisexual?'

'No, not that. I'm afraid something awful happened. He died last week, well not even a week ago, a few days ago. You didn't know? You don't know?' I reach across and touch his wrist. He doesn't move it. He actually smiles at me briefly before standing up and turning his back. This is what you call composure. I stare at his beautiful three-quarter-length grey cotton coat and wonder if it would suit me and if I could ask him where he bought it – at a better moment maybe, when we're friends.

'I'm sorry.'

He turns around and lowers into the only chair, takes a sip of his chocolate.

'I've been flying all over the place the last three days. I hadn't heard. How? I mean he sounded so cheerful last …' His voice breaks.

'I'm so sorry. I don't really know the details. I think his front door was open and someone found him. You'd be better to talk to the police in the morning. Maybe you should go home. No, I suppose not, well maybe … No, well maybe you should try to get some sleep before you attempt to take in any more, there is only so much … You look dead beat. Listen, you can sleep at my house if you like. I mean, maybe that would be the sensible thing to do.' I can't quite believe I'm saying this, it's impossible of course but he looks so kind and so destroyed and so old suddenly. 'My girlfriend, Megan, would—'

'You're kind, really you are. I'll book into a hotel – you can't possibly offer a complete stranger—'

'No, well I'm just so sorry, that's all. Can I call somewhere for you?'

'That would be very kind.'

I phone the Balmoral. I give him our number and he promises to call and find out how Rachel is.

He leaves and I go back to Rachel's bedside to wait. An hour later, the nurse tells me to go home.

It's almost six when I zombie through our front door. I switch the tree lights on and stare at the presents around its base, not seeing them really – not seeing anything, except a blur of reflective wrappings. I long to slope off to bed, collapse for twenty-four hours, let things settle. It's amazing that Callum's not woken already. Panic stirs in my stomach. I must wake Abi. I must wake Abi now and tell her. Now. As I wait for the kettle to boil, it's all I can do not to curl up beside the Aga with Nevis and sleep.

'Abi? Abi it's me.' I have my hand gently on her shoulder. If there was any way I could spare her this I would, any way at all. She wakes up all sleepy eyed and stares blankly at me for a moment. Without her make-up she looks like the young child I used to know so well. My heart is breaking up with love. She smiles at me and looks towards her stocking at the end of the bed.

An awful dread steals over me.

'You should have told me first. I should have been there. It's me who lives with her, not you. You had no right! I should never have left her alone!'

'She's okay. I knew her life wasn't in danger, that she wouldn't even be conscious. I couldn't bear to wake you.'

'That's the problem, isn't it! You couldn't! You couldn't! It's all about you again, it's always about you! Well, she's my mother, she chose me! I should have stopped it, stopped her. I should have checked up on her. I should have rung Dawn, made sure she was there. I should have called her – she wasn't … she's not strong enough. Oh God, how could she? How could she?' And then Abi howls. 'Why did you do that, Mum?'

'Listen to me, Abi. What she did is not about you, it's about her. For God's sake, you didn't make her take pills, or try to kill herself. You've done everything you could to look after her, you're exhausted. This isn't about you, it's about her!'

She pushes out of bed, drags on her jeans and sweater over her pyjamas and storms across the room kicking out at the soap and chocolate pennies that have spilled from the bulging stocking.

'Don't you even think of following me. Don't you dare!'

I think perhaps she's turning back to hit me and to my shame

I flinch, but she's just retrieving her boots from under the bed. Along with them, she scoops up a handful of tiny forlorn gifts and throws them at me in disgust. 'You can stuff your fucking Christmas – I'm spending mine with my mother!'

'There was nothing you could have done, Abi.' She must believe me. I get up now and take her arm.

'Get stuffed, Dad. Just fuck off. You are unbelievable! This is my problem, it was my problem. Let me go! You've done enough damage.'

She flies down the stairs, takes out her phone and concentrates on the screen.

I follow her from room to room.

'What are you doing?'

'Going to see her of course – getting an Uber, fifteen minutes.'

'Listen to me, Abi – I'm going to tell you something.'

'Something that'll get you out—'

'Something that shaped the way your mum behaves, something that happened to her.'

'Go on then.'

'Carl, her Dad ...'

'Yes I do know Carl. I do know he was her dad actually. Get on with it – my cab will be here in a minute.'

'He abused Rachel, both of them, her and Sheena, when they were little – that was why she didn't—'

'What do you mean abused them? Hit them? What do you mean abused? What the fuck do you mean?'

'I'd always hoped you'd never have to know, but now, well you've got to stop blaming yourself – Mum was never—'

'For fuck's sake, Dad!'

'He played with them at bath time – it was his time with his girls and he played with them. He didn't rape them, but what he did was maybe worse because it left Rachel utterly confused about, about trust and about what love means – I can only try to imagine what it must be like and I can't get close, not really—'

'Fuck you! Fuck you, Dad. Just stop it, I've heard enough. You'd say anything—'

She storms through to the hall snatching a scarf and gloves off the chair.

'Granddad would never have touched her, not like that, you're lying, you're fucking lying. Why are you doing this, Dad – why are you trying to blame Granddad?'

She's backing into the loo by the front door.

'Just get out, fucking let go. Because I loved Granddad, and … and why didn't she tell me? I hated her for hating them and that's – so unfair. This is so fucked up – I mean I can't bear this … Why didn't she tell me?' Her voice breaks.

I wedge my foot in the door, praying Callum doesn't wake up, and keep my voice low and steady.

'I don't know. I probably should have told you but I didn't know where it would lead. I didn't know what to do. I think you should have known, but Mum, well it was up to her wasn't it?'

She lets go and the door springs open with my weight. She pushes past, collapses on the bottom stair and rests her head in her hands. 'And Gran – I mean, did Gran know?' She half turns towards me.

'No. Well, not until recently.' I perch at the far end of the same step.

'How?'

'I told her. I shouldn't have, but Rachel was so cruel to her. I wanted to explain that it wasn't her fault. After the barbecue.'

'So after all those years you told her that Granddad had … Poor Gran. I mean, how did she take it?'

'She couldn't take it on board, so she had a series of tiny strokes, got ill. I haven't got much right really. I'm sorry Abi, I am so sorry – I don't know what to say except that none of this is your fault.'

'And it isn't Mum's fault either, is it?'

'No, of course not, Abi, but it's up to her how she deals with it. It's not up to you to stop her messing up her life – sorry, but it's not.'

'So what you saying, Dad? That I should give up on her too – like you did?'

'She needs help, Abi, professional help. I can see what she's doing to you. I mean, leaving school, giving up Jamie, going out with Ash, that's all about—'

She rounds on me. 'Just shut the fuck up will you? I make my own choices – don't you dare do that. I like living with her, I like my life. It might be convenient for you and Megan, but I'm not like you, she's my mum and I'm not just going to give up – I won't.'

Her screen lights up and a look of relief flits across her face. Shooting me a look of pure hatred, she grabs her stuff and leaves. I flop sideways on the bottom step in as much of a foetal position as it will allow and sometime later wake to whoops of joy coming from Callum's room followed swiftly by Santa's outsize stocking bump, bump, bumping from stair to stair towards me.

Abi

Mum drifts in and out of sleep and I hold her hand. She has drips and monitors and stuff all around her. I'm not sure how much more of this I can take. It's all so unfair and gross and I don't know what's going on, or what to feel or do or anything. I sit and stare at her for a long time. I try to picture her young, a child. And Granddad. And Gran. It's all so fucked up and it sort of bunches up inside me and I think I'm going to be sick, but it's like I can't even puke because something in my brain is stuck – please, someone help me …

When I get home Dad's on the phone to Sarah. Callum is in the sitting room pushing a car around the floor. I join him, vrooming as best I can. He doesn't say a word. I tell him Mum'll be okay. I ask him if he wants a drink and he shrugs a 'yes' shrug. I start to get up off my knees and he turns towards me and pushes into me and we hug each other tight and I start crying, no noise really, just tears and an aching throat.

'She'll be okay. She was just sleeping.'

Dad comes through and crouches down and hugs us both. 'Abi.'

'Yes.'

'I've just been speaking to Sarah.'

'I gathered.'

'She's distraught.'

'Dad, I'm not sure I'm interested in Sarah right now.' But he isn't listening to me.

'Apparently David pitched up at the house yesterday, all tears and apologies and took India out. She didn't go home last night. Maybe it's okay. I said she was probably in some hotel somewhere, that she wasn't to worry. What do you think?'

'What do I think about what? If India would stay out and not tell her mum? Why not? It would hardly be the first time.' And then I start wondering. Would David know it was India who ... Oh for fuck's sake ...

'Dad? I didn't say anything because I didn't know for sure or care for that matter, but I think India might have – oh I don't know, I don't really know anything.'

'Go on.'

'She and Mum – I suppose it was a couple of days before the police were here, before they took your computer—'

But I don't get to finish, because Dad's mobile goes off and it's Sarah and India is dead.

RACHEL

'I GATHER YOU SAVED my life.'

'Inadvertently, I assure you. I was merely coming home. It seems like we both have a lot to come to terms with. How are you feeling?'

I'm not even going to answer.

'Stupid question.'

'Yes.'

'You have a beautiful daughter and son.'

'Yes.'

'You must have loved Ryan a lot.'

'Yes.'

'I'll go. I just wanted to say that if you'd ever like to talk to someone else who loved him, then please do come and see me – sometimes it can help.'

'Thanks. Winston, isn't it?'

I wait for the click of the door. As if.

Andrew

'Hold this will you Dad, please?'

I kneel down and take the photo off Callum and hold it flat. He picks up his large paintbrush and spreads glue on the back, carefully turning it face up and pressing it firmly across the newspaper headline, 'ACCIDENT, SUICIDE PACT OR MURDER? GIRL FOUND DROWNED.'

Sarah picks up another one. This one is of India posing in her bikini pointing at her belly button piercing. Sarah rips it in two and pastes one half of it at right angles to one of the hundreds of 'GIRL FOUND IN RIVER' and the other half over one of the 'BAILED MURDERER DRIVES OVER BRIDGE WITH EX-GIRLFRIEND.'

'You want a coffee?' I say, feeling sick at the compelling brutality and yes, beauty of her work. 'You should get some sleep you know – we need to be at the church in a few hours.'

'Nearly done, aren't we, Callum?'

'It's good isn't it, Dad?' he says, grinning up at me.

'It's extraordinary. People are going to be shocked. Are you sure about this?'

'That's typical of you, Andrew – I mean, we wouldn't want to shock anyone would we? We wouldn't want anyone to feel anything real – to feel what really happened last week. Well fuck them, Andrew, if they can't face this then they can fuck off – they shouldn't be here. Look at her, my baby …'

'I think it's nice,' Callum adds, sticking on a photo of India as Sarah saw her in the morgue. Her hair lank and matted, her naked body cut and swollen.

'Whatever you want. I'll get the coffee then. Want something, Callum?'

'Ice cream, please.'

'You've only just finished breakfast.'

'Pleeease.'

'For God's sake, Andrew.'

'Okay, okay.'

Sarah gets up off her knees, apparently satisfied. 'I think I'll have ice cream too. Get the toffee one – it's at the back.'

I hold my arms out and Callum jumps down and runs through to the kitchen and I follow.

'Ice cream, Todd?'

He sends me a worried glance.

'No thanks. And thanks, Andrew. She's still in shock isn't she?'

I hand Callum his ice cream and take some back through to the hall.

'Sarah?'

I look in her studio. She's not there. I put the bowl down on the coffin, which looks smaller than it did when we first lugged it in through the front door.

'Todd?' I say through the kitchen door. 'I think she's gone outside. I'll not be a minute.'

I half run down onto the beach.

She's by the large rock staring out to sea. 'I used to come here when I was pregnant.'

'Yes. I remember.'

'Do you know what I want to do? What everything inside me is crying out to do?'

'Tell me.'

'I want to go into the church and scream at them all to fuck off – that I'm okay on my own.'

'Yes, I imagine you do. It's what you've always done.'

'But I'm not though, am I?'

'Probably not.'

'And I never was, was I?' Her voice is breaking up now.

'None of us are really, are we? But you manage pretty well.'

She turns towards me and starts to sob.

'Where's Todd?'

'With Callum. Waiting inside.'

'I've been horrible, haven't I?'

'He seems to love you anyway.'

'He does, doesn't he?'

'Yes, he does. Very much. Come on, let's go and have that ice cream.'

We cling to each other and kind of half stagger, half run along the beach. We've hardly slept for a week. I see a small figure walking towards us and for a minute I am sure it is Megan. But it isn't.

Todd and I persuade Sarah to go and rest for a few hours and by the time she wakes up, Guy and Abi and Rachel have arrived from Edinburgh and we are all having a cup of tea.

ONE MONTH LATER

ANDREW

Abi's waiting on the pavement.

We drive in silence. The rain's holding off, though only just. It looks pretty raw out there, but as we park along the front, cracks break through the leaden grey, and yellow winter light pours through the gaps like paint, turning the bleak expanse of sea into a Turner masterpiece. The tide is miles out – we should make it to the island dry footed.

Abi is so thin.

I doubt she'll ever forgive me for not holding it all together, for failing, but never is a long time and I'm trying not to tie myself up with definitives and absolutes. I ask her how her mum is.

'You saw her. She's okay – she's doing okay. You and Megan?'

'Good. We're taking things slowly. And I go back to work next week.'

'That's sooner than you thought, isn't it?'

'Things blow over, I suppose.'

'Yeah I guess.'

We come to a halt and stare out to sea.

'You're not coming home are you?'

'No. It's fine, Dad. I'm doing fine.'

'Yeah. And work? Are you going to keep working? You don't have to, you know.'

'I do, I need to get out of the house. What else am I going to do?'

I daren't say anything.

'Oh and you'll be pleased to hear I've given up Ash.'

'Oh yeah? Gosh Abi. How does that feel?'

'Okay. And before you say anything, no, I'm not seeing Jamie.'

She stands up, calls Nevis, and with unlikely skill throws the stick she's been fiddling with far out into the surf. She's still got that swing in her hips and that easy flick of the wrist.

I remember that day on the beach outside Sarah's, teaching her how to throw over-arm, she must have been about nine. Her jeans are still falling off her skinny hips. I was worried then she wouldn't make it. But she did, is. With a bit of luck we'll all make it.

She stands laughing as Nevis dips his head into the waves searching for the sunken stick, and I lay my arm around her shoulder. She takes my hand and pulls down and wraps her other one around my waist. I fold my head over hers, pulling her in to me as tight as I can.

'Shall we go and get Callum? Get some tea somewhere before I take you both back to Mum's? She'll be okay for a bit longer?'

'Sure. Winston's with her. He's cooking us one of his *mild* curries for dinner, which means I'll need to buy a bucket of yoghurt.'

Resources

If you have been affected by any of the issues raised in *Call Billy* the following organisations can offer help and support.

Abused Men in Scotland (AMIS)
Telephone: 0808 800 0024
www.abusedmeninscotland.org

Home Education Support
www.gov.uk/home-education

Legal Guidance
www.gov.uk/divorce/overview

National Centre for Domestic Violence
Telephone: 0808 2000 247
www.nationaldomesticviolencehelpline.org.uk

Victim Support
Telephone: 0808 1689111
www.victimsupport.org.uk

Thanks so much for buying and reading *Call Billy*. If you enjoyed it, I'd be grateful if you left a review on Goodreads or Amazon or both.

Call Abi will be released in 2019 (see next page for a synopsis and extract). If you would like to pre-order *Call Abi*, or to receive an email when the book's available, please contact me at sam@sammccoll.co.uk or via my website www.sammccoll.co.uk.

Also by Sam McColl
Short Cuts, a collection of short stories

CALL ABI

Things have been lonely for Liam since the accident. Brian, his best buddy, had moved to Oban and there was no one else down the lane to play with. He's always worshipped his dad but he's never at home and his doting mum gets on his nerves.

Looking forward to high school with the prospect of seeing Brian is about the only thing that keeps him going.

But Brian blames Liam for the death of his wee sister. He's been looking forward to seeing Liam too – to get even.

He starts by sabotaging Liam's relationship with Abi. And Abi, blackmailed into silence by Brian, who knows about her crazy mum, finds herself falling from the dizzying heights of her first romance to a world of deceit, drugs, and dark secrets.

First chapter:

Six Years Earlier
'Come on, idiot! Run! Run for your life!' Liam yelled, bending low outside the garden gate, about to lift Brian's wee sister, Carly, and carry her in.

Her sweet face crumpled, and she stamped her foot in the mud.

Brian grabbed Liam by the back of his jacket and spun him around. His eyes were playful and fiery. 'She'll be fine. Come on, or we'll miss the beginning.'

They ran through the garden gate, across the waterlogged lawn and in through the back door, grabbing coke from the fridge and crisps from the cupboard. A minute later they were wriggling their tummies into the soft pile of the carpet in front of the telly.

'You think she's okay? Want me to go back?' Liam asked, licking salt off his fingers.

'Nah. She'll be in those puddles by the gate. Eat up before she gets here and steals the lot.'

Liam went out anyway. But Carly wasn't in the garden or on the path where they'd left her.

'She's not there,' Liam shouted from the door.

'Aw … it's a really good bit,' Brian whined.

'C'mon. Your mum'll be back soon,' Liam said.

'I'll kill her when I find her. She'll be in yours, I bet.'

But Liam's back gate was locked.

Brian's mum arrived home to an empty house. After calling out for a long time she found the boys by the ford.

'You left the back door wide open and the telly on,' she shouted at them. 'I told you … Where's Carly?'

It seemed like the rain would never stop.

Carly looked so happy on the TV, and when Liam saw her smiling out at him from the corner of his living room or from the posters in the village he would sometimes forget he was meant to be sad. But when the relief was snatched away, a black hole yawned open and swallowed him up.

Three weeks later, Liam was on the golf course with his dad. Bored, he slipped under the wire fence and into the woods. The river here was slow. Liam threw a stick into the water and followed it, until it got stuck in a pontoon of matted twigs and debris that had built up over the winter. He lay flat on the bank and tried to fish it out. Caught up in the solid thatch was a piece of pink spotted fabric.

Everyone was at the funeral. Light drizzle clung to felt hats like spider webs. An old woman in black sprawled over the fake lawn around the pit and howled like a cow torn from her calf until someone pulled her to her feet and took her off. Brian and Liam found each other and stood dry-eyed and side by side as Brian's dad and uncle lowered the tiny coffin into the ground.

When Brian and his family moved to Oban a month later, Liam waved goodbye and found himself crying for the first time.

'Too late for tears,' his father said, taking his hand off Liam's shoulder and giving him a push towards the house.